The

Bloodletter's Daughter

The

Bloodletter's Daughter

A Novel of Old Bohemia

LINDA LAFFERTY

amazonpublishing

Published by Amazon Publishing
P.O. Box 400818
Las Vegas, NV 89140

ISBN 13: 9781612184654
ISBN 10: 1612184650

DEDICATION

To my beloved parents, Fred and Betty Lafferty,
who taught their daughters the magic of books

ACKNOWLEDGMENTS

First and foremost, my profound gratitude to my husband, writer and editor, Andy Stone. For twenty-seven years, he suffered the heartache of publishers' rejections along with me.

Just keep writing, he said. *A writer writes.*

Andy, my "touchstone," taught me to write well by writing more…and loving the art and craft, published or not. *The Bloodletter's Daughter* is the result of that love.

To my parents, Fred and Betty Lafferty, who taught their children the love of books at a tender age. We are a family of readers as a result.

A tremendous amount of research went into this novel. I would like to thank translators and Czech friends who offered assistance. Thank you, Zuzana Petraskova, Jiri Vaclavicek, and Mirka Gamarra. For housing me with great Czech hospitality, my thanks to Jakub Rippl of Dum u Velke Boty bed and breakfast in Prague.

Screenwriter Vladimir Vojir helped me procure a DVD of his documentary for Czech television illustrating the story of Don Julius and Marketa Pichlerova. Gratitude to him and to Ceska Televize for this valuable resource.

A highlight for me as a writer was to hold the Coded Book of Wonder (the Voynich manuscript) in my hands. Immense gratitude to Marty Flug, Yale president Dr. Richard Levin, and Yale University for this opportunity. (Beinecke Rare Book and Manuscript Library is magical.)

Thank you to another Yalie, Jonathan Rose, for your help.

Thank you, photographer Nora Feller of NoraFeller.com for the extraordinary author portraits. My white shepherd, Rosco, sends a lick on your cheek, whether you want one or not.

Writing is a solitary process, but a few friends gave me vital encouragement. Thank you, Nancy Elisha, my beloved sister who has read every word I have ever written. Her belief and love of my books carried me through the darkest hours for nearly three decades.

Other dear friends and readers: Sarah Kennedy Flug, Anne Fitzgibbon Shusterman, Lucia Caretto, Judy Sharp, and Elizabeth Haas White. Thank you, dear ones, for the support over the years.

To Caroline Leavitt, who swooped into my life, buoying me up when I was heartbroken by the publishing industry. Caroline, you are a talented writer and an extraordinary human being. God bless you.

Thanks to David Forrer, who worked with me on early versions of this book.

My editor, Melody Guy, guided me in rewrites with a gentle, supportive hand. I loved working with her. I trusted her judgment absolutely and worked to meet her expectations. Thank you, Melody.

Jessica Fogleman's expert eye reviewing the manuscript was essential and much appreciated.

To my author team of Danielle Marshall, Nikki Sprinkle, Jessica Poore, and PR rep Gracie Doyle, a debt of gratitude for helping readers connect with my book.

To those at Gelfman Schneider, who help in all matters—Victoria Marini and Cathy Gleason, thank you.

To the Production Department, thank you for all your meticulous work.

My boundless gratitude to Betsy Robbins and the translation rights staff at Curtis Brown.

Special thanks to the Aspen Writers' Foundation, and especially Executive Director Lisa Consiglio; Programs Manager Natalie Lacy; AWF Board Vice President Julie Comins Pickrell; the entire AWF Board of Trustees; and Founder Kurt Brown. Attending the Aspen Writers' Conference and Aspen Summer Words for over thirty years has paid off! I always enjoy those terrific June workshops and the talented writers who share their experiences and the craft of writing. Aspen Summer Words is truly a "Writers' Mecca in the Mountains."

Bravo to Amazon's art department. You dazzled me with the cover design.

To my acquisitions editor, Lindsay Guzzardo, who believed fervently in *The Bloodletter's Daughter*. You are this book's fairy godmother. Lindsay, thank you for your faith and persistence. Amazon Publishing—you made this book possible. Thank you for taking a chance on me.

Finally, to my spectacular agent, Deborah Schneider—who took me back as a client after an eighteen-year absence and secured the perfect home for three books at once. *Chai, Deborah, Chai.*

PROLOGUE

Little Giuglio and the Coded Book of Wonder

Within that awful volume lies the mysteries of mysteries!
—Sir Walter Scott

There was no snow in Prague in February 1599—only freezing rains and a heartless cold that crawled into the marrow, chilling the bones of all Bohemia. From the dense Saxon forests bordering Dresden to the dark mountains of Sumava north of Vienna, to the curing waters of Karlovy Vary in the west and the wet, pine-studded mountains of the eastern Polish frontier, the cold winter rains lodged in aching joints and spawned melancholy humors, making the weary, mud-splattered Bohemians yearn for a blanket of fresh white snow.

Icy raindrops clung to the windows of Prazsky Hrad, the royal castle towering over the ancient city. Meandering silver fingers of water ran slowly down the glass, distorted by the warp of the thick, uneven crystal.

A boy, not more than thirteen, sat with his head propped in his hands, his elbows resting on either side of an open book. The beige vellum, soft and fragile, was illuminated by a smoking tallow candle on the mahogany table. Even in the early afternoon, the thin gruel of midwinter light entering the windows did not offer enough illumination for the boy to read.

As if anyone could ever read this book.

The boy who gazed so hungrily at the book had honey-toned hair that grew in unruly waves. He pushed his hair out of his blue-green eyes, eyes the color of the North Adriatic Sea.

Giuglio studied his precious book in his mother's apartments, for the royal nursery was far too noisy for a boy of such an intense nature. That morning he had begged and wheedled his grandfather, Jacopo Strada, curator of the king's vast collection of curiosities, into lending him this priceless book of indecipherable code and mysterious origins. He pushed his disobedient hair back again and bent low over the strange, colorful illustrations.

Giuglio particularly liked the pictures of bathmaids, the naked women in tubs of green water. His mother teased him that he was becoming a man and their white breasts were what attracted him.

"It is only natural, Giuglio," she would say, stroking his hair tenderly. Mistress to King Rudolf II, she understood such things well. "Soon you will find your way to the bathhouses of Prague and see the bathmaids for yourself."

But Giuglio frowned, shaking her off. His mother did not really understand. It was the *secret* he was searching for. He was certain the laughing women understood, particularly one slim-hipped maiden who stared at him from the pages. She held the secret to the mysteries, he was sure. If only she could speak to him.

He struggled to concentrate. *Was it the bathmaids' voices that filled his head?* No, what he felt was a lightning bolt that rattled his spine, making his face shake with palsy, his cheek quivering like a raw egg in hot grease.

And after the lightning in his spine came the thunder in his head. It wasn't a voice.

Not yet.

It was an overwhelming urge, a passion to do horrid things, things that would make his beautiful mother cry. He longed to call his mother a whore. There! Now that he'd thought it, the word filled his mouth, bulged his lips, and almost burst out into the room. Had Giuglio been born to a legitimate wife of King Rudolf, the entire Hapsburg Empire would one day be his, and his alone.

Whore!

His left eye began to twitch, and he pressed his fingertips against it to stop the spasm.

Giuglio watched the silhouette of the beating rain, the heavy drops of water licking the glass. The shadows painted trembling patterns against the bare plaster between the tapestries, as if the veins of water were boiling instead of near freezing.

Suddenly, the winter light illuminated his mother on her bed, a radiant spear of sunshine lancing through the window, piercing the heavy gray clouds, if only for a few seconds. Giuglio studied her profile, the perfect white skin and rounded bosom that had enchanted a king, filling the nursery with bawling children. Her eyes looked like aquamarines set in wet glass. She inclined her neck to study her glossy black hair, which was hooked around an ivory comb.

A servant entered with a message from the king. Giuglio bent his head once more over the fantastic illustrations, his hand over his eye to still its spasm. He traced the green cascade of water as it ran through cylinders—just like the maidens' bathing barrels, only bottomless—and then splashed into a pool where the naked women frolicked.

Or did the barrels look like the segments of a telescope, Galileo's device for studying the heavens? He must write down that idea. He started to reach for the stack of parchment across the table.

"Ah, *benissimo!*" cried Anna Maria, scanning the note in her hand. "Your father is going to pay a visit."

Giuglio's hand froze in midair.

"The king is coming? Now?"

The skin around his eye began to jump even more. He quickly gathered up his papers.

"Yes, dear! Now behave and make me proud. You know he dotes on you. Try not to act—so odd, *tesoro.*"

"Mother! He is ill-tempered with me."

"No, no, Giuglio. He boasts of your future by his side! You will one day help him govern as Lord of Transylvania; he has told me so. You must indulge his humors. His melancholy too often colors his vision. You are his treasure, *figlio mio.*"

There was a sharp rap on the door.

"The king," the servant said, stepping aside.

Rudolf II entered with a sweep of his long cape, a feather jauntily stuck in his velvet hat. He smiled slowly at his beautiful mistress, reclined on the bed, combing her long black hair, her jewel-green eyes beckoning him.

"You look ravishing, Anna Maria," he growled. "Leave us!" he snapped to the servant.

The man bowed and backed out the door, the heavy latch clicking into place.

"Now," said Rudolf, striding to the bed and throwing her ivory comb to the floor with a clatter, "I will tangle your hair in such passion, no comb's teeth will chew through the knots!"

Rudolf began to unlace his breeches with eager hands, his eyes never leaving his mistress.

"Wait, Your Majesty! Please! Did you not see our Giuglio at the table?"

Rudolf turned. He saw Giuglio with a quill, an ink pot, and blotter. And quires of parchment.

The king stifled his lust with an exasperated sigh. He lay back against the silk cushions and studied his son from his mistress's bed. He waited for his passion to cool.

Even a king should not disgrace himself in front of his children.

Giuglio, his first-born and most beloved son. The child had inherited the handsome looks and passion of his Italian mother. Rudolf had doted on young Giuglio and spoiled him with a generous allowance, the best tutors, horses, expensive clothes—and a collection of valuable clocks.

The king had noted with satisfaction Giuglio's fascination with the clocks' intricate workings, spilling their metal guts onto the parquet floors of the palace nursery. Part of his genius—*so similar to mine*, thought Rudolf—was this facility with mechanical reasoning. The king had spent hours watching his little boy play, puzzling over countless tiny parts, deeply absorbed as he dismantled and reconstructed the clocks.

But Giuglio was hunched over something on the writing desk. It was not a clock.

"Boy, what do you have there? A book?"

Giuglio swallowed hard. He swatted at the voices—no, no, the urges!—in his head.

Not now!

"The Coded Book of Wonder," he answered, clenching and unclenching his fist.

Rudolf's eyes narrowed. "I told Jacopo to keep that book under lock and key and to supervise you personally when you are looking at it. Where is my antiquarian?" the king roared.

Anna Maria crawled hurriedly off the bed and laid a soothing hand on the king's shoulder as he rose and approached their son.

"You forget that I am Signor Strada's daughter. I am supervising his grandson's work, Your Majesty."

The king's shoulders softened as he felt her touch, and his flesh tingled. But the book was one of his most treasured possessions.

"Work? What work?"

"Giuglio, show the king your tables and graphs."

Giuglio ducked his head in a nod of acquiescence, took a deep breath to still his tremors, and began reluctantly unrolling the sheaf of parchments he had so recently put away.

"Oh, Your Majesty! Giuglio is decoding the book," said his mother. "Such a clever boy!"

The king dismissed this with a snort.

"I have had every linguist, mathematician, and alchemist try to break the code, and in thirteen years no one has succeeded. This boy will not unlock its secrets!"

Still the king was curious. He looked at his son's work. He saw mathematical tables, series of quadrangles, graphs with segmented lines, and foreign words scribbled in the margins of the notes. He saw with pride that they reminded him of his alchemists' annotations, the work of sages three and four times the boy's age.

"What is this?"

"I have been comparing the usage of symbols with all the languages of Europe," said Giuglio, his green eyes glittering feverishly, his mouth dry and moving mechanically like one of

Rudolf's windup toys. There was nothing he loved more than talking about the Coded Book of Wonder. But he also showed the side of himself that his mother feared most—the peculiar side that was haunted by the specter of Hapsburg lunacy.

"Blocks of meaning," he continued, his hands gesturing wildly. "Recurring combinations of letters. Some only at the beginning of the word, some only at the end, and others exclusively in the middle. The royal chess maker, the Saracen, says it is a characteristic of Arabic. He said it may also be true in Hebrew, but I will have to consult a literate Jew to confirm this. I thought the next time you meet Rabbi Lowe to discuss the Kabbalah, I could—"

"What!" roared the king. Giuglio's head shrunk into his shoulders, and he put an arm up, shielding himself. "My son conversing with a *Jew*? Do you know what damage you could wreak with such stupidity? If a Hapsburg is seen asking advice from a Jew, both the Catholics and the Protestants will want my blood!"

"But, Father! I would see him in secret when he visits the court—"

"Do not call me Father!" said the king, slapping his son hard across the face. "Leave us at once, and do not touch that book again! You should be out prowling the streets and taverns, or in the woods hunting—not hunched over a book like a puny, castrated hermit, hiding under your mother's skirts!"

The king hadn't meant to hurt his son, but his flaring temper had outweighed love and caution, and his rings had hit hard against Giuglio's face and teeth. Blood ran inside the boy's cheek and flooded his mouth. Giuglio wiped it away with his sleeve, staining his blue satin doublet.

"Oh, my dear Giuglio, you are bleeding!" cried Anna Maria, running to him and pressing his head to her breast.

"Leave the boy alone!" thundered Rudolf, rage and frustration bursting forth. "He is weak and timid enough as it is, petted and coddled! It is good for him to be bloodied, by God! He should be pleading to chase the stag, the boar, the bear, instead of this girlish pastime with a book!"

Giuglio clapped his hands over his ears. The book was his only refuge from the urges and vile visions. His father grabbed his hands and wrenched them away from his head.

"You listen to me! Do not dare cover your ears when the king speaks. You should be out seeking women, drunk in a tavern, sowing your wild oats. Be a man I can be proud of! Come home covered with blood from a bear hunt or even a street fight, damn it!"

He turned back to his mistress, scowling in disgust.

"Even my best hunting hound growls at this weakling! The bitch knows. There is not enough courage in his heart or spunk in his balls to command respect, even amongst dogs!"

"Your Majesty, please, I beg of you. He is just a boy!"

"Get out of my sight, boy! Woman, get into bed where you belong! I have waited long enough—I shall have my pleasure!"

Giuglio ran from the room, his hand pressed to his face, the inside of his cheek still bleeding copiously. He ran out of the castle, through the courtyards, and across the covered bridge to the stables. He knelt in the stall of his favorite pony and cried in her straw, where he could not be seen.

But then, too busy fleeing his father's rage to control his own, he heard the voices come calling him again. Yes, they *were* voices, now he could understand them, pouring seething spit and hatred into his ear. They had come more and more in recent months, and he could do nothing to quiet them, except to lose himself in feverish study of the book.

Now there would be no book, no silence. His teeth clenched, and he tasted the blood in his mouth, salty and sour, mixed with the bitter, sulfurous taste of bile in the back of his throat.

The voices urged him to do things. Cruel things. They would not cease, louder and louder. Ever louder.

The taste of blood lingered on his tongue until he grew accustomed to it, even fond of it. He felt his fury growing, running through his veins. He listened to the voices now; they understood his rage.

He spat blood and strode back to the castle to find Minister Rumpf, his father's closest advisor. He brusquely told the king's minister he wanted to visit the bathhouse across the Vltava, just beyond the walled Jewish quarter.

"Not to be bathed, I will assume," said Minister Rumpf, raising his eyebrow.

"It will please my father," said the boy, spitting out the words like bitter seeds. Rumpf nodded sadly, knowing it to be true.

Giuglio lost his virginity that night with a beautiful bathmaid who gave the young boy great pleasure with her experienced hands and ample bosom. When she had finished with him and he with her, she eagerly collected the shiny gold coins he thrust at her in a laced leather purse. Giuglio returned home in Rumpf's own carriage late that night, drunk on ale and smelling of his own spunk and the tangy juices of a woman twice his age.

The next morning, the king's best hound was found stabbed to death, its entrails strewn about the bloody straw of the royal kennel.

PART I

Before the Fall

LATE SPRING 1605

CHAPTER 1

MUSLE OF CESKY KRUMLOV

The bathhouse on the Vltava River was pale yellow, the color of winter sunlight. It had stood in the Bohemian town of Cesky Krumlov for nearly three hundred years, wedged tightly among houses built as close together as fingers in a fist. But in all that time, thought Marketa Pichlerova, no one had hated it as fiercely as she did. The young bathmaid disliked many things about that pale-yellow house, but most of all, she hated the profession to which she was born.

Yet Marketa was not one to accept life meekly. Over the years, lecherous men on the streets of Krumlov watched her grow up, licking their lips. She'd felt their greedy eyes run over her body as if she were a fattening calf. But she would brush her wavy hair out of her storm-colored eyes and stare back at the offender, raising her chin. The gesture exposed her heart-shaped face and the ruddy color of her cheeks, which would flame with color if her passion was stirred.

The color of her cheeks contrasted with her wild hair. Just as a person can be born with two different colored eyes, Marketa's hair was a blend of shades—russet, gold, and chestnut strands, reflecting the colors of a Bohemian autumn.

But her chin was her most prominent feature—not large, but strong, determined; it was emblematic of her personality. Despite the opinions of others, despite her own fears, she raised her chin and proceeded through life with a directness that startled those who did not know her well.

There was only one person in the world who could best her in passion and determination—and that was her mother, Lucie Pichlerova, who ran the town bathhouse.

Marketa was the daughter of Lucie and her husband, barber-surgeon Zigmund Pichler, the town bloodletter.

A bloodletter inspired respect in Bohemia. Men and women alike drew coins from their purses to purchase a leeching cure. When Marketa was in her father's company, she held her head high as she assisted him in bleedings, carrying the fine ceramic trays that caught the blood from the patient's veins. Marketa knew the meandering tracks of bloodways and pulse points as well as her father. And how to harvest and handle the leeches. She could have applied them herself to a patient's veins if only the barber-surgeon guild would allow women to practice the trade.

But that profession was closed to her—as were, apparently, all others. The daughter of a Bohemian bathmaid, Marketa was fated to be a Bohemian bathmaid herself. She was a slave to the business run by her mother, Lucie—the business of bathing the townspeople and giving men sexual pleasure. Randy men dug even deeper into their purses for bathmaids than they did for a leeching, hunting for silver thalers to purchase a young maid's attentions and a hand in the right place.

Marketa had dreaded the day when she, too, would be for sale. At age fifteen, she was ripe for a patron and was expected to earn her way in life. For more than two years she had ignored her mother's pleas that she trade on her young woman's body to help the family. She had reached the age when she was expected to begin entertaining men in the bathhouse and accepting their favors.

Since she was twelve years old, men had squeezed her budding breasts and groped under her bath shift as she fought them off, once even scalding an aggressive hand with boiling water. Her mother had pinched her arm and told her she was no longer a child to be protected, but a woman to be admired and handled—for a price, of course.

Marketa had learned that this was part of her life as a bathhouse girl, indulging a grope or two, especially when men were in their cups, drunk on the ale and mead Lucie sold. Marketa knew it was her job to make their visit "pleasurable."

"Marketa! What harm does it do us to make a weary man's life more bearable here in the bathhouse?"

What she meant, Marketa thought, was what harm would it do to earn tips and favors that would benefit the Pichler family. Those tips would give Lucie more money to purchase tasty meat in the market. Marketa's mother had a strict rule that her daughter should never allow boys her own age to touch her, as they were penniless fools and there was nothing to be gained from their affection.

"Of course they will lust for you, but there are no coins in their pockets. Only greedy hands reaching for heaven," Lucie said, chucking her daughter under her chin. "Now is the time to find a rich patron. A wealthy burgher or a merchant. Two would be better, for they vie for your favor and raise the price."

Marketa sometimes wondered how her mother had ever settled on her father, a member of a guild, yes, but as a barbersurgeon, hardly a burgher. Both her mother and father worked hard to keep bread and ale on the table and saved their money for scraps of meat when they could—and books for Zigmund

Pichler. And then there were the trips Pichler took to Vienna to further his studies of bloodletting, which were financially ruinous. He left his family at least twice a year to visit the barber-surgeon guild in the old capital.

Pichler, for his part, was very much aware of the demands of the bathhouse on the seven women who worked there. This bathhouse on the Vltava had, in fact, been in his family for generations. He had met Lucie when she came to work for his parents as a very young bathmaid. He had only married her after learning for certain that she accepted that life and would run the family business with authority and even a kind of enthusiasm for its demands. The fact that a neighbor's hand wandered over her body only made him the more hungry for her at night. Marketa had been awakened many times by their gruntings and squeals, the rustle and snap of the straw under the ticking as her parents rutted.

But Marketa's father played no part in the bathhouse trade; he left that business to his wife. His profession was cutting hair and veins...and leeching. The bathhouse was his wife's vocation.

Marketa longed to join him and leave the sordid business, the smell of the dirty bodies and sweat, the lusty thoughts and talk of both men and women. She wished she, too, could dedicate herself to some higher calling.

In time, her mother's pleas that she must find a patron became more insistent. One day, Lucie waited until her husband had left the house for her brother Radek's tavern and began her attack in earnest.

"How long are you going to steal food from our mouths and watch contentedly as the twins grow more and more lean? It is your time to help make ends meet."

Marketa swallowed her groats guiltily, choking a bit on the rough chafe. Her mother never spoke this way to her in front of her father, but she did not hesitate to scold her in her sisters' company.

"I do not want to be a bathmaid," Marketa whispered.

"What did you say, girl?" asked her mother, rising from the bench. She grabbed Marketa's long braid and twisted it around her hand. "You think you are too good to follow in my footsteps? A bathmaid is a dependable profession that ensures a future—there will always be dirty, aching bodies that need a good scrub and a soak. And a hand in the right place to make a man forget his woes. Or is it beneath you, Your Highness?"

Marketa stared at the millet mush, the rising steam warming her face. Her eyes were stinging with tears.

"I do not want to be touched by old men, Mother! I hate their groping paws and lecherous looks!"

"Then you go out in the fields and dig your fingers to the bone. And eat boiled roots every night and morning, too. And you think the men will not lift your skirts when they choose? And without a cent crossing your palm."

Lucie let her daughter's hair slide from her hand. Then she sighed, gathering up her eldest daughter in an embrace.

"Daughter! This is who we are. This is what we do. Why can you not understand this? God has set our course, and he provides the means for us to survive."

Marketa ducked her head and looked down at her lap. She hated the day the blood had seeped through her skirt for the first time and made her mother smile, so proud her daughter was a woman at last.

Marketa looked up at her mother and held her gaze steady. This battle had gone on long enough. And it was true, her twin sisters looked puny, their eyes sunken and huge in their scrawny faces.

"What do I have to do?"

Her mother smiled so wide Marketa could see the empty space from the tooth that the blacksmith had pulled last year when it turned dark and rotten. The stench had driven away clients, and she had no choice but to have the smith take his iron pliers to it.

"I have just the right one picked out for you," Lucie said. "A rich burgher, of course. One who can provide for us."

"Who?" Marketa said, her eyes clenched tight.

"The brewer."

Marketa's eyes flashed open.

"But he is married and older than you!"

"He has pockets jingling with gold coins, and he has lusted for you for years. I watch his prick swell when you walk into the bath-house carrying buckets of water. No, he is the one. Trust me—he will provide well for us and give us a good price on beer and ale."

Marketa felt tears sting her eyes, and she wiped them away angrily. She was no more to Lucie Pichlerova than a means to procure a good price on beer, she thought. Yet her mother scorned the prostitutes on Virgin Street, considering herself and her daughters to be "ladies."

"One thing you must promise me. You will never ever speak of this arrangement with my father," Marketa said bitterly.

Her mother sniffed. "He will wonder how it is we can afford meat on the table," she said. "Besides, he knows it will happen one day—you are a bathmaid, Daughter."

"Think of an excuse or I shall never agree!"

Her mother nodded, chewing the inside of her mouth. This was how she looked when negotiating a price in the market, whether it be for cabbages or a larded piece of meat.

"All right," Marketa whispered. "For the twins' sake."

Marketa's mother's mouth split into a gap-toothed smile, and she pulled her daughter close to her, smothering the girl in her ample breast.

"There is no shame in it, Daughter. God means us to fend for ourselves. You will bring happiness to an old man's heart—and good meat and beer to our table."

She threw a shawl over her head against the cold. "I will go and see him immediately. He will be at the tavern, no doubt. I will drive a hard bargain, you will see!"

Marketa winced to hear how she was to be bartered and sold like a fattened pig at market.

"And the twins will each put on a half a stone by Christmas, thanks to you, Marketa!"

~

The brewer came to the baths that Saturday night. Marketa ran out to the bank of the river across from the castle wall that rose above the bathhouse. She crouched in the reeds and cried, muffling her sobs with the damp hem of her shift.

Lucie came out looking for her daughter, her flesh showing pink and white through her wet tunic, steam rising from her body in the cold air of the riverbank.

"What do you think you are doing out here?" she said, staring down at the shivering girl in the reeds. "Pan Brewer is here to be bathed, and he has asked for you."

She did not wait for Marketa to speak, pulling her daughter to her feet and leading her by the hand toward the bathhouse.

"I won't let him hurt you, I promise. Just let him have his pleasure, and it will be finished."

"I cannot do it, Mother! Please, help me. Send him away."

Lucie narrowed her eyes at her daughter. If Pan Brewer was not satisfied, there would be no meat, no pitchers of ale on the table. Marketa's mother, even with gray in her hair, still allowed prowling hands to roam her body, if only for a quick grope or cupping of her sagging breasts, although she made it clear to the randy men that she would never make a cuckold of her husband. Old men tipped for the titillation, and what harm did it do?

But her aging body could not bring in the extra money and sustenance the Pichler twins needed. A hard winter or fever could carry them away, they were so puny.

But she also understood the fear that her daughter had. It was her first time.

"It will get easier with time," she whispered to Marketa. "You will see."

"No, Mother!"

Marketa began to weep again, violently.

"Shh! Enough of this! There now, enough!"

But Marketa only sobbed louder, her shoulders heaving.

"Hush, Daughter! Patrons will hear! Let me speak to him. Perhaps we can meet his desires without him taking you."

She left Marketa crying on the wet grass of the yard and returned to the bathhouse.

The twins were already helping Pan Brewer remove his clothes.

"Pan Brewer, we must discuss some business. I have a proposal for you."

She whispered in his ear, and the brewer at first frowned, shaking his thick head stubbornly. But Lucie was not deterred. She whispered all the more fiercely, her face furrowed in determination.

"Just time to let my little girl become accustomed to you, Pan Brewer. Think of your pleasure when she finally gives herself freely."

At last he nodded, and Lucie went to find Marketa. She would also have to negotiate with her daughter, she sighed, but Marketa was a good girl and wouldn't let her sisters starve during these hard times.

"Here is our timid fawn," called Lucie at last, her voice as sweet as medovina, the honey wine the family served as refreshment. "Fetch a mug of ale for our guest, girls. We'll leave Marketa to attend him."

Marketa entered the bathroom dry-eyed. She could not refuse her mother this time, especially since Lucie had secured special terms from the patron.

Marketa helped the brewer to remove his kidskin boots. Their softness reminded her of live animals, and she cradled them in her hands as if they were kittens, stroking them with her fingertips. Marketa had owned but one pair of shoes in the past two years, and she only wore them in the winter, lashed with sackcloth and strips of pigskin to protect her feet from the cold and snow. The boots Pan Brewer wore were a luxury of which Marketa could only dream. Her mother said the brewer's pockets were lined with gold, for everyone in the town drank his beer and ale by the barrelful. He even sold his brews in Budejovice, the Bohemian capital of beer. Soon his money would buy lard, meat, and beer to fatten her skinny sisters. It was up to her to help the family.

She was born a bathmaid.

"Come, come, Marketa—help me with the rest of my clothes," said the brewer, stretching his arms wide.

One of her sisters came in carrying a tankard of ale, and her mother followed.

"What?" she shouted, hands on her stout hips. "You are still dressed. The water will grow cold. Dana, fetch some hot stones from the hearth and drop them into the soaking barrel. Marketa, help Pan Brewer out of his clothes."

Marketa drew off his linen shirt, the armpits stained brown as the ale he brewed and smelling sour of old hops and yeast.

When she untied his breeches, her hand brushed his penis. It leapt up straight as a stick, pink as the underside of a white pig.

"Pan Brewer, you put the young bucks to shame!" said Lucie.

He laughed, making his penis bob at the compliment. He took a long draught from the tankard of beer.

Marketa felt sick and dizzy. The pork knuckle her mother had fed her as a special dinner for the occasion worked its way up her throat, and she tasted pig's meat and ale in the back of her mouth.

She wanted to run, run and not stop running until she reached the mountains, where the pines were thick and she could hide forever in their darkness.

"I think you have impressed our Marketa," said her mother. "Look at her, not a word from her mouth."

The fat brewer looked at the girl, licking his lips as if there were grains of salt at the edges of his mouth. Marketa struggled to keep her dinner down, merely belching quietly.

"Here," said her mother, handing her the sponges and the reed brush. "Marketa will bathe you," she said sweetly to him. Lucie helped her patron to the bath stool.

Marketa dipped the sponge in the bucket and squeezed the water over her patron's great beefy shoulders. She kneaded his thick neck and back, massaging the muscles the way she had been taught since she was six.

Her hands had grown strong, as strong as many a man's from years massaging and pounding at knots in bathers' bodies. Muscles melted under her touch.

The brewer sighed. His old prick flicked up and down, like a stick lashing out at a donkey.

Her mother watched from the corner of the room, nodding and squinting, gesturing and pointing, urging her daughter on.

When Marketa reached his buttocks, he turned around and grabbed her by her waist.

"My darling," he whispered in a hoarse voice. "*Milacku!*"

Marketa tried to squirm away.

"No, no, your mother and I have come to an arrangement."

He pawed at Marketa's breast.

Marketa screamed with indignation and slapped the brewer across the face.

"Get your hands off me!" she said.

"Oh, *Berusko!*" the brewer said, ignoring her protests. "Come here, my little bug!"

Marketa saw her mother out of the corner of her eye. Lucie had been keeping one eye on the bathers in the barrels in the next room and one eye on her daughter, making sure Marketa pleased him and did not spoil her hard-won deal. But she was also keeping watch to see that the brewer did not hurt her daughter.

"Get away from her, Pan Brewer!" shouted Lucie, lumbering toward him. When she saw his greedy hands grabbing at Marketa's body, Lucie began beating the old brewer about the head and shoulders with a long reed brush, like a washerwoman breaking up a dogfight.

"You get off my daughter this minute! Enough! Remember our agreement—no touching!" she bellowed, still thrashing her patron with the brush. Then she grabbed a bucket of icy river water and dumped it over his head.

The fat man yelped. He wiped the cold water from his eyes, shivering.

Lucie handed him a dry bath sheet, scowling. The brewer snatched it from her, rubbing himself vigorously.

"There will be no touching, Pan Brewer," Lucie said, shaking her finger in his face.

Pan Brewer turned away from her growling, his skin puckered and red from the sudden cold shower.

"Sit!" he told Marketa angrily. He rubbed his back, aching where she had pounded her fists. "Sit on the stool and let me see you!"

Marketa began pulling her ripped shift back over her hips.

"No, you sit there naked. I want to study my purchase."

Now she understood. This revolting old man would study her body. She thought of how many times she had studied the courses of the veins and the anatomy of the human body, fascinated. She thought of the drawings her father owned, copied from originals in Vienna. He had taught her the magnificence of the physical body, the intricate pathways of blood—the interplay of muscles, the functions of some organs, the mystery of others. She had gazed at sketches of both men and women in amazement, marveling at God's superb creation.

Now this old rutting goat would gaze at her body for his sexual pleasure.

She thought of her skinny sisters, their hollow eyes bulging from their sockets. Dana's sharp elbows and bony knees. Kate's sunken belly and raw cheekbones, cutting like white knives through her pale flesh.

He wants to see my body. All right, she thought. *Let him!*

Marketa threw her shift to the ground and looked at the brewer defiantly. She would imagine herself nothing more than a naked drawing on parchment.

She no longer felt the fear of this man, only disgust.

"Open your legs, girl."

He touched her knees with his clammy hands and drew them apart.

The stink of sour hops mixed with sweat from his balding scalp rose from him, and she turned her head to one side to gasp for fresh air. She felt his beady eyes staring at her womanly parts.

Parchment, she reminded herself. She had no fear—this man could not hurt her. She was no more than a drawing in a book, a figure in ink.

"Ah, there it is. The lips of the young *musle*."

His hand reached down between his legs.

Why did this old fool speak of mussels? she wondered. Then she thought of the open lips of the bivalves in the waters of the Vltava, their tender flesh creeping over the shell halves.

She felt the sweep of his stumpy fingers touch between her legs, and she drew back in revulsion. "Mother!" she shouted.

"*Musle!*" he said. "Ah, sweet *musle!*"

"I said no touching!" said Lucie, blistering his back with the long-handled brush. Hunkering like a stubborn beast, his brute attention to his task unbroken, the brewer ignored her.

Then he shuddered once, twice, three times, and his hand fell loosely from his penis. He groaned with pleasure. "Moosh-layyy."

Marketa's mother helped him up, muttering curses in Czech.

"Pan Brewer," she said, "you stubborn old goat! Come with me to your barrel. It is steaming hot and ready for you."

She gave her daughter a congratulatory look over her shoulder and disappeared with the brewer, who stumbled as if he were in a drunken stupor.

The girl was left on the stool alone.

Foolish old man, she thought to herself. She did not understand the allure of sex—a repugnant act, reducing men and women to the level of rutting animals.

Well, she would not think of it. The brewer's proposition did not involve her affection or even her regard.

I am only a drawing on parchment, she told herself.

He can never hurt me.

When Marketa finally composed herself and looked around the open doorway to the bathers' barrels, she saw her mother place the lid over his head and tip a long draught of beer down his throat.

His eyes were drowsy and a lazy smile of satisfaction spread over his fleshy face.

All the heads in the barrels surrounding him swiveled in his direction, leering in admiration.

"You have been feasting on young mollusks, Pan Brewer," said the cooper, who made barrels for the brewery. "We could hear your joy! *Dobrou chut!*"

The entire room erupted in laughter, and the full barrels shook with mirth, splashing the stone floor with little puddles of herbed water.

"This is the season for mussels, tender and young," said the greengrocer, trying to best the cooper. "We should all have *musle* and dive for her pearls!"

She knew from that instant that the name would stick. By the next day, her given name Marketa disappeared from the mouths of the townspeople and was replaced forever by "Musle." She was christened anew.

Pan Brewer visited weekly and was allowed to see Marketa naked, although Lucie was always present and never allowed him to lay a finger on her daughter. His pleasure in seeing the young girl naked before him, seated on a three-legged stool, was enough to supplement the Pichlers' income. The brewer looked forward to the day Marketa's body would be his to touch and take at will. The price would go up.

Marketa dreaded his visits and could not be persuaded to eat the days he bathed. Though she no longer feared him—she realized he was an old man who finished his business quickly—she found his dazed stare repugnant. She grew thinner the more often he visited the bathhouse.

But the twins gained weight, and meat appeared several days a week on the table. Her father never questioned how it was that Lucie could afford such good cuts from the butcher or the bottomless jug of ale always present on the table.

He never questioned, but of course he knew.

WINTER 1606

VIENNA

Landesirrenanstalt Lunatic Asylum

CHAPTER 2

THE MAD BASTARD OF PRAGUE

"He's here!" cried the ragged servant boy, his bare feet slapping across the paving stones in the great hall of the asylum. "King Rudolf himself! Glory to the Austrian Empire…" the boy shouted, then trailed off, realizing he had nothing else to say. Deflated, he concluded, "He's here, Herr Fleischer!"

"Stop screaming and empty the chamber pots," hissed the head attendant, cuffing the boy's ears. "You should be invisible, not galloping about like an unshod pony in front of the king!"

The asylum director nodded nervously in what might have been agreement and then stroked his black robe, picking lint off his sleeves in the capricious light of the flickering sconces. His breath cast a foggy halo in the cold air. He swallowed hard, his heart pounding as he stationed himself near the barred door of the stone prison. The toothless woman in the far room cackled, her slick gums shining red in the torchlight. A man wailed a curse at the arriving monarch.

"Damned Hapsburg! One more mule-chinned ninny!"

"Silence, Herr Schiele. A lunatic can lose his head as easily as any other," snapped the attendant, motioning to a guard.

"Gag him," the director said, his lip twitching wildly.

The broad-shouldered guard raised his leather whip and stormed off to silence the offending heckler. The director stretched and twisted his short neck like a curious turtle, trying to straighten his posture before he greeted his noble visitor.

It was not every day that a Hapsburg emperor paid a visit to a lunatic asylum.

Two assistants pulled the wooden latch-beam aside and opened the iron-girded door. The hinges groaned as the great doors swung wide, giving way to the cobbled street where the king's entourage surrounded the royal coach, helping the monarch descend and lighting his way with flaming torches held high.

Dressed in an ermine-trimmed cape, the Holy Roman emperor, King Rudolf II, strode into the asylum, accompanied by a half dozen advisors and servants. He stopped after just three paces, arrested by the smell of human feces and rancid urine.

The director bowed.

"Your Excellency, I am honored beyond words at your visit."

The king looked at the man as if he were examining a dead insect.

"This is where you treat the mentally diseased?" he asked. "It smells worse than a Spanish slaughterhouse!"

The king snatched a lace handkerchief proffered by a servant. He covered his nose and mouth and breathed in exasperated gasps, his long Hapsburg lip quivering below the white cloth.

"The diseased mind produces an unclean body, Your Majesty. It is one of the many vices we must purge."

"The place smells of shit!" protested the king, his lips curling in disgust.

At this, several men hooted from the darkness at the end of the long hall.

"And a Hapsburg farts roses, I hear!"

The king sucked air between his teeth, and the flesh at his temples tightened.

"Let me see these men who dare to insult the Hapsburg name!" he roared.

"You understand, Your Majesty, they only insult you because they are bedeviled by disease," pleaded the director.

"Show me the offenders!" the king shouted.

Reluctantly the director led the way down the dark hall, reaching for a torch from the entry.

As he strode ahead, the light illuminated the dirty, bloodied faces and brown, decayed teeth of the patients, who for the most part retreated hastily from the flame like night beetles, scurrying into the recesses of their filthy cells. One man ignored the commotion and stared straight ahead, pressing his louse-scabbed forehead hard against the rusted bars and leering at the naked women in the cell across the way. The light of the torch reflected off the oily skin of their bald heads.

"These women have no clothes!" said one of the king's entourage, squinting hard to focus on them.

"Has the disease made their hair fall out?" asked the king's advisor. "They are as bald as baby mice!"

"We can clean them more readily this way," said the director. "It is easier to undress them once than to fight them every day. The lice bury their nits in the fabric of their skirts, and the fleas infest their underclothes. We shave their heads to keep them free of the vermin, for unlike the men the insects drive them to distraction."

The king wrinkled his face in disgust. At the far reaches of light, he saw movement on the ground. It appeared as if a cluster of animated melons were watching him approach.

"What in Jesus's name is that?"

"These are the men who called insults, Your Majesty."

In the flickering light, the king made out three heads with no bodies, twisting on the ground. He started at the sight, unable to make sense of the dark vision before him. He grabbed the torch from the director and strode toward them.

In unison, the heads swiveled in the dirty sand and straw. Now he realized that they were men, buried up to their necks.

"Hail to the king!" said a head, now beseeching, not mocking.

"This way, my lord!" cried one. "Free me from this hell!"

"Just liberate me and I will not cut flesh—not by my mother's eyes, will I! Fetch the spade and loosen me from the earth, so that I may walk again!"

"I have an itch that bedevils me between my legs. Unbury me so that I might scratch the vermin who bite me!"

The director jumped in front of the king and seized the torch.

"Please, I beg of you, Your Majesty. Do not approach them."

As he said this, one of the king's ministers bent over the man closest to him, marveling at the foam-flecked chin that rubbed against the ground, the body buried deep into the packed earth. He brought a pair of spectacles to his eyes, studying the talking head at closer range.

The head swiveled futilely, dirty teeth snapping.

"Get back!" shouted the director. He circled behind and yanked the buried man's head back by a shank of his greasy hair, as his teeth gnashed the air. An attendant sloshed a bucket of water full in the man's face, causing the snapping head to gag and cough.

The king's attendant screamed in terror.

The small entourage circled the king and pulled him away from the heads that now laughed in unison, their breath raising dust in small puffs around them. They coughed and spat viciously at the monarch and his men, hissing a litany of profanity in labored gasps.

"Come away from here," motioned the director. "Let me show you what you have come to see, Your Majesty."

The king, wide-eyed, let himself be led away.

Across the courtyard, there was an empty cell. The director held the torch high so that king could see the straw mat and chamber pot. A rat scuttled out of the straw, startled by the sudden light. It bared reddish-yellow teeth at the intruders.

"This is where we mean to keep him, Your Majesty. He can have his own furnishings, of course, tapestries, and wardrobe. Meals prepared in the castle kitchens can be brought here and served on linen and silver plates. He would be treated as—royalty, of course."

King Rudolf stared at the dark cell, his nostrils quivering at the stench of old urine.

"No," he muttered. "No son of mine will be fettered in such squalor!"

"But, Your Majesty!" protested his advisor, Herr Rumpf. "Don Julius cannot remain in the streets of Prague. He shall be imprisoned if he commits another crime. The magistrate has said as much, and the Bohemian lords will insist upon it. The municipal dungeons are as dark and the prisoners more savage than this! He will end up on the gallows if we do not intervene now."

The king turned to his minister.

"That is why I have brought him with me to Vienna. A new start in a city that he does not know so well as fair Prague—that's all the boy needs. Let the wretched Viennese deal with him."

"Your Majesty, I beseech you! His conduct will lead him to death even as it sullies the Hapsburg name and endangers your empire. Your brother Matthias is waiting eagerly for such an opportunity to seize the throne!"

"Vienna is a new start for the boy."

"Vienna will have far less tolerance than Prague for his conduct, I promise you."

King Rudolf set his jaw in anger, a scowl contorting his face. Rumpf retreated a few steps, bowing his head.

"No! Never!" roared the king. "No seed of mine shall come to such an end. He has my blood, even if he is a bastard. No Hapsburg shall ever live in such debased conditions. He shall not share his bread with rats, I swear it!"

The king swept his cape around him in an angry gesture and walked quickly toward the street where the royal coach stood waiting.

A cacophony of raucous laughter chased him out as the great door slammed shut, leaving the director alone holding the single torch in the cold blackness of the stone hall.

CHAPTER 3

ANNABELLA AND THE MAGIC PEARL

The rash began the night after Marketa's first service to Pan Brewer. A bright red blush appeared around her mouth, and when she undressed, she saw the rash staining her breasts and between her thighs. Wherever he had touched her, her flesh was inflamed and the heat burned her from inside, making her thrash on her straw bed and whimper in pain.

Marketa's mother caught her by the chin when she came to eat her soup for breakfast.

"What is this?"

Marketa pulled her face away from her mother's hands.

"Probably a disease I caught from the brewer."

"Nonsense!" Lucie said. "Any sickness you would contract would take days to show through." She knew of such things quite intimately.

"No, these are the devil's marks!" she declared and crossed herself. She looked at Marketa as if she wanted to drown her in the Vltava and save the rest of the family.

"What do you mean, 'the devil's marks'? What dealings do you think I have had with the devil, other than serving my body to a married man?"

Her mother scowled and said nothing. She ladled some cabbage and barley soup into Marketa's bowl and went back to cutting onions for another pot of soup. After a few moments she asked, "Have you been touching hair bits from your father's barbershop?"

Marketa focused her attention on the soup. When she did not answer, Lucie pursued. "Have you, girl? Have you picked up the hair?"

"No, he would never allow it. But I think your fear of hair is all foolishness. Science will someday prove it is nothing but superstitious ignorance."

Marketa's mother narrowed her eyes.

"You think you know the dark world? Say a prayer that your soul is not snatched by the devil for your haughtiness. Spit, Marketa! Spit now on the ground and take back your words before the evil eye sees your confidence and boasting and strikes our hearth and home."

Marketa knew better than to argue with her mother, so she gathered up the juices in her mouth and spat copiously on the stone floor.

"So what am I to do about this map of red on my body, Mother?"

Now her mother was truly worried. She stopped cutting onions and stared at her.

"It is beyond your face?"

"It laces every spot the brewer touched. You can imagine the burn between my legs."

Lucie pinched up her face like a mole emerging from its burrow, peering out into daylight.

"I swear to you I will not let him touch you again. Not yet."

"Mother, that may be so, but look at his mark."

Lucie looked at her daughter in exasperation, flinging down her knife on the cutting board so that chopped vegetables scattered about the table.

"You must get rid of this ugliness. How will the brewer ever look upon you again with lust if we do not erase the devil's touch?"

Marketa said nothing but broke off some bread and dipped it into her soup. With the promise of more money, her mother had been generous with the marjoram and pork bits.

"We have to return your fair skin," she said, wiping up her daughter's spit from the floor with a rag. She paused. "You must go see the cunning woman Annabella on Dlouha Street. She will concoct something to cure you and ease your pain. So that you can go back—to work."

Marketa winced. Work. What she was expected to do with her body from now on. But she made herself focus on her mother's other words—she must go to see the witch.

She had heard of the cunning woman Annabella and her mother, also Annabella, the old crone who had died last winter. Every woman who lived in the house on Dlouha Street was named Annabella, and they passed on their spells—and their home—from mother to daughter. The current Annabella was only a few years older than Marketa and lived alone in the house. No one ever knew what happened to Annabella's father or grandfather or any of the men of that family; it was only women who lived in the old house.

The house was near the home of the alchemist who used to keep his laboratory in the first courtyard of Rozmberk Castle that towered above the town. He was rumored to have been close to producing gold from lead and brewing the Elixir of Life. But then Wilhelm Rozmberk died and his brother Petr Vok spent his money on women and drink and the war against the Ottomans, not alchemists' secrets.

"You must go to Annabella and see if there is an herb or potion she can give you. Wear a scarf around your face and walk straight there. You do not want people to see you until you are cured. Finish your soup and go!"

Marketa pulled her cloak from the peg and wrapped a wool scarf around her blistering face.

"If she is not at home, try the cemetery. She may be there."

Marketa shuddered. She did not like to visit the cemetery. Sometimes she had to go that way, by the crook of the Vltava, to look for mussels when the Pichler family was short of food for the day. Her father would give her a basket and a dull iron knife, though she would still cut her hands on the sharp-lipped shells.

Too often as the girl searched for mussels she felt a cool draft from the graves thread its way around her legs like a cat. She looked over her shoulder at the tombstones, her eyes scanning the crowded Franciscan field. She never saw anything, but she thought she heard whispers as she scraped her knife against the river rocks. When she cut her hands on the shells, the blood dispersed in wispy red clouds, carried slowly downstream by the current.

Today, Marketa walked through town, her head lowered and her face covered by the scarf. Because it was cold, no one asked her why the wool was pulled up around her mouth, and she greeted them one by one.

"*Dobre den, slecna.*"

"*Dobre den,*" Marketa answered, nodding her head.

When she reached the house on Dlouha Street, she banged at Annabella's door, stamping on the cobblestones to warm her feet. She had pulled her shoes out of the wooden trunk, although her mother had frowned, knowing the more she wore the shoes, the sooner they would wear out. But it was cold and the cobblestones made her feet ache. She bent over and tightened the rawhide straps that lashed the worn wooden soles to her feet. Three cats appeared out of nowhere, threading their soft-furred bodies around her legs, purring as they examined her.

"She is not there," said a voice.

Marketa turned around and saw a wizened old man making his way down the street.

"I saw her leave early this morning with a basket," he said. "She may be gathering mushrooms, though it is not the season. More likely roots or mussels. At the cemetery, most likely."

"You are the alchemist," Marketa said, through her scarf. Warm air puffed through the fabric, vapor clouds rising in the cold air. "I am Marketa Pichlerova."

"Ah, the bloodletter's daughter!" said the old alchemist. "A pleasure to meet you," he said, offering a hand.

She shifted her left hand to hold her shawl and shook hands with him. He kept his milky, scarred eyes focused on hers.

"Why are you hiding behind that scarf, *slecna*?"

She sighed and dropped the shawl. "A rash. I came to visit Annabella to see if she could give me a potion to cure it."

"It looks like a transmutation to me," he murmured, his icy fingers touching her face. There was a professional kindness in this act, not a judgment of character or repugnance at her condition.

"Is there a change in your life or something you want changed? Your body is struggling to throw off a poisonous state."

She gulped and strained to compose herself. This was a stranger. What did he know about her struggles?

"How do you know such things, sir?"

"I have studied transmutation and the Kabbalah all my life. Rashes like these are often a sign of the body and soul rebelling." He looked deep into the girl's eyes. "Is there something troubling you, *slecna*?"

Marketa looked down at the cobblestones, icy and slick.

He coughed. "Yes, well, I have overstepped the bounds, I fear. Seek Annabella, she may have something to help you. She is a wise woman, like her mother, and shows signs of having strong powers at such a young age."

She thanked him for his trouble. He nodded his head and turned to walk around the corner, to his house on Siroka, or "Wide," Street, where the market stalls hummed with haggling and bartering.

Marketa hurried back down Dlouha Street toward the river, avoiding the town square and distancing herself from the busy market.

~

Annabella was at the edge of the cemetery, digging for roots among the graves. The red-haired witch was on her knees, her fingers searching through the dirt. Marketa recognized the fresh mound of the grave of a drowned boy Krumlov had buried just a few weeks ago.

"These roots have special powers, given up by the departing spirit," the witch said, without looking up. "You are the girl the bathers now call Musle, are you not?"

Her words startled Marketa, for Annabella had not looked up. Marketa's eyes were uncommonly keen, and she had seen the sorceress's young body huddled under the dark cloak from a distance, but she did not know it was Annabella for sure until she saw the tangled red hair. Not once did the cunning woman look up.

"How do you know me? How do you know that name?"

"Oh, now, do not blush," Annabella said, turning at last to look at Marketa with her hazel eyes. "There is no need to ever worry what people think."

"It hurts me," Marketa said, choking.

"Do not let it. Gossip is only meant to weaken your powers because people are afraid of anything but the most common and familiar. Your name has great power, did you know that?"

Annabella brushed her hands clean of the dirt and rose from the grave site.

"Now take your shawl away from your face and let me look at what you hide behind it," she said, stretching her back like a cat.

Marketa swallowed and let the shawl fall.

"A nasty one. Does it affect your womanly parts?"

Again Marketa blushed. "Yes. Even more severely than my face."

Annabella made a clucking sound with her tongue. "We must do something about it."

"How much will you charge me? I do not have much to give you."

"Oh, that is where you are wrong, Marketa. You have much to give me. I will prove it to you."

Annabella took Marketa by the hand and walked to the edge of the river. She pointed down to a bed of mussels under the ripples of water.

"I will rid you of the rash if you will help me. Show me which one of the mussels has the great pearl."

Marketa looked at her as if she were mad. "I know nothing of pearls. Even the old shellman at the market does not know which mussel might contain a pearl. If he did, he would be a wealthy man."

"Musle," Annabella said. "You were given this name in a moment of passion. The spirit speaks truth in these seconds, even when spoken by the most fetid and base human beings. But most are fools who cannot comprehend their message. It is like the mussel. A piece of sand irritates it, and the shell wishes to expel it as rubbish. But what occurs is a miracle of beauty, a pearl.

"Point to the mussel, Marketa. But promise I will have what is contained within."

Marketa touched the rash that was burning her left breast and sighed. She knelt above the rocky ledge of mussels just below the water's surface. Under the ripples, the shells seemed to be moving, growing, retreating. River grasses and mosses grew fuzzy beards on the shells, making them look like the Jews who huddled together as they stood every morning, waiting for the town gates to open and let them enter.

How would she find a pearl among the dozens and dozens of mussels here?

She reached down and her left hand broke the surface of the water. There was one mussel, no different from the rest, neither smaller nor larger, shinier nor more covered with moss. She touched its lip and it closed, tight.

"This one," Marketa said.

Annabella nodded and bent down beside her with her knife. It was crooked and better suited for loosening mussels than the one Marketa had.

Annabella worked the edge of the knife back and forth behind the shell and severed its hold on the rocks. She smiled as she looked into Marketa's eyes, and, quick as the shellman in the market, the witch slipped her knife around the mouth of the shell and pried it open with a twist of her wrist.

Inside was an enormous white pearl, the largest Marketa had ever seen. It lay glistening in the spit of the mussel.

"Here, quick—put it in your mouth for good luck. Then spit it into my hand," said Annabella.

Marketa did as she was told. The mineral taste of the mussel was fresh on her tongue and she smiled.

She spat the pearl into Annabella's open palm. The red-haired woman took out a little leather purse and popped the pearl into it and drew the purse strings tight. She tucked the buckskin bag into her bodice.

"Now," she said, "let us do something about that rash."

Marketa accompanied her back to her house. Again, the three cats appeared, meowing this time in chorus. Annabella bent over to stroke their chins.

"My beauties," she purred to them as she opened the door.

The great room was cluttered with clay pots on shelves, full of ointments and rendered fats. An open fire pit stood in the center of the room, though the fireplace on one wall was clearly where she did her cooking.

This must be where she performs her spells and witchcraft, Marketa thought. She said a quick prayer but did not want to leave. One of the cats, a bright orange tomcat with green eyes, lingered at Marketa's side, watching her.

The ceiling was hung with dried herbs, an upside-down garden, the flowers and leaves blossoming from the rafters down.

Marketa sneezed and sneezed again.

"That is normal until you get used to it," said Annabella. "There are half a hundred different herbs and flowers drying overhead. I will brew us some chamomile tea, and we will get started curing your rash."

She pulled a clay pot with a wire handle from a shelf and filled it with water from a jug. She fed the embers in the hearth with twigs and blew on them until they burst into flame. She added a birch log and wiped her hands on her apron. With tongs, she hung the little pot from the hook in the hearth.

Marketa could smell the smoked hams, redolent with fat, tied in the chimney above the fire. Amid the strangeness of the herbs, it was a familiar scent; Krumlov families stored meat and sausages in strings from the chimney so the smoke would cure the meats.

Annabella took her knife and reached up into the chimney. She smiled as her hand emerged with a fat sausage. The three cats came meowing, and Annabella squeezed some fat on the floor for them to lick.

"Here, we will have this with some bread and ale. We must celebrate the pearl!" she said, bringing out a big jug of ale and two clay mugs. The two young women sat on the bench by the fire and shared the bread and sausage while the tea water boiled.

"How did you find me?" Annabella asked.

"Your neighbor, the alchemist, told me where you might be," Marketa said.

"Ah, Pan Alchemist. Yes, he is an observant one. Do you know he is an astrologer as well? A wise man, though he failed as an alchemist."

"He told me my rash is a result of my body and spirit rebelling."

Annabella chewed thoughtfully on her sausage. At last she smacked her lips and asked, "Do you think he is right?"

"I do not know. I thought you would know."

"I am not inside your body and mind. It was not I who found the pearl."

Marketa sighed, confused, and looked at the leaping flames.

"There are some moments in my life I am ashamed of," Marketa said. "Things I would like to change."

"Dare to speak them aloud, Marketa. Tell me."

Marketa swallowed hard. "I hate being a bathmaid." She said the words as if she were spitting out a bitter herb. "I hate showing my body to a man for his lust and pleasure, especially an old married man. I despise his smell and touch."

Marketa gasped as the big orange cat leapt into her lap.

Annabella looked at the fire as she leaned over to stroke the cat, who purred at her touch.

"It seems your body despises his touch as well. You must seek a way to escape. Is there a dream you wish to pursue?"

Marketa ducked her head and looked down into the cat's orange fur.

"Tell me," Annabella said. "Tell me what future you want, no matter how unlikely. Declare not what you are, not what you have to be, but what you want to be."

Marketa could smell the healer's breath, fragrant with herbs as if she were part of the dried garden hanging overhead.

Marketa spoke the words she had never said to anyone before, words she had hardly had the courage to think, much less speak. "I want to be a physician. I want to be a bloodletter, *ne*, a full physician, one who can heal with the teachings of Paracelsus as well as Galen."

"Ah, Paracelsus," Annabella said. "Do you know that many of his methods and medicines are ones we cunning women have used for hundreds of years? His bible of herbal remedies came from our mothers and grandmothers, handed down woman to woman for generations."

Marketa ducked her head in disbelief. Paracelsus was a scientist, not a sorcerer. Annabella's words were blasphemy.

"I can see that you do not believe me," Annabella said, shrugging. "Well…" She left the word hanging in the air as she rose and opened an oak chest that groaned in protest. Bending and straightening, she carefully lifted out a book, the Book of Paracelsus.

"What is this?" Marketa was astonished. "You could afford to have this? It is a treasure!"

"Yes, well. It was a gift. Let us just say that I did a very rich and powerful man a very great favor." Annabella smiled. "Shoo, Prophet!" she said, waving her hand at the cat on Marketa's lap. She laid the tome on Marketa's lap. "Open it."

Never did Marketa think she would see the writings of Paracelsus, let alone in a witch's house in Krumlov. She handled the book carefully, savoring the animal smell of the vellum, the finely inked writing scratched on the pages.

It suddenly occurred to Marketa that Annabella could read.

"Who taught you to read?" she asked.

"That same good neighbor you met earlier, Pan Alchemist. Now, look, see what it says about skin inflammations. I have a potion for you—Saint-John's-wort tempered with soaked oats."

Marketa carefully lifted the pages one by one, to find cures for skin inflammations.

"Yes," she said, as a smile broke over her face. "Yes, Paracelsus calls it 'red oil.'"

And as Marketa said this, Annabella reached her hands toward a jar, shining red as a sunset.

"I have infused these oils since I gathered the flowers on Saint John's Day. They have a special power when plucked on that date. You must take this home and pour enough oil to cover just the bottom of a cup, fill the cup halfway with cooked oats, and make a poultice to cover wherever the rash afflicts you."

Marketa nodded.

"But that is not all. I want you to take three drops of the tincture three times a day and concentrate on your dream. You must do this or the tincture will do no good for you."

Marketa hung her head. "What good will that do? My mother has contracted me to the brewer, and we need the money. I am a woman, and if I practice bloodletting or other medicine I will be accused of being a..."

She broke off.

"A witch? Is that what you are afraid of?" Annabella said. "Well, my sister, have some courage and heed your dreams, not your mother's demands or what the gossips may say or expect you to be."

Marketa nodded.

"If you have hope, the medicine will work for you. If you settle for despair, there is nothing I or anyone else can do to help you. Now let us have some of the chamomile tea with honey. It is also good for your nerves."

Then she reached over and caressed Marketa's hair.

"Such special hair," she said. "I have never seen so many colors at once. It is like mottled amber."

Then she stared into Marketa's eyes, holding her gaze.

"There may be a day when you again need my help, sister. Do not forget that I am here to serve the innocent and deserving. And remember this: Do not fear the good spirits who come to aid you in your life."

Prophet the cat began to purr at Marketa's feet as she settled down to examine the book again.

When Marketa left Annabella's house two hours later, she felt a new sense of determination, like a young colt galloping and bucking in the tall grass of summer. The cold wind that curled around her chin seemed gentler than she remembered it, and she dropped her scarf, not worrying whether anyone saw the red blisters on her face.

LATE SPRING 1606

CHAPTER 4

ARCHDUKE MATTHIAS, YOUNGER BROTHER OF RUDOLF II

A tall, bearded rider raced along the spine of low hills flanking the Danube. The wind blew the white mane of the Andalusian stallion into the rider's eyes as he crouched low on the horse's withers, its pounding hoofs churning up loam at breakneck speed.

Matthias, Archduke of Upper and Lower Austria, glanced back to see his entourage far behind him; no one could keep up with Royal Ducat, his gray stallion.

Trained to ride in his father Emperor Maximillian II's Spanish Riding School at the age of five, Matthias had grown up on the back of Lipizzaners. These Andaluz horses were brought from Spain to Austria by his father and uncle and bred exclusively for the Hapsburg monarchy. Matthias felt his father's passion for horses in his blood. And although his elder brother Rudolf—stocky and short—shared his enthusiasm for the Andaluz breed, it was Matthias's long leg on a horse and fearlessness in the saddle that made his father proud.

Emperor Maximillian knew this young son was the warrior Hapsburg.

Matthias reined in his horse along the rocky ridge, trampling the carpet of red poppies under hoof. He had ridden several miles beyond the walls of the great city of Esztergom—the "jewel of the Danube bend" and ancient capital of Hungary. King Rudolf's younger brother was determined to defend the city that his armies had fought so hard to take back from the Ottomans scarcely more than a decade before.

The archduke scanned the low green hills of the Hungarian countryside. There were rumors of an Ottoman incursion in the southeast beyond Buda, but so far he had seen no smoke from campfires where the Janissaries would have been cooking their rations in enormous copper kettles.

More than any other army, thought Matthias, an Ottoman's heart for war was determined by the rations in their dinner bowl. The sign of honor and high rank was a soup ladle, distinguishing the officers from the soldiers.

Not a star. Not a crescent moon or gold stripe. A soup ladle signified the *corbaci*, the captain of a unit.

Matthias had learned much about the Turks in the past years, mostly from one of his chief commanders, the wealthy Transylvanian Ferenc Nadasdy, whose gold had financed a large portion of the Hapsburg defense against the marauding Ottomans.

Despite the financial backing and Nadasdy's appetite for war, Matthias had not been sorry when he heard last year of the warrior lord's death in battle. The brutal Transylvanian had made his skin crawl. Matthias dreaded the nights of the Ottoman campaign when he was quartered in Nadasdy's ancestral castle of Cachtice, a drafty stone fortress at the foot of the Little Carpathians. The frightened eyes of the castle servants and the cowering peasants in the village made Matthias wonder which the people feared more—the Turks or the Nadasdy family.

Nadasdy was a man who loved war—and was especially fond of torture. Even the Turks feared him, calling him the Black Knight of Transylvania. It was rumored his wife, Elizabeth Bathory, niece of the king of Poland, was as sadistic as her husband.

Still, distasteful though they might be, these alliances with the rich and powerful families of Europe were critical to the Hapsburg dynasty.

Nadasdy taught Matthias the savage customs of the Ottomans and their beliefs. *Know your enemy, Matthias,* he had instructed him. *Know your enemy better than he knows you.*

Matthias learned how the Ottomans dyed their horses for battle, how their Janissary troops were kidnapped Christian boys, circumcised and raised as Islamic warriors. He learned that the bloody heathens, who impaled their enemies' heads upon stakes as trophies, stopped to pray five times a day. Before they prostrated themselves before God, they washed themselves. He learned that on the battlefield, where there was no water, they rubbed themselves with sandy dirt, cleaning behind their ears and rubbing their hands from the forehead to the nape of their necks, as a cat would lick itself clean with the crook of its paw.

Heathens, thought Matthias, leaning to spit over his boot in the stirrup. Yet the barbarians were banging a mighty fist on the front gates of Europe, once again threatening Vienna itself, as they moved ever closer to the heart of civilized Christendom.

It was Matthias and his Holy Roman armies—led by men like Nadasdy—on the wild Hungarian front that held back the infidels' armies. His brother, King and Emperor Rudolf II, had given him a perilous honor: commander-in-chief of the Ottoman War.

Rudolf would like to see my head stuck on the tip of an Ottoman spear, the crows pecking at my eyes, thought Matthias. *At last he would be rid of me.*

Rudolf feared Matthias, for the king had no legitimate children. He put every obstacle in his younger brother's way to keep him away from Prague and the throne.

Matthias looked down at the crushed poppies on the ground and thought of his lovely cousin, Anne of Austria. He swallowed hard, knowing that as long as King Rudolf was alive, Matthias could never ask for her hand, or any other woman's for that matter.

It was not enough that the king had begrudged Matthias permission to marry; the warrior archduke was called away from his home in Linz to plan and fight battles, both offensive and defensive, against the encroaching Ottoman armies. He had no life but war, year after year.

How he wished he could shift this burden to his older brother's shoulders! But Prague did not concern itself with Hungary and its scorched lands, the wounded, the dead. King Rudolf spent his gold on alchemists, astrologers, and the occult. He washed his hands of Hungary, leaving its defense to Matthias and his allies.

The king's only concern with Royal Hungary was taxing the Protestant majority into poverty and ruin as they fought to save their ancient kingdom. If it weren't for the money that Petr Vok Rozmberk now poured into the Turkish campaign, the Ottomans would have long since taken Moravia, Bohemia, and Vienna.

Matthias saw a thin wisp of smoke snake up over a hill in the distance. His stallion nickered, no doubt calling to the mares in the Ottoman camp.

We will attack at dawn, he thought. *If we circle the encampment and cut off escape into Buda, we stand a chance of halting their progress into Royal Hungary.* The scouts to the north and east would no doubt report other incursions that evening, for the Ottomans were always on the march.

Matthias reined his horse back toward camp, where he and the commanders would plan their attack.

But before he spurred his horse, he took a second look at the flower-strewn countryside and the rolling green hills. Someday all this would be part of his kingdom. Someday he would rule as Holy Roman emperor.

His numerous spies in Prague kept him informed. They came to the Hungarian front to find him, all with the same report, eager for the silver their sharp ears and wagging tongues earned them.

The king's son Don Julius is mad! The people of Prague spit and whistle at the rogue when he walks the streets, yet the king does nothing to contain him.

The Achilles' heel of his brother Rudolf was his favorite son. Matthias's informers told sordid tales of scandals in the streets of Prague and Vienna, and in the brothels of both cities, dark stories of the lunatic bastard, who even prostitutes feared.

Now there were whispers that Rudolf considered incarcerating Don Julius—his own son.

Know your enemy, Nadasdy had said. And find his weakness.

One day my young nephew will help me claim the throne, Matthias thought, and he smiled as his entourage finally caught up to him on the ridge.

CHAPTER 5

THE WHITE LADY

The first time Marketa saw the White Lady of Cesky Krumlov, the girl was kneeling by the banks of the Vltava, rinsing a ring of blood from a white ceramic bowl. Her father had performed a bloodletting that morning, and his finest dish was crusted brown with a stain that clung to the ceramic after she had fed the garden soil with what remained of the patient's bad humors.

Her fingernails scratched at the crusted blood, and the sparkling cold water of the river flooded over the rim of the bowl, clearing the stain at last. Suddenly, she had the uneasy feeling that someone was watching her from above. She lifted her eyes from the water, up the stone walls that rose directly from the riverbank to the castle.

The woman who stood there, far above the racing waters, was as fair as snow, dressed in white satin, her pale arms encased in transparent gauze. A gray sash draped to one side, looping down to a long train of white folds. Her hair was fashioned in ringlets, hay-colored and long against her neck, in the old style of a century ago.

She smiled sadly down at Marketa from the heights of the palace wall. Marketa dropped the bowl in the mud of the river and heard it chip on a rock. She bent her dirty knees under her homespun dress and wet apron in a curtsy. She supposed the lady to be a Rozmberk of the Five-Petal Rose, the noble family of the castle and the same as kings to those of the village. Even as she curtsied, Marketa stared down at the chipped ceramic and thought of what her mother would say when the surgery bowl came back damaged. Her father's patients noticed such things, especially the rich ones.

When Marketa lifted her eyes, the woman in white had vanished. Marketa collected the crockery in the wet folds of her apron and turned back to the bathhouse, her heart thudding within her chest.

Viennese peddlers often lodged in Marketa's uncle's tavern, and he would tell the family their tales at Sunday dinner. Uncle Radek had never married and grew up eating his sister's Bohemian cooking. He felt it was his birthright to have a place at the Pichler table, whether or not they could afford to feed another mouth.

The evening following the appearance of the lady in white, Radek invited himself to dinner. Marketa saw him leering at the meal on the table when she peeked as they said grace. He lusted after her mother's cooking like a dog chasing a bitch in heat. The way he eyed the dumplings made Marketa blush, which did not come easy. Working in her mother's bathhouse, Marketa had seen all manner of lechery.

After the Pichlers had thanked God for his bounty, Zigmund Pichler nodded his head and pronounced, *"Dobrou chut"* before the family broke bread.

As Lucie ladled out cabbage and lentil soup and *jatrove knedlicky*—liver dumplings—into his bowl, her brother Radek stuffed his mouth with fresh bread that the twins had baked that afternoon. He rolled his fat tongue over his food and addressed the table with an open mouth, his words making their way through a brown wad of buttered bread.

"Another rich trader came bringing fine cloth and bright jewels for the Rozmberks," he said, taking a long draught of pilsner and filling his mouth with a dumpling. "He says it was a waste of a hard journey—they no longer have the gold to buy his goods."

"As if the Rozmberks cannot buy anything their heart desires!" Lucie scoffed. "They drive coaches of gold, and the lady wears loops of pearls around her neck! The old bears in the moat dine on fattened calves—I have seen the carcasses with my own eyes! How could they not afford to buy pretty things?"

"I am only telling you what I hear from my customers, and they have no reason to lie," said Uncle Radek, digging with his thumb at a plug of dumpling between his molars. He sucked at his thumbnail and the dislodged food, smacking his lips in satisfaction. "The Rozmberks have come onto hard times and may even sell the castle."

"Sell the castle!" Marketa echoed. "Maybe that's why the fair lady in white is walking the walls. I should like to look upon her again!"

Suddenly the clatter of dishes and lip-smacking stopped.

Marketa's mother stared, her dark eyes bulging.

"When have you seen a lady in white, girl?"

"Leave her alone now, Lucie," said her father, setting down his knife, a chunk of dumpling still speared on its end. "Let her finish her dinner."

"You heard me, Daughter!" her mother insisted. "When did you see a woman in white?"

"Today, as I was washing the surgery tray," Marketa said. "She startled me so that I dropped it and took a chip out of the rim. I am sorry. She was looking at me, and I've never seen her like before. Fair-haired and bejeweled, with skin whiter than bleached bedsheets in summer."

"It is the White Lady," murmured Uncle Radek, swallowing at last, his hairy nostrils flaring. "She's seen her. One of my own family! Musle, you have the gift—"

"Do not dare call her that vulgar name in this house!" roared Pichler, his dining knife raised and pointing at his brother-in-law's face. "This is not the tavern, and you will keep a civil tongue!"

Marketa felt the blood drain from her face, and her cheeks went cold and numb. No one had ever dared to use that lecherous nickname in her father's presence before. She wanted to seep into the cracks of the stone floor and hide under its darkness forever.

She had hoped her father did not know what the townspeople now called her.

Her mother jumped up from the bench. She knelt by her daughter's side and grasped her hand so hard, Marketa thought she would cry out.

"What color gloves was she wearing, Marketa?"

"Gloves?"

"Were they white or were they black?"

Marketa could feel her mother's hand trembling. She could smell her sweat and the onions from her cooking clinging to her skin.

"I—I did not see any gloves. No—she did not wear gloves. She was bare-handed and fair-skinned as a marble statue."

"Liar!" said her mother, suddenly smacking Marketa with an open palm. "You chipped our good bowl and made up a lie about the White Lady just to frighten us!"

Marketa pressed her hand against her stinging cheek. She was too stunned to cry, for her mother had never struck her before. She looked at her twin sisters, whose faces blanched, and they clutched each other in fear.

Pichler pushed his wife away and sent her tumbling on the floor. Marketa gasped. Her father had always been a gentle soul, and now he was shouting at Uncle Radek and shoving her mother to the ground.

"Our Marketa does not lie! If she saw a woman in white, it could have been a Rozmberk relation or guest. If she says she had bare arms, it is the truth. Do not dare to strike her again, lest you feel my own hand on your face!"

He hugged his daughter close, sheltering her in his arms. Marketa could smell her mother's meaty cooking in his beard and ale on his breath.

She whispered to him, "Who is this woman and why is Mother so angry?"

"Finish your dinner, Marketa. You are looking pale and thin. It will not do for my patients to see my assistant, my own daughter, ailing when you carry away the trays of blood."

"But the White Lady?"

"Never mind now. Eat, Daughter."

He scraped a gravy-covered dumpling off his plate onto Marketa's with his knife. The scratching of the blade against the pewter plate filled the room, otherwise silent in obedience to her father's rage.

Her mother struggled to her knees and hoisted herself back onto the bench, gathering her skirt under her. She held her head erect, her back rigid with resentment.

For the rest of dinner, Lucie glared at her daughter across the table and seemed to have no appetite. Still, every now and again Marketa noticed a shiver catch her and shake its way up her spine.

~

The next day, Pichler set out for Vienna and the barber-surgeon guildhouse, where he kept abreast of the latest phlebotomy studies. He kissed his daughter good-bye and warned her to behave and keep peace with her mother while he was away.

Marketa sighed and promised to make herself useful in the bathhouse. She worked hard that morning washing a mountain of linen bath sheets and hanging them out to dry by the banks of the Vltava. When her mother nodded approvingly at the rows of flapping white laundry strung between the trees, Marketa smiled.

"Daughter, you deserve time away from the bathhouse. Dana and Kate can help me this afternoon."

Marketa kissed her mother's cheek, knowing she was trying to make amends for striking her the night before. Her mother embraced her quickly and shooed her away, encouraging her to enjoy a few hours of free time in the sunshine.

Marketa sought out her best friend, Katarina Mylnar, the miller's daughter. They sat side by side on the riverbank, their feet dangling in the water, looking at the great walls of Rozmberk Palace looming above them. The Mylnar family's waterwheel groaned behind them as the girls took pleasure in a few rare moments of leisure, basking in the afternoon sun.

Marketa found her friend's company comforting, especially after her mother's strange outburst the night before.

Katarina smelled of flour and sugar, especially on Saturdays. That was the day her mother did the most baking and provided cakes for the town and the Rozmberk family.

Katarina was plump, and the flour and fine sugar would find their way deep into the folds of her damp skin, nestling in her neck and cleavage, elbow crooks and fingers. She was fair-haired and laughed at everything as if she were pleasantly drunk at a holiday feast.

The millers's daughter had many admirers, for who would not love a woman who loved life with such passion—and whose family baked buttery cakes for nobility? As they exchanged secrets, their feet splashing in the cool water, Katarina whispered to Marketa that she wished one day the blacksmith's son would taste her skin all night long, his tongue savoring every sugared crevice.

Marketa laughed in conspiracy at her friend's confession, but she knew Katarina's desire would never come to pass. Katarina's father was not keen on the match and scowled at the sweaty-faced lad with sooty fingers. He felt his daughter could attract a better suitor, perhaps a butcher or even a wealthy merchant.

In fact, Katarina's father forbade her to spend time with any man. His daughter was to be surrounded by women and girls until he found her a suitable husband. Katarina chose to spend most of her time with the bathmaid, although Marketa could not understand why the town's beauty would want to spend time with the bloodletter's daughter.

But Katarina loved Marketa's strong character and admired her fierce interest in science. Her stories fascinated the miller's daughter, for Marketa could read, a skill that was rare among women.

In the winter, the two girls loved to skate down the icy cobblestones on hilly Meat Street in their wood-soled shoes, slipping and falling to the hooting of the butchers. The meat cutters would cheer them on with muffled claps of their fingerless gloves, their bodies wrapped tight in woolen cloaks while they stamped their feet against the cold. Marketa's cheeks flushed red and hot from the contrast of the steaming barrels of the bathhouse and the damp, frosty air. Katarina's pale skin would glow warm pink, sticky with sugar, like a frosted cake.

The two were inseparable, and Katarina spent many an afternoon combing and braiding Marketa's long hair, particularly on lazy warm days such as this one.

"The most peculiar and enchanting hair in the world," she sighed in wonder. "It has every color of every girl's hair. Amber, chestnut. Look! Here is a strand of blonde the same hue as mine, and here is one the raven black of the gypsy girl, Ruby!"

"Oh and this!" she said, plucking a hair from her friend's head.

"Ow!"

"This one is the flaming red of the witch Annabella!" Katarina teased, twisting the orange strand in the sunlight. "Your hair must be bewitched!"

"Do not call her a witch!" Marketa snapped, twisting her head around to admonish Katarina. "The Church burns witches! Annabella is a cunning woman, capable of great cures."

"Calm down! I am neither the Church nor the king. I do not wish to harm our village healer," said Katarina. "Now relax for goodness' sake. Let me finish your hair."

Katarina went back to lifting Marketa's tresses and braiding it with her soft hands.

"If it were not so perfectly mixed, I could plait it into individual braids and no two would be the same color!" Katarina said.

Marketa felt herself drifting off as Katarina pulled her hair gently with her soft hands and tugged it into long braids. The girls would sit in the soft grass by the river and Katarina would adorn Marketa's hair with wildflowers, which thrived in the rocky soil and laced riotous colors through the fields and meadows of Krumlov.

Katarina asked endless questions about Marketa's father's profession, about the sharpening of the blades, the four humors of the body that were released by surgery, the people he had saved, and the patients he had not. She wanted to know about the fleam, the razor-sharp blade he used to nick the skin, the cupping glasses to pull out blood, and the leeches themselves.

Katarina had a curious habit of crossing herself anytime she asked a question, as if the science of Zigmund Pichler's profession were somehow a sin.

"Tell me again," she would implore, her hand fluttering about her face and bosom. "About the humors. I have them all muddled up, Marketa. I am not as clever as you."

Marketa sighed because she couldn't believe that a miller's daughter, with a hundred recipes in her head, couldn't hold on to four simple humors.

"The black bile. Now that one stays with me, Marketa. The sadness, melancholy humor."

"Just the opposite of you, Katarina. It's strange that you should remember only that one!"

"Maybe it is because I have heard it said that King Rudolf is haunted by melancholy. But tell me the others!" she begged. "And how your father brings them into harmony."

Marketa smiled because Katarina was paying her father a compliment. A good barber-surgeon could cure the sickest man, woman, or child, if he could manage to balance the four humors.

"Blood, the sanguine humor, is for laughter, music, and passion. That one you have in your veins, my friend, by the bucketful."

Katarina laughed, throwing her head back so that her white teeth gleamed in the sun and the light caught the granules of sugar that clung to her plump throat.

"The others, Marketa. Please."

"Phlegm. The dull and sluggish."

"Like the grave digger's son, who is not saddened at his occupation, but is just like an old mole, bored with life itself. Oh, how I wish he wouldn't stare at me in the streets with his sad face."

"The last is yellow bile. It is the cruelest of them all. It causes outrage, ravenous lechery, even—murder."

Katarina widened her eyes. Legends and fairy stories captured her like nothing else. And to her, the cholers were a witch's tale.

"Murder," she whispered.

"Too much yellow bile causes lunacy. It boils up in the veins and scalds with burning lust or murderous passion. That is what the book says."

Katarina looked at Marketa in admiration, nodding her head.

"You and your books. Ah, what a gift it must be to discover the world in those squiggly lines."

Marketa heard her mother call from across the river that she needed help in the bathhouse.

She rose to her feet and kissed Katarina on the cheek.

"I have to go now," Marketa said. "But as always you have given me cheer, dear friend. Let me teach you to read, Katarina. Then you too can decipher those squiggly lines!"

Katarina looked at her friend, stunned.

"Me? Read?"

"Of course. Why not? It is not magic. Reading only takes instruction and practice."

Katarina reached for her friend's hands, kissing them.

"Oh, Katarina," said Marketa, snatching her hands away. "Don't make such a fuss!"

Marketa waved good-bye as she hurried to the Barber's Bridge.

It was true. Reading was a rare gift that Pichler had given his daughter, and Marketa had the opportunity to practice with tutors who were too poor to pay for bloodletting and traded their bookish skills for her father's services. Books were mainly in Latin, and she struggled with her father's help to decipher them. But she could understand Czech and German well enough to read and write simple correspondence, her mouth working over the sounds and threading them together into a word.

Her skinny twin sisters, Dana and Kate, age ten, could neither read nor write. Like most of the children in Krumlov who did not attend the Jesuit Latin school, they did not seem to mind in the slightest. The girls shook their heads as they saw their sister sitting with a book in her lap, her finger tracing the words to sound out their meaning. They never resented Marketa for having the education they did not, for neither of them had any desire to spend precious minutes of free time bent over a book.

Lucie would stomp over to the table in the evening where Marketa leaned over a precious book, poring over the words. With a wet pinch of her finger and thumb, she would snuff out the sputtering tallow candle, leaving Marketa in the dark, with only the glow of the embers in the hearth to illuminate the room.

"Do not waste candles," her mother scolded. "We are not Hapsburgs! Go to sleep. Your reading will do you no good in the baths and is useless for a woman. It can only ruin your eyes!"

Marketa would sit in the sudden darkness as the rancid, smoking fat of the candle spread its last greasy fumes across the room. She breathed in the thick air, touching the parchment with her fingers.

Her father thought it was important for her to read, especially as she had taken an early interest in his profession. There was no such thing—there could be no such thing—as a woman barber-surgeon, but Marketa quickly excelled as an assistant. She knew how to keep his scissors and blades sharp, and when he performed surgery, she held the bowl to catch the splashing course of blood in a modest manner that reassured the patients. She learned the bleeding points, the system of veins, and how to stanch bleeding.

And Marketa knew she was never ever to touch hair that was cut with her father's barber's scissors. The spirit left in the strands could be malevolent and strike her dead. At the very least it might invade her soul, make cows' milk curdle, or leave her infertile.

Marketa also took a keen interest in the humors and the diseases they created when out of balance. Marketa felt that her father's profession was akin to the divine working of miracles. It was said that she was much more like her father than her mother, but some of the older folk in Krumlov whispered she was much like her revered aunt, the mother superior of the convent of Poor Clares. They nodded their white heads in silent agreement when they saw her in the street. Indeed, the girl possessed the same mysterious air the holy Mother Ludmilla had when she was the same age.

Marketa's father whispered to her when she was a mere toddler that he was sure she had the gift of healing. He thought his daughter too young to understand and remember his words.

But she did.

As Marketa walked over Barber's Bridge to the bathhouse, she thought wistfully of her father in Vienna. How she wished she could be at his side, listening to the latest discoveries in human anatomy and phlebotomy.

Little did she know that another discovery—a chance encounter in the streets of Vienna with a Hapsburg—was about to change her father's life forever.

He would be the first to bring the unspeakable news to Cesky Krumlov.

CHAPTER 6

RUDOLF II AND THE CODED BOOK OF WONDER

King Rudolf scratched peevishly inside one nostril with his manicured fingernail. It wasn't a particularly elegant act to perform in the Viennese court, but then what did it matter? He was emperor of the Holy Roman Empire, the king of Hungary, king of Moravia and Bohemia and Croatia. And the Eastern kingdoms paid him tribute and asked for his mighty protection, so he could include these in his possession.

And given the daily news of the outrageous behavior of his bastard son Giuglio—now known to everyone but the royal family as Don Julius—what condemnation could a little nose-scratching merit? He had divine right, he was...

One of his many dwarfs, the pimply one, giggled and whispered something behind his pudgy hand.

"Do you mock me, you ugly sprite?" snapped the king. The finger so recently engaged in scratching now pointed ominously at the little man. "Approach me, you warty little toad!"

The dwarf widened his eyes in horror and tried to swallow his fear. The king was known for sudden fits of rage, and a court dwarf was disposable, just one among the many given to Rudolf for his amusement. The man trembled at the thought of being plunged into the darkness of a Viennese prison.

"Of course not, my lord! I'd sooner cut off my right arm than to insult my king!" he said.

"Of what do you speak, then, so full of mirth?"

The dwarf hesitated, his eyes darting like scared minnows as he conjured his lie. "I—I was wondering if life in Prague and the *hrad* is as marvelously amusing as I've heard. The music, the feasts, the Vltava River that sparkles green—"

Everyone in the Viennese court knew of His Majesty's preference for Prague, where he could escape the pressures and royal duties of Vienna and indulge his melancholy, his love for art, astronomy, exotic animals, beautiful women, and clocks.

The king's minister, Wolfgang Rumpf, stepped in, perhaps saving the dwarf's life.

"Yes, indeed. This little man does praise well the charms of the capital city Prague for one who has never laid eyes on her eternal beauty," he said, casting a sardonic look at the trembling dwarf. "What an astute observation from someone so humble."

"My holy city of enchantment," murmured the king, momentarily forgetting his wrath. "Bah! Vienna sickens me with her air—the Danube cannot compare with the Vltava. Did I not proclaim Prague as City Eternal of the Holy Roman Empire? Why do state affairs continue to draw me back to this old whore of a city and the nagging voice of my mother? We shall prepare for Prague immediately. You, Rumpf, shall address these tedious councilors who suck my very marrow with their questions and pleas. They tire me with their wheedling."

Minister Rumpf, who was long accustomed to taking charge of the reins of the empire, especially when His Majesty suffered a bout of melancholy, consented with a low bow.

"However, before your imminent departure, my lord," said Wolfgang Rumpf, addressing the king's polished boot, "if you please, we must discuss the fate of your son, Don Julius Caesar d'Austria."

"Giuglio has the corrupt blood of his Italian mother in his veins. This is my punishment for coupling with the foreign wench."

Minister Rumpf's eyebrow twitched. It had long been assumed by the European royal courts that Emperor Rudolf's own mental failings—bouts of melancholy and fits of temper—were a direct inheritance from his great-grandmother, Juana La Loca of Spain, the maddest perhaps of all the Hapsburgs. And now Don Julius, in turn, manifested undeniable signs of the Hapsburg lunacy. The bastard son did not share the dark, brooding melancholy of his father, but displayed a belligerent choler that endangered all near to him.

At least King Rudolf was more eccentric than macabre and his tempers were short-lived, blessed be, thought his minister. It could be worse. His ancestor, Juana La Loca, had kept the dead body of her consort with her for years, caressing and sleeping with the decomposing corpse. Certainly it was best not to have a rotting corpse at court and a queen who made love to it, especially with the Turkish sultan Suleiman waging war and demanding tribute in the southern regions. Still, the nagging problem of the bastard son had to be addressed.

"Last night, my lord, Don Julius attacked his own servant with a knife and thrust the blade through the man's hand. He has been detained by the authorities and rests in a guarded room in the courthouse."

The king's face contorted, but he said nothing. Rumpf waited silently, hoping the king would gain control of his temper before he spoke.

Then Rudolf exclaimed, "Damn that bastard! Damn him and his brothers and sisters, all six bloody bastards! Well, set him free at once, by my order."

Rumpf lowered his voice. He was nearly whispering. "This act was the culmination of a night of debauchery, Your Majesty. Don Julius is reported to have taken two whores into the streets and performed his sordid business in front of a crowd of drunken louts, who cheered him on. His servant tried to pry him from the thighs of the prostitutes and throw clothes on his naked back. The man received this unmerited assault as thanks from your son. He nearly bled to death, but a barber-surgeon in the crowd rushed to stanch the bleeding."

The king said nothing. He remembered the one afternoon years ago when he had struck his son, the day he had found him trying to decipher the Coded Book of Wonder. He thought how his young son had been intrigued by the workings of clocks and other mechanisms such as music boxes and windup toys.

Perhaps it was this instinct for logic and order that had led Giuglio to study the incomprehensible text of the mysterious Coded Book of Wonder.

Why had he lost his temper that day? The memory from seven years ago still gnawed at the king.

What had happened to that boy with the curious mind, the intellectual? The king had pinned all his hopes and pride on his eldest son, the handsome boy who had inherited the good looks of his mistress.

And now...his son had grown cantankerous and fat, gorging himself on cakes and ale, ordering outrageous repasts from the palace kitchens, one after another, each more sumptuous: game, hams, ducks, pies, cheeses, and fancy Viennese pastries, laden with butter and heavy cream. At night, he whored and gambled, came home staggering drunk, and brutally attacked his servants.

He had disgraced himself in the streets and taverns of Prague and now Vienna.

How the boy had disappointed him! He was now twenty and Rudolf could make no more excuses for his outrageous behavior. His appearance, fleshy and swollen-eyed, disgusted his father. What had happened to the sea-green eyes, the color of Venetian glass, he had inherited from his mother? Submerged now in his swollen face, like raisins stuck deep in risen dough.

Had the boy no shame?

The minister dared to touch the king on the sleeve. Rudolf's eyes focused on the light pressure of his hand.

"Your Majesty," Rumpf said in a quiet but urgent tone. "We must do something immediately or your son will be assassinated or worse."

"What do you propose, Minister Rumpf?"

The minister clenched his teeth and closed his eyes.

"The asylum."

"Never! Not that nightmare we witnessed! Mention this to me again and I will have you dismissed."

The minister sighed. "Then, if he cannot be confined to an asylum, Your Majesty, you will likely see your own son murdered by one of your subjects. Or perhaps your brother Matthias will use him as an excuse to seize the crown. No Viennese citizen would oppose Matthias if your son continues his present conduct."

Rudolf's back stiffened at the words.

"May the plague take Matthias and send my brother's soul to hell!"

"You must not let him have an advantage. Show your supreme strength and banish your son before Matthias plays his hand."

The king looked at his minister. He swallowed hard.

"Suggest a solution! I cannot condemn my son to that place we saw!"

Rudolf thought of the bald women, the screaming heads of the wild men, begging to be freed.

"Yet the bastard shall not cost me my throne, I swear it! Perhaps the astrological prognostication was right, and it will be a member of my own family who will bring me to my death."

The king worked his ruby ring around his finger, thinking of the prophecy.

"Tell me, good Rumpf, tell me! What do you propose?" the king said. "But I will not commit my son to the hellhole we visited."

"I have tried to have him enstated in Transylvania as you hoped, but they will not accept him, my lord," said Minister Rumpf. "We would have to go to battle with the Wallachians again to gain him the post."

"No," said Rudolf. "That would give us another vulnerable front to Suleiman's Ottoman army."

The minister reminded the king of the other alternative they had already tried, interning Don Julius in a monastery.

"My lord, you well know that eighteen months with the monks in the Alps did nothing to extinguish his disease."

"That was my mother's idea," grumbled Rudolf. "She always insists he is lacking in religious discipline."

"Yes, well, you know how I feel about the clergy," whispered Rumpf. "They only seem to complicate matters. However, I do have one more idea that might appeal to Your Majesty, and I have taken the liberty to investigate the possibilities. There is a township in southern Bohemia, less than two days' ride from Vienna. It is a place called Cesky Krumlov, on that same Vltava that flows through Prague. Petr Vok and the Rozmberk clan have fallen on hard times financing the Bohemian resistance to the Turks. I think we could persuade them to sell you the castle, and we could keep Don Julius under guard there."

"A prisoner?"

"Under guard only until his humors improve. He will be ensconced in a beautiful castle that rises on a hill above the village. The Rozmberks have furnished it lavishly. It rivals your *hrad* itself. They keep wild bears in the moat to remind the people that they are of the royal Orsino blood of Italy."

"A Bohemian family related to the Orsino? Impossible!" sneered the king.

Rumpf nodded, knowing the Bohemian lords and especially the Protestant Rozmberk clan were thorns in the king's side. Rudolf could not even raise taxes without the consent of the Bohemian estates.

"Certainly, it is highly disputed, but my point is that they have spared no expense or luxury in the castle. Surely your son would find solace and his wits in such a situation."

A smile spread across the king's face. He pulled his ear, contemplating his son as master of his own castle and Bohemian estate.

"The matter is settled! Negotiate a good price with Petr Vok and acquire the castle and the township, too, while you are at it. My son will become Lord of Krumlov. The matter is settled.

"Now I must ready myself for Prague. Dwarf, fetch my valet."

"Then I have your permission to send Don Julius to Cesky Krumlov?"

"I have just said so. He is a nuisance and a menace. But I must insist that a priest accompany him, to appease my mother—she and my uncle Felipe would never let me hear the end of it were he not administered by a Jesuit."

The king stopped, his hand in the air.

"And, Rumpf. I know that it will be difficult to persuade Giuglio to go willingly, let alone cooperate once he is confined to the castle. Yet he must improve his conduct or I shall take even sterner consequences—I will cut off his allowance and send him back to the monastery in Austria and let the bloody monks deal with him again!"

Rudolf tightened his lips, remembering that the monks had no success at all with his belligerent son. No one spoke and the hall resounded with the ticking of over a dozen clocks.

Then the thought came to him.

"Ah!" he said, looking at one of his favorite timepieces, a colossal silver piece with a figure of Bacchus playing the bagpipes. Upon the hour, the figure would come alive and a miniature wooden pipe organ would play music. This was one he had forbidden Giuglio to even touch, let alone dismantle.

"One carrot for my donkey of a son that is sure to snap his head around. Tell him, should he acquiesce to a more moderate life, I will reward him. Yes, tell him I will loan him the Coded Book of Wonder. Tell him I will loan it to him to decode, but only if he shows proper conduct as reported by a priest or responsible caretaker."

"I shall see to it."

"I have not let him touch it since he was a young boy, before he began this bestial conduct."

"It sounds like a perfect occupation—translating a mysterious text. A worthy and dignified use of his intelligence and education."

"By God's holy name, yes!" said the king, smiling broadly. "If I could renew his interest, the Coded Book would keep him occupied for years! Even my most brilliant mathematicians and language experts have failed in deciphering it. I should like to see his mind engaged in something other than debauchery. I have invested a small fortune in tutors and books. Now Don Julius spills his seed in the gutters of Prague and Vienna for the drunks' amusement!"

"A strict regimen will cure him of that," said Minister Rumpf, trying to animate the king before he slumped into one of his dark spells of melancholy. "The Jesuits will see to his discipline."

Rudolf thought about this and wrinkled his brow.

"Ah, yes. The Jesuits. I remember their cold touch when I was a boy in Spain. Rumpf, I want a doctor to treat him as well. Consult my physician, Jan Jesenius, and see if Doctor Mingonius can arrange to treat the boy in Krumlov for a few months. Mingonius could have some luck with him—an engaging sort who would not put up with my son's threats and wheedling. Yes, I shall give Giuglio the Coded Book as a reward after successful treatment for his malicious humors."

Minister Rumpf nodded. Doctor Mingonius had an excellent reputation at court, second only to the Polish Herr Doctor Jesenius. The only drawback was that he was a devoted husband and father and would surely balk at having to leave his family in Prague while he attended Don Julius.

"I will see that Doctor Mingonius makes arrangements to treat Don Julius. In the meantime, I have already sent Jakub Horcicky to make inquiries about hiring a staff and readying the Krumlov castle for Don Julius. He should be there by tomorrow at the latest, inspecting the castle to determine the appropriate apartments to confine Don Julius. We will have to estimate the expenses, along with that of the purchase price, to the royal treasury. He will prepare a report."

"Horcicky? My botanist?"

"Yes, Your Majesty, our imperial chemist. The doctor was born in Krumlov and raised within the walls of the Jesuit monastery there. He can oversee the preparations and secure a reliable staff. He speaks their dialect and has connections through the Jesuit order."

The king pinched his lip. "See that Horcicky does not spend too much time away from the botanical gardens. There is no other man who can coax my orchids into bloom. If he could only distill a potion to cure my son of his madness.

"And see who the barber-surgeon was who saved the life of the servant," said the king, rising from his throne. "He shielded my son's life by preventing a death on the streets of Vienna. Reward him!"

~

Wolfgang Rumpf was never able to find the barber-surgeon who had intervened to save the life of Don Julius's servant.

That barber-surgeon was Zigmund Pichler, Marketa's father, and he had saddled his horse and departed for his home in Cesky Krumlov that very day.

The disgusting encounter with Don Julius had left him even more eager than usual to escape the streets of Vienna, where violence thrived and debauchery rang in the laughter of the drunks and whores. Despite his continuing visits over the years, he had never been comfortable in the foreign city. He had been brought up a strict Catholic by his mother; his much older sister, Ludmilla, was the abbess of the Convent of St. Clare, known as the Poor Clares for their vows of poverty. A yearning for knowledge had attracted him to Vienna, for he longed to better his skills and cure more patients, but he had no stomach for the ribald comportment of the city and his animosity was reciprocated. The Viennese dismissed his German as unintelligible through the thick accent of his native Czech, and they laughed rudely at his prudish, parochial behavior.

He might have protested that he was the owner of the Cesky Krumlov bathhouse and he could hardly be considered prudish—he simply knew what behavior was appropriate for the bathhouse and what behavior for the streets. But he never mentioned the bathhouse to anyone, especially not strangers.

This visit had been more difficult than most. He had been forced to try new accommodations, and this rooming house, though near the guild, was far rougher, less civilized than the one he had stayed at so many times before.

Pichler crossed himself when he heard a curse at breakfast, and the other boarders had snickered at his innocence. They mocked his antiquated clothes, his sack trousers and worn jacket, clear signs of a rural Czech rube.

Still Pichler had endured their teasing, just to study with his mentor, Master Weiss, at the barber-surgeon guild. For it was Weiss's unparalleled erudition he sought—with a burning hunger to learn.

Each day of his stay, Pichler approached the bright, cream-colored guildhouse as his elder sister might approach the altar of God. He felt the thrill in the quickening of his heartbeat and the cold shiver that worked its way up his sweating back.

Master Weiss traveled the world, collecting secrets from other barber-surgeons. He had most recently been to London where he heard the lectures of the distinguished William Clowes, chirurgeon to the Queen. Clowes's book, *A Proved Practice*, graced the polished table of the guild.

Master Weiss invited Pichler to study the book. It was the New Testament to the barber-surgeon profession. The master also unrolled scrolls that sketched the anatomy of the human body and the veins that had been identified. That knowledge was precious indeed. The English Parliament had passed a law that the barber-surgeon guild was to receive four bodies—hand-picked and delivered by the beadles of the gallows—every year, so that the science of medicine could advance. Family members were known to pursue the cart carrying off their loved one for dissection. Still, Henry VIII had decreed that science must prevail, and his daughter Elizabeth I, who reigned now, did not protest the law.

The thirst for knowledge had grown so acute that members of the guild squabbled over the corpses and were even driven to robbing graves. Paupers and whores were rarely missed when they disappeared from the overcrowded cemeteries, where no mourner would ever visit the departed.

Pichler copied the charts of the veins as best he could onto scrolls of parchment and thought how they would delight Marketa, who took an almost uncanny interest in the course and conduits of life's blood.

But the morning after the debacle of Don Julius, Pan Pichler heard news that sent him packing immediately for home.

"It seems you are going to have a royal visitor in Cesky Krumlov," said Master Weiss.

Pichler took a few seconds to sort through this statement, the German tongue confounding his comprehension.

"A visitor?"

"The mad bastard son of Rudolf II is to become the new master of Cesky Krumlov and reside in the palace."

"But the Rozmberks have lived there for centuries!"

"They need the emperor's gold," said Herr Weiss. "And so you are to inherit the king's bastard son. I am sorry to have to give you such sore news, for he is no prize. He is Prague's most sordid sot, and they will sing at full lung in the Old Town Square when the news comes they are rid of him. I hope the guards keep the wretched bastard under tight control, for the women—and the men—of Cesky Krumlov are not safe from his lunatic humors."

Herr Weiss dropped his voice and bent close to Pichler's ear.

"I hear last night he rutted with whores in the streets, just to cause mirth and let his infamy be announced throughout Vienna."

Pichler realized that the man Master Weiss was describing was the same young barbarian who had attacked and almost killed his own servant—indeed, would have killed him had not Pichler intervened to save the man's life.

"That fiend is to come to Cesky Krumlov! How can it be? I shall alert the ministers, and we shall howl a protest that even the deaf shall hear!"

Weiss smiled sadly at his protégé. "You may howl like dogs at the moon, but the moonlight will not change its color." He leaned even closer and whispered, "Our emperor is strange in the head himself. Although everyone knows that, I could be beheaded for saying it. Still, our Rudolf is more melancholy than choleric. His son, however, harbors the most choleric bile and should be legally obliged to bleedings to rid him of his murderous humor and protect the citizens."

"I must ride home," muttered Pichler, carefully closing the precious Clowes book and fastening the latch. "I must warn our town at once."

"I suppose you must. It's a pity you cannot indulge your mind in more knowledge, for there is much I wanted to show you. A cauterizing procedure that could save many lives. The effects of housing surgery tools safely, far from malodorous airs and away from the hair of barbery that can give off evil humors of its own."

"I only use my surgery tools for surgery," said Pichler. "I keep them in an oak chest that my daughter organizes for me. My barber's razors and scissors are kept out on a separate tray. The two never mix, any more than milk with meat for a Jew."

"You have good intuition, for it is said that hair has a power all its own, both good and evil. If I were you, I would burn or bury the sweepings so that your daughter will not touch them by accident."

"Thank you for your advice," said Pichler, gathering up his knapsack and notebooks. "I will try to return next summer, if I can save enough for the journey."

"No, come sooner. In late February, the royal surgeon Jan Jesenius will perform the first public dissection of a corpse. Over a thousand observers are expected to attend from all over the world. Save your crowns for that journey, my friend."

"Here in Vienna?" asked Pichler in astonishment.

"No, by King Rudolf's orders, it shall be performed in Prague."

CHAPTER 7

DROWNED FLEAS

The bathhouse on the banks of the Vltava River stood in the shadow of Rozmberk Castle, like a mushroom growing on the root of a host tree. Gazing up at the castle with its high windows and colorful tower, a tall man in clothes cut of Italian silk and fine wool slowed his pace as he approached Barber's Bridge. Jakub Horcicky de Tenepec, court physician, imperial chemist, and director of the royal gardens, dropped his gaze from the castle walls to the pale yellow bathhouse just below.

It was just as he recalled it from his youth. A place that Jesuits considered a den of iniquity, where the villagers bathed communally, without modesty.

Jakub smiled, remembering the Jesuits' admonishments. Now in his service to the king, he found himself again in his old hometown, gazing at the same blasphemous bathhouse.

He had been sent by Minister Rumpf to inspect Rozmberk Castle to ensure suitable lodging—and containment—of Don Julius. When it was ascertained that a secure confinement could be arranged, along with all the luxuries, staff, and fine dining befitting a son of the king, Jakub had finished his task.

It had been a long, hard journey from Prague; the thick mud of the road had hidden a boulder that shattered the axle of the coach. Jakub was forced to spend two days in Cesky Budejovice, sleeping in a filthy inn, eating rancid food, and enduring the service of a surly innkeeper and his mouse-faced wife. The inn owners were stingy with their guests, offering only gristly meat and watered-down beer. But worst of all they had bed pallets with dirty straw. Jakub suspected the straw hadn't been changed in several seasons, and he scratched at the fleabites on his ankles until they drew blood.

As he stepped on the bridge he saw a girl wading into the river on the Latran side. She was barefooted and was drawing two buckets of water. Her hair looked shiny and clean, and she was taking pains not to get her shift dirty on the rocks.

Jakub watched the girl in the glittering water and rubbed his fingertips over the welts on his ankles. The girl's tunic was wet with perspiration and steam from the bathhouse, and her skin was mottled with red as the cold water of the Vltava stung a blush on her flesh. As she leaned over to dip her bucket, the sunlight caught her hair and he saw the flickering highlights— flame red, sunny blonde—blended among the strands of black and chestnut.

Just then a flea skipped over his silk doublet. A bath! He would drown the cursed vermin in a hot soak and end this infernal itching.

~

"Marketa," called her mother from the entrance of the bathhouse. "Marketa, come here right away!"

The young bathmaid was carrying a bucket of water from the river toward the hearth, but set it down and rubbed her sore back, kneading the strained muscles with her long fingers. She turned toward her mother, who stood at the doorway, welcoming a tall man with fine clothes who pulled off his gloves as he addressed Lucie Pichlerova.

The sight of this handsome, well-dressed man stopped her short, as she wondered how he had found his way into a simple village bathhouse.

"I have traveled for five days from Prague," he said. "I am aching and in need of a bath and a good soak. And I...I have fleas."

"Of course, my lord," Lucie said, curtsying and showing him her gap-toothed smile. It amused her that a rich man would complain with such shame of what all the poor of Bohemia endured as a natural course.

"We run a good bathhouse here, clean and savory. Would you like some sweet herbs in your bath, sir? I will have my daughters prepare the barrel for you, and Marketa here will tend to your scrubbing."

Marketa swallowed. There was something about the man—more than his fine clothes and bearing—that made her heart race. She stared at him, scanning his face. He smiled and she ducked her head, her cheeks burning.

"Marketa!" said her mother, nudging her with an elbow. "Where are your manners? Take this good gentleman to the bathing quarters and give him a good scrub."

Marketa bobbed her head and helped the visitor take off his coat, hanging it on a peg near the front door. She gave a little gasp as she took his scarf, an exquisite garment that seemed made of spun cobwebs, the color of the forest canopy when the morning sun shone through its leaves.

"Do you like it, *slecna*?" asked the stranger, watching her hands delicately handling the silk scarf.

"I have never seen anything as beautiful, not even the priest's vestments," she said, staring at the scarf in her hand.

Marketa turned to hang the bather's clothes on the wooden pegs by the door.

"No," said Lucie, grabbing the cloak in her hand. "Garments as fine as these, we will put in a special place for safekeeping. And this bewitching scarf, it is made from worm spit—silk you call it? It won't do to leave such a rare treasure in plain view. Excuse us, sir, I will just show Marketa where to store it, among our valuables. It won't do to have them hang next to the door where a thief might snatch the lot. Please wait, it won't be a moment."

Lucie folded the coat and scarf over her arm and arched an eyebrow at Marketa to follow her into the recesses of the house.

"Here is your chance, girl!" said Lucie to her daughter, laying the coat on the straw pallet bed and standing back to admire it. "You wanted to get away from the brewer! The greedy bastard is haggling over the supplement he is paying, saying it is too much just to look, not touch. This is a chance to make him realize what a prize he has in you."

The color that had flooded Marketa's face just minutes before drained.

"What are you saying, Mother?"

"This man is ten times as rich as the brewer—maybe a hundred times! Do you see the cut of his coat, the richness of the material? He is from the king's court, I swear it!"

"And?"

"Give the man pleasure, Marketa. Good hands in the right place and we will let Pan Brewer know what price he ought to pay for a bathmaid who entertains visitors from Prague!"

"But Mother!" she protested. "You told me if I submitted to Pan Brewer, it would be enough to feed the family. I did what I promised to do."

Lucie hugged her daughter, pulling her close. She whispered in her ear. "We could triple our payment with some rivalry. If he hears that you have touched a nobleman and given him pleasure, who knows what price he might one day pay for taking your virginity? Come, Daughter. Just slide your hands in the right place when you soap him. Enough to make him moan so the gossips will carry the news to Pan Brewer that you are servicing a member of the king's court. And what a handsome man he is!"

Lucie did not wait to hear Marketa's response but hurried back to the gentleman waiting at the entrance, beaming her split-toothed smile.

"My comely daughter, Marketa, will escort you to the bathing area. I will see to it personally that the barrel is a perfect temperature. Do you like it warm or hot so the water is nearly quivering on the surface?"

"Warm to the touch but pleasant. I do not want to stew, please, *pani*," he said, laughing at her. "Just water to drown these damnable fleas."

He looked at Marketa, his eyes still dancing with amusement.

"I am Jakub Horcicky," he said. "Court physician to King Rudolf II. I am pleased to make your acquaintance, Slecna Marketa."

Marketa accepted his hand and shook it formally. Then she curtsied because she was not sure what manners were appropriate with a physician of the Prague court.

"Please, come with me, Herr Horcicky."

"Pan Horcicky," he corrected her. "Or Jakub would be more suitable as you are about to bathe me. But I have not addressed you in German, so 'Herr' is not appropriate."

"But all those from Prague speak German."

"I speak German, of course, but in my hometown, I prefer to speak my native language."

Marketa realized now that he had, all along, been speaking colloquial Czech with a Krumlov accent. And he was a physician, one who distilled medicines from herbs, just as Annabella did. But she had never seen this man before.

She showed him to the stool where she would bathe him with soap and a reed brush. She helped him remove his finely cobbled shoes and his dark blue doublet.

"You are a physician!" she said, trying to contain the excitement in her voice. "Galen or Paracelsus?" She was suddenly eager to show him she was not just another bathmaid.

Jakub stopped his hand on the lacings of his britches. He cocked his head at her.

"What does a bathmaid know of Galen, much less Paracelsus?"

Marketa jerked her chin up at the insult.

"I happen to be studying his methods of distillations and recognition of medicinal herbs and plants, Herr Doctor."

"Jakub, please—*you* can read?"

Marketa chewed the inside of her mouth in irritation. But of course he would be surprised that a bathmaid could read.

"Yes, I can read, and yes, I know about Paracelsus and his methods, and Galen's four humors as well."

A slow smile spread over Jakub's face.

"Ah, so you must be the bloodletter's daughter!"

Marketa was not certain how he could come so quickly to this conclusion, but a spark of pride ignited in her breast.

"Yes," she said, wiping her wet hands on a bath sheet. "My father is Barber-Surgeon Pichler. I am his assistant."

She noticed that her bemused client was picking clumsily at the knot in the laces of his breeches, and she approached him out of habit, shooing away his hands and working at the knot with her fingernail.

"I have a friend who has the Book of Paracelsus, and I devote hours each week to studying his methods. You see, I want to learn. I want to know. I want to—"

"Marketa!" interrupted her mother, peering around the wall to the soaking area. "The bathwater is hot and you have not yet begun to bathe the gentleman!"

"I am sorry, Mother, we were just talking—"

"Cease talking and let the poor man relax. He did not come here to listen to a bathmaid chatter on!"

"Mother, we—"

"Give the man his bath, Marketa. And remember what I told you."

Marketa unraveled the knot to Jakub's breeches, and suddenly she felt the heat rise to her face. She helped him to the bathing stool and bade him sit. The girl kept her eyes averted as she pulled off his pants and folded them on a bench. She knew the man sat before her naked now, like hundreds of men before, but she could not look him in the eye.

Then she caught sight of a little silver cross on a chain around his neck. It stopped her short, and she drew in a sharp breath.

"Would you like me to remove your chain?" she asked. "It might tarnish in the soapy water."

"No thank you, *slecna*. I never take it off," he said. "Some clean water and soap will do it good."

He sensed that something was wrong. He said, "I am not a priest, *slecna*. Treat me as you would any man in the village who has come for a bath."

Marketa nodded. "Yes. Of course."

She approached him from behind, bending down to retrieve a warm bucket of water and a flat bar of soap. She was determined to treat him like anyone from Krumlov.

"Close your eyes, sir," she said.

She poured water over his head. Then she slipped the bar of potash soap through the warm water and worked up a good head of lather.

Her expert hands massaged his head, working the suds through his dark wavy hair. She pulled the lather away from his eyes with her fingertips, molding the whitecap of foam where she wanted it, like a sculptor working wet clay. His shoulders relaxed as his muscles melted under her fingers.

"What hands you have," he sighed. "Truly you have a gift."

As he exhaled, she drew in his breath. She leaned closer to him. When he blinked open his eyes and smiled up at her, she snapped back her head, mortified.

"Do not be frightened, my little bathmaid," he said, tilting his head back and gazing at her. "See, I shall close my eyes again, but please do not stop your hands from their miracles."

He squeezed his eyes shut but could not hide a smile.

Marketa worked the lather longer than she normally would and listened to his sighs of pleasure. She, too, did not want to stop.

Finally came the time when she needed to work the lather around the front of his torso. Out of the corner of her eye, she saw her mother motion to her, urging her on. A patron called from his barrel for more ale, and Lucie disappeared to fill his stein.

Marketa swallowed hard and reached her hands around Jakub's stomach, his chest, rubbing the lather in wide circles.

"Ahh," he moaned.

She moved around the stool and faced him. She stared down between his legs, his penis slightly aroused. The dark pubic hair stretched to his navel in a thicket of tangled hair.

She raised her eyes and stared hard at the little silver cross, sparkling through the suds.

Marketa swallowed hard and reached for his groin.

But her hands betrayed her. Instead of the assurance and deft touch she had working his muscles, her fingers froze, numb and useless.

She moved closer to him and reached again for him, determined to complete the bath. But her hands merely hovered, paralyzed.

Jakub opened his eyes and saw the girl frozen before him, her face stricken with fear. He reached out gently toward her shaking hands, soapy and wet. He held them in his own and looked up at her terrified eyes.

"You do not have to touch me, *slecna*," he said quietly. "I'll wash myself there."

Marketa's eyes filled with tears, and she tried to wipe them away, but the man held her hands like trapped birds.

"All right," she whispered. "But please do not tell my mother. Promise me you won't."

"I promise," he said. Then he realized what had transpired and looked in her blue-gray eyes. "Your mother was looking for a supplement, was she?"

Marketa nodded, not trusting herself to speak.

"Well, she shall have it," he said gently. "Bring me water to rinse."

At last her hands were released, and they flew back to her sides.

"Yes," she whispered hoarsely. "I will fetch the rinsing bucket."

As Marketa returned to the bathing stool with a bucketful of water, she saw Jakub's lips moving, his head bowed. Then he quickly kissed the cross around his neck. As he let it go from his hand, it bounced on his chest and swung like a pendulum, in a little arc.

"Doctor Horcicky, I fetched your rinse water if you are ready."

"Yes, yes, by all means before the soap dries. Thank you."

She poured the warm water over his head and back, and he took the bucket from her and finished rinsing the rest of his body.

"Are you preparing to take the orders, sir?" she asked him as he shook the water from his face.

"No, not at all. I am the king's imperial chemist and physician," he said. "Do not allow this cross to confuse you. I was raised in a Jesuit monastery. I have had it since I was a boy. But again, I have not the virtues of a priest, I assure you."

She gave a curt nod and handed him the bath sheet. She did not look up at his eyes or down at his groin. Her eyes were fixed on his chest and the cross.

Jakub wrapped the coarse sheet tight around his waist. He saw Marketa's eyes were fighting back tears and she bit her lower lip.

Jakub reached his hand out and tilted her chin up, urging her to look into his eyes.

"You have done nothing wrong, *slecna*. I will not tell your mother, I promise."

Her eyes sought his, begging for confirmation of his promise.

"Come here," he whispered, looking into her eyes.

Jakub's lips met hers, warm and moist. It was a kiss as surprising as it was brief. Without thinking, she stepped closer and for a moment their bodies were pressed together and Marketa drank in the smell of his clean skin and hair.

At the sound of Lucie's booming voice from the next room, Marketa jumped back. She straightened her kerchief, her cheeks aflame.

"Come, *slecna*," he said, his hand still resting gently on her shoulder. "Show me the barrel."

As Marketa accompanied the physician to the soaking barrel, all the other bathers' heads pivoted toward the tall, well-muscled man. He walked with a posture and grace that spoke of his years at the Prague court.

No one recognized him as the poor, awkward boy raised within the walls of the Jesuit monastery, just a quarter mile from the bathhouse.

As was the custom throughout southern Bohemia, bathers at the Pichlerova bathhouse were not segregated by sex; men and women were set in wooden barrels side by side. Instead, they were grouped according to their choice of conversation. The brewers would often prefer to soak next to the tavern-keeper to discuss ale and beer and conduct business. The shopkeepers were placed near the purveyors, the greengrocers alongside the farmers, who enjoyed a nice soak after hour upon hour toiling over their crops.

And on this day, the bloodletter's daughter and the elegant young man from the royal court formed a group of their own.

Marketa moved the stool over so that he could climb into the barrel and submerge himself.

"Ahhh!" he sighed, closing his eyes as the herbed water lapped over his shoulders.

"Marketa!"

Lucie came bustling toward them, a bucket in her hand.

"How have you bathed our guest with such haste," she said, her voice cross. "Have you made the gentleman—comfortable?"

Marketa's lips moved to utter an answer, but a reply came from the gentleman himself.

"Your daughter has greatly pleased me, *pani*. Far greater than the bathmaids in Prague—she has the hands of a goddess. The only thing that would please me more would be for her to sup with me. Bring cheese, bread, and ale for us both. I should like to finish my conversation with Marketa."

Lucie bobbed her head, staring openmouthed and gap-toothed at the stranger.

"Yes, my lord," she stammered. "And cake, I will bring you cake."

Marketa stared at the man in the barrel.

"I cannot take food and drink with you," she whispered. "I am working."

"I will pay for your daughter's time," called Jakub from his bath. "I will pay you well, *pani*."

"Just to talk?" said Lucie, her hands on her stout hips.

"My bath is losing heat. Fetch a warm stone, *pani*. And then bring the refreshments for the two of us."

Marketa sat down on the stool, not knowing what else to do. She studied the old tarred wood of the barrels, splintered on the outside from decades of use. The wet wood smelled of fresh lavender and river water.

"You must know Annabella," said the voice from the barrel.

"Yes, my lord," said Marketa. "Do you know her as well?"

"Ah, yes, the good healer of Krumlov," he chuckled. "She has a superior knowledge of herbs and medicines. I have known her most of my life."

"She has the Book of Paracelsus," said Marketa.

"I know," he said, and his voice was obscured by the splashing of his arm adjusting to more comfortable position.

Marketa looked up as her sisters, Dana and Kate, brought a plank to place across the barrel. Lucie followed carrying heavy platters of food and two steins of ale, her sweaty cheeks puffing with effort.

"And that hot stone, *pani*," said Jakub as the plank creaked with the weight of the food.

Lucie motioned to Marketa, out of habit.

"No," said Jakub. "She is my guest. She shall remain at my side. And do not worry, *pani*. I shall pay you handsomely for her—services."

Marketa smiled into her hand. She looked around the bathhouse where every face was staring at her.

For the next hour, no one spoke a word in the bathhouse but the physician and the bathmaid, who chatted on about medicines, herbs, bloodletting, and other cures. They spoke of the impending public dissection of a human body to be performed in Prague by Jan Jesenius himself.

Marketa argued the virtues of balancing the humors through bloodletting, while Jakub dismissed it as fraud.

"You do not believe in Galen's humors?" said Marketa, rising to her feet to peek over the rim of the tub. She stared at the bathing physician, forgetting altogether her earlier shyness.

"Charlatanism," he pronounced, raising the stein of beer to his lips. "Chemistry is the secret to medicine. I am a scientist, not a sorcerer. In my laboratory I distill medicines from herbs, roots, and flowers. I isolate healing minerals from stone, water, and soil. *Slecna*, I cure my patients without stealing their blood."

Marketa scowled at the bather, not knowing what to think about this doctor who mocked her father's profession.

"Do not frown, Marketa," said Jakub, wiping the foam from his mouth with the back of his hand. "It is unbecoming and mars your natural beauty."

Marketa didn't know if she was being complimented or insulted. She started to frown again, then paused, confused between anger and a new emotion—could it be vanity? She sneaked a look at the handsome court physician and saw that he was smiling widely.

In an instant, she realized he had been teasing her. It was a revelation. In the king's court, men teased women just as boys teased girls in the streets of Cesky Krumlov.

She smiled back at him for an instant, then deepened her frown and said, "Better frowning and plain than to distract your lordship from his important study of science, and his colossal self-importance."

Now it was Jakub's turned to begin to scowl, before realizing that he was being teased in turn.

He broke into a broad smile and splashed her from the barrel. She sputtered, shaking the water off her face and hair and growled a curse in Czech—a particular Krumlov curse that she knew he would understand.

The other bathers roared in laughter for they had been watching intently. Jakub raised his beer mug at her, smiling.

Marketa smiled in return. She could not remember when she had been so entertained by one of her mother's clients.

When Jakub finally rose to leave, the water in the barrel was stone-cold, and black fleas floated among the sprigs of lavender. He dried himself with a bath sheet and called for his clothes.

Marketa did not help him dress, but waited patiently at the door. When he emerged from the bathing rooms, he had his magnificent green scarf in his hand.

"Here, Slecna Marketa," he said, lifting her chin gently with his fingers. He tied the scarf around her neck as if she were a child.

His touch raised the downy hairs on her neck as his fingers fussed with the knot. He stepped back to admire her in his garment. There was a propriety gleam in his eye.

"Something to remind you of Prague," Jakub said. "A magical city lies waiting for you, Marketa Pichlerova."

He bowed to her, mounted his horse, and rode away.

CHAPTER 8

News of Don Julius in Krumlov

Pichler arrived home the following day, a week earlier than planned. Marketa heard the hollow clip-clop of his mare's hooves on Barber's Bridge as she was hanging out bath sheets in the afternoon sun. She looked up to see him waving to her. She ran out with her arms open wide.

"Easy there," cooed her father to his mount, who had shied as Marketa ran from the house. "You are home to rest and eat hay. No reason to bolt."

He slapped his horse on the neck and dismounted. Marketa could tell by the hitch in his leg that he was saddle-sore and had not stopped long to rest along the way. He was more than thirty years old now and could not manage such a hard ride as if he were still a young man. The mare's coat was lathered white and her flanks were drawn up tight in thirst.

"Father! What is the matter? Why have you come home so early and run your horse so hard?"

He smiled at Marketa's observation; above all he had taught her that a good physician was alert to symptoms and discrepancies.

He gave his horse to the servant boy who slept in the small shed at the side of the bathhouse.

"Let her have her fill of water," he said. "Do not feed her until sundown. She has run hard and will colic."

As the boy started to lead the horse away to the grassy bank of the river, the barber-surgeon stopped him.

"Wait, let me untie my saddlebag. I have something there, Daughter, I want to show you."

He untied the canvas bag and delicately withdrew a rolled parchment.

Marketa stopped breathing as she gazed at the sight.

The parchment displayed the human body and the course-ways of blood, penned with exquisite precision. Marketa had long tried to learn what she could by tracing her white skin and blue veins with her index finger, referring to her father's notes, but here was a wealth of new knowledge.

The human body lay unveiled before her in all its mysterious glory.

"This comes from England, where they have charted the veins from humans themselves," said her father.

"But look at the detail—and there are interior veins here that would kill a man if he were cut so deep!"

"Not if that man were already dead." Her father smiled. "In England and France, bodies can be procured legally for science's sake. It is the law, Daughter. Science is the law!"

She dropped her jaw in awe.

"The law?"

"Ah, they say there are still grave robbers, but in a country as wild and ruthless as England, it is no surprise."

He paused a moment as Marketa's eyes drank in the tracings, then murmured, "How is your mother?"

Marketa lifted her eyes slowly. "She complains every day about my ineptness in the bathhouse and my clumsy manners with the customers. I caught Pani Schmidt's curls in the lid of the barrel and made them limp. She howled like a cat in heat."

She gave him a glance. If only he would intervene and save her from her work in the bathhouse.

"I could not wait for you to return!" Marketa said, taking his arm. "And we have at least five patients who desperately require your services—they were almost prepared to let me bleed them myself."

She meant this as a joke, but her father gave her a stern look.

"You would never do that, would you, Marketa?" he said. "Not that you do not have the knowledge—even the gift, I believe."

"No never, Father," she said. "I do not belong to the guild."

He took her chin in his hand. He squeezed it tight, almost as tightly as her mother did in anger.

"And that is the only reason?"

"I do not belong to the guild," she said stubbornly. "It would not be right."

He released her chin, and she dropped her eyes to the ground and made a quick excuse to leave to fetch water for the bathhouse.

But instead Marketa ran to her straw pallet and retrieved the green silk scarf from under the feather pillow. She stroked the scarf and then brought it near her face. She could still smell the scent of Jakub Horcicky deep in the fibers.

~

Pichler wasted no time in talking to the town council. They met at Radek's tavern. Marketa helped serve pitchers of beer and spiced mead.

"No Hapsburg bastard will rule us!" shouted the mayor, pounding his fist so hard that the creamy foam on his ale quivered. "We shall send a delegation at once to Prague and take up this matter with the king."

"But what of the Rozmberks? Should we not approach them and challenge their right to sell the castle to a madman?"

"Gold is gold to them," muttered the municipal judge. "We will not have a legal right to challenge them."

"But if they leave, so will the courtiers go—over three hundred! Who will buy our goods? How will Krumlov survive?"

"I would like to throw them in the moat with their own bears," sputtered a member of the council. "What right do they have to seat a Hapsburg idiot above our town? What if he takes a liking to one of our women, or worse yet, one of our boys as his father is rumored to fancy? No one will be safe."

At this, Pichler told them the stories of debauchery he had heard in Vienna, ending with his own experience with Don Julius. The men muttered in anger, and the mayor himself declared that the Hapsburgs had copulated so frequently with their own family members, they were no better than pink blind mice at ruling an empire.

Marketa stood silently in the shadows and listened. Her father had never kept sex a secret from her. It was a normal function of the human body, and Marketa knew both men's and women's anatomy as thoroughly as the four humors. Her father had a theory that the yellow bile, the murderous and most dangerous, caused excesses of sexual acts and was a symptom of imbalance in either a man or woman.

Marketa's father said that Don Julius would be accompanied by a Jesuit priest, a Spaniard from the court of Felipe II.

"That is all we need, a Spanish Jesuit!" grumbled the mayor, a staunch Protestant. "A Papist, mumbling the pope's bidding in a foreign tongue. Plotting against our church."

The meeting dispersed well after midnight, the men not having settled on any plan. As they drank more and more beer, they grew hoarse from uttering threats, but there was no way of counteracting the king's will.

As Marketa walked home alongside her father under the black sky, she heard him puzzling aloud.

"Who knows if I could cure him with regular bleedings? It could be the miracle he needs."

She whispered a prayer and looked up at the few twinkling stars that were etched in the night sky. Her thoughts wandered to Jakub Horcicky, and she wondered if he gazed up at the stars tonight, just as she did.

The Vltava roared in the blackness, winding its way through their town like a serpent.

~

Within a week, the town council had drawn up a petition and selected a rider to carry it to the king in Vienna.

They did not know that the king was already in Prague and Rumpf had invited the Rozmberks to Vienna to discuss the sale of the castle. By the time the messenger came back, the affair was settled. He brought news of the sale and the impending arrival of Rudolf's notorious bastard in Cesky Krumlov.

The church bells tolled, and people left their bakeries, taverns, shops, and fields to come hear the news in the town square. The mayor stood by the well on a sturdy wooden box.

"The king's minister promises that Don Julius will be kept under lock and key until he is controllable," announced the mayor. "We have begged the Bohemian lords, especially Petr Vok, to intercede on our behalf at the Prague court. This is their response."

"What if he gets out? Who will he stick with his dagger, and what will become of our women?"

"No, I have the king's word—Rumpf's word—that he will be confined to the palace and will never cross the moat. Until he is cured."

The men in the crowd began to grumble and spit on the cobblestones.

"There has never been a Hapsburg who did not have his way. The bastard will descend upon our village and defile our women."

"This is what a Hapsburg does to his subjects? Send a lunatic to dwell amongst us?"

The mayor furrowed his brow. "You had best learn to control your tongue before the Hapsburgs arrive. If a guard from Prague heard your slander against the king's son, you would be searching for your head."

Again the people hissed. The cobblestones glistened with their spit.

Marketa's father always said it was right for men—and women—to spit and cough up any phlegm that might poison them. The phlegm that welled up from an excess of the phlegmatic humor was easily concentrated into disease. So the glistening cobblestones of Cesky Krumlov that day should have pleased him, but Marketa saw no smile on his face.

CHAPTER 9

A Holy Conspiracy in Hungary

The freshly minted coin winked up at him, silver glinting in his hand. Engraved on the thaler was the image of his older brother, King Rudolf II.

"You say the pope himself has protested?" said Matthias, turning the coin over in his palm.

The pope's emissary, Melchior Klesl, bishop of Vienna, raised his chin in confirmation.

Klesl had voyaged down the Danube on a merchant's barge, from Vienna to this outpost at the edge of the Royal Hungarian city of Esztergom on the violent border where the Holy Roman Empire battled the Turks. The thud of an Ottoman kettledrum drifted up from beyond the gates below, and Klesl shivered with apprehension. His mission was crucial to the pope and to the empire, but the borderlands were still scorched and smoking, the Ottoman frontier lined with rotting heads impaled upon bloody stakes.

There was never true peace with the Ottomans. Ever.

The old stone fortress above Esztergom looked down upon the embattled city, a strategic stronghold recaptured from the Turks in 1595 by Matthias's armies. The Ottomans camped within sight of Esztergom's walls, like snarling wolves, encircling their prey.

Klesl imagined the flashing yataghans of the bloodthirsty Saracens who had spread the word of the Prophet Mohammed into the heart of Europe. The pope's blessing must be brought to Matthias far from the luxuries and safety of Vienna. As his coach had rattled up the hill away from the Danube, the bishop kissed the gold crucifix around his neck. But this was God's work, and he would bring the pope's word directly to the younger brother of Rudolf II.

This Matthias, unlike his brother, was a man of few words, a soldier who never shirked from a battle. He spent much of his time here on the frontier, on the long, narrow tongue of Hungarian land that still belonged to the Holy Roman Empire.

The bishop mopped his temples with a white kerchief, attempting to compose himself. "Our Gracious Holiness has denounced King Rudolf's image on the coin as an alchemist, an adeptus. No mortal, certainly no Catholic, should aspire to communicate with the dark spirits of the netherworld. Now the entire Holy Roman Empire shall be reminded of his dalliance with the evil spirits and the Jews each time a merchant draws a coin from his purse."

A slow smile tugged at the corners of Matthias's mouth and widened the breadth of his close-clipped beard. He flipped the shining coin into the air and caught it as if it were deciding a bet.

The bishop lowered his voice, though they were alone in the drafty castle chamber. The acrid scent of gunpowder wafted in through the high windows, and he could hear the not-so-distant sound of cannons, thundering.

"Rudolf is said to converse on a regular basis with Jews. Rabbi Lowe is admitted to court and lingers in the king's presence to discuss the Kabbalah and the Elixir of Life."

"Hardly a Catholic notion, is it?" said Matthias. His eyes twinkled with conspiracy.

The bishop sniffed, indignant. "The elixir of everlasting life is our Lord, Jesus Christ, that God sent down from heaven to save us from eternal damnation!"

"Yet as Holy Roman emperor, Rudolf is the guardian and moral authority of the Catholic Church."

The bishop winced.

"Pity," said Matthias, studying the image of his brother in the robes of an alchemist. "Good likeness, though—finely minted. Indeed, it will remind everyone in Europe of the alchemists' quest. And silver finds converts..."

Melchior Klesl's face grew red as the Turkish paprika the Hungarians used to flavor their stews. He looked about the room, devoid of furnishings except a tattered tapestry, a few rough-hewn chairs, and a straw pallet.

The clergyman whispered, "He must be stopped, Matthias. I bring word from the pope in the most confidential manner that should you as a good Catholic succeed him—in a most timely manner—you would have the pope's blessing and the full support of the Church."

"These are the pope's own words?" said Matthias.

"From his holy lips. King Rudolf must be stopped. His conduct is intolerable."

Matthias smiled and pinched the silver coin tight between his finger and thumb.

"I shall keep this, good bishop," he said, pocketing the coin. "As a token of the promise and good will of His Holiness."

Bishop Klesl leaned closer to Matthias. "His Holiness has confidence in you as a staunch defender of the Catholic faith. He trusts you to lead our flock away from this blasphemy. Protestants infest the Bohemian states like maggots on a rotted corpse."

"His Holiness overlooks the sin I commit by having Lutheran advisors at my side, trusted friends who practice their damnable faith? He condones my siding with William of Orange and the Netherlands at the age of twenty?"

The bishop folded his hands over his robe. "He believes these are the follies of youth, and as a Hapsburg you will find your way back to the True Faith."

"That is a risk," said Matthias, his voice blunt. "I am the least Catholic of all Hapsburgs."

The bishop sighed and opened his hands, his palms facing Matthias. "His Holiness believes you will bring peace to the empire and stop the encroachment of the Ottomans, before they besiege Vienna and overrun the remainder of Europe. Then you will lead the vermin back to the Truth Faith."

Matthias walked to the window and looked down at the waters of the Danube, sparkling below. Beyond the walls of Esztergom, in the grassy fields he could see the corrals of Ottoman warhorses, painted red or green up to their bellies, the colors fading slowly in the rain and sun.

Facing the window he sighed. "They are not maggots, these Protestants, but men who hunger for freedom to practice their faith. This is their land, my good bishop."

He turned to the pope's emissary. "Has His Holiness's opinion been swayed by the Ottoman armies' proximity to Vienna? Perhaps the unrest has benefited my standing."

"Your brother's inept handling of the Turkish campaign has made all of Europe anxious," said the bishop. "We are certain you will be declared king of Royal Hungary."

The bishop approached Matthias, who stood in the small pool of sunlight that stole across the stones. *How fine this younger*

Hapsburg would look with the gold crown of the Holy Roman Empire upon his noble—and Catholic—head, thought Klesl.

"No Hungarian would ever swear allegiance to Rudolf now! They need a true soldier, a leader in battle against the Turks. They will follow you, Matthias. And His Holiness believes many more Catholic kingdoms will demand your strong hand leading their destiny, rather than a deranged fool who dabbles in the black arts."

The bishop leaned closer to Matthias. "But His Holiness must know how we can take power from your brother without bloodshed. The Protestants are too numerous—indeed, the vast majority in the Bohemian states—and can turn against us, should we move too quickly. Rudolf has indulged them in his court, including that Lutheran Johannes Kepler and physician Jan Jesenius."

"Brilliant men, these Protestant heretics. Or so I am told," said Matthias. His eyes twinkled as he watched Melchior's face redden again.

"The pope wished to know how we can bring Rudolf down without war, sire."

"With patience, good bishop. With time." Matthias stared north, toward the distant borders of Bohemia. "My brother Rudolf digs his grave with his own hands. My sources in Prague tell me there is a storm brewing now in the town of Cesky Krumlov that may bring matters to a head. My bastard nephew Giuglio may be the unlikely key to our triumph. The reign of my brother Rudolf rests in the balance, if I am right. All we have to do is wait...patiently."

The bishop nodded solemnly to the younger Hapsburg and bid him adieu. He was anxious to begin his journey back to Vienna, far from this savage Ottoman border, as soon as possible.

Matthias watched as the pope's emissary swept out of the room, his black robes flowing behind him above the gray stone.

SUMMER 1606

CHAPTER 10

A Strict Regimen

King Rudolf II did not talk to his son before he left Vienna. That duty, among so many others, was left to Minister Rumpf. Preparations were made for Don Julius's imprisonment in Cesky Krumlov, though Rumpf was careful not to speak of it until the last possible moment.

In his hands Minister Rumpf had official orders from the king, affixed with the Hapsburg seal. He looked out the window for the last time at the waiting coach and swallowed. He beckoned to the guards to accompany him as he entered Don Julius's chambers.

"Cesky what?" Don Julius roared in response to the minister's announcement, rubbing his aching head, throbbing with the excess of strong spirits that still poisoned his blood, as they did almost every morning. "You mock me, and I have no stomach for it."

Minister Rumpf sighed. Among the many tasks distasteful to him as Rudolf's chief minister, dealing with his bastard son was the worst.

"Don Julius, I neither mock you nor jest. My orders come from your father, His Majesty, the king. I shall follow them faithfully. You shall leave for southern Bohemia with utmost haste."

"Shut up, you miserable little German! Your voice is splitting my head like a hatchet."

The king's minister longed to spit on this surly son of the king, but he wisely sucked the juices to the back of his mouth and swallowed. He studied the youth's face, and despite the flabby countenance and fleshy body of his overindulgence, he recognized the traces of Anna Maria da Strada, the king's mistress. Don Julius had inherited her fine skin and high cheekbones, and his blue-green eyes, buried in the fat of his round face, were unique and brilliant as jewels. Were he not so bloated with excess drink and food, he would be quite handsome.

The only features he seemed to inherit from his father were the pendulous lips of a Hapsburg, red and full as if he had just been eating bloody meat.

Minister Rumpf interrupted his contemplation to duck as a porcelain vase came flying toward his head. It shattered in shards against the wall.

"To hell with you!" roared Don Julius. "As if could I survive in a godforsaken Czech town where they probably do not even know how to speak proper German and their wenches grow hair out of their bumpkin ears. Go away, Rumpf. It is time for my breakfast, and your prattle spoils my appetite."

"That is another thing, Don Julius." Rumpf took special pleasure in this. "Your father has given strict orders that your meals are to be no more than three a day. You are to learn the life of the ascetic as he did in Spain with his uncle, Felipe II, when he was your age."

"God damn you and your presumptions!" shouted Don Julius, scratching at his groin. He motioned to a guard. "You, wretched man, fetch the cook's assistant to serve me."

The guard hesitated and looked at Rumpf, who twitched his mouth in impatience.

"Don Julius, you are under guard. There is no special cook, no valet, no attendant to serve you. You will reduce your meals from twelve to three, you will have no contact with women, and a priest will travel with you and be installed in the chapel at Cesky Krumlov to hear your confession."

"Confession!" Don Julius focused his bloodshot eyes on Minister Rumpf. "I will confess nothing to some Papist!" The aroma of bacon wafted through the air.

"See! When Don Julius commands, the servants leap to please me, as they should for the eldest son of their king. Bring me my breakfast, you miserable dung beetle!"

Rumpf stood aside as a guard laid a plate with lean bacon and coarse black bread at the little table.

Don Julius twisted his face in disgust.

"What meager rations are these? Where are the cheeses, the chicken, the herring? Where is my ale, damn it! My head aches for it."

"Sit and eat, Don Julius," said Minister Rumpf, looking at his pocket watch. "It will be hours before luncheon, and we have many preparations to make. The guards will escort you to the coach once you have finished your repast. I bid you farewell, my lord."

The outraged howling of Don Julius could be heard across the fields as the royal coach rattled along the old road to Bohemia. He was tied with soft linen gauze, in an attempt to reduce the injury to his limbs and flaccid skin as he thrashed within the carriage.

Men spat in the dust of the road as he passed, and the women crossed themselves behind lace-curtained windows.

Minister Rumpf was not able to accompany him as he was occupied with more serious matters of state, running an empire while the king danced with his court in Prague. Instead, the Jesuit priest, Don Carlos Felipe, escorted the young bastard prince. Carlos Felipe had been raised in Madrid, the youngest son of a noble family of Ronda. He was a confessor to some of the most influential families at the Spanish king's court, although not to the royal family itself.

He had helped tutor King Rudolf II and his brother Ernst when they were sent to their Spanish uncle's court as young boys. He understood the erratic behavior that was a trait of the Hapsburgs, but this bastard son, this Don Julius, was far worse than any he had seen. True, the bastard's first cousin Don Carlos, son of King Felipe II, was known to spend hours lying in the family vaults of El Escorial, preferring the company of his dead ancestors to the living. But the Spanish prince's madness was of a morbid nature; he did not lash out violently as did Don Julius.

With a shudder, the priest thought of the legends of Juana La Loca and her love for the corpse of her dead husband, Felipe the Handsome. Juana was great-great-grandmother to both boys.

Don Carlos Felipe knew that Don Julius must be possessed by the same demons as his Spanish relatives and posed a danger not only to himself, but to the entire Hapsburg dynasty. The priest passionately swore an oath to the king that he would do everything he could to purge the devil that inhabited this young man's soul.

"You know, of course, of the Jesuit monastery in Cesky Krumlov," Minister Rumpf had said when explaining the mission to the priest. "Perhaps you could entreat some other Jesuit brothers to aid you in your mission. I fear Don Julius will not be an easy convert."

Carlos Felipe looked down at his black wool robe and fiddled with the hemp rope that encircled his thin waist. He had dealt with the strange habits of Don Julius's great-uncle, Felipe II, and his feebleminded son, Carlos.

The priest felt certain he could deal with this bastard son, Don Julius. The Eastern branch of the Hapsburg dynasty had become soft. Their precious Austrian manners were too indulgent—they needed the rigor and discipline of the Spanish court.

As if reading the priest's thoughts, Minister Rumpf said, "I fear he will not be an easy patient, but he shall not be indulged."

"Indulging gross habits only encourages new ones," the priest said, bowing his head. "Yes, I shall inquire of my brothers to see if there are some willing and suitable to assist me in our work."

As Rumpf dismissed him, he warned, "See to it that Don Julius is not unbound until he is safely ensconced in a secured palace room. But he is to be allowed exercise at least three days a week. The king suggests you let him hunt in the hills above Cesky Krumlov, to improve his health and stamina. He should be encircled by mounted guards—no fewer than half a dozen—to see that he does not escape or stray into the town."

The thin priest nodded. The rigor of riding and pursuing the hounds would be good discipline for Don Julius's mind and body.

"One more thing. As King Rudolf is a patron of the sciences, he feels it is necessary to send along a physician. I have received word that a highly esteemed member of Prague's barber and surgeon guild will join you soon in Cesky Krumlov. He has strict instructions to monitor the king's son's health and report back to Prague as to his diagnosis. The king forbids bloodletting at this time unless Don Julius agrees, but he thinks this surgeon, Mingonius, could bring his observations to court and prescribe treatment."

"God's judgment alone would be treatment for this royal sinner," remarked the priest dryly.

"Perhaps you are correct. But never forget that this young man is our emperor's eldest son, bastard though he may be. The king would not tolerate any—shall we say—untoward treatment suffered by his favorite son. He has ordered that you keep your diaries legible and send the entries by courier to Prague."

Minister Rumpf bowed in respect—and relief—as he dismissed the priest to make the journey to Cesky Krumlov.

~

Don Julius still howled in pain, not at the bite of the gauze fetters, but at the gnawing hunger in his belly. For years now he had shown no restraint in his gluttonous habits. Excesses of sex, food, and violence were his steady diet, and he knew no limits.

The coach made a stop at midday at a small town in Bohemia. The innkeeper could not speak German and was so astonished to see the royal coach that he could barely manage to serve a welcoming ale to his clients. The driver ordered everyone out of the establishment to make way for Don Julius and his entourage. The townspeople gathered dumbfounded in the dusty street outside the tavern, trying to catch a glimpse of the king's son.

Don Julius was unbound, although the priest and two guards stood by his side, alert to his every move. The innkeeper's wife struggled out with trays heaping with stews and roasted chops, sauerkraut, and fat, oozing sausages.

Don Julius's eyes gleamed at the sight.

"Wait," said Carlos Felipe, holding up his hand. "We must test the food."

Don Julius salivated at the smell of the good Bohemian cooking.

"Hurry up, then," he growled. "If there is poison in the stew, may you die a quick death!"

Don Julius often went without a taster, in order to speed the act of moving food to his eager mouth. He watched as the first guard warily took a taste of the stew.

"And the millet pancakes. Don't forget them. The duck and the sausage," instructed Carlos Felipe.

"Enough," roared Don Julius, pounding his open hand on the wooden table. "Serve me, I command you."

But Carlos Felipe was not done yet.

"You must learn patience, Don Julius. Your father has asked that I teach you many virtues, and patience and abstinence are among them. He learned such lessons at the court of your great-uncle Felipe II."

The guard hesitated, but he remembered Rumpf's strict instruction, which came from King Rudolf II himself: take your orders from the priest.

Looking eagerly at the food, he took his place at the table and gorged himself.

Don Julius stared slack-jawed.

"Away, you vultures! This is no tasting—you feast on my dinner!"

"Ignore him," ordered the priest.

Don Julius jumped from his chair and overturned the table, spilling pitchers of foamy beer and hot food over the earthen floor. The tavern-keeper's wife shuddered and called to her husband. He appeared moist with sweat from the kitchen and gasped at the scene.

"My lord, was the food not good? We are but humble people and served the best we could! Take mercy upon us!"

"The food was splendid," said the priest. "Was it not?"

He looked at the astonished guards and frightened footmen, who sheepishly nodded. A poor groom was brazen enough to take a goose leg from the floor and start gnawing at it.

"We will pay you amply for your cooking and service. One thing, before we depart. Do you have some good coarse bread to serve to our king's son? He would do best with that, I should think."

Don Julius clenched his fists and raised them toward the rafters.

"Brown bread? I shall dine, you demon!"

The priest took out a purse of gold coins given to him by Minister Rumpf.

"Here, take this," he said, putting a pair of coins in the hand of the bewildered woman. "And fetch us a cool draught of well water in a jug. We will take both the bread and the water with us." He motioned to the guard to bind the prisoner again.

And so began the new life of Don Julius.

CHAPTER 11

THE ARRIVAL

Saturdays were always the busiest for the bathhouse. The people of Cesky Krumlov wanted to be bathed and shaved before Sunday prayers.

"It is the clean-faced man who can receive the Holy Spirit," said Pan Mann. "To approach God with a four-day growth of beard is blasphemy."

When Marketa asked how Jews were so pious and yet so hairy, her father signaled to her to be silent with a wave of his hand.

"Marketa! What do you know of Jews?" said Pan Mann, turning to the girl in astonishment, his face creamy with soap.

"I see them in the marketplace during the day, peddling their wares. And I watch them retreat at sunset, outside the city walls. My mother told me they were Jews. They wear tight caps and have long beards. They look pious and humble."

"Even if they were to pluck each cursed hair from their puckered skin so they looked like a Sunday roasting chicken, they could not purge their sin."

"Marketa, fetch me the long razor," said the barber.

"But Pan Mann," Marketa insisted, "some of them are the most skillful surgeons, they say. Isn't it so, Father, for you have told me so?"

"The razor, Marketa. Pan Mann's face is drying. I do not want to cut his fine skin."

The man in the chair screwed up his mouth and stabbed a pudgy finger at Marketa. "This is what happens when you expose a girl to the world of men. They begin arguing with you about Jews! Next thing you know, she will be arguing to become a bloodletter and inherit your practice."

Marketa's father laid a hand on her shoulder, and she remained silent.

She trembled in anger under his touch, but in deference to him, she said no more. She found herself thinking of the young physician Jakub Horcicky and how they had spoken so freely of medicine. And how he had kissed her.

"Go help your mother in the baths," said Pichler.

Marketa nodded, bidding farewell to Pan Mann.

As the steam of the bathroom hit her face, she heard her mother call.

"Ah, good! I was about to send Kate to fetch you. Please help Miklos into a barrel and put a plank across the rim so I can serve him ale and sausage."

As Marketa helped a young farmer into the barrel, her eyes were drawn to his anatomy. From hard work with the hoe and shovel, scythe and pitchfork, his veins stood clearly defined and blue against his skin, especially that skin that was normally protected from the sun by clothing. Marketa traced the blue threads eagerly in her mind, trying to commit them to memory.

She felt her mother's quick cuff on her ear and her admonishment.

"Avert your eyes!"

Marketa blushed red and realized that the farmer had mistaken her study of his veins for admiration of his body. Already his penis had begun to thicken and was levitating, swaying this way and that, to the bawdy guffaws of the other bathers.

"Miklos, submerge yourself this minute," shouted his mother, embarrassed, although secretly proud of her son's prowess.

"Musle," Miklos whispered to Marketa. "I would love to discover your pearls."

"Fetch water, Marketa!" ordered her mother, her face reddening. "Now!"

Miklos smiled at Marketa in a way that made her skin crawl. Another boy who would pester her.

When the men were safely submerged in their barrels where Marketa's curious eyes could not study their anatomy, she was allowed back in the bathhouse, to the snickers and loud whispering of the bathers.

Still, this was a good night, for Pan Brewer was sick at home with a cold and Marketa was not forced to attend him.

She struggled with the heavy buckets of hot water from the cauldron. Her younger sister Kate followed with baskets of wild thyme she tossed into the water to make it sweet. Marketa returned with a poker, hot from the coals, and plunged it into the water, watching it sizzle as the bubbles tossed the dried herbs across the surface.

Before the bathers soaked in the barrels, the girls scrubbed them clean with brushes of reeds, gathered at the shores of the Rozmberk carp ponds. Marketa's sisters harvested them, while Marketa tended the cow, tethered deep in the reed bed. The cow attracted the leeches Barber Pichler used in his practice, and when they had attached, Marketa led the beast out of the water onto the surrounding meadow. When the leeches were gorged, they dropped one by one, onto the green grass where they were easily gathered.

That summer night the bathhouse was full to capacity, and the air buzzed with gossip. Marketa's mother hurried from one barrel to another, testing the water. If a bather was scalded, he would never return. She stood on a little wooden stool and dipped her elbow in the water; her hands were too calloused from washing to be sensitive to temperature.

All anyone wanted to talk about was the Hapsburg prince.

"Pan Brod said that he is only a few hours' ride from here, probably staying the night in Budejovice."

"And your own husband, Pani Pichlerova, witnessed his filthy acts in the streets of Vienna."

"Yes, you are right, Pani Pstruh. The man is a lunatic. But just the same, he is the son of the king."

"A Hapsburg at Cesky Krumlov! Who would ever imagine a Hapsburg living amongst us in southern Bohemia?"

Marketa's mother smiled at this as she fluffed up the linen bath sheets in her large basket.

"Yes, and I hear that he is unmarried."

Pani Pstruh pulled her lip down into a frown.

"And what of that?" she muttered. "Look at his father. Sired six children with that Italian whore but cannot bring himself to marry, even to produce a Hapsburg heir. And this son's the mad bastard. Married or not, what does it matter?"

"Still," said Lucie, "Rudolf's Italian favorite lives like a queen in the *hrad*. And the young prince will be wanting services, won't he, same as the Rozmberks?"

"He is not a prince—he is a bastard son," growled the mayor from a barrel nearby.

Lucie ignored him.

"You, Pani Mylnar, your good breads and cakes made from your husband's flour. Once the Hapsburg smells the baking on Saturday mornings, he'll send a servant soon enough to fetch him some sweet rolls and cakes for his royal belly. You will be working in the castle kitchens again, just as you did for Wilhelm Rozmberk when he was alive."

Katarina's mother smiled to herself, her fat cheeks crinkling up so high her eyes were pinched tight under folds of flesh.

"And you, butcher's wife. Do you not make the best sausage in southern Bohemia? Did not Petr Vok dine on your meats and wursts and even take them with him to Trebon Palace?"

The *pani* nodded so vigorously, the water reciprocated with little splashes all around her stout neck.

"Ah, but I don't think the son of a king will be bathing here," Lucie said sadly. "All of you will profit, but what do I have to trade for royal gold coins?"

"A bloodletting!" exclaimed Pani Pstruh. "Perhaps Don Julius will employ your husband to cure him of his tempers."

At this all the bathers laughed until their barrels shook, to think of young Marketa carrying bowls of Hapsburg blood to pour into the garden and feed the earth.

When the royal coach crossed the Barber's Bridge, there were at least a hundred villagers lining the banks of the river. It was not often that a Hapsburg traveled to Cesky Krumlov. Only old Friar Damek remembered a visit by Rudolf's father fifty years before.

And now one was about to live above them in Rozmberk Castle.

Several riders preceded the coach, and a young nobleman with blond hair and Viennese clothing winked at Katarina when he saw her alongside the road. She blushed and lowered her face, almost missing the coach itself.

"Look up—here he comes!" Marketa whispered to her.

The red velvet curtains were shut when the coach rattled across the bridge. An old hand, dry and withered, slipped through the curtains and drew them open for just a second.

Marketa saw the face of a priest in a black cassock. Beside him was a stout youth who looked to be bound and gagged. He stared at her intently, and as the coach moved along, his head suddenly thrust out the window. She could see the gag plainly as he twisted his head to watch her until she was out of sight.

Marketa was the first person he saw in Cesky Krumlov. She often wondered if that was her moment of destiny.

~

That hot summer of 1606, few could sleep soundly in Cesky Krumlov. The howls that pierced the night air disturbed even the most profound slumber, and the oppressive humid heat of the Bohemian plains settled uncomfortably into the little river town.

The people of Krumlov resembled sleepwalkers in the day, stumbling through their errands on the cobblestoned streets.

"Who can sleep at all with that bellowing?" they complained in conspiratorial whispers. Every resident knew that it was treason to speak ill of a Hapsburg, but going night after night without sound sleep made their nerves raw.

"The priest who cares for him is trying to drive the demons from his flesh. He lives on black bread and water."

"Imagine a Hapsburg eating like one of us. Worse!"

Don Julius himself could not imagine it. He cursed the priest, throwing any object he could find. His apartments were stripped of anything that could be hurled at those who attended him.

"I want cake!" he sobbed, holding the loose folds of skin that gathered around his shrunken belly. "I want sausage! I can smell the meats frying in that wretched town. What torture! Barbaric fiend!"

Carlos Felipe looked coldly on his charge. His kissed the crucifix he held in his hand and stowed it again under his woolen robe.

"You are just beginning to realize life's pleasures," he said. "Have you ever savored smell so keenly?"

Don Julius spat back at him. "You sack of Spanish bones! What do you know of pleasure, you spineless, ball-less demon? You wouldn't know how to enjoy a sausage pie or a whore between your legs!"

"It is only with an empty belly, dry lips, and purged heart that you can receive the grace of God," said the priest.

Don Julius lunged at him. The two guards retrained him easily; the lack of food had made him weak. Still his curses condemned the priest to a painful death and a damned afterlife, threats wrapped in a host of references to his mother.

Carlos Felipe, in fact, suffered in his own way. He keenly appreciated food and wine, but the fare of the Bohemians bordered on cattle feed to his Castilian tastes. He could not abide the smells of Cesky Krumlov, where the river valley retained the local cooking's pungent aromas like a hovering cloud over the land. The air was laced with vinegar from pickles and hops from the brewery. The breath of the men in the streets was heavy with yeasty ales and pickled cabbage. But above all was the caraway! The priest lay awake at night on his cot, his nostrils yearning to breathe fresh air, uncontaminated by caraway. Even the skin of the people exuded this vile spice; they feasted on foods stewed in the wretched seeds, even bathed with it in the vast barrels where they submerged their white flesh, their heads bobbing above the waters, draining great tankards of beer.

Miserable spore! Carlos Felipe believed the Bohemian fondness for the strong essence of the caraway seed bordered on sin, just as the Andalusians took such delight in smothering the good, simple taste of God's bounty with heathen saffron, the spice of the infidels. Harvesting the stamen of the crocus and infusing their rice with the yellow-orange seed struck him as vulgar and worse...Moorish.

All such strong tastes of foreign spice smacked of the devil.

The Spanish priest longed for the succulent roast pork of Avila in the clean plains of Spain, simple foods, unspiced except for salt—the grain of God.

AUTUMN 1606

CHAPTER 12

ROZMBERK CASTLE

Two months after Don Julius's arrival at Cesky Krumlov another visitor came to the town.

It was Doctor Thomas Mingonius, renowned across Austria and the empire for his bloodletting techniques. When a letter announcing the visit came from Herr Weiss to Barber Pichler, the news left him astonished.

"This doctor is one of the finest in Europe, second only to Jan Jesenius!"

Marketa said, "Ah, but the physician Horcicky who stopped here for the baths when you were in Prague...I think he must be a remarkable doctor, Father."

Her father dismissed her remark with a wave of his hand. "Doctor Horcicky works with insipid plants and pretty flowers, not with the raw blood of humankind. The weak medicine he practices is nothing more than old wives' cures for the sick. Now Mingonius, he is a true surgeon—a renowned bloodletter! To have a few moments in his company to ask him questions, I would give my eyeteeth on a silver tray."

And, as if the offering had been heard across the hills and plains, Pichler's prayer was answered. It wasn't two days after the new visitor's arrival that a groom brought a message to the barber from Doctor Mingonius himself—written in a steady hand on fine parchment.

"I find myself here in the service of Don Julius and wonder if you might attend me. I will require some assistance in the near future, and Herr Weiss in Vienna has informed me of your skill as a barber-surgeon."

Pichler could not believe his good luck.

"I am to assist Doctor Mingonius!" he said, his hand trembling as he read the letter. "One of the king's own physicians!"

"You are to attend royalty! You will see Hapsburg blood stain your bowls!" said his wife, clasping her hands.

He frowned at her, opened his mouth to say something, but thought better of it.

"Marketa!" he said. "Gather my things for a bloodletting. Only the best implements, and sharpen the fleam's blade. The crystal cupping glass, yes, the best one. And bring the ceramic bowl that is not chipped."

"I will give you a fresh shirt," said his wife. "The white one you use for church baptisms."

And so, within the hour, Pan Pichler climbed the steep road from the bathhouse to the castle.

The smell of decaying meat greeted Doctor Mingonius as he entered the hall leading to Don Julius's chambers. He covered his nose and mouth.

"My God! What is that stench?"

The priest nodded. "Look into the antechamber and you will see."

The guards opened the door. Strewn about the room were uncured animal skins, stag heads, and carcasses. A great bearskin writhed with the workings of maggots.

"Don Julius insists on keeping his trophies from hunting in his room. He is quite adamant about it."

"As his physician, I order them to be removed immediately and burned!" shouted Doctor Mingonius. "What vile unhealthy scene is this? Remove these putrid carcasses and have the servants scrub the floors and walls with lye!"

At the doctor's words, Don Julius looked up and turned his head. "Ah, the good Doctor Mingonius," he said, rising from his writing desk, where he was composing his daily letter to his father, imploring for his release. "Has my father sent you here to inquire about my health?"

Doctor Mingonius studied the boy he had known from childhood, now a young man twenty years of age. While still heavy, his weight had decreased several stones on his peasant diet, and the brilliant green eyes of his beautiful Italian mother gleamed against his skin, brown now from weeks of exercise on horseback in the Bohemian hills. He could see, more clearly than in many years, the traces of the young boy who had studied his books with such ferocity.

"Your father is eternally concerned about your health, Don Julius. He sends his affectionate greetings and wishes you well."

"The swine!" roared Don Julius, lunging at the doctor. The guards quickly restrained him.

"I see that you are physically fit, but your bile is as rank as ever," said Doctor Mingonius, composing himself and pulling down his coat where it had bunched in his hasty retreat. "Well, perhaps we will continue our discussion after our midday meal. And after these disgusting bits of carcass and vermin have been removed from your chamber."

"But these pets are my only companions," Don Julius whimpered, his personality changing in an instant from raging attacker to lost soul. He reached past the guards' strong arms to stroke the bear's head, moving with maggots. "Am I to have no friend to keep me company in this damnable prison!" His forehead creased and trembled, his eyes pinched tight. His fingertips stroked the fur like a child with a puppy.

"Remove every one of them immediately—and burn them," Doctor Mingonius repeated to the guards.

As he closed the door behind him, he could hear the rants and screams of Don Julius, struggling against the guards.

"My beauties!" he wailed. "My beauties!"

The priest and the doctor consulted in an antechamber where their conversation could not be heard.

"He looks remarkably better. Physically, that is."

The priest bowed at the compliment.

"I am trying to purge him of the demons that haunt him. He has had strong discipline, and I kneel and pray for his soul each morning and night. May God deliver him from the demon that resides in his heart."

Doctor Mingonius rubbed his chin.

"This is where you and I differ, sir."

"How is that, Herr Doctor?"

"I believe that there is a scientific reason for his rage and savage behavior, while you insist it is a spiritual one."

"We are all sons and daughters of the Creator, Herr Doctor."

"I do not deny that, but I wonder if your strict regimen of water, bread, and broths is the cure. Has he called for any..." The doctor hesitated, studying the priest's face.

"Whores?" supplied the priest, his lips curved downward. "Not in the past fortnight. At first he did, studying most often one particular girl who passed by below. He said the most sordid things."

"Who is the girl?"

"A daughter of the bathhouse keeper. They live beside the river, just below the palace. Don Julius's window gives on the river where he can spy on her and the others who cross the bridge below. They are all fodder for his filthy thoughts, and he shouts insults at them. But I shall weaken him further with fasting," said the priest, a ghost of a smile haunting his face. Just as suddenly it disappeared. "These are God's ways. God's work."

"So the regimen has weakened him, at least temporarily," said Mingonius, considering the Jesuit's words.

"I mean to keep him this way until he has made his soul clean. He harbors a devil in his soul."

The priest pulled his thin lips together in a brittle smile, folding his bony fingers as if in prayer. Mingonius noted his skin, dry parchment pulled tight over blue veins, blotched with spots from years under the blazing Spanish sun.

"I want to bleed him," pronounced the doctor, drumming the wooden table with his fingers.

Carlos Felipe pressed his thin lips together. "Minister Rumpf has said that the king will not allow him to be bled. He told me that before our departure from Vienna. Surely you must know that."

"Yes, but he has sent me here to examine him and to hear the treatment I prescribe. Apparently the burghers below have sent word of his wails and salacious conduct as he rides through the town, to and from the hunt. The king does not want to alienate the southern Bohemian estates. Petr Vok, the Rozmberk lord, is intervening on their behalf. I was given the responsibility to calm him and restore peace to the town."

"No bleeding. It is an insult to God."

Mingonius shook his head. "You live in the world of God. I tread in the world of science, and Don Julius is insane. We cannot ignore his present state of mind, for the king wants him to have full liberty to wander free in Cesky Krumlov. He cannot abide the idea of his son held prisoner here."

"No!" the priest protested. "You have seen him. He cannot be permitted to leave the palace walls, except under close guard on his way to the hunt—the people will not be safe from his violence and lechery. He must remain under my control."

Doctor Mingonius considered this—it was highly unlikely that the emperor would leave a Jesuit in charge of his son for very long. He suspected this was a temporary situation, more of a punishment for Don Julius and an appeasement for the king's Spanish mother.

"I will need express permission from our king for a bloodletting, of course," said the doctor. "But once I have obtained that right, I shall proceed immediately. I have sent for the local barber-surgeon to assist me. It may be that Don Julius will need regular leeching until the next time I can visit. I cannot leave my family and the court permanently."

Carlos Felipe looked toward the window.

"Do you think it wise to involve any of the local people?"

"I have known this boy since the day he was born. I want an unbiased eye to give an observation and aid me in his bleeding— the task will not be an easy one with such a patient! The barber must build up a familiarity with Don Julius so he can continue to administer to his health once I depart."

The priest nodded, grim-faced. "I have considered having a priest from the Jesuit monastery pay me a visit as well."

Doctor Mingonius's mouth pinched in consternation.

"What use is a local priest in this case?"

"The same excuse you use. An unbiased eye."

Knowing that a Spanish Jesuit was attending the son of Rudolf II, Abbot Bedrich Prochazka of Cesky Krumlov's Jesuit monastery was pleased when the Castilian priest Carlos Felipe finally invited him to visit the castle. The pleasure was diminished only by his acute consciousness of the many weeks that had passed while he waited for the invitation to come.

"It is fitting that the nephew of Felipe II should be in the care of the Jesuits," said Abbot Prochazka, accepting a cup of tea with his pudgy hands. "It is the same kind of spiritual care and guidance the queen gave her two sons, His Majesty, Rudolf II, and his brother Ernst."

Carlos Felipe nodded his head in agreement. He settled into his chair with his teacup perched on a little saucer. He stirred sugar into his tea with a tiny silver spoon and watched the whirlpool of dissolving sweetness.

"Yes, it is fitting and part of the Hapsburg tradition. I personally accompanied both His Majesty and his brother to Madrid when they were but small boys," said Carlos Felipe. "It was quite difficult for them the first year, although both were quite adept at learning Castilian. The monastery life at Montserrat was a shock to them, however, after the life in the degenerate streets of Vienna."

He toyed with his spoon. "I really do not have complete control over the charge," he said at last. "My assignment is to calm his appetites and keep him from harm."

Abbot Prochazka looked up at the Spanish priest and set down his teacup.

"Do you give him the holy sacraments?"

"He refuses them."

Abbot Prochazka clasped his hands nervously.

"Refuses the host? If this were to be known, our enemies would surely take advantage of us. The Hussites and…"

"Yes, I know. But the fact remains that he is intolerant of any spiritual guidance and spits at any attempt to lead him to a holy path."

"What engages his interest then?"

"Food and drink. And when those appetites are satiated, women."

Abbot Prochazka stroked his double chin thoughtfully.

"That is all he thinks about?"

"Well, he can be quite violent, although he has grown so weak lately from this regimen that he doesn't quite have the will or strength to indulge those vices with as much exuberance as before," said Carlos Felipe. "But given enough sustenance, he would. I try to starve the devil out of him, and it seems to have diminished the violent tendencies. He is easier to manage this way."

Abbot Prochazka traced his fingernail along the rim of the porcelain cup.

"We must break his will, then," the abbot said. "For the good of his soul and the soul of the Hapsburg Empire, we must bring him to God. Only God can cure his infirmity and mind."

At the same time the abbot sat drinking tea with Carlos Felipe, Doctor Mingonius addressed Pichler in the antechambers of the first courtyard. It was in these rooms that the Rozmberk astrologers and alchemists—at one time, more than a hundred—had practiced their craft, and some of the old glass and copper distilleries and assorted beakers remained, covered now with dust.

"I do not yet have permission to bleed Don Julius. The king is reluctant to proceed in these areas of science. Still, I expect to procure his permission," said Doctor Mingonius, pacing the stone floors. "If I am not able to attend to the bleeding personally in the months to come, I would like to know I have a competent barber-surgeon who could act in my stead. I shall initiate the process and complete the first moon's cycle and then know you will be here to follow my example during the winter months."

"Thank you, Herr Doctor. I am humbly grateful for your faith in me."

"You have been highly recommended by Herr Weiss at the guild in Vienna. He says that you have a sharp mind and intuitive nature. I warn you that Don Julius will not be an easy patient. Especially as the moon waxes—his humors turn deadly."

Pichler remembered the night in the street when he had to apply a tourniquet to a man to stanch the bleeding and save his life. All because he dared to throw a garment over Don Julius's naked buttocks.

"Yes. I realize that Don Julius will not be an amenable patient."

"Indeed, but we must balance his humors if we are to cure him and the festering wound he has inflicted on the empire. And think what credence will be achieved when the people realize that science can cure a man's soul and temperament!"

Pichler nodded.

"Yes. Of course, Herr Doctor."

"We shall examine the patient together first thing tomorrow, before he has had time to eat his breakfast. That will be the best time to diagnose his humors."

Pichler arrived at the gates of the palace before sunrise the next day. He could hear the bears in the moat grunting in the dark, feasting on the bones of a calf, along with the scrabbling of rats as they gnawed on bits that fell from the toothless jaws of the oldest bears.

"Barber Pichler," said the guard, Miklos Chaloupka, scratching his red nose in the cold morning air. Chaloupka was a frequent visitor to the bathhouse and an even more frequent visitor to Radek's tavern. "You come early. Enter."

The iron and wood-plank doors creaked as two sentinels opened them to admit the visitor. The burly guard nodded to him.

"Wait here, I will tell them that you have arrived," he said, leaving Pichler alone in the courtyard.

Wispy patches of clouds raced over the moon. A muted silver light danced on the gray stone of the castle, painted to mimic the marble of a faraway Italian palazzo. The barber lifted his eyes to the second story, where a pale light spilled out the leaded-glass windows.

Pichler's eyes widened and blinked in the cool air as he saw a woman there, dressed in a fine white dress in a style of an earlier century. She stood by an open window, pale and fair, with an elegant air that would seem to be that of a Rozmberk. But they had all departed, he thought. Surely they would not leave behind a woman such as this, not under the same roof as a madman. But in his heart he knew she was no living Rozmberk. He had seen her once before, when he was a child.

She turned away, toward a closed door behind her. She hovered near the door, perhaps listening. She stood alone in grace, but seemed to have a strong interest in what lay beyond the door.

The White Lady looked over her shoulder to the courtyard, turned, walked to the window again, and looked directly at Pichler, raising her candle so it illuminated her pale face and black gloves.

"The Spanish priest will see you now," announced the guard from the doorway. "Pan Pichler, what are you looking at there in the darkness?"

The bewildered barber could not utter a word, but pointed his finger in the direction of the apparition.

The moon cleared a tattered rag of cloud and illuminated the courtyard and the castle. Pichler felt foolish as he pointed at an empty corridor beyond an open window. He could see no one now.

"How did you know which room housed Don Julius?" whispered the guard. "Keep it to yourself, Barber. The priest will think I told you."

With this conspiratorial whisper, the big guard ushered the stammering barber-surgeon into the cold, dark corridors of Rozmberk Castle.

Although Pichler had spent time in Vienna and had been born in the shadow of Rozmberk Castle, he had never dreamt of the opulence within those stone walls. The fine tapestries and thick velvet curtains astonished him, their rich colors and designs too intricate for his eyes to absorb in one glance. The walls were covered with a plush fabric that raised the five-petaled rose, Rozmberk's seal, exquisitely in each panel. Portraits of elegant lords and ladies were weakly illuminated by the elaborate sconces. Sparkling crystal chandeliers twinkled in the relative darkness.

The floors gave off the rich odor of beeswax, and his worn leather soles squeaked on their immaculate surface, heralding his approach. He wondered if the sound was scorned by the aristocracy—perhaps their own kid-leather slippers glided silently across such a finished surface. The dark wood and heavy furniture—secretaries, tables, great spiral-armed chairs—stood guard in the shadows of the room. Each one was grander than the next. He entered one room painted with biblical scenes: Abraham sacrificing his son, Lot being tempted by his daughters. What strange themes to decorate the walls. Sacrifice and sin. Were these concerns of the noble families who had lived here?

He stopped, staring at the painted scenes until the candles of the attendants left them in the shadows.

The coffered ceiling displayed the gilded five-petal roses carved into wooden panels. He spun around slowly, mesmerized by the grandeur and opulence.

He felt a gentle but firm grasp at his shoulder.

"Pan Barber—we must continue. The priest is waiting."

Pichler swallowed hard and shook his head mildly, trying to compose his wits. He had almost forgotten why he had been summoned to the castle.

The door was open to the assembly room. A long, narrow table took up most of the available space. In the corner, an enormous ceramic-tiled stove, measuring the girth and height of three men, crackled and spat as it churned out heat for many rooms and corridors beyond. The barber marveled at the smooth white surface of the behemoth. A necessity for the cold Bohemian winters in such a vast rambling drafty castle, its surprising warmth in the early morning of an autumn day was a stunning luxury.

At the head of the table, his head bowed over a large tome, sat the Spanish priest, writing fiercely with a quill. He looked up and studied Pichler before finally uttering a meager greeting in his nasal Castilian accent.

"Ah, Herr Barber. The good doctor Mingonius will join us shortly. I am afraid he may not be accustomed to rising so early as we Jesuits."

He smiled at his insult to the Protestant doctor and made a little temple of his hands.

Pichler waited for an invitation to sit. He stood, shifting his weight on his feet.

"You come highly recommended from the barber-surgeon guild in Vienna, I am told. Doctor Mingonius was surprised at your qualifications and good reputation with that establishment in such Bohemian wilds, so far from any cultured metropolis."

"You are very kind, Father," said Pichler, tightening his lips at the insult to his town. "I try to learn what I can in my practice and trips to Vienna and Prague."

Carlos Felipe ventured a sour smile, not much of a welcome, thought Pichler, watching the priest's nose wrinkle as if he had a whiff of a foul smell. Then the priest turned and gestured over his shoulder to the window, high above the Vltava River.

"And you live just below us, do you not? The bathhouse at the side of the river."

Pichler walked near the priest, still not having been invited to sit down. He smoothed his cloak so it would not hook on the empty straight-back chair and approached the window.

"Yes, just there. I can see the candles burning in the kitchen as my wife makes breakfast and boils the cauldrons to wash the sheets and heat the bathwater. I could hit the window with a rock if you were to give me one. Ah, how she would be surprised!"

The priest did not acknowledge the attempt at levity. Instead he pursed his lips sourly. The barber's skin smelled of sweet rosemary and ale, more like a woman than a man. Carlos Felipe had heard how the Bohemians bathed often, steeping their bodies in barrels of hot water and herbs. He thought that such a custom of regular baths was barbaric and unnatural, an affront to God who made a man sweat honestly and copiously in the first place. Water was for baptism and holy sacrament, not for soaking a man's body.

And they bathed communally with women! These Bohemians were incorrigible. Even the pope did not know how to expunge their sinful habits.

Meanwhile, Pichler smelled the rancid sweat of the priest's cassock and turned his head to find a breath of fresh air. What a foul odor, he thought. To receive visitors, reeking the way he did, was offensive. But then this was a foreigner, and he had heard of the strange customs of these Latin people, how they consumed vast quantities of garlic, spicy sausage, and acidic red wines that burned the throat and the stomach.

He thought fleetingly of offering his wife's services to scrub the odor from the rough cloth and hang it to dry in the fresh fall air. She would add plenty of dried thyme to the wash, perhaps lavender. He could see her bending over the garment, sniffing the coarse fabric like a hound to check that it was sweet-smelling at last and all traces of bodily odor had been banished.

Pichler did not smile at the priest. The Spaniard's manner was cold and even hostile, for he had not extended his hand nor had he even yet invited his guest to sit. Pichler did not know why he had to deal with the foreign clergy at all, especially as this was not a spiritual matter but a medical affair. The Church always got in the way of science, fettering progress, scowling at new knowledge.

And Jesuits were the worst.

The two men eyed each other in silence.

"Ah, good," said Mingonius, sweeping into the room, "I see you two have met." His face was bright pink from the ice-cold water he had splashed on it, and his skin flushed even more in the heat of the room.

"You are very good to come," he went on, extending his hand. "And so early in the morning. These Jesuits keep the most ungodly hours!" He threw a quick look at the priest, hunched again over his papers in the corner. "But then, it's a hard task keeping pace with God."

Carlos Felipe gave the doctor a withering look, his cold gray eyes looking down his aquiline nose.

"Your remarks border on blasphemy, may I warn you, Doctor Mingonius."

"Only border? Well, it is still early. I am out of practice. Herr Pichler, would you like some ale for breakfast? A bit of bread and cheese, some soup, perhaps? I am afraid that is about all we can offer, for our rations are meager here. We seem to be forced, one way or another, to adhere to Don Julius's regimen, although I cannot for the love of God understand why we should."

"Gluttony is a vice," snarled the priest. "It is an affront to Christ, who suffered for our sins."

"And so is a lack of charity and appreciation for God's wondrous bounty," replied the doctor, snapping his fingers at a page in the corridor.

"Send up bread and cheese, ale, and whatever other fare you have in the larder for our breakfast. We want Herr Pichler to think we are hosts, not jailers."

The priest glowered, muttering under his breath in Spanish.

Pichler recognized the young page to be one of the town baker's sons, Jiri, a brother of Marketa's friend Katarina. He nodded his head and then winked at the boy, who scurried away down the cold hall in search of food and drink.

"Come, Pan Pichler, sit. I cannot for the life of me understand why you were not comfortably seated before I entered the room."

The priest did not look up.

◊

Katarina's little brother, Jiri, brought in a board with fresh rye bread and cheese. A great tankard of ale was set in front of Pichler, a creamy froth blossoming from the rim.

"Will that be all, sir?" Jiri asked, looking down at his shoes.

"Yes, lad. But stay close in case we need your services." Mingonius smiled briskly and dismissed the boy with a wave of his hand.

"Eat, Barber," he said. "I will explain our plan. The priest has asked to remain and hear of the treatment. You see, we are competing stewards of Don Julius's welfare. Our great King Rudolf, embracing both the spiritual and the scientific worlds, has given us equal charge of his son. Even as we talk, a messenger should be on his way from Prague bringing me a letter of permission to bleed the boy."

"Those who meddle with God's work will not be redeemed with the word of man!" spat the priest.

"Are you saying that King Rudolf, ruler of the Holy Roman Empire, is a mere mortal, priest? Your words border on treason, I should think, against His Highness the sole protector of the Holy Roman Empire. Perhaps you should say them only in whispered prayers, in Spanish, under the protection of the cathedral."

Pichler chewed his bread quietly, not venturing a word.

"What I plan is a great purging," said Mingonius, his long finger lashing the air. "We will need to procure leeches, but not just any leech. The Rozmberks have ponds near here with proper leeches. I have procured them in the past—we have had them carried to Prague in buckets for the spring lettings. As the cusp of winter will soon be upon us, it is a most auspicious time to let blood."

"I can procure them tomorrow," said Pichler, eagerly. "I use the ponds to stock my own supply."

"And, pray tell me, how do you harvest them?" asked Mingonius before nibbling at a crust of bread.

"The caretaker lends me his cow, in exchange for a bleeding and a bath. The leeches attach as she stands in the waters, chewing her cud. We lead her into the grass and she stands until they fall off, gorged. The farmer will not let us unsuckle them any earlier, for fear of tearing the flesh of his fine cow."

"So they must fast for weeks before they feel ready for more blood."

Pichler smiled and wiped the foam off his lips with fingers.

"I plan ahead, Herr Doctor. I have hungry leeches harvested from the early spring, in buckets in the back of the bathhouse. We can use them if you want a deep letting."

"Barbaric!" pronounced the Spaniard. "Animals sipping blood from man's veins."

"I should think you would find it in keeping with your own traditions. Is it not the blood of Christ your faithful sup on each Sunday?"

The priest crossed himself and hissed a prayer in Latin.

"In any case, I am afraid, Herr Barber, we cannot use those leeches," said the court doctor to Pichler. "I cannot allow a blood-sucker who has feasted most recently on a cow to touch the son of the Holy Roman emperor."

The barber looked confused.

The doctor continued, "We must attract and harvest the leeches on finer bait. I have heard you have a daughter, a good pious virgin, I would imagine."

Pichler did not answer.

Doctor Mingonius noted his reticence and rushed ahead to break the silence.

"She does her washing just below us in the river?"

"Yes, she cleans my tools and trays for me at the end of the day."

"Perfect, she will do. When I document the procedure for King Rudolf, I must mention how we procured the leeches. He would not like the prospect of a cow's blood mingling with his son's. A Hapsburg—you see my point?"

Pichler had never considered such things, he realized. He was shocked at his own ignorance and felt embarrassed in front of the court physician.

"Certainly, sir," he murmured. He realized he had eaten most of the bread and cheese and felt like an ignorant bumpkin.

"But leeches procured by an innocent virgin, well, now that would be another matter altogether. More fitting for a king's son."

Pichler pushed his tankard away.

"I will see to it, Herr Doctor."

Mingonius smiled. "Yes, and I think we still have time on our side. The waters are not so cold as to lull the creatures to sleep, though the maiden may find herself cold enough in the Rozmberks' ponds."

Suddenly a scream pierced the air.

"Ah, I see that our charge has awakened."

The priest rose to his feet. "I will lead him in prayers," he said.

"You will not lead him anywhere," smiled the doctor. "Any more than I can."

The shrieking came again, and then a low moaning wail.

"God is with me," pronounced the Jesuit. "And I can see the devil is with you both."

~

Pichler shuddered as Mingonius knocked on the door. He could hear the shattering of crockery and the ranting of Don Julius.

"I trust you have quick enough wits to jump away from him should he attack," said Mingonius, studying Pichler's sturdy build. "He is quite agile, though the guards seem to anticipate his moves. But with your beard you would be an easy target."

Pichler stroked his beard with an open hand and nodded, his eyes registering Mingonius's concern.

The guard standing beside them turned the key in the great lock and opened the door slightly. A hand reached out, fingers curled, seeking something to grasp. The fingernails were broken and dirty, the fingers without rings or adornment. Nevertheless,

Pichler could see by the smoothness of the skin that it was the hand of an aristocrat.

"Come back, I pray you, Don Julius," said one of the guards inside. "Come and sit in your chair while we welcome the good doctor."

"Fie and dog's dung on the doctor! He and the priest hold me prisoner."

Pichler slipped into the room, standing well behind Doctor Mingonius.

He looked around. A canopy bed of stained mahogany was still unmade, and the red jacquard bedspread lay twisted in a heap. The porcelain washing basin was overturned on the floor, and the jug had been shattered. Shards littered the floor.

The disheveled Hapsburg allowed the guards to lead him back to his chair. Carlos Felipe stood off to one side. The sour expression on the Jesuit's face was hardly that of a man who had led another in a moment of satisfying sacred prayer.

"Approach," Don Julius commanded Mingonius. "Who is this peasant you bring here?"

"He is a fellow guild member, the barber-surgeon of Cesky Krumlov, Don Julius."

Pichler removed his cap and bowed to the king's son.

"At least he has manners and recognizes me for who I am," mumbled Don Julius. "You there, Barber. Why do you not apply your profession to your own face?"

"I prefer my beard," said Pichler quietly. He looked up as far as Don Julius's knees. "My wife and daughter like it."

"You mustn't trust women, especially in matters of men," pronounced the pendulous Hapsburg lips. "Look at me, Barber."

Pichler looked up.

"I know you," said Don Julius, stabbing his finger at the barber. "I have seen you from my window there. You live and work in that house just below."

Pichler could not answer. He wondered how much Don Julius knew about him and his household.

"Oh, yes, I know you. I watch your family. There is one, a wild-haired girl. She rinses crockery in the river every night."

Pichler lifted his chin. The horror of Don Julius's knowledge of his family could not interfere with his duties as assistant to Mingonius. He was here in a professional capacity.

"Yes. She rinses the bloodletting bowls and cupping glasses. She is my assistant."

Mingonius interrupted. "Which is why the good Barber Pichler is here today. We are awaiting permission from your father to bleed you. It is high time—the cusp of the season. It will do your body good to have—"

"Barbaric fiends!" cried Don Julius. "Is it not enough that you have kept me under lock and key for months? My father told me that I would be free to walk the streets. This place is my kingdom, I am Lord of Krumlov!"

The barber's forehead wrinkled as he thought of the madman let free.

"That is impossible in your present condition," said Mingonius. "Perhaps after a bleeding or two, when the humors are vanquished—"

There was a knock at the door. The guards tensed, ready to grab Don Julius if need be. The door opened and a dusty messenger with a leather pouch slipped in. The door was closed behind him and the lock snapped shut.

"Let me see the letter," said Mingonius.

The messenger hesitated.

"Ah, it is addressed to me," said Carlos Felipe as the man bowed and delivered the envelope with the red royal seal to the priest.

No one spoke as the priest opened the letter.

"Come, Jesuit," shouted Don Julius. He suddenly sprang toward the priest and snatched the letter from his hand.

He bent over it and read to himself. There was a slight wrinkle in his forehead of concern, but then the forehead released and his face buckled and twisted in mirth.

"Ah, yes, Mingonius. You can bleed me. What are a few leeches sucking at my body when I am to be a free man in the near future!"

"What?" gasped Pichler.

Mingonius bowed and requested permission to read the letter. Don Julius flung it in his face.

"Read, good doctor. Bleed me and set me free in health. That is my father's compromise. He seems to be having second thoughts about locking me up in this godforsaken castle."

Carlos Felipe crossed himself and kissed his fingertips.

"It cannot be," he whispered.

Mingonius read the letter, his brow knitting tight in consternation. He passed it back to the priest.

"I am afraid so. Once we have completed a two-moon course of bleedings, he is to be set free to be Lord of Krumlov."

Pichler did not say anything. He was thinking of his daughters.

"Yes, let your leeches have at my veins," crowed Don Julius. "But only if you bring your comely daughter with the wild brindled hair to attend me, Herr Barber-Surgeon. I should like to see her close up."

Then he turned to Doctor Mingonius, and a palsy tremor ran up the left side of his face. When the physician reached out to inspect the spasm, Don Julius swatted his hand away.

"And what about the Coded Book of Wonder?" he demanded, his voice cold and distant. "The letter mentions it. Why have you not told me it is in your possession?"

Doctor Mingonius had the book hidden in his room. He played Don Julius as carefully as he would an opponent in game of cards with a huge wager at stake. Now was the time to deal the first hand.

"It will be yours to decode, Don Julius, but only after the Jesuit priest and I determine you are cured and can be trusted with such a great treasure. It is the king's command."

Don Julius looked away. When he turned back to face the men again, his face was composed and there was no trace of the spasm.

"Bring your leeches. And bring the girl as well."

CHAPTER 13

A Letter for Marketa

A weary rider in rumpled clothes and mud-stained boots approached the bathhouse. He was a stranger to Cesky Krumlov, his accent indicating he was from the northern reaches of the empire. Across his saddle was a thick leather bag, weathered and battered.

He dismounted and banged his reddened knuckles against the door.

Lucie Pichlerova opened it a crack and eyed the stranger.

"Is this the residence of Slecna Marketa Pichlerova?" he asked, wiping his sweaty face on the sleeve of his shirt. The gesture left a smear across his right cheek.

Lucie nodded.

"Yes, I am her mother. What would you want with her?"

The man opened the leather bag and withdrew a letter, a large red seal of wax stamping the vellum folds closed.

"I must deliver this to her."

Lucie opened the door wider and stretched out her hand. "You can give it to me. She is down tending the baths."

The rider shook his head. "The gentleman who penned the letter and paid for its delivery said I must give it to her in person."

Lucie frowned. "Marketa!" she bellowed back into the house. "Come here!"

"Coming, Mother."

While the two waited, Lucie crossed her arms over her bosom and looked the rider up and down. She took in his travel-worn appearance—his dirt-streaked face and neck; his tired, puffy eyes; and the stiffness in his back as he bent over toward the cobblestones in a long, wincing stretch.

"You look in need of a good soak, Pan Courier. Why not let our stable lad take your horse for a feed and rubdown. Then let my daughters bathe you. My Marketa has the hands of an angel. She will melt those knots in your aching back and render you a new man."

The rider shook his head, for he was in the habit of hoarding every coin he possessed. He knew the cost of a bath in Krumlov would be a fraction of what it was in Prague, but he was loathe to part with any pennies. He was determined to buy a more comfortable saddle for the long rides that were his livelihood.

But when Marketa emerged, drying her hands on her white apron, he reconsidered. The dirty skin on his face creased in a smile.

"This gentleman says he has a letter for you," Lucie said, pointing her chin toward the rider.

Marketa's eyes widened. She had never received a letter before.

The courier placed the large folded parchment in her hand, nodding to her. Marketa's fingers cradled the fine vellum as if she were receiving the host in mass.

"Well, open it, girl. Who is it from?" asked Lucie.

"I have no idea."

"Open it!"

Marketa shook her head. "I need a proper blade to break the seal. I will ask Papa for a good knife."

The rider watched her as she hurried away from her mother. Then he turned to Lucie.

"Good *pani*, I think I will take the bath after all."

"Humph! Smart man." Lucie whistled for the stable boy. "You won't be sorry."

Lucie's curiosity about the letter was replaced by her immense satisfaction of attracting a new client to the baths and coins to her pocket.

The stable boy Vaclav had taken the reins of the horse and was leading him toward the feeding shed.

"You will be back to bathe me, won't you, *slecna*?" called the rider to Marketa's back.

~

Barber Pichler was not in the bleeding room. He was still at Rozmberk Castle with Doctor Mingonius. Marketa hesitated. She was forbidden to touch his instruments without supervision. But she couldn't wait for his return. She opened the oak trunk and reached for the case that held the bloodletting fleams and blades, her hand trembling. She opened the leather flap and pulled out a sharp knife. Its short iron blade shimmered darkly, honed to an exquisite edge.

Marketa slipped the blade under the seal with the same care as if the parchment were live flesh. Her hand worked the blade with precision, careful not to nick or tear the vellum.

She unfolded the document. Two silver thalers dropped to the floor, ringing brightly against the floor stones. Marketa stooped to pick them up, her mouth dropped open in amazement. The figure of Jachymov, the Virgin Mary's father, gleamed in the dim light from the face of the coin.

My Dear Slecna Marketa:

I hope this letter finds you in good health. I remember my exquisite bath at your establishment and your capable hands, easing my tired muscles. I remember much more detail of our brief encounter, but I will not digress as this letter is of an urgent and professional nature.

You professed an ability to read, so I have decided to exercise that ability with this missive. I am intrigued with your curiosity in the matters of science and medicine—perhaps we could discuss these matters in correspondence.

I understand that Doctor Mingonius has contracted the services of your father in the attempt to bleed Don Julius. You told me that you often serve as your father's assistant, though I am quite certain that he would not let you near such a dangerous patient. Still, you may be in a position to learn how the patient is progressing. This information is of the utmost importance to the king.

The priest who accompanies Don Julius prepares a weekly report, as will Doctor Mingonius. However, the casual comments and observations your father may relate to you could be crucial to our understanding of Don Julius's progress. What you overhear may serve our purposes more than any formal report.

As I related to you, I am not a believer in Galen's humors but a follower of Paracelsus and the chemistry of the human body. Doctor Mingonius has persuaded the king that this should be the course of treatment. His Majesty does, however, want me to monitor the reports from both Mingonius and the priest. He also seeks reliable eyes and ears in Krumlov to gather information.

I would be most appreciative if you would serve in this role. In return, I can offer you reports of medical progress, scientific discoveries, and new experiments here in Prague. You will be in service to the king, His Majesty Rudolf II.

It is necessary that this correspondence remain strictly confidential, as it relates to royal matters. The king will know only that there is an impartial informant who reports to me.

Would you consent to this arrangement?

I will wait for your reply. Obviously you will need time to consider and to compose a letter. Please know that if I write to you again, in order to avoid arousing suspicion I will send my letters through our mutual friend, Annabella, who I know can be trusted.

I enclose reimbursement for the purchase of ink and parchment. And a little extra for curing me of my damnable fleas!

Your companion in service of our King Rudolf II, I wish you good health.

Jakub Horcicky de Tenepec

Marketa's hand cupped her throat, and she realized she had stopped breathing. A letter, news from Prague! Reports of scientific progress and communication with a physician of the Imperial Court. She fingered the thalers in her hands and made up her mind immediately.

One thing she knew was how to keep a secret. Especially for a man as handsome and learned as Doctor Jakub Horcicky, a man whose lips had touched hers and whose gentle hands had lingered on her skin as he tied a scarf around her neck.

Throwing her shawl over her shoulders, she hurried off to the market to buy parchment from the tanner, forgetting all about bathing the courier.

CHAPTER 14

LEECHES FOR A HAPSBURG

Pichler came home from the palace that night and would hardly touch his supper. He held his head in his interlocked fingers, thumbs pressed against his temples.

He poked at the sausage and peevishly nibbled on the cabbage, complaining there was not enough caraway in the dish and it tasted bland. Marketa knew some trouble was brewing, because it was rare for him to complain about her mother's cooking. And even more rare for her not to bristle at such an insult.

"Marketa, I must ask you a favor," he said finally, dropping his knife on his plate, surrendering to a force stronger than his appetite.

"Anything, Father."

He wiped his forehead with his sleeve and then rubbed his temples. He did not return her look but studied the glistening fat oozing from the sausage on his plate.

"You will need to go to the ponds tomorrow and fetch some leeches. I shall accompany you."

Marketa cocked her head in puzzlement.

"Do you not trust me with Pan Brener's cow? How many times have I led her to the pond to harvest leeches? Have I ever failed? And we have a goodly supply already. We must have over thirty lean ones in the barrels of the cellar."

Her father looked away and scanned his wife's face. She jutted her chin out at him, a stubborn gesture urging him on.

"Tell her, Husband," she said folding her arms across her stomach.

The barber drew a great breath.

"The leeches we are gathering cannot be harvested in our usual manner. They must be attracted to human flesh, not an animal's. I have strict orders, Daughter. Otherwise I would not ask you."

It took Marketa a few seconds to understand his meaning.

"I need you to wade into the pond, Marketa. Your tender skin and blood must be their bait, pure as you are. These leeches will be for a bloodletting for the king's son, Don Julius."

Marketa shuddered. She wondered if it was the idea of the leeches waiting under the muddy waters of the pond or the idea that her blood would be in some way mixed with that of the madman in the castle.

"Don Julius? The howling prince?"

Her father looked at her with a dull reluctance in his eyes.

"I am sorry, my daughter. But it is for the king's son's health… and science."

Marketa nodded her head. "Of course, Father. For science. I will be ready in the morning."

Pichler nodded with satisfaction. Then his eyes grew serious.

"I want you to go now and see why the twins are tarrying so long at the tavern fetching the ale. Your uncle has probably set them to work scouring pots."

"Yes, Father."

Marketa pulled her cloak off the hook and wrapped a wool scarf over her head and neck.

"Tell him to send them home immediately," he called to her as she shut the door. A gust of autumn wind blew in a spray of brown leaves, littering the stone floor.

"Wife, I must talk to you," Pichler said, his jaw working over the gristly meat in the sausage. "Of a matter of great importance."

"Yes, what is it, Husband?" said Lucie, sitting at his side. "Tell me."

"Marketa—is she—"

"What is it?"

"Is she still a virgin?"

Lucie's eyes dropped to her plate.

"I know I said when we married that I would leave the business of the bathhouse to you, but this is information that is of importance to the king."

"The king!" cried his wife, looking up at him, her hand flying to her throat.

"It must be a virgin who harvests the leeches. If Marketa has already lost her virtue, you must tell me at once."

Lucie's mouth dropped open in a gasp.

"Oh, no! She is pure, I swear it. She has never lain with a man!"

"Good," muttered Pichler. He sighed deeply, and his shoulders relaxed. He reached back with a crooked elbow and rubbed the muscles between his shoulder blades.

"I know she is of age for a patron, but it is our good fortune she remains a virgin, Wife. The leeches she harvests shall be the only ones that can touch the skin of a Hapsburg."

Lucie Pichlerova swallowed hard. She thought of how she had almost bartered away her daughter's virginity and her service to the king of Bohemia, the emperor of the Holy Roman Empire, for meat scraps and beer.

~

That night, Pichler called the town councilors and the elders of Cesky Krumlov together at Uncle Radek's tavern. There in the stone-walled cellar, with the door barred and shutters pulled closed, they sat talking, arguing, and when it seemed necessary, shouting at one another through most of the long night. Over tankards of ale, they pounded their fists on the wooden barrels and threatened treason.

"King Rudolf cannot let that madman loose on our town," said the tanner from the corner where he sat alone, his smell having driven the other men away. "How can we protect our women?"

"I saw the letter myself," said Pichler. "The king's orders were clear. And then Don Julius asked me about my daughters. He leers at the women from his chambers in the castle."

The baker shuddered and pounded his fist. "I will kill the bastard before he sets his fingers on my Katarina."

"Watch your tongue," warned the jailer. "A spy from the castle hears you say that and you will be hanging from the gallows come morning. Have a care what you say, all of you!"

The blacksmith, sooty and red in the light of the tavern fire, stood up, towering above most of the men. His raised a meaty fist.

"I won't stand aside and let that filthy bastard defile our women. I've heard the stories from Prague and Vienna. We are a God-fearing town, but I'll not be afraid of a hanging if he touches one of our own."

Pichler rose again to speak. The side conversations stopped, for he was the only one in Cesky Krumlov who had met Don Julius face-to-face.

"I appeal to your reason," he said.

"Oh yes, you're a man of reason," the rope-maker said over his beer. "Until he touches one of your girls!"

Pichler stared the man down.

"You think I do not worry about my girls, especially Marketa, who is old enough to catch his eye? He talked about her today. He has watched her from the castle when she rinses the letting bowls in the river. I live in horror at the thought of him walking freely in our streets, but I know what I heard today. The king has declared he shall be free, once he has undergone a cycle of bleeding. I know that I cannot protect myself and my family from the wrath of a Hapsburg. Don Julius will descend upon us as soon as we have balanced his humors."

"Bleed the whore's son dry," said a drunken sot in the corner. "Let that lancet slip, good barber, and you will do all of Bohemia a favor."

The jailer growled at the drunk and went to check the door and windows to make sure no royal guards were straying close to the tavern.

"Listen to Pichler, you drunken fools," he said. "Not enough of you have witnessed the kicking and choking of a hanged man, or you wouldn't be so quick to tie the noose around your miserable necks."

Pichler continued, "Doctor Mingonius is a respected physician. Together we will work to bleed out the bilious imbalance of the king's son. But I have witnessed his crudeness in Austria, and I cannot but warn you to lock up your womenfolk. They will not be safe from his lechery for long, for we have permission to bleed him but a couple of months."

~

Pichler woke Marketa at what seemed the middle of the night to set off for the Rozmberk carp ponds. Lucie had packed some buttered bread and a piece of cheese and pickle for each of them. Marketa carried hers in her apron pocket wrapped in a rag. She tied up her skirt in a knot at the side of her waist so the cold morning dew and mud would not soil the cloth. If she returned with muddy skirts, her mother would make her pound the hem on the rocks with urine collected from the chamber pots to get out the stains. Marketa avoided getting her clothes dirty at all costs.

Her father knew the way even better than she, and Marketa marveled at how he could thread through the meadows so quickly. She realized that he had spent many summers there before she was born, gathering leeches for his practice. He carried two buckets with a long pole across his back, slipped through the wooden handles of the pails. Despite the burden, he ducked agilely through the brush and around the trees.

Petr, the caretaker, was milking his cows in the pale light of daybreak when Pichler and his daughter reached the dams. He waved, his toothless mouth spreading wide in a smile.

"I have a fresh carp for your *pani* to cook tonight," he said. "As big as your shoulders are broad!"

"Thank you, Petr, you are too kind."

Marketa's eyes welled up with tears as she thought of Old Petr's only grandson, her first childhood love, who had died of the pox five years before. She could see Petr the younger in his grandfather's kind face.

"Ah, but you want the cow. Let me just finish with her," Petr said. "Just a moment and she'll be dry."

Pichler shook his head.

"We don't need the use of your cow this morning. Marketa will wade into the water and collect the leeches."

Petr sat up so abruptly from his milking stool that he nudged the cow's flank with his head and she bellowed, slapping his neck with her tail.

"The girl?"

"Yes," said Pichler, setting his jaw. "These leeches are for Don Julius, the king's son. I've been told to fetch them with a—with a girl."

Petr stood scratching his head. His rheumy eyes looked distractedly at the bloodletter. "Marketa will harvest the blood worms?"

Pichler nodded at him solemnly and thanked him for the gift of the fish. He assured him his wife would be delighted and cook the fish and they would toast to Petr's good health.

They walked to the pond, the reeds waving high above their heads as they stood side by side at the edge of the shallow water.

"Are you ready, Marketa?"

"Yes, Father."

"You've never been bled before. You need to know that their mouths make a little stick, but then like magic, the pain goes away like nothing ever happened. You won't even feel them except the tug of the water current as they start to wave."

Marketa swallowed hard. She knew them from the buckets stored in the dark corner of the bathhouse. Her father never let her touch them when they were ready for feeding; only he could pick them lean and hungry from the murky water, and only he could apply them to his patients.

Marketa had picked them up after they had fed, either from the wet grass when they fell off Petr's cow or from the cold stones of the floor after they had sucked the bad humors from a patient's body.

Then they were sated, their oval mouths and sharp, tiny teeth sucking listlessly.

But now they would find her flesh in the muddy water of the carp pond. They would smell and attack her, tapping into her blood. Marketa looked at her father and nodded. She wanted him to know that she was aware of what she was doing, that she would sacrifice anything for him.

Marketa stepped into the pond. At first there was nothing. Perhaps the water was too cold, she thought. She shivered and her father put his wool jacket over her shoulders. It smelled of beer and tavern fire, comforting in the cold dawn.

Then she felt something. A slight trembling in the water, a soft brush of a weed or twig.

And then a prick.

"Ow!"

"That's the girl," said her father. "In a minute, you won't feel a thing."

She looked down and saw a leech, no bigger than her baby finger, attached to her calf. Then two swam toward her legs.

"Ow! Ow!"

"Stand still now, let them attach. You have got to give them a chance to bite firmly or you will knock them loose and they might not come back."

Marketa trembled now in the water, feeling unsteady, but trying hard to stand still. She studied her father's face; he encouraged her every time they bit and she yelped. Soon the water was rippling with the small leeches, waving like tiny brown flags from her legs.

"You must have hit a nest of them," he said eagerly. "Now wait just a moment. We can't risk knocking them loose or scaring away the others. But they cannot fatten too much on your blood. They must be lean and hungry, ready for a meal on Don Julius's veins."

Marketa nodded her head. She no longer felt the pinch and prick of their sharp teeth. Instead there was a strange numbness, and her skin no longer felt so cold in the water. She felt as if her legs were drunk on mead.

Marketa's mind raced to the thought of the leeches as they fastened to the king's son's skin. Would they be as eager to sup on a Hapsburg's royal blood, her blood mingling with his in the worms' bellies?

The idea made her shiver, and she crossed her arms over her heart.

"Everything all right here, now?" said Old Petr, limping down to the water's edge.

He saw Marketa in the reeds and his face went white.

Marketa looked down. At the mid-shin she could see the water churning with shiny brown leeches, twisting against each other as they vied for her blood.

"Get that girl out of the water," he roared, his bleary eyes watering. He raised his fist in the air. "You get her out of the water, Zigmund, or I'll carry her out myself!"

Marketa's father looked at him and then at her.

"Slowly, Marketa. Don't disturb them from their feeding. Walk back to the grass and I'll harvest them."

As she walked through the reeds the water became more and more shallow. In the frigid sunrise, she could see a dozen or more glistening bodies drape down her leg, no longer buoyed up by the water.

Petr cursed as if he were warding off the devil himself. He used words in a Moravian dialect the Pichlers could not understand.

Marketa's father's eyes shone as if she had brought him gold from the center of the earth. He carefully applied a grain of salt to each wet mouth, and one by one they dropped into the grass.

He greedily snatched them up and placed them into the buckets.

"Aren't you going to attend to your daughter's wounds, Barber?" growled Old Petr.

The barber looked up as he picked up the last leech, still sucking, and dropped it into the bucket.

"Her wounds are what anyone will get in a leeching. There may have been many at once, but they have stolen little blood from her in those few minutes."

Petr approached the shivering girl and kissed her head like a doting grandfather.

"God bless you and protect you from this wickedness," he said, his red eyes brimming with tears. "This is the devil's business. No angel such as you should be mixed up in such a thing."

"Calm down, Petr," said Pichler. "It's not the devil's business at all. It's science."

"It's all the same," said Petr sadly, crossing himself with his gnarled right hand. "There are some matters better left to God, and not to the meddling of men."

He blew his nose into his rough-skinned fingers and slid his sleeve against his face. Marketa could see he was crying. She had never seen a man cry before. Without warning he kissed her cold hands and then embraced her, mumbling a prayer to the Holy Virgin.

Marketa stood as still as a stone in his embrace, not knowing what to say.

CHAPTER 15

KATARINA'S WARNING

Katarina's eyes grew wide when she heard how Marketa had harvested the leeches. They were sitting in the kitchen of the Pichler house, enjoying the warmth from the stove. A sudden cold spell had brought a reminder that winter was lurking not that far in the future.

"Marketa! Were you not afraid? To think of those horrid worms fastening their teeth to your flesh and drinking your blood!"

She flung her hands to her face in disgust and shivered in horror. Marketa tried to calm her, but she begged to see the wounds.

"See, they are but a prick," Marketa said, rubbing her thumb across the small red marks. "My father treated me like a princess afterward. He had the twins bathe me and wait on me hand and foot while I sipped Uncle Radek's best dark ale. I soaked in a barrel scented with lavender for almost an hour."

Katarina again wrinkled her beautiful face, the skin on her nose folding up tight like an accordion. Marketa could see she was thinking of something more sinister.

"There is much evil in it. I feel the touch of the devil. Remember the fairies and the tales of the Water Demon."

She raised her finger in warning, for she was a deep believer in the ancient Czech tales.

"Those worms are the Water Demon's pets," she pronounced, nodding her head at Marketa's pricked skin. "You are lucky the demon himself did not pull you down with his gnarled claws to his cave at the bottom of the lake."

Marketa laughed. Katarina's fears were based on nonsense and fairy tales. Marketa's own mind was shaped by science, she thought. It was as if the two girls were speaking different languages.

Katarina narrowed her eyes at Marketa.

"You know the story of Lidushka," she said, murmuring. "It's a warning, Marketa."

Everyone knew the ancient tale of Lidushka. One day while she was washing her clothes in the river, a frog had begged the young girl to become godmother of her children. Lidushka followed the frog down a crystal staircase, transparent as layers of water, until they reached a sparkling room, where Lidushka blessed the tadpoles. As she wandered through the cavernous palace, she came across a room lined with shelves. On the shelves were glass jars upside down. When she lifted one, a dove flew out. She realized that these were trapped souls, and one by one, she let them loose.

Marketa thought silently about Lidushka.

"What silly ideas stuff your head?" she said. "What does Lidushka have to do with a bleeding?"

"These Water Demon pups were sucking at your soul, Marketa. Evil times lie ahead."

Marketa laughed at her friend, until Katarina's lovely face pinched together so tight that Marketa realized she was crying. She reached out for Katarina's hair. Katarina tried at first to shrug off her friend's touch, but then finally she allowed Marketa to smooth her sugar-dusted locks. To make her laugh, Marketa tasted her fingers, and indeed they were sweet like a Christmas candy.

"These leeches are medicinal," Marketa explained to her. "They have nothing to do with fairy tales. Their tiny mouths do not suck at your soul. They release the bad humors from the body. Think of the four humors draining away from the body, just the way Lidushka freed the doves from the jars. They free the good spirit inside."

Katarina furrowed her forehead and then quickly released it again.

"I prefer to think of the white doves rather than those evil brown worms!"

Just then, Pichler entered the room. He seemed ill at ease and his movements were fidgety.

"Yes, Father?"

He looked at his daughter and then Katarina.

His wife appeared and pushed him closer.

"Tell her," Lucie said.

Marketa could see from her mother's sudden color and dancing eyes that she was as excited—and as happy—as Marketa had ever seen her.

"Don Julius has insisted I bring you as my assistant to the bleeding," he said. "He has refused the bleeding entirely if you do not accompany me today."

Marketa dropped her hand from her friend's sticky locks and stared openmouthed.

Her mother's normally creased face suddenly released into a laugh. It was a rich rumble in her throat that startled her daughter, for it was so rare.

She rubbed her hands together and twisted her fingers, fidgeting with pleasure.

"The son of King Rudolf himself requests my daughter at his castle! Is this not the most fortunate day of our lives?"

Marketa watched Katarina and her father exchange a look that belied any happiness.

"Come, my girl, I will bathe you myself," said Lucie, shooing away her daughter's friend. "So much preparation, so little time!"

Katarina stood motionless, her fingers plunged into her mouth like a child.

"A Hapsburg," she said, pulling her fingers away from her mouth. "My God in heaven!"

Marketa waved a good-bye to her astonished friend and allowed herself to be led to the bathhouse by her mother's eager hands, with no chance to question her father for more details.

Marketa's mother dressed her in a treasured Bohemian *kroj*, the jewel of Lucie Pichlerova's possessions. The *kroje* represented her identity—it was sewn according to the Krumlov traditions and embroidered intricately by her own hand.

Marketa's hosiery was held up with ribbons, and the starched skirts stood out as if they had legs of their own. The *halenka*, the blouse she wore on feast days, was embroidered with elaborate stitching, as was the laced bodice that just barely skimmed the girl's slim hips.

After Lucie brushed her daughter's hair until it gleamed, she twisted it up in a tight knot. Then she tied on the white embroidered cap, the black velvet ribbon stretching across her forehead to keep it centered.

Her eyes gleamed as she stepped back to inspect her work.

"You look like I did as a girl," she murmured. Marketa could see by the wistful look in her eyes that she was lost in the past.

Marketa could smell the faint odor of her mother deep in the fabric, though Lucie had washed the material fastidiously. She had been a maiden in this dress, as well as a matron, for this was part of her dowry. The costume was only worn on special occasions: feasts, Christmas, baptisms. But in recent years, Marketa's mother had grown too stout to wear it.

The final piece, a white starched apron, was embroidered with dark red cotton thread and colored sequins. The sequins were the scales of carp, dyed a myriad of colors.

Marketa stared down at herself, at the fine clothes, and suddenly felt silly.

"But I am attending a bleeding," she said. "Why do I wear a costume meant for a celebration?"

Her mother sniffed at her ignorance.

"And what else would you dare wear in the presence of the king's son? Your old woolen shawl and linen bathmaid shift? You are ignorant of the ways of nobility—they would not let you enter their grand palace dressed like a peasant."

"But what if Don Julius's blood stains your fine white blouse? The blood splatters against the tray and often paints my clothes."

Her mother smiled.

"I shall peddle a look at it for a koruna apiece. The fabric merchant's wife would give her eyeteeth on a plate to see the bloodstain of a prince."

Marketa shuddered.

"He's not a prince," Marketa said in a low voice. She watched her mother's eyes flash, but went on. "He's the king's bastard son."

Marketa's mother grabbed her daughter's ears, scratching them with her broken nails, and shook the girl's face.

"Never utter that insolence again!" Lucie hissed, her face close to her daughter's. "He is—and will always be—the king's eldest son. He has the blood of an emperor flowing in his veins."

She looked at her hands and must have realized she was crushing the white dove-cap. Her fingers released their grip and she smoothed the material, trying to erase the creases.

"You must remember that you are blessed with opportunity. Do not waste what God has given you. Don Julius is the Lord of Krumlov now, the same as the Rozmberks were."

As she tightened the bodice with black ribbons, Marketa wondered exactly what her mother was referring to when she spoke of opportunity. Was it Marketa's able assistance in her father's practice of medicine or was it something else she had in mind?

Pichler and his daughter heard the howls of Don Julius as they entered the courtyard of the palace. Marketa listened as her father conversed in German with the royal guards and one left to give notice to the priest and Doctor Mingonius.

Her father's eyes scanned the second floor of the palace, his face alert, his eyes nervous.

"Is he up there in that room?" Marketa asked, motioning with her chin in the direction of his focus.

"Yes," he said. Then his face narrowed again, as if he were worried.

"What troubles you so, Father?" she asked. "You have bled hundreds of people—surely a Hapsburg has the same blood and courses as we of lesser birth."

"It's not that, Marketa," he said. "If I told you what I saw just yesterday morning, you would think me—unsound."

"Tell me, Father," she said, finding his hand and squeezing it. "Nothing could ever inspire an ill opinion of you."

He cast a look over his shoulder toward the one guard.

He lowered his voice.

"It was still black with night. As I waited for the guard to announce my arrival, I looked up at that corridor and I saw..."

"Her!" Marketa said without thinking, her heart leaping inside her chest. She felt an insatiable thirst for his words. "You saw the White Lady, didn't you?"

She grabbed both his hands, joyous that he had shared the same vision as she had. Now he would never doubt her, she thought.

He looked at the buckle on his boot and nodded his head.

"I think I must have. They said there were no women in the palace except in the kitchens by the stables. Doctor Mingonius has forbidden any womankind near the prince. But you must swear never to tell anyone, especially your mother."

"It is our secret." Marketa took a deep breath. "Father, why am I here?"

He gripped her hand now.

"I already told you, Marketa. He will not consent to a bleeding unless you accompany me. Unless you are there, he will not allow Doctor Mingonius near him. As the moon waxes, his behavior becomes more and more erratic, Doctor Mingonius says."

It was Marketa's turn to look at the ground and study her hosiery.

"It is not because...because I know something of the science you perform that you bring me?"

Marketa realized as soon as she said the words aloud, they were foolish.

Her father squeezed his lips together and shook his head.

"Marketa! We have discussed this matter, and nothing will change. You are a girl."

"Of course," she mumbled, her cheeks burning.

"Listen to me. This man is unsound in his body and soul. He has no appreciation for science, no respect for woman, man, or beast. Forgive me, he is—"

"Barber Pichler!" shouted the guard.

"Come, Marketa. You are to remain quiet and assist as you always do. Speak your best German to Doctor Mingonius—he will see what an educated girl you are. Hold the trays and replace them as needed. Neither look at Don Julius, nor speak, nor encourage him in any way."

~

Marketa took rapid, shallow breaths as she was led through the grandeur of the halls. Never had she imagined such beauty on earth as she saw that day. The paintings in golden frames, the burnished woods of inlaid furniture. Velvets, plush and richly colored. The parquet floors and the carpets—carpets that she dared not walk on, until the guard smiled at the girl and insisted.

"That's what they are there for, girl," he said. "Plant your foot on them and walk. They will not disintegrate!"

Before Marketa reached Don Julius's room, she could smell the sickness. There was an odor of evil humor—like hot vinegar.

Her father watched her as she sniffed the air.

"You can smell it, can you not?"

"Yes, Father."

"It's the yellow bile. He reeks of imbalance."

Doctor Mingonius stood outside the room. He greeted her with the air of a fond uncle.

"So this is the fair Marketa, the only one to whom Don Julius will offer his blood. You have charmed a Hapsburg, my dear. Congratulations."

Marketa winced and dropped her gaze.

Doctor Mingonius held out his hand to her as if she were a man. She looked at her father, who nodded his consent.

She shook the famous physician's hand and felt the firmness.

"Forgive me for being so indelicate," he said, his voice softening. "Your father tells me that you are an assiduous student of Galen's medicine."

"I am devoted to it," Marketa said, raising her eyes to meet his. "And also to the studies and medicines of Paracelsus."

Doctor Mingonius drew a breath as if startled by her affirmation. Then he offered a quick smile.

"Unusual for a girl. A fascination with science, that is."

Then his face grew serious.

"Today you will have the opportunity to observe a very sick patient. I have agreed that you are to assist us only because the king's son has been so reluctant to seek medical intervention. I have had to bribe him, if you will. I am negotiating with a lunatic."

At this remark, the doctor stuck out his lower lip. It was a stubborn but troubled face, as if he were wrestling with something in his mind.

"You must remember, Marketa, do not speak to him, no matter how he pleads. If he is unseemly or rude, you must avert your eyes and block your ears. He is sick—very sick—and has no manners with young women, despite his upbringing. He can seem to be the prince that he is, our king's eldest son. And he can be a sad, lost child. But his behavior is mercurial, and when he is possessed by the choleric humors as he is now, he is as vulgar as a grave digger and as dangerous as a mad dog."

Pichler coughed.

"Yes, well. We must begin. I will ask you to wait. Perhaps we can begin treatment without you—perhaps he will forget that you were to accompany us."

The doctor motioned to the guard, who in turn knocked on the door.

"The doctors are here," he said as another guard opened the heavy door a crack.

"Let us get him seated to receive them."

A harsh shout pierced the air. "The sons of whores can cut out their own vitals! Leave me in peace."

Doctor Mingonius squared his shoulders and walked into the room.

"Good morning," he said, his voice booming and bright. Marketa's father glanced at her, put a finger to his lips, and gave her the satchel with his knives and the bucket of leeches nestled in wet grass and muddy water. Then he disappeared into the room.

Marketa waited in the hall, feeling like a trussed-up goose ready for the oven. Her breasts were squeezed under the tight fabric of the bodice, and her mother's shoes pinched her toes. She felt foolish dressed up in a *kroj* when she was used to a simple dress in her father's practice or a plain white shift in the bathhouse.

The guard, an occasional customer at the bathhouse, licked his teeth and winked at her. Marketa looked him straight in the eye, smoldering with anger. She was here to assist in the medical procedure. How dare he treat her like a bathmaid? After an uncomfortable moment, he lowered his gaze and studied the parquet floor.

The howls of protest persisted in the room. There were shouts and curses from Don Julius, his guards, and perhaps even the two men of medicine.

The door opened and Zigmund Pichler came out. His neat hair had been mussed, and there was a deep scratch down his cheek.

"Father, you are hurt!"

"Marketa," he said, ignoring her remark. "Doctor Mingonius has asked you to please enter."

He took the satchel from her and motioned ahead, the blood making little rivulets down his jaw.

"Stay as far away from him as you can, even when holding the trays. Extend your arms to catch the blood, but keep the rest of your body out of reach of his teeth. He is fettered now, but should he come loose, he is very fast. Be ready to jump aside and run for the door."

He was breathing raggedly, still catching his breath. "He is consumed by yellow bile, the choleric humor, and is deadly dangerous."

Marketa entered the room, and in the corner by the great window that looked out over the river and their bathhouse sat Don Julius, bound to a heavy carved chair. He heard Marketa's steps and turned his head to see her.

Don Julius was still stout, though leaner than weeks before. He was a Hapsburg, she could see that at once. His lower lip hung loose, full and red. But mercifully he had inherited his mother's reported good looks as well, the Italian chiseled nose and fine cheekbones. He had an oval face, thoroughly royal, and sharp green-blue eyes that darted restlessly.

"Now, here is something worth looking at!" he snapped.

His eyes flashed at Marketa, and she watched as his right hand strained against the rope toward his groin.

Marketa dropped her gaze, her face flushing red-hot. Her father moved nearer to her, clenching his fists at his side.

"She will attend us now, Don Julius, in your bleeding, and you shall behave as a gentleman," said Doctor Mingonius. "Or she shall depart."

"No!" shouted Don Julius, his hands struggling against the ropes. He squinted at Marketa as if she were perhaps someone he knew. A wave of emotion registered on his face.

A sudden innocence softened his countenance, as if he were a little boy once again.

"I know you!" he said in a whisper, the ropes tightening as he leaned toward Marketa. "You are queen of the book, the Angel of the Baths!"

"What's he talking about, Father?" Marketa said under her breath. She trembled as she heard this Hapsburg call her a queen and angel.

"It is the humors speaking, Marketa. Look lively and stay out of his reach."

Don Julius had lost all color and his mouth hung open. He began to mutter under his breath and rock his body back and forth in the chair where he was bound.

Doctor Mingonius approached, but was careful not to touch him. Instead he spoke in a kind voice as if he were addressing a small child.

"This is the barber-surgeon's daughter, Don Julius. Remember, you insisted she visit with Herr Pichler. Perhaps it is too much company for one day," he said, signaling for her to leave the room with a nod of his head.

"No!" wailed Don Julius. A shrill voice, the haunting scream of a dying rabbit. "Noooooo! I shall *die* if you take this heavenly creature from me, I swear it! She is one of the angels from the book, come to speak the secrets of the universe at last!"

Marketa looked at her father, suddenly terrified. The man was truly mad!

She heard the door groan as someone entered.

"Come now, Don Julius. You have only just met her. Women have never stolen your heart," said a black-robed priest, coming in the open door. "You abuse them and take devilish pleasure in their tears."

"Shut up, Jesuit! You will scare her away!" whispered Don Julius. "She is from a different world and possesses unspeakable powers."

"You should have announced your presence," said the doctor in a cold voice. "I thought we agreed that I would care for his body and you his soul. Please leave at once."

"The king has asked that I witness the first bleeding," the priest said simply, sitting on the edge of a taffeta-covered chair. "His Majesty wants to see that you in no way mistreat his son and that he does not endure any treatment to which he does not give his express consent."

The priest studied Marketa with cold eyes. His pinched look was foreign to her, and she could barely understand his German through his thick Castilian accent.

"She is hardly a beauty," he said finally, examining the girl as if she were a stick of wood. "Far too thin. She has the mottled hair of a fox! Still, she seems to have captured Don Julius's attention. Am I correct?"

"You fool! I worship her as you do your God!" Don Julius said. "I have watched her for weeks now from the window, those honeyed tresses. Come to me, my angel," he cried, turning to Marketa.

His arms wrenched against the ropes; the hemp bit into his skin. "Tell me how you walked off the parchment to be at my side."

Marketa stared at him in astonishment and remained immobile.

"See what the humors have done to his mind?" muttered Doctor Mingonius. "Don Julius," he said in a loud voice, "there are no women in the palace because your sickness leaves you with beastlike tendencies and you forget your royal manners. But if you behave, we will be able to employ maids from the village to make fine things for you—breads, sweets, music. We will then unlock the door and let you walk the courtyards and gardens. And you may gaze once more upon your Coded Book."

Don Julius snarled at the doctor and snapped like a mad dog. Then he turned his eyes up to Marketa. The sudden bad humor that clenched his face melted like ice in strong sunlight.

"You must be of vellum and paint, but you appear so mortal. Let me touch her, I beg of you, Doctor!"

"No. There will be no touching," said Mingonius.

"She is my heart and has been since the day I was born when my father bought the book for me," he said. "Six hundred and fifty ducats, he paid, a royal sum. 'Someday you will make me proud, my son.' Proud, he said! 'You will learn the Hermetic principles, the Kabbalah, and the secret Elixir of Life—'"

Don Julius broke off muttering, his eyes staring at nothing. He seemed to have forgotten them completely.

"A very impressive book, indeed," said Doctor Mingonius, examining his patient as he spoke, noting his color, his rigidity. He even stooped to smell him.

Don Julius's eyes had grown large, the whites exposed like a horse frightened by a fire. He twitched periodically, and a tremor ran down the right side of his face. He rubbed his fingertips mechanically, as if he had grains of sand between them.

"She possesses the very secrets of the universe. I must touch her!" he said, suddenly lunging and making the ropes cut against his flesh. The guards secured the chair, holding it in place.

"Well, she is about to go away," said Mingonius. He motioned for Marketa to leave.

"No!" Don Julius shrieked, struggling against the guards and making the heavy wooden chair hop across the floor. Marketa jumped back in horror and willed herself not to run for the door.

"She will go away immediately unless you are cooperative. If you allow us to bleed you, she will come near."

"How near?" the mad prince said, suddenly stopping his struggles.

"Close enough."

Don Julius looked heavenward as if hearing a voice.

"Yes, by God. I will spill my blood for her in sacrifice."

"That will not be necessary. The fleam and leeches shall do that for us."

"Leeches?"

"Yes," said Pichler. "We have brought fresh leeches to dispel your injurious humors. They will purify the regions of concentrated poison the fleam cannot touch."

"Remember, Don Julius," said Doctor Mingonius. "We discussed this last night."

"I will not let you fasten those loathsome creatures to my veins!" He struggled against the ropes again. "A common worm to sup on Hapsburg blood! Jesuit, you are my witness. I refuse treatment from these frauds! Cut the ropes that bind me at once or I shall tell my father of this torture!"

Doctor Mingonius flicked a glance at Pichler. The doctor knew he was about to lose.

Marketa lingered in the doorway. The words that emerged from her lips surprised her.

"Do not worry, Don Julius."

"Marketa!" whispered her father. "Do not address him."

"They drank of my blood only yesterday," she said. She walked to the prince's chair where he could see her better and her scent could reach his nostrils. He reminded her of a horse in his stall, thrashing about to free himself. She approached him cautiously, whispering to him gently, and he quieted.

"All you will feel is the slightest prick, and then it is as if you are drunk with strong spirits. There is no further pain, my lord, I swear it is so."

Don Julius stared at her, his green eyes scanning her features. He cocked his head, turning his ear toward the sound of Marketa's voice.

"She speaks like an angel of God! Listen!"

"Blasphemy!" snarled the priest. "Guards, untie him. He has refused bloodletting, and I am his witness."

"Silence," ordered the doctor. "This is not your domain, Priest!" He looked at Marketa as if realizing something for the first time. "Yes, Don Julius," he said, nodding toward Marketa. "Yes, these same mouths have kissed the skin of this fair Bohemian maiden, just as she says."

It took a second for the doctor's words to dawn on the king's son. Then a lopsided smile emerged on his face, growing slowly.

"If these worms have touched your skin and carry the precious elixir of your body," he said, staring at her, "may they mix our bloods together, may we be conjoined forever! I shall have the secret of the Coded Book and an angel as my wife."

A shiver rocked the girl. Her breast grew cold at the thought.

"Pichler," whispered the doctor. "Bring your implements and the leeches at once."

"Oh God! What a blessing you have sent with this angel!" cried Don Julius, clenching his fists in prayer. "Open my veins and let them receive."

"Hold him tight," her father warned the guards.

Pichler's hand dipped down into the torn grasses and extracted a moist brown leech. Its round mouth sucked the air, and Marketa could see the tiny, file-like teeth inside.

"Join our bloods!" screamed Don Julius. "Oh merciful God, let the divine communion begin."

"I will not witness such references to our Holy Father!" shouted the priest. With a sweep of his robe, he rose from the chair and stormed out the door.

Pichler placed the leeches on Don Julius's wrists, forearms and neck. Don Julius smiled in ecstasy.

"Now we shall open a vein," said Doctor Mingonius. "Only for a few seconds, to ensure we reach the depths of the bad humor, where the leeches cannot reach."

"And she—she shall hold the tray," Don Julius murmured.

"Yes, if you remain quiet."

Marketa approached him, and he swiveled his head to watch her every move. He seemed peaceful now, as if the leeches' sucking mouths had already reduced his choler.

Still, Marketa stood well away from him as her father cut the vein in his forearm, and then she approached cautiously, praying the ropes and guards would restrain him.

The blood splashed into the gleaming white tray. She removed the tray by placing another just under it, not spilling a single drop.

Don Julius's eyes rolled back in his head.

"I can smell her," he uttered in a hoarse whisper. "I cannot see her anymore, but I can smell her."

"Enough," ordered Doctor Mingonius. "Stanch his bleeding. He has given enough blood. We will wait until the leeches have had their fill, but no more blood shall be taken today."

Already two or three leeches had fallen to the floor, bloated with Hapsburg blood. Marketa knelt and gathered them up, weaving them into the coarse grass to be carried back home.

"Fräulein, give me the leeches," said Doctor Mingonius, taking the basket from her. "I must dispose of them in a way that will satisfy our king."

Marketa dipped in a curtsy, bowing her head. As she did so, she could see the water worms in the basket, resting peacefully in the damp grass.

∼

The walk home from Rozmberk Castle was silent. There were no more cries from the Hapsburg lord echoing through the town.

The only sound in the air above Cesky Krumlov was the wind off the river and the chirping of birds.

Pichler kept looking furtively at his daughter, but she kept her eyes trained ahead, greeting her neighbors who stood outside their shops and homes, staring after her.

"Pan Pichler's daughter accompanies him to treat the mad prince," Pani Kovak whispered to her mother-in-law. She dried her wet hands on her apron without taking her eyes off Marketa.

"He lets her assist him! She sees the wretched man in his madness."

Pan Dvorak stopped dusting the porcelain jars of his apothecary. He saw the sloshing bucket of leeches and watched as Marketa stooped to pick up one that had climbed to the rim and slipped out onto the cobblestones. She dropped it gently from her fingertips into the wooden bucket without a word.

"How could he allow her to see a madman?" Pan Dvorak asked himself, shaking his dust rag in the open air.

Marketa nodded, her white kerchief clean and neat over her hair, as she met the stares of Krumlov with a smile.

The greengrocer's wife waved and called after Marketa to send greetings to her good mother, adding that she would be bathing on Saturday.

"Musle looks pretty today," said Pani Kranz to her husband, who was stacking and arranging cabbages in a pyramid display. She kept a knife at the ready to pare away the wormholes.

"Look at her, she's radiant," she said, poking her husband.

He sighed and rubbed his back, sore from bending and moving crates of vegetables and roots.

"Yes, Wife," he said. "She is comely, although Pan Pichler should feed her more. With the supplement Pan Brewer is paying her mother, they could afford to give her more meat and cheese."

"Yes," said Pani Kranz. "But there is something special about her today."

It was not just the greengrocer who noticed Marketa's unusual radiance, but the sausage-maker and his son. Marketa stopped at the shop to buy some wurst for the family's dinner, and the butcher, known for being a skinflint, refused her money.

The butcher's son Andrej ducked behind the scales and stole a piece of bacon from the larder chest. He ran the fat-streaked strip across his unruly red hair, to make it lie flat and shine for Marketa.

"Your father's medicine has eased the ill humors of the prince," said the butcher. "My hand will be steadier on the knife, thanks to the silencing of his infernal screams."

Andrej wrapped the sausages in a clean rag, and when he passed them to Marketa, his hand lingered on the package. He, too, noticed the sparkle of her eyes, the radiance of her skin, and he wanted her to linger a moment longer.

Marketa pulled the package gently from his hands.

"Thank you," she murmured, smiling down at the sausages.

"What's he like?" whispered the butcher's son. "Is he as mad as they say? Does his royal blood look different than ours—is it blue? Does it smell any different?"

"Does a lamb's blood look different from an ox's?" she asked, still smiling. "Can you smell the difference as you hack open the carcasses?"

"Ah, but the meat has a different taste, doesn't it, Marketa?" His eyes danced with mischief. "One is sweeter than the other."

Marketa dismissed him with a cluck of her tongue.

"I do not taste the prince's blood. But thank you for the sausages, Andrej. It is kind of your father." Her voice was now raised so the butcher could hear her.

As Marketa repeated her gratitude and turned to depart, she gulped hungrily at the fresh morning air. The butcher smelled of meat, the sharp metallic odor of blood clinging to his skin and breath. He smelled of coins being rubbed together in greedy hands. And his son—smelled of bacon lard.

~

Jakub received the letter from the courier, his hands eager for the parchment. He smiled as he looked at the writing, for it was smudged and spotted with ink spots, signs the writer had labored to write the missive. He had waited almost two weeks for her reply. Still the Czech was legible and he was impressed by the bath maiden's ability with the written word.

Her father's interest in her education had not been wasted, he thought. Some students at the Latin school could not write as well as this girl.

Esteemed Physician Horcicky:

I was surprised beyond all measure to receive your proposal. I accept, willingly, and swear to keep all communication between us confidential as requested. I am flattered to act in service to His Majesty, King Rudolf.

I am in a perfect position to observe the patient, for I have accompanied my father to a bleeding now. I do not have to rely on hearsay. My information is gathered with my own eyes and ears.

Don Julius rants and behaves most rudely—he despises his doctor and must be tied to a chair for Physician Mingonius to even approach him. He snarls and spits, shouting blasphemous curses not only at his physician, but at the priest as well.

For some reason his malevolent humors calm when he is in my presence. Sometimes he reverts to the character of a little boy, confused and lost. He makes the most bizarre comments, but he will allow bleedings if I am within his sight. My father and Doctor Mingonius work quickly while I speak to him.

He raves about a book. A book with fantastic illustrations of maidens and waters, spells and incantations.

He is a lost soul. Dare I say I feel sorry for his torment? Was he once a normal man such as you? I have now met two men from the royal court—you and Don Julius. What a curious place it must be to have created two men so different in almost every way.

Your servant in service to our noble king, Rudolf II.

Marketa Pichlerova

~

There were no howls from the castle for over a week. Pichler brought back reports each night to his family, saying the prince was resting quietly and taking food.

"His behavior is quite docile," he reported over a midday meal of dumplings and sausage. "Even the Spanish priest has remarked on his improvement. He has said a rosary with the priest at his bedside. The choler has vanished."

He chewed his gravy-covered dumpling, contemplating.

"What is it, Father?"

He looked up at his wife's back as she stirred the night's soup.

"He still begs to see you," he whispered. He held his finger to his lips, glistening with fat, in warning. He did not want Lucie to hear.

"So is there a bonus for curing the king's son?" asked his wife, casting a look over her shoulder. "There should be some compensation for letting him breathe easy again—and not keeping us up at all hours of the night with his howls!"

"There is no compensation."

She grunted and shifted her weight to her other leg.

"Poor leavings these Hapsburgs give us," she said in a growl. "No orders for fine cakes or sausages, no washing of linen, no shaves, no baths. No courtiers to buy our goods, give us trade.

Those who lived at the castle once sustained this town. How will Krumlov survive?"

Pichler poked at his sausage and let the juices ooze out.

"I have been summoned again."

Lucie stopped scraping the vegetables and turned to him.

"They asked you to return?"

"Doctor Mingonius has requested a meeting this afternoon. I do not know what it is about. Perhaps he will employ me after all to bleed Don Julius once he departs for Prague."

Lucie dried her hands on her apron.

"Did I not say that this Don Julius would bring us good fortune!"

Pichler put down his knife for good. He threw his daughter a look, and Marketa ducked her head, concentrating on her sausage.

"He asked if I might bring Marketa back as well."

Lucie's face warmed, the corners of her lips taking an uncustomary turn up.

"The king's son has taken a fancy to our Marketa, has he?"

Pichler's eyes flashed at her. He set his jaw so that the muscles bulged.

"The man is a lunatic! And a dangerous one."

He stole a glance at his daughter. She looked up from her plate and set down her knife.

"Would you consent to accompany me, Marketa? We must be there at four o'clock."

Marketa was startled, feeling like someone watching a puppet show when suddenly one of the puppets spoke to her.

"I—I do not know."

"Of course you will, girl!" insisted her mother. "I will get the *kroj* pressed and ready."

"No!" Marketa said, jumping to her feet in defiance. "I will go, yes, Father. But I do not wish to dress in a *kroje*. If I am to accompany you, I shall wear the same skirt and blouse as I use every day."

Her mother's face fell.

"And have him see you as a common girl!"

"I *am* a common girl, Mother. I do not want to go about tied up in ribbons."

"The girl wants him to see her gentleness, and her mind," said her father, softly. "Her presence calms him."

"Who cares about her mind? This is a Hapsburg, and he has had book learning since he was at his milk nurse's teat. What he wants is a bit of Bohemian beauty—a real woman."

"Stop, Mother!" Marketa cried.

Pichler pounded his fist on the table, making his empty tankard jump and the cutlery rattle.

"My Marketa is not a common prostitute. He shall not have her!"

Marketa took a deep breath, savoring his words. How long she had yearned to hear him take a stand for her.

Lucie approached her husband, her eyes lit up in fury.

"You fool! You are the doctor who is supposed to heal him. Why not believe in your own skills—and in your daughter. It is your job to save that poor young man from the demons who torment him. And then our daughter's charms will soothe his injured soul. Why can we not believe that? And if we do, well then, think what a Hapsburg's attentions could win this family. We could have a life you could never dream of. Perhaps Marketa would move to Prague to be near him, maybe in the palace itself. She would be dressed in fine silks and furs, walk the streets of Prague on the arm of the king's son. And she would not forget us. Think of her influence at court and what wealth those ties could bring us!"

Pichler stared at his wife as if she were a stranger. Then he rose to his feet slowly, looking at Marketa and saying, "Meet me on the bridge at three o'clock. We shall go together to the palace."

"Yes, Father."

Neither one of them looked at Lucie Pichlerova.

~

As Pichler prepared to leave the bathhouse, there was a knock on the door.

He opened the door to see the red-haired cunning woman, Annabella, standing outside, a basket in her hand.

"*Dobre den, slecna*," he said. "May I help you?"

"I have come to visit with your daughter and to bring your good wife mushrooms gathered from the mountainside," she said.

Pichler escorted her into the bathhouse and called for his daughter.

"Marketa, you have a visitor."

Marketa, who never had visitors other than Katarina, smiled to see the healer at the door. Annabella winked at her. Marketa was puzzled for only a moment and then thought, *Ah! She brings correspondence from Prague!*

"Thank you, Father," she said hurriedly. "And I will see you on the bridge at three o'clock."

"Be punctual daughter."

"Of course, Papa."

He kissed her on the cheek, a preoccupied look on his face. He nodded and bid Annabella good afternoon.

As soon as he had closed the door, Marketa asked eagerly, "Is it news from Prague? Oh, tell me!"

Annabella smiled and retrieved a letter from her basket.

Dearest Slecna Marketa:

I thank you profoundly for your correspondence and, most of all, your agreement to write of Don Julius's progress.

I was amazed to hear that you are in the position to actually witness the bleedings. While it is a perfect arrangement to observe and document the treatment, I have grave concerns.

You must not feel sorry for the patient. Don Julius is a very dangerous young man, ruled by his madness. He stabbed one of his servants and has committed the most sordid acts. It is for this reason he was sent so far away from Prague for treatment—and confinement.

I have struggled with the idea of writing Mingonius to remove you from Don Julius's presence to protect your innocence. He might break his restraints and hurt you!

But I also will not break our confidence by letting Mingonius know that we have been in communication. Still, this is no place for a young woman to tread. It is simply too dangerous.

Meanwhile, even as I write, Doctor Jan Jesenius prepares for the public autopsy. Physicians from across Europe have expressed interest in attending. There may be hundreds in attendance, convening not only to see the dissection, but to discuss and share medical discoveries from other lands.

The king is pleased with the attention as the eyes of Europe, Africa, and Asia turn toward Prague. He feels it is only fitting that the seat and capital of the Holy Roman Empire is recognized for its accomplishments. His mood has been one of elation and pride lately.

One thing more. This book that you allude to, with maidens in water. It sounds as if this might be the king's great treasure, the Coded Book of Wonder.

I look forward to your next report. I trust you are still in possession of the green scarf and wear it in good health. It gives me great pleasure to think of its silk caressing your soft throat, especially as the days grow cold and bitter.

Your colleague in service to His Majesty, I bid you good health and caution you to keep safe.

Jakub Horcicky

"Is it the news you hoped for?" asked Annabella, studying Marketa's face.

"I am not sure," said Marketa. "He fears for me. Annabella, I must tell you a secret that you cannot divulge to anyone."

And so Marketa told the healer how the king's son had appeared bewitched by her presence. It was a secret in equal measure terrifying and entrancing, though it made Annabella unusually quiet and contemplative for the remainder of the day.

CHAPTER 16

THE POOR CLARES CONVENT

Marketa wondered why her father wanted to meet her so early on the bridge. The castle was only minutes from their house, up the steep cobblestone road.

She lingered on the bridge, watching the ripples of the Vltava below her and the dark shadows of the trout under the bridge.

A shrill whistle pierced the air, and Marketa turned to see who it was. High above she could see Don Julius waving a white cloth from his window. When she looked up, he stopped waving and pointed directly at her.

She hesitated, not knowing what to do. Should she curtsy, should she incline her head in deference? Perhaps she should wave back to him—or would that be an affront to his royal status, an impertinence?

He let the cloth fall from his grasp, and it fluttered down to the banks of the river, settling on a heap of rubbish from the castle.

Don Julius looked down at her and began to laugh, pointing at the white cloth on the small hill of waste, where food and slops mounded against the castle wall. His cackle echoed across the valley.

Marketa turned her back to him and watched the trout, holding steady against the current. Her heart thumped hard against her chest, so hard she could feel it in her throat.

She heard her father's voice calling her from the Latran side. He walked briskly to where she was standing.

Marketa tried to calm herself, not let him see her flustered. He seemed unnaturally grim. Had he seen the exchange between Don Julius and her?

"I am pleased you are so punctual, Daughter. Let us hurry. There is someone I want you to meet before we go to the palace."

He took her arm, and they hastened back across the bridge. Marketa looked up and saw Don Julius still staring at her, silently.

The Poor Clares convent stood alongside the Franciscan monastery on the banks of the Vltava, only a few hundred paces from the cemetery where Annabella dug for mushrooms.

The heavy wooden door creaked open and the two—father and daughter—entered. The smell of an open hearth and stale air rushed into Marketa's nostrils. The heat of the fire pressed against her skin like an insistent cat. She could barely breathe.

The nun who opened the door seemed to know her father.

"Sir, you will be kind enough to wait outside? I will take your daughter to her."

"Yes, of course."

"Why are we here?" Marketa whispered to her father as the nun took her arm and ushered her into the dark hall.

"You must speak with your aunt," he said, his face dissolving for an instant, then steadying. He composed himself, straightening his back and firming his jaw in determination. "She will give you courage and guidance that I cannot."

The old nun at the door smiled, but her dull brown eyes were studying Marketa as if she were a curiosity, an interesting trinket in a peddler's bag.

"Yes, you have some of the mother superior in your countenance," she murmured. "I can see more than a little resemblance, especially when she was young."

They came to an ancient door, worm-riddled beneath the thick coats of beeswax. The nun knocked and lifted the creaking latch as she pushed a palm against the door.

"Mother, I have brought your visitor."

At a small desk near the lone window of the room sat Marketa's aunt. Marketa had never seen her before—only a drawing that her father kept safe in his room. Marketa had thought of her aunt as dead to her, enclosed forever in the convent.

The nun struggled to her feet. Her wimple framed a sweet, albeit aged, face, the kindness Marketa knew in her father's eyes. They were sadder, though, as if they had known great tragedy.

"My dearest niece!" she said, her voice collapsing into a cry. "Marketa, come to me!"

Marketa was embraced in her arms and drank in her scent—smoke from the fire and incense that infused her clothes. She did not bathe as often as they, but how could she, confined to a convent? Still, her smell was comforting, and Marketa thought of how dogs knew the scent of a family member. Yes, they were flesh and blood, she could sense it.

The mother superior held her niece for a long time until she finally pushed herself away, swallowing tears.

"Sit, please," she said, gesturing to a wooden stool. "We do not have much time. Sister Milana, please wait with my brother and send for Marketa when he indicates it is time."

Despite the fact that it was broad daylight outside, little light entered the room. Ludmilla lit another candle and studied her niece's face as if it were a familiar map she was eager to trace.

"Now, my child. My brother has told me of your trouble. It seems that you have captured the eye of a Hapsburg, be it an illegitimate one."

"Yes, madam. Don Julius has given me unwanted attention."

"Unwanted. I see."

Marketa shifted uncomfortably on the little stool. It was barely wide enough to support her.

"I was only to hold the tray for the bleeding."

"And you spoke to him, I understand. Even though you were told not to utter a word."

Marketa drew a quick breath.

"Yes, but only to encourage treatment. He refused to be leeched. The only way to cure him is to balance his humors."

The nun leaned back a bit in her straight-back chair. Marketa noticed her breathing was irregular and she cleared her throat often.

"The only way, you say—your father has told me of your great interest in medicine."

"Yes, madam."

"And you are quite sure that this—bloodletting—is the cure for the king's son?"

"Yes, quite sure. He is clearly unbalanced—the yellow choler is overflowing."

"And this yellow choler—the symptoms are?"

"Rage. Violence. Cruelty. Unsound mind."

"And lechery? Your Hapsburg is hardly a gentleman."

Marketa felt her back tense.

"He is not my suitor. He is my father's patient. He is—mad. Surely you have heard his wails from the castle above?"

Ludmilla looked around the room, contemplating Marketa's answer.

"Niece, do you have any other gifts?"

Marketa stared back at her in the dim light.

"I do not understand."

"Have you ever had a calling from—another form, another world? Dreams that follow you throughout the day? Voices?"

"I am afraid I do not have your spiritual calling."

Her aunt raised her eyebrows and pressed her lips together tightly.

"Do not be so sure, Marketa. You can sense an imbalance in the humors. Perhaps you can perceive other things ordinary people cannot."

Marketa listened to the faint sound of a girl's voice singing, penetrating the walls. It reminded her of her mother's finch, chirping behind the wooden bars of its cage.

She shook her head.

"I am not so gifted," Marketa muttered. "I am merely my father's assistant."

Ludmilla reached out and held Marketa's chin squarely in the palm of her hand. She studied the girl's eyes, making Marketa look at her own.

"You are very stubborn," she said, finally dropping her hand to her lap. "Your father has told me you have seen the White Lady."

Marketa could see she was watching her reaction.

"He has told you that?"

"My brother and I are very close. Would it surprise you if I were to tell you that I have seen her as well?"

"When? Where?"

"She appeared to me when I was your age. In the same place—above the river in the palace corridor window. She was beckoning to me."

Marketa asked the question her mother had asked her.

"What color gloves was she wearing?"

"Gloves? No, that time she was bare-handed as a maiden. But I speak of this only to open your eyes to your gifts. The woman you saw was the ghost of Perchta of Rozmberk, Bílá paní. She was a kindhearted woman who gave porridge and bread to the poor of Krumlov. Then her father married her off to a wealthy land baron, Jan von Lichtenstein, who severely mistreated her. He beat her when he found that her dowry was not sufficient, and the other women of his family made her work as a maid. She was beaten and abused. When her husband was on his deathbed, he asked her to forgive him for making her life a misery."

"And she did?"

"No," said her aunt, slowly. "She refused. Her husband then cursed her with his dying breath. When she died herself, she was destined to walk Rozmberk Castle."

Ludmilla studied her niece with her clear blue eyes.

"There are many who see her shadow or smell her scent on the air. Very few have the gift to see her. You and I, Marketa, share that gift."

Marketa supposed she should have bowed her head. She should have thanked her for her compliment, for saying they were alike and shared the ability to see spirits from the other world.

She did none of this.

"Why?" Marketa asked, setting her chin rigid in a challenge. Had her mother been there, she would have pinched it, calling her daughter rude and stubborn.

"Why what, my daughter?"

"Why do I have this gift? Why can I see spirits—the White Lady? Why can you?"

Her aunt looked away, at the cross fixed above the door.

"She has come to warn you. And because you have not made a decision, she appeared bare-handed. Once you have made a decision, she will choose the color of her gloves, white for good fortune or black for bad fate."

Marketa sat in silence, pondering her words. She remembered the White Lady's bare hands.

"Come, my child. Think. You have a gift and the blessing of the spirit. Make your decision wisely."

"What decision is that?"

Her aunt's eyes stared at her piercingly. Marketa thought indeed she and her aunt looked much alike, even now, despite the difference in their ages. Rarely seeing the sun, Ludmilla's skin was still fair as hers, and she had Marketa's nose and chin. Marketa wondered if she once had the same brindled hair.

"You can seek sanctuary here. You will develop your spiritual devotion and join the Clares. We have sisters who have the ability to see beyond, and they use their powers to serve God."

Marketa jumped off her stool, shocked by her aunt's earnest invitation, for even thinking she would consent. Had her father planned this? He had—he must have!

Realizing her rudeness, she curtsied and then took her aunt's hand and kissed it.

"Forgive me, dear Aunt. I could never become a Poor Clare!"

Her aunt nodded sadly and sighed. She looked away from her niece and up at the figure of the Virgin Mary at the foot of the cross.

"I can see that. No, the convent would not endure your obstinate nature and impulsiveness. You are too ambitious to marry Jesus in spiritual vows. To worship God, you must be humble. You, despite your simple upbringing, are not humble at all."

Humble. Why *should* she be?

"You, my dear niece, look to something else. Science has taken you as a devotee, regrettably. The worship of God and his son, Jesus Christ, is all-consuming. You cannot follow both paths, I am afraid. You have missed the all-important call of God, of saving your soul and praying for the souls of others."

Marketa stared at her. Her aunt's chin was raised and sharp with conviction, condemning her niece for not following in her footsteps. Marketa was filled with fury. Ludmilla's words were an accusation, a declaration that Marketa was spiritually starved because she was dedicated to science.

Marketa bit back, not caring how she hurt her aunt.

"Aunt Ludmilla, how many people have you helped while locked away in this dark convent for so many years? It is safe to worship and to serve God in the darkness, but in the light, people suffer and we bear witness to that suffering. At least we try to offer more help than posing on our knees, hands clasped and useless."

Ludmilla's face mirrored Marketa's own defiance.

"How dare you speak to me so! I am mother superior of this convent, and we serve God in our simplicity, poverty, and devotion."

"Better not to dirty your hands with the suffering of the outside world where you could truly make a difference."

Marketa stood up, knowing how rude she had been and not caring. As she reached the door, she spun around to ask a last question.

She had to know.

"Did my father ask you to invite me into the convent?"

"Yes. He saw the White Lady, too."

At this, she bit her lip and turned her back on her niece. But Marketa could hear her sobs.

The girl ran down the hall, her feet slapping the old wooden floorboards and sending an echo through the convent.

CHAPTER 17

A Woman Surgeon

The nuns moved aside, a parting of the black sea of habits as Marketa fled the convent. She raced past them, sweeping out the door, breaking into a run. One of the youngest, a novice named Fiala, felt her eyes well up with tears as she watched Marketa emerge into the light of the morning, free of the darkness of the convent, her clothes already airing and losing the heavy scent of incense and old women in the freshness of the morning.

"Will she join us?" she asked no one in particular. "I should like to have a friend like that."

A withered nun sat in the dark corner by the hearth, embroidering a priest's robe.

"Ay!" she cried out, pricking her finger with the needle. "What nonsense you speak, Fiala! Your friends abide in the heavens, angels to God and our Lord himself."

"I should love to have an earthly friend," the girl sighed, her murmured answer inaudible to the old nun.

"Close the door, Fiala. You are letting the warm air out."

"Yes, Sister Agnes," said the novice, a reluctant hand pushing the massive door closed.

Marketa looked back at the convent as the heavy door shut. She spun around, running toward her father, who stood waiting on the bridge.

"Why did you send me to see my aunt?" she demanded. "Why, Father?"

He turned away from her gaze and looked down into the waters of the Vltava.

"I fear for you," he said quietly. "I have seen the power of the Hapsburgs. Even a mad Hapsburg has power. You cannot imagine. The convent would keep you safe and pure."

"Pure? Safe? Is that that all you can wish for me in my life?" she said, her fingers tight in fists at her side. She thought of the brewer, and her eyes stung.

Her father met her eyes, and his shoulders sagged.

"You are but a girl," he began. "A gifted girl, but still a girl. We cannot change that fact. Your knowledge of medicine must remain a secret or you will be regarded as a freak. Or worse, a witch."

The words stung Marketa as if a swarm of bees had smothered her. She stared at him openmouthed. He suddenly looked old and frail to her, though he was still a robust man in his thirties.

"Oh, Marketa, if anything should happen to you, I don't know what I would do," he said.

She noticed his nose was running, and he wiped his eyes with the cracked red skin of his knuckles and then looked down at the river, so she couldn't see his face. She swallowed hard and put a soft hand on his wrist.

"Father! Nothing is going to happen to me. I will learn from Herr Doctor Mingonius and from you. I will stand no closer to Don Julius than you say."

"You do not understand, Marketa! King Rudolf will not allow his son to be fettered for long. It is a blow to his pride. He wants to believe that his son is sane, that he is worthy of the Hapsburg name. A king's pride is a dangerous thing; it consumes like fire all that it touches."

Marketa looked up to the castle, looming above them. She heard the hollow cry of the crow circling above.

"And the moment Don Julius is free, he will come for you."

Marketa swallowed hard. "Then I shall run away, Father. I shall run away to Prague."

Her father shook his head. "No, Daughter. You do not understand the determination of a Hapsburg."

Marketa fidgeted with her apron, twirling the fabric round and round. "No, Father. You do not understand my determination. He shall not have me. No man shall have me without my consent."

Her father did not answer.

"Come, it is getting late," her father finally said. "We must walk up to the castle now."

Don Julius was far calmer this time. When he saw Marketa, his thick lower lip firmed up in a smile, a smile that would have been dazzlingly handsome on a man whose sanity was not so utterly compromised. But Marketa thought of what her father had said, and she kept her distance, giving him only furtive glances so as not to attract his attention.

Besides, thought Marketa, *Don Julius is far too stout, though he is slimmer than when he first arrived in Krumlov. He must be greedy at the dinner table, feasting on butter, cakes, and ale. I could never find such a fat man attractive, especially after the jowly brewer and his fleshy hands, grabbing for me. Men who have such appetites must be stingy in their love, feeding only themselves like the big-bellied men who sweat hunched over their dinners at*

*Uncle's tavern, sucking the meat bones dry of marrow and cast-
ing them into the hearth's fire to crackle and burn. A gentle man
who can give of himself in love must have discipline and satiate his
appetite slowly, savoring the flavors shared with his lover.*

She found herself remembering the lean physique of Jakub
Horcicky and the feel of the soapy water slick on her hands as she
massaged his taut muscles. A man with disciplined tastes, a man
of rational thought. And a generous heart.

It was of no use. Don Julius did not care whether Marketa
fancied him or not. He was obsessed with her, and his obsession
would not be diminished by her lack of interest.

"Fair Marketa," he said as he stretched out his left arm and
leg to the surgeons who applied the leeches. "See how the worms
linger on my flesh, looking for yours instead. How proud and
particular they are to hesitate at a Hapsburg's blood once they
have tasted your own sweet nectar. You have spoiled the creatures, my darling."

Pichler flicked an eye up at his daughter and then back at
the particularly large leech he held. He pricked a hole in Don
Julius's flesh with a lancet to excite the sucking mouth. Marketa
held the white porcelain tray under the incision and watched as
thick drops of blood splashed into the basin.

Finally the leech bit hard at the small wound, and Don Julius
rolled back his eyes in ecstasy.

"We are united at last, fair angel!"

Marketa noticed a bulge in the king's son's breeches, straining at the leather laces. He saw her eyes travel to his erection and
leered at her, the tip of his tongue sweeping around his mouth,
his breathing hoarse and erratic.

This was not the innocent, bewildered boy she had seen at
the end of her last visit. Nor the eloquent gentleman of just the
moment before. She gasped.

Fury sparked in Marketa's father's eyes, and his hand let go of the next leech. It slipped with a splash back into the murky water of the bucket.

"Work more quickly," Mingonius said under his breath, his own hands attaching the leeches to the patient's torso. "Pay no attention to what he says or does. You know his condition."

But Pichler would bear no more.

"Marketa, leave at once!" he ordered.

"No!" shouted Don Julius, wrenching at the ties. "If she leaves, you will pull all these worms from my flesh!"

"Come now, Don Julius," said Doctor Mingonius. "Surely, you can do without the girl's presence. We are half finished as it is."

"No! No!" he roared. He threw his body side to side until the chair tilted and crashed to the ground, splintering the armrest. Don Julius groaned, his cheek already bruising from the fall.

He heaved and struggled against the two burly guards who restrained him. They untied him from the broken chair, brought him across the room, and tied him in an ornately carved chair, its armrests wrought as lion paws.

Mingonius stooped to the patient's ear and whispered to him.

"Calm yourself, man. Let the leeches do their work. They will drink up your rage and purge the ill humors."

Don Julius looked at him, his eyes narrowing in rage.

"You will obey the rules of this sordid game, Mingonius," he hissed. "You agreed to let me see her, for her to hold the pans of my blood. That was the condition, or you may go to the devil!"

Mingonius glared back at the bastard prince, the muscles of his face stiff and cold. He nodded.

"She stays," he said.

"But, Herr Doctor—" protested Pichler.

"Enough!" said Mingonius. "This is a Hapsburg, Herr Pichler! You do not want King Rudolf as an enemy."

Pichler had no answer to that.

"Come here, girl," said Doctor Mingonius.

Marketa approached, her hands trembling on the pan, making the blood creep from one edge to another.

"Do you have the will to stay, Marketa?" Mingonius asked, wiping the sweat from his brow.

She looked at the wild-eyed prince.

"Yes, of course," she said, swallowing hard. "He is our patient." Then she added, "Just do not untie him and I will remain."

Mingonius nodded. He glanced down at the enormous erection of the young prince, the head of his penis peeking crimson over the rim of his laced breeches. He threw a white linen cloth over the sight.

"Control yourself, man," Mingonius said, disgusted. "Have you no shame at all?"

"Pichler," Mingonius said, "I think I can apply the rest of the leeches without assistance. Would you be so good as to wait in the hall?"

Pichler stared at the doctor.

"But—"

"I think I can finish this best if you leave," Mingonius said coolly. "Marketa will remain here to assist me and finish the treatment."

"But, Herr Doctor—"

"Please," he implored. "Trust me. I will let no harm come to your daughter. But I need her and it will be easier for all if you wait outside."

Pichler looked from Mingonius to Marketa and back again. He nodded curtly and left the room.

"So we are almost alone at last," sighed Don Julius. "Your père is gone."

"And her guardian is here, may I remind you, sir," said the doctor.

Julius's lips pressed together in scorn. He snarled.

"Then you must leave as well—and let her apply the worms," he cried. "Let her hands touch those eager mouths that suck at my flesh, seeking her own."

"That is out of the question," said Mingonius.

Once again the chair lurched.

"Guards!" shouted Mingonius.

"Let her! Let her!" cried Don Julius, twisting in the chair and making it rock wildly.

"What is the matter?" cried Pichler from the hall, trying to push past the sentry. "Marketa! Come here at once!"

Marketa looked coolly from her struggling father to Mingonius to Don Julius. She thought of the lonely darkness of the convent, the oppressive incense, and the sad look of the young novice. Her father had wanted her to stay there, to become one of them. He was ready to trade away her life, her hope, in order to keep her from witnessing the raging of an insane man. It was as if his lessons in science and reason meant nothing.

Then she thought of how her virginity would one day be traded to the fat old brewer.

And now, here was the great Doctor Mingonius, known throughout the Holy Roman Empire, who pleaded for her help, who needed her help to treat the king's son.

It was the first time in her life she had a taste of power. She was the one Don Julius wanted. She was the one who could finish the treatment and please the great Mingonius. Her father should be proud of her because she could accomplish what no one else could.

"Leave us," she said, lifting her chin. "Both of you. I will finish the treatment."

"Marketa! You will leave with me this minute!"

"No," she replied calmly. "I shan't. I know exactly where to apply the creatures. Leave me alone with him. The guards shall stand by and protect me. Please, Father." She thought, for an instant, of Jakub Horcicky. Now she would truly be a doctor, like him.

Mingonius studied her, listening as if hearing her for the first time.

"Is it true she knows the system of veins and the points of application?"

"As well as I," replied her father, grudgingly.

"Then let her, Pichler," said Mingonius quietly. "She is right."

"But his behavior, his intentions—"

"I know men's intentions, Father," said Marketa, her voice strong and clear. "I was raised in the baths. I know men's urges, their bodies, their nakedness. Nothing he can say will shock me. And he cannot touch me, no matter how hard he tries. Unlike the bathhouse, I have control now."

Pichler dropped his gaze. It had not occurred to him that his wife's bathhouse had so educated his daughter. He had taught her science, literacy, anatomy. The bathhouse had taught her other subjects he could only guess at.

The thought made him suddenly sad.

"She's right," said Mingonius. "And he must be bled, at all costs! We can wait in the hall. We will hear any screams for help should he frighten her."

"He will not frighten me," Marketa said, looking calmly at both of them. "He is my patient. And if he does not comport himself properly, I shall leave immediately." Looking into Don Julius's eyes. "Is that understood, Your Highness?"

The young Hapsburg nodded acquiescence, eyes round with wonder.

"Leave us, I command you!" he ordered suddenly. He sat up in his chair and straightened his back. "As son of King Rudolf II, I command you to leave at once!"

Marketa turned her back on the two older men, knelt down next to the bucket, and fished out another leech, firm and meaty between her finger and thumb. It wriggled wet and cold in her grasp, its mouth already open to suck.

"Recline your head, Don Julius. I will apply a worm to your forehead to drain the bad humors and make you rest in peace from your anguish. You are my patient, and I will care for you."

"I am yours, good angel. Please never leave me again," said Don Julius, his voice suddenly high and trembling. "The demons retreat at the sound of your voice."

As the two men retreated into the hall, they could hear the contented sighs of King Rudolf II's son.

There were no more screams.

CHAPTER 18

The Coded Book of Wonder

Alone with Don Julius, Marketa continued to apply the leeches. He winced, not at the nip of the leech, but at his awkward position.

"This chair is damned uncomfortable," he complained, grimacing. "I have an ache in my back that consumes me. A deep pain has dug into my shoulder blades. But those men—they do not care about my torment!"

Marketa moved quietly behind him, slipped her hand between his shoulders, and eased him as far forward as the ropes would allow. She dug her strong fingers into his aching muscles, loosening them with her experienced touch.

"Oh, oh!" Don Julius groaned. "What healing hands you have, fräulein!"

Marketa said nothing, but continued softening the knots on his back, her brisk movements warming his muscles and encouraging blood to return into his stiff body. Under her fingers she could feel his vertebrae and ribs, and she realized that he was growing leaner more swiftly than she thought.

"*Mein Gott!*" he sighed. "How you give me comfort!"

"We must have the carpenter build you a proper chair for bleedings," murmured Marketa as she rubbed, melting the pain. "One that reclines so you may lie comfortably on soft cushions. Your spine needs to be supported. And an armrest that splays wide." Marketa's mind conjured up the details of the chair as she continued to massage Don Julius. "An elevated leg rest, so you can recline and we can reach your inner thighs. And slats to allow my hands to touch your spine, unimpeded."

Don Julius swallowed hard and purred to her, "Think how much easier it would be to administer the leeches were I untied and lying in my own bed, with you beside me."

Marketa stopped the back rub and dropped her hands to her side. "I will speak to Doctor Mingonius today about commissioning the carpenter to construct the chair."

"So that your hands can more easily reach my groin," whispered Don Julius. "How could I not beg for such a chair!"

Marketa felt the gaze of the smirking guards. She reminded herself she was practicing medicine. She cleared her throat and lifted her chin.

"You will not speak to me in that fashion or I shall leave. You must understand that. Now, with your permission, my lord, we shall continue treatment."

"By all means, Fräulein Doctor," murmured her patient, drowsily. His flesh had melted under her hands, and he still felt the flush of heat in his back.

Marketa moved around to face him. Her hands dipped into the bucket, and she retrieved a torpid leech. She warmed it in her hands, letting it smell the blood that lay close to the fine skin of her fingers.

"Pray tell, Don Julius," she said, to keep his mind engaged as she rolled the mouth of a leech to the thin skin of his ankle. "What is the Coded Book of which you and Doctor Mingonius speak?"

Don Julius leaned back, savoring her touch as she held the leech to the prominent vein above the sole of his foot. It bit and he flinched, smiling slowly.

"You pretend you do not know the book, and yet you are one of its principal players! As you are in the bathhouse below."

Marketa's skin prickled. She did not like that Don Julius knew anything about her life, but the bathhouse was in plain view from his window. Clients arrived rumpled and dirty and emerged wet and clean.

"What does my mother's bathhouse have to do with an enchanted book?" she demanded.

"Ah," said Don Julius. "When you stepped from its pages, you must have lost your memory, your mind is befuddled. You have always been a bathmaid, and a most seductive one. You are the one of slim hips with a cherub hiding behind you, peeking around your waist."

Marketa pressed her lips together tight in frustration. "I have a perfectly good memory, and I have never seen or heard of any such Coded Book, nor of bathing angels and cherubs. This is a delusion, a product of the humors that swirl unbalanced in your head."

Don Julius sighed, a sad look overtaking his face. "Pity to forget your origins. Still, you must hold the secrets, if only we could persuade you to remember."

This conversation is not going well, thought Marketa as she moved a leech to another point on his leg. *He does not follow reason; he lives in his own fantastical world.* She took a deep breath. She needed to know more.

It was she who would play mad now.

"Perhaps you are right—I have forgotten my origins," she said. "But if I were to see the pages, I might remember."

Don Julius straightened and looked down at her.

"You are so clever! Yes, I will procure the book and share it with you! You will help me decode it, once you see your world again in its pages. And then my father the king will find favor in me once more and we will return to Prague together to be married!"

Marketa fished another leech from the bucket. The king indulged his eldest son generously, even if he was mad as a rabid dog. His fine clothes, his stable of horses, a dozen servants. His own castle and estate. What would he give his son were he to behave as a normal man? The stars in the heavens above, all manner of riches. But marry a common bathmaid? The thought was, itself, a symptom of his madness.

Marketa knew better than to argue with a madman.

She realized that his behavior at this point was beyond his control, but perhaps if he had some objective clearly focused in his mind, his behavior could change. After all, they were wringing the bad humors from his blood, drop by drop.

"I want you to pretend that I have never seen or lived in the book," she said. "Imagine you were speaking to a stranger and explain the contents of the magical book in all of its splendor."

"Ah!" he said. "A game? But you will laugh at me, because I cannot know its depths—it is undecipherable to man."

"Ah, but that is what I want—to know what a mortal perceives. While the leeches purge your humors, tell me your story."

Don Julius looked down at the leeches at his legs and ankles, and then back to Marketa's face.

"It is the work of a magician, a sorcerer, a hermetic," he began, closing his eyes. "The symbols speak of the marriage of the moon and sun, the polar opposites, as in the Kabbalah or the Hermetic Principles of Egypt. The first section deals with all sorts of plants, flowers, and herbs used for medicines. A catalog collected by witches and sorcerers. Recipes conveyed from an ancient's toothless mouth to the tender ear of the next generation through the ages.

"The next quires are dedicated to the zodiac and the stars, a study of the heavens. You and your sisters mark the twelve signs of the zodiac—bathmaids crowded into the circle, your breasts and nipples erect above the barrel's rim. All are pregnant, except you. You appear slim-hipped, by far the most beautiful and the most seductive. You are the only virgin."

Marketa blushed but was too fascinated for the color to remain in her cheeks for long. What was the point of being modest in front of a madman?

"It is you who hold the deepest secrets," he went on. "You protected me." He fell silent for a long moment, then spoke in a smaller voice. "You kept away the evil voices. You saved me from them. And then..." His voice tapered off, halting, uncertain, as if it came from far away.

And then, silence. Don Julius slumped in his chair in a swoon, tears running down his cheeks, as the bleeding finally took its toll.

CHAPTER 19

A CHANCE FOR PEACE

In the hunting lodge near Katterburg, Austria, torches flickered in the darkness. Here, amid the dense foliage of pine and beech, not far from the front lines of the war against the Ottomans, lay the sanctuary of Matthias, archduke of Upper and Lower Austria.

Matthias's father, Emperor Maximillian II, had inherited a hunting lodge on this spot, but it had burned to the ground. One day when Matthias was hunting, he had seen the charred remains of the lodge and, near it, the clear waters of a spring. The bubbling fount pooled against the green grass and rocks, shaded by a canopy of great beech trees.

The waters sparkled innocent and pure. Matthias tied his horse to a nearby tree, removed his riding boots, and dangled his bare feet in the cool waters.

He called it Schönbrunn—beautiful spring.

And though the Katterburg property lay within the domain of Rudolf's empire, it was Matthias who fell in love with the spot and swore to restore it.

Being one of sixteen children, Matthias did not have a close relationship with his father, and really only knew him by gazing at the oil portraits of the emperor in Hofburg Palace. Emperor Maximillian had brought peace to the kingdoms of Moravia, Austria, Bohemia, and Hungary. Though he had no time for his many children, he had found time to cultivate tulips in his beloved *hrad* gardens in the city of Prague.

How Matthias longed to behold a tulip now, a sign of peace and tranquility. Only with respite from war could one occupy oneself with planting bulbs and pruning fruit trees.

Matthias spat on the ground, thinking of the lush beauty of his brother Rudolf's *hrad* gardens, cultivated by a royal physician no less. What was his name—Horcicky? A physician should leave the pruning shears to a gardener and instead administer to the ranks of the dying soldiers littering the countryside of Hungary. But Rudolf kept the doctor tending orchids in Prague.

How could his brother dare breathe such sweet perfumes as lilacs and jasmine when the borders of his own kingdom burned!

Their father had brought peace during his reign. He had turned a deaf ear to the pope and had given Protestants equal rights, stifling the beginnings of the Reformation. Maximillian had paid tribute to the Ottomans to purchase peace in Hungary. He ruled a far-flung empire without the fires of war.

Matthias felt a connection to his father in Schönbrunn that did not exist during the emperor's lifetime. The peace and tranquility of the Austrian countryside gave him strength and clear vision after the stench and smoke of war. He longed to find a way to bring peace to the Holy Roman Empire, just as his father had once done.

On that first day by the spring, Matthias had stared down at the clear waters, untainted by battle, greed, and power. Upon his return to Linz, he had commanded that the lodge be rebuilt, so he could enjoy his solitude in the green hills of Austria.

Matthias had grown weary of war. As a young man of twenty, he had joined forces with the Protestants against his own uncle, Felipe II of Spain, in the battle for control of the Netherlands. It was a reckless adventure that enraged the entire Hapsburg family, but it branded him as the Soldier King, distinguishing him indelibly from his hermit-like brother Rudolf.

But his tranquil moment of discovery by the spring and his youthful daring in the Netherlands were long behind him. Now his eyes were rimmed bright red, burning and raw from the constant smoke of the battles against the Ottomans along the Hungarian border and the scorched scent of fires perfumed his woolen clothes. He woke at night, gasping for breath, from a recurring dream of long tongues of flames licking his beloved Schönbrunn.

On these nights, it seemed to him his entire life was defined by war and nothing else. He was weary of death and dying, of bloated bodies, and most of all, endless battles under religious flags, flapping pointlessly in the wind. So when the messenger rode up to the lodge at a full gallop, Matthias had the rider sent to him immediately.

Matthias was eager to see the proposal for peace.

It was on a sleepless night that the seed of compromise was planted. Matthias's stewardship of Hungary would forever be defined by the Peace of Vienna.

Matthias held the tallow candle low and closer to the parchment map, being careful to catch the dripping wax with a small pewter plate in his other hand. Outside a peahen screeched in the night, her ugly cry stabbing the silence.

The flickering candlelight illuminated a new map of Hungary, drawn by Istvan Bocskai of Transylvania, with the blessing of the Ottomans. This was their proposal to settle the

Hungarian-Ottoman War. To the north and west was Royal Hungary, a possession of the Holy Roman Empire. The map-maker had slyly chosen a cardinal red to denote its imprint. To the extreme east was Transylvania, bulging to the Black Sea, in a moss green.

And the middle section, dun-colored, was the Ottoman Empire, including the great city of Buda.

Matthias frowned at the map. The bright color of Royal Hungary could not camouflage the fact that Ottoman Hungary was an oppressive bootprint, larger by half than the Hapsburg share. And—this could not be!—Transylvania's proposed principality dwarfed Hapsburg Hungary.

The traitor Istvan Bocskai had been granted the vast principality as a reward from the Ottomans for fighting in their legions. Matthias had heard just that day of Bocskai's gold, jewel-encrusted crown, a gift from Sultan Ahmed himself. Because Ottoman sultans did not wear crowns, it was modeled on the miter of an Orthodox patriarch, heavy and clumsy, but cast in pure gold, adorned in rubies, turquoise, emeralds, and pearls.

Istvan Bocskai. The filthy swine. A renegade Calvinist who had once fought for the Hapsburg crown, Bocskai had sided now with heathens. King of Transylvania, be damned!

A knock on the door was followed immediately by a draft of air from the cold hall, making the candlelight flicker.

"You are up late tonight, Matthias," said Bishop Klesl. "Was it that damned peahen or do you require any spiritual counsel?"

Matthias tapped his finger on the parchment.

"I am reviewing the map. Bocskai's kingdom will be larger than ours," he muttered. "Rudolf's suppression of the Protestants has provoked a war we can never win."

Klesl sighed. "There once was a time when I thought as Rudolf did. Rid the Hungarians of the scourge of Protestantism and return the country to the traditions of its founder Saint Stephen."

"I remember. You called the Protestants wriggling maggots on rotted meat."

The bishop stared at the map. His eyes were sunken into his head from lack of sleep and his jowly skin was ashen. He too was weary of war.

"Even bishops can be fools. I underestimated the Protestants and their zeal for their religion. Men who thirst for freedom will find it, even if they drink at a poisoned well. I have searched my soul, looking for answers."

"And what have you found, Bishop Klesl?"

"Only a recurring question: How can the Protestant Christians be allied with barbaric Saracens? These are our brothers in Christ we fight."

The bishop crossed himself, his pale hands white ghosts in the candlelight.

Matthias nodded and then gazed down at the map and the proposed division of the Hungarian kingdom.

"Pride," he muttered. "My brother's pride. Rudolf now curries favor with the pope and the House of Hapsburg, boasting he will transform every Protestant church to a Catholic house of worship. He who worships the occult and drains the treasury in search of the Elixir of Life."

Melchior Klesl sighed.

"His Majesty has a better chance of filling those Catholic pews with Muslim warriors than staunch Protestants. They will never give up their religion now."

The peahen screeched again. Matthias's back stiffened. He thought he smelled smoke, but decided it was the scent he carried from the front lines.

"I shall wring that peahen's neck in the morning and make soup of her, with your permission, sire," said Klesl, shuddering.

"My brother has turned every Hungarian against the crown! Ninety-five in every hundred are Protestant. We cannot wage war both on the Ottoman borders and within the country itself! What madness plagues him?"

Klesl did not reply.

"What counsel can you offer me? Not of spiritual nature, but of an astute politician."

"Politician, my lord?" Bishop Klesl raised an eyebrow.

"Every clergyman who holds a title, be it bishop, cardinal, or pope, is a politician."

Klesl nodded in the dim light. He grimaced, then squared his shoulders and answered.

"I think you have no choice, sire. You should secure your bargaining terms from our king as soon as possible and negotiate peace. Force him to accept terms if need be, or he will be at war with his own Hungarian subjects."

"He will roar and bellow at relinquishing land and tribute. And he has promised Catholics they will acquire the estates of the Protestants. Their greedy mouths water at the prospect."

"Our king is blind to what transpires beyond the walls of Prague. The Ottomans will burn the land and take it as their spoil, moving closer to Vienna. A compromise, a treaty must be made before the Ottomans swallow us whole."

Matthias rubbed his hand through his sleep-rumpled hair. The Soldier Hapsburg was faced with concession and the wrath of his powerful brother.

"I hear wisdom in your words, but I am loathe to approach my brother with words of compromise and defeat."

Klesl touched Matthias's sleeve.

"Pray listen to my counsel, my lord. Send your emissaries to meet with Bocskai in Bratislava. Give Hungary its religious freedom, or they will be at war against the empire and fill the

Ottoman ranks alongside the Janissaries. Nothing will stop them from marching to Vienna."

Matthias listened carefully, his brow wrinkled in consternation.

"Place Protestant on equal footing with Catholic?" he asked. "My brother will never consent. It will make him look weak in the eyes of the pope."

"The pope could think no less of him than he already does. And even the pope recognizes the danger of the Ottomans and their stranglehold on Europe. And our blessed pope does not live cheek by jowl with the Saracens and their scimitars."

"And Bocskai emerges from our disgrace with the principality of Transylvania?"

"It is a wild and perilous land. I doubt Bocskai will make it through a year without being murdered. Give him Transylvania— it is overrun with Roma and other heathens. There are cutthroats at every bend of the road and witches who brew poisons to kill kings. The wretched Bathorys will seize the crown yet again, mark my words."

Matthias looked hard at Klesl and retrieved a key from his belt. He unlocked his desk and withdrew a parchment. The broken wax seal made a click as he threw it on the mahogany wood.

"Read, my good priest. See how God has seen fit to bless me."

Klesl bowed at the honor of seeing Matthias's private correspondence, sealed with a Hapsburg ring.

"What is this?"

"A secret letter drafted by my younger brothers. They have asked to meet with me in Linz. Ferdinand and Maximillian see the inevitable ruin of the Hapsburg Empire if our brother is not stopped."

Klesl jumped to his feet.

"My lord, is it—Are they supporting your succession to the throne?"

Matthias closed his eyes. "Yes," he said. "Yes, good Klesl. They pledge their support. They are convinced that the other royal families will do the same. My brother's incompetence stains the Hapsburg name across Europe."

"Oh, blessings upon you and our kingdoms! You, King Matthias, shall save the empire from the torn vein of bloodshed."

"It is your counsel I shall count on, now and in the future as emperor. Damn it, I will speak to Bocskai and begin preliminary negotiations in secret, though we must push our military advantage now to strengthen our hand. The borderlands near Esztergom are still in peril.

"I will restore the equilibrium of freedom—neither Catholic nor Protestant shall prevail. Hungarians will return to their Christian home without threat of persecution. We shall stand united against the Ottomans, I swear it before God!"

The candle in his hand guttered and died under his fierce breath, leaving the smell of smoke in the sudden darkness.

CHAPTER 20

MARKETA'S CHARM VS. THE CODED BOOK

Doctor Mingonius quietly shut the heavy door. Don Julius was sleeping soundly.

The doctor sighed. It echoed through the empty halls of the castle. He shivered at the cold air that whispered back his regret.

He realized he had come to think of Rudolf's son as a "problem," not a man of flesh, bone, and spirit. This girl, a simple Bohemian bathmaid, had reduced Don Julius to hot tears. Even though his behavior was erratic and could be dismissed as a symptom of his lunacy and the imbalance of humors, there was something in his tears that moved Mingonius's heart.

Certainly there was a man's soul somewhere deep within the mad bastard, whose vile behavior had humiliated the most powerful sovereign of Europe. Could it be possible that the violent cruelty of Don Julius would be pierced and vanquished by love? He thought again, for a moment, of that young boy, the clocks that had fascinated him and the book he had treasured. Where had that boy gone?

As the physician stood in the palace corridor, he smelled the ancient wood, polished with coat upon coat of beeswax. He looked up at the gallery of Rozmberk portraits, powerful men and women who had inhabited this castle for centuries.

Doctor Mingonius contemplated their fine clothes and icy stares. Their glittering jewels and privileged scowls were preserved forever in the paintings. These Bohemian lords were the equal of kings within their own lands and their courts had numbered in the hundreds. Now the castle was devoid of merriment. Gone were the boisterous courtiers that had packed the halls and ballrooms. Only his solitary footsteps echoed in the hall.

He stopped in front of a haunting portrait, a pale blonde noblewoman, her hair in ringlets, in a white dress, with a long train that swept around her ankles. Who was she, he wondered, for she had a peculiar quality about her face that made him stop and study her alone among the dozens of portraits.

His finger rubbed his lip, and he again thought of his patient. Perhaps this was the time to bring him the Coded Book to study. Perhaps that was a path that could lead back to that young boy, lost within the madman. And perhaps now was the time, now that Don Julius's spirit was softened by imagined love for a simple bathmaid.

Mingonius smiled. Barber Pichler had passed her off as a virgin to collect leeches. A bathmaid a virgin, at age sixteen—highly unlikely. The doctor knew full well how bathhouses operated and how destitute the townspeople of Krumlov were now that the Rozmberks had left the castle. They would do anything to scrape by and survive, including bartering the virginity of a maiden. Poor peasants could not afford moral scruples.

And yet, there was an honorable tradition about the women of the Bohemian baths. It was said that King Wenceslas himself, the father of Czech Christianity, would visit the bathhouse of Prague for trysts with a beautiful bathmaid, Suzanna, his most beloved mistress. Some said that he took her as a lawful bride. Bathmaids were illustrated in the holy Wenceslas Bible, as the Bohemian king sought to raise their social status. Bohemian bathhouses were infused with a special significance that even the Catholic Church could not touch, let alone the Protestant Reformation.

And there was something special about this girl, Marketa. There was some mysterious quality she possessed that had touched Don Julius when nothing else could. And maybe he could take advantage of the prince's obsession with Marketa, so jumbled up with the Coded Book and bathing women.

He would present the book as a reward and gain sway over his patient. Once Don Julius had engrossed himself in decipher-ing the text, he would have no interest in the fantasy of Marketa. His mind would be engaged in a more rational discipline. As he compiled his endless tables of syntax and semantics to decode the manuscript, science and rational thought would triumph!

It was at this moment that Doctor Mingonius realized he was jealous of Marketa, how she alone could command respect from Don Julius. But should the Coded Book replace her, then the doc-tor would regain his stature as the man who could cure the Royal Bastard of Prague.

One passion could easily replace another. If he presented the manuscript now, Don Julius would latch onto the book as a leech would a vein—and forget the bathmaid. Then the doctor would be in command, before the king's ministers came to inspect and report back to Rudolf II.

Mingonius jumped. Out of the corner of his eye, he was sure he had seen the portrait of the lady in white move her hand. He reached an open palm for his racing heart, wild-eyed and gasp-ing. He struggled to compose himself, taking deep breaths as his eyes fixed on the white hand of the woman in the portrait.

He was a rational man, and the steady, logical part of his mind focused defiantly on the painting, daring the woman to move again.

And of course she remained motionless, a figure in paint, forever pigment and shadow on canvas.

What is happening to me? thought Doctor Mingonius. *I have always been a man of science. And yet here I am, like a flighty woman, imagining a painting has the ability to move! Pfah!*

Still, to reassure himself and prove his scientific mind, he touched the raised oil paint with his fingers, tracing the swirls and shadowing of the woman's white dress.

Fool! he thought, shaking his head. *The sooner I give Don Julius the book and capture his attention, the sooner I will be in control. Then I can finish the bleedings and return to my family in Prague and the sciences of the court. The wilds of Bohemia are starting to wear on my nerves.*

The physician walked swiftly down the hall toward his apartments to retrieve the book from the chest. He felt a prickle of the skin on his neck but refused to turn around to see if anyone was following him.

CHAPTER 21

THE ROYAL GARDENS OF PRAGUE

Late fall was always a sad time for Jakub Horcicky. The beauty of the royal gardens, the florid tangle of exotic blooms, faded and slowly died as the sun dimmed and the ground cooled with the first hard frosts of the season.

Jakub instructed his gardeners to cover the tulip bulbs with an extra layer of soil and horse manure, to protect the precious flowers from the harsh Bohemian cold. He had personally purchased these bulbs to augment the original strain dating from 1554. He had bought them from a Turkish trader from Constantinople, just as he had negotiated with a Syrian merchant to bring hyacinths and narcissi from the Middle East.

Jakub pruned back the grape vines and fruit trees himself, not trusting any other hands to touch the gnarled branches that had sprung miraculously from the northern soil, nurtured from seedlings and grafts with the tender love of Ferdinand I, King Rudolf's grandfather.

Jakub sighed, leaning on his garden spade. Everything around him seemed to be dying. Or slumbering, he thought, checking his morbid thinking. It is time to rest, to nourish and prepare for spring, so many months away.

Redemption, he thought. Spring came no matter how dark and cruel the winter might be.

Jakub found himself thinking of the snowy winters in the monastery and the beauty of the little town of Krumlov under a white blanket of snow. He wondered how another beauty of Krumlov, the bathmaid Marketa, was faring with her study of Paracelsus. Her determination brought a smile to his face, though he knew how impossible her dream was.

Marketa had enchanted Jakub, he realized. As a botanist—director of the fantastic gardens of the emperor—whenever he encountered a new species of plant, he made a point of drawing it in his journal. He would carefully sketch the root system, the leaves, fruit, flowers, stems, seeds, the drooping tendrils. When he had seen Marketa that first morning in the bathhouse, he had the same urge—to draw her with her wild hair and luminous blue-gray eyes.

He remembered Marketa's remarkable hands, so strong and capable on his back, coaxing the soreness from his body. And he thought how she had frozen before him, unable to wash between his legs as bathmaids were expected to do.

What a strange little bathmaid she was. How oddly innocent. He removed the latest letter from the pocket of his gardening coat and read it again.

My Dear Doctor Horcicky:

I read your letter with great interest, especially delighting in the news of Jan Jesenius's public dissection. Ah, but Prague must be the jewel of the world. You are so privileged to live in such a city where science and reason reign.

The patient continues to change before our eyes. He has lost so much weight you would not recognize him. His body is fit from the hunt, and his eyes sparkle with health.

He speaks of love. I seem to be the object of his affection, as he continues to confuse me with a figure in a book he knew in his childhood. It may indeed be the Coded Book of Wonder, which you spoke of in your last letter.

Doctor Horcicky, you must not concern yourself with my welfare. I am perfectly capable of taking care of myself. You must not consider betraying our confidence and approaching Doctor Mingonius.

While I find some of the patient's behavior despicable, I remind myself it is a product of the humors that poison his veins. He is not capable of reason, and for that I feel a certain sadness. He is adrift in his madness, a soul lost in the horror of his mind. Sometimes I see glimpses of a forlorn, lonely boy, begging for affection.

He is a human being, is he not, and thus worthy of our sympathy?

I hope this letter finds you well and serving our king in good faith.

Marketa Pichlerova

Jakub shivered as a cold wind from the north blew and rattled stiff branches of the apple tree above him. A shriveled apple fell to the ground, rolling and coming to rest near his feet.

How could Mingonius let her near Don Julius! Love? And what is love, in a madman's eyes?

Surely this love could not be reciprocated!

Jakub remembered taking the girl's trembling hands, slippery in soap, into his own. She had been so shy about touching him. What rudeness would she encounter now with Don Julius? The king's son kept company with prostitutes and thieves; there was no tenderness about him. What was this talk of a lost, for-lorn boy?

About twenty paces from the fruit orchard was the fig-tree house, a stone building with a removable roof. The team of gardeners and workmen had replaced the roof for the approaching winter and were working on patching holes with slate tiles. They, too, looked up and faced the cold north wind, blowing from Poland.

Jakub entered the fig-tree house and drank in the rich scent of orange blossom. The humid breath of the tropical trees and plants enveloped his senses, their heady scent making him dizzy.

Here, among exotic botanical gifts and acquisitions from around the world, Jakub felt at peace. He liked to think of his accomplishments, how far he had come in his life. As a boy, he slept with a coarse blanket on the refectory floor and was fed scraps from the monks' meager meals. He was not allowed to mingle with the townspeople, so, at age six, he might as well have been a monk himself.

And then he had met young Annabella, wandering the hills above Krumlov, searching for mushrooms. The two children became lifelong friends, their solitary natures and love of botany nourishing one another. The two never acknowledged each other in town, but they met in secret places in the forests to compare knowledge gleaned from nature and books.

Jakub was startled from his reverie by the petulant roars of Mohammed, the king's pet lion, who begged to enter the warmth of the fig-tree house, clawing deep marks on the wooden door.

Ah, Mohammed, thought Jakub. *Indulged by the king even more than his favorite mistress. How the king would suffer were he ever to lose you.*

Never content to remain idle, Jakub's fingers plucked the dead leaves from a mulberry tree, a gift from an Asian sultan.

How could a son of Rudolf II profess love for a simple country bathmaid? Impossible!

An ache stabbed his chest as he thought of Marketa's blue-smoke eyes close to his face as she bathed him. How she had drawn back like a startled bird when he had smiled back at her. How she had stepped closer when his lips brushed hers.

Nonsense! Don Julius's attention would fly away from her, for his thoughts were as errant as mountain winds. The bastard son did not know love. He knew nothing of tenderness.

Jakub's gaze fell on the blossoming of a forced tulip in the greenhouse. He felt a stab of pain in his heart as he looked at the shiny, tender petals, red as blood.

He thought of the Dutch ambassador who first gazed upon a tulip here in the court of Rudolf II, more than a decade before. His eyes had shone with tears at the beauty of the blood-red flowers.

WINTER 1606-1607

CHAPTER 22

The Insult

Katarina held the mill door open for Marketa, ushering her in from the blustery wind that stung her eyes and played an eerie tune through the paddles of the waterwheel. The enormous millstone groaned and creaked on its scaffolding in the center of the room.

Katarina's mother, Eliska, and little brother, Jiri, stooped before the open fire and the huge iron cauldron suspended over the flames. They were mulling wine, boiled with honey, for Jiri to take to the castle when he returned to work later that evening. It brought in a few thalers each month for the family, whose fortunes—like those of all Krumlov—had suffered since the departure of the Rozmberks.

Each night the miller's wife sent a cask of the wine to be peddled to the guards and servants at the castle. Pan Chaloupka, the head guard, rationed the sale of the sweet spiced wine, just enough to fortify his men to brave the watch between midnight and dawn, silent hours when the men's only company was the hard gleam of the stars in winter's heartless sky.

"Come, join us," said the plump Eliska, ladling mulled wine into a clay cup for Marketa. "Sit by the fire and tell us stories of the Hapsburg prince."

Marketa kissed her cheek and sat next to her on the rough-hewn bench.

"Ack! You are chilled to the bone," Eliska said, pressing the warm cup into Marketa's hands. "Your cheeks are like the frozen dead!"

"What is Don Julius like?" asked Katarina. "Tell us!"

"Why not ask your brother?" Marketa replied, holding the cup to her cold lips and taking a sip. She was grateful for the warmth of the mug that drew blood back into her fingers. "Jiri works at the castle every day. My father is only summoned a few times a week to bleed the prince."

"Ah, but Jiri hasn't the stories you have, Marketa," said Eliska. "He only fetches food and drink, logs for the fire, and runs errands for the doctor. He never even sees Don Julius. You know that."

Jiri nodded his head solemnly. "I cannot enter the rooms, nor can any of us. They will not allow me even a glimpse of him. The maids clean his room and change his linen only when he is on the hunt chasing stag and boar, so none of us sees the king's son."

Marketa looked at the fire and felt three pairs of eyes staring at her. What could she tell them? They knew Don Julius was mad, but they did not know, they could not imagine that he had declared her an angel out of some strange book. She dared not tell them that Don Julius refused to let the king's physician lay the leeches on his body, that the task had fallen to her. Were she to tell Eliska, the news would spread through Krumlov like grease on a hot griddle.

"He is strange," was all she could say.

"Does he speak to you?" pressed Katarina.

"Sometimes. Yes, he addresses me, though I cannot understand what he means. Ravings." She was unwilling to tell them more.

"Well, Marketa, you are blessed to lay eyes on a Hapsburg and to be allowed to see and handle royal blood. Where do you pour your trays?" asked Eliska, as she moved to refill her guest's empty cup.

"Doctor Mingonius disposes of it himself. We leave the trays, and it is said that there is a special oak tree on the north side of the castle that receives the blood to its roots, after it has been blessed by the Spanish priest."

Eliska nodded her head, knowing that the priest's holy incantations would keep witches or sorcerers from using the blood in spells. And with that blessing, beasts that licked the ground could not carry away the spirit of the young Hapsburg.

"I wish I could stay and hear more," she said regretfully, "but I must go to the market to buy food. They say that a merchant from Budejovice has brought an oxcart full of cabbages and salt to be sold today. The cabbages have been stored in a cold room under sawdust. The cartwright's wife has seen them herself. She says the weevils and worms have hardly made a mark on them."

She pulled her cloak off a peg and wrapped the woolen garment tight around her head and shoulders. "Come, Jiri—bring the wheelbarrow and we will buy what we can. Load up two buckets of the wine and a serving cup. We will fetch a good price with this batch—it is worth a few cabbages and salt to a merchant standing in the frozen muck of Siroka Street, especially when the wind blows from the north."

When her mother and brother had departed, Katarina took her friend's hands and pleaded.

"Now tell me more about Don Julius. Is he bound in soft ropes made of silk as they say? Does he fear the leeches and twist when your father brings them near? We have heard his curses on bleeding days."

Marketa hesitated and drained her cup. "Can you keep a secret, Katarina? You must swear—"

"I swear, I swear, by all that is holy, only tell me!"

Marketa licked the last drops of honeyed wine from her lips.

"It is I who treats Don Julius. He will not let Doctor Mingonius, let alone my father, near to him."

Katarina gasped. "You—a woman! You treat a Hapsburg!"

"You have sworn to me—"

"No, no, by my honor I shall not whisper a word. But—but how is it that you can touch Don Julius and His Majesty's physician cannot?"

"Don Julius must agree to undergo the treatment, as ordered by the king. And he will not let Doctor Mingonius near him. Hate burns in his eyes. It is only with me that he…finds peace."

Katarina's eyes were as round as Shrovetide pancakes. She stuck her fingers in her mouth as she always did when she was perplexed or astonished.

"Does he—does he find you attractive?" she asked at last.

Marketa scowled at her.

"What does it matter? Katarina, I have my own *patient*! Don't you see! My father was wrong. Not only do I have a patient who responds to me and me only, but he is a Hapsburg!"

Katarina nodded warily.

"But he is not right in his head," she said. "And would not the king himself object were he to find out that a woman is treating his son?"

"No one will ever know. What the doctor says is that King Rudolf is overjoyed with the progress in his son's health. He would not care whether it was Satan himself who cured him as long as his sanity returns and the Hapsburg name is unblemished."

Katarina moved a step away from her best friend, closer to the fire. She said nothing for a moment. Marketa could tell that she was deep in thought and digesting the story. But when the silence began to drag on, Marketa touched Katarina's shoulder.

"It is all right, Katarina. He is my patient, no more. No harm will come of it."

Katarina turned to face her friend.

"What does it feel like to treat royalty, Marketa, to see a prince lashed to a chair? Do you ever wonder what it would be like to…"

"To what?"

"To make love to him," she said, turning her head away to the fire so Marketa could not see her blush.

She was thinking of her own love, the blacksmith's son Damek, whom she was forbidden to see.

"Don't be foolish, Katarina! Don Julius is a Hapsburg and is besieged by malicious humors."

"He is still a man, Marketa—and you a woman. You are in control, are you not? Sometimes I like to think of my blacksmith lashed to a chair, with only the two of us in the room. My father would have no say in the matter—"

"Your father will never let you see Damek; you know he won't." Marketa had to turn the talk away from Don Julius, even if it meant hurting Katarina. "Why torment yourself with such silly ideas? Forget him—he is just a lovesick pup with a sooty face."

Katarina swallowed hard, her hand flying to her breast as if she had been wounded. She turned to Marketa in fury. "Can I not dream the same as you, Marketa? What is so impossible about a miller's daughter marrying a blacksmith? Who would think a bathmaid named Musle would lay healing hands on a Hapsburg?"

Her words were a hard slap across Marketa's face. She tasted the tangy bite of bile in the back of her mouth. Katarina had never before uttered the name Musle in her presence.

"Forgive me, Marketa!" Katarina said, desperate to take the word back almost in the same instant she said it, her hand trying to clasp her friend's, seeking a pardon for the insult.

Marketa snatched her hand away from Katarina and pulled her woolen cloak tight against the wind as she opened the oaken door and left, slamming it closed behind her.

CHAPTER 23

A Hapsburg's Addiction

Marketa's mother made sure her daughter had an extra portion of pork that night. Dipping the wooden ladle deep into the pot, she drowned the meat and dumplings in thick brown gravy. It was a gesture of such forced exuberance that Marketa knew it was penitence for her mother's blunt insistence that she court the favor of the Hapsburg prince at all costs. Lucie realized she had pushed too hard—and Marketa knew her mother would try another tack, once she thought she had been forgiven.

Lucie always apologized—and persuaded—with food. She believed anyone who disagreed with her would be more easily convinced to come around to her way of thinking on a full stomach.

"Eat, Marketa. It will not do for Don Julius to see you so pale. The pig's meat will return the color to your cheeks. Is that not right, Husband?" she said, waiting for his approval.

Pichler said nothing, but continued chewing his dumpling, washing it down with beer.

Marketa bit her lower lip but nodded, yes, please, she would like some more meat. She was voraciously hungry. Still her mother's reference to her cheeks irritated her.

"Don Julius does not care if my cheeks are red or pale as snow," she said. "He is a madman, and his visions of beauty are colored by the bad humors in his blood. He could just as gladly make love to the meat of this pig as me."

Lucie froze, her hands suspended in air. Her face turned red, as if she were over a steaming barrel in the bathhouse.

"The prince finds you attractive," she said, her voice sharp. She shifted on the bench, making it groan under her weight. "What talk is this, love of pigs? And who are you to question a Hapsburg, *slecna*?"

The Czech word for "miss" was intended as an arrow to Marketa's heart. Her mother was afraid that with her daughter's strange obsession with medicine, she would never find a husband.

Marketa did not answer. Better to let her mother indulge herself in the illusion of a daughter who had charmed royalty. It was to her advantage to have her mother happy with the time spent in Don Julius's company; it could only help further her plans to study medicine in Prague.

"The pork is delicious and will surely make my cheeks as red as apples," Marketa said, keeping her voice sweet. "I can feel the blood rising to my face this minute, coloring my humors sanguine."

Her mother smiled, cautiously. She didn't like it when her daughter spoke of blood.

～

At dawn, Doctor Mingonius met Marketa and her father at the door of Rozmberk Castle.

"He has rested comfortably all night," the doctor said. "I dispatched a letter to the king reporting the progress. I persuaded Don Julius to write a short letter in his own hand, to bear testimony to the change in humor. His Majesty will be overjoyed!"

At this Doctor Mingonius thrust his hand out to grasp Pichler's. He pumped it vigorously and then turned to Marketa.

"I did not report anything, of course, of your intervention, Fräulein Pichlerova. You understand, of course."

"Yes, of course," Marketa said. "It would seem odd to mention a woman's intervention in a medical matter."

"Precisely," answered the doctor with satisfaction, though his eyes studied her carefully. Was there impertinence in her answer?

There was a spark in her blue eyes that worried him.

Mingonius led them to a room near the enormous porcelain boiler, where water bubbled into the great pipes that warmed the castle. A fire roared, and the kitchen staff had laid out a rich breakfast. Sausages and bacon on fine porcelain plates. Fresh cheeses—none of them edged in mold or riddled with worms, Marketa noted—were sliced beside brown and white breads from Katarina's mother's bakery. There were crocks of creamery butter and fresh soured cream, and two great pitchers of dark ale.

"Eat," said Doctor Mingonius. "Eat and then we will discuss our medical procedures for the day."

But Marketa could not finish even half a sausage. She looked nervously at Doctor Mingonius, his face flushed and throbbing from the warm air and strong ale. His voice boomed, filling the room with cheer and good spirits. He was obviously very pleased with his letter to the king and the fact that he had been able to induce Don Julius to write to his father.

"The bleedings have restored balance to his psyche," he said. "The bad blood that tormented him has been released."

"He has asked blessings from God," said an accented voice. "Praise be our most merciful Lord."

Once again, the Spanish priest had entered a room unannounced and unnoticed. What a knack for secrecy and stealth, thought Marketa. Was it Jesuit training or his Spanish blood that allowed him to blend into the shadows and move invisibly? If he were not a priest, she would guess him a sorcerer or a thief.

The warm atmosphere in the room cooled as the priest approached. The fire did not warm their backs now, and the ale did not heat their blood as it had a moment earlier.

Marketa shivered and pulled her woolen cloak tighter around her shoulders.

"He knelt by my side and asked forgiveness," said the priest. "I have written my own missive to our king. He shall be pleased with this spiritual progress."

"Come, sit and partake in breakfast, Priest," said Doctor Mingonius. "We are planning our medical intervention now."

"I have already eaten my brown bread," said the priest. "I broke my fast after prayers an hour ago. I have my own spiritual intervention to plan. Much work is to be done."

Mingonius eyed the Spaniard suspiciously.

"You must not push him to a limit that will break his mental peace," he said. "Don Julius despises the Catholic Church, and too much time with God will make him rebel and impede his cure."

"What blasphemy!" snapped the priest. "The more time he spends on his knees to ask our Lord's forgiveness, the more chance he will be forgiven for his sins and enter heaven."

Mingonius took a long draught of ale. He stared at the little priest whose face was a map of angry wrinkles, like creases on parchment that had traveled hand to hand for months.

"You forget the weeks of hell and torment you endured before we began the bleedings, the rotting carcasses of animals and the screams that haunted this castle and all Krumlov," said the doctor. "If you push him too far, he will fight back. You know this as well as you know the scriptures. If we let a week go by without a bleeding to purge his choleric humors, you will be shaken from your prayers by his raving screams. Priest, he will not kneel beside you like a lamb without the suck of the leech. And it will be you and you alone responsible for his lunacy."

"How dare you accuse me of anything, Mingonius! I have the backing of the Jesuits, of the pope, and of the king."

"You forgot to mention the backing of God himself. And I doubt the king will back you if his son begins raving again. Everyone knows that King Rudolf is not particularly fond of the Catholic Church. His melancholy nature was born in the dark days at the court of his uncle, King Felipe. The Spanish corrupted his sanguine nature, something that even the great physician Jan Jesenius himself cannot correct. A happy boy in the Viennese court returned as a melancholy prince after too many years in El Escorial and Madrid."

"King Felipe taught him discipline and God's word," hissed the priest.

"It does not matter what you think, Priest," said Mingonius, nibbling on a piece of cheese. "If you and I do battle for Don Julius's well-being, I am certain our good king will come down on my side and not that of a Spaniard who wears his son's knees to bone, praying on cold granite."

"Let me know when you have finished with him," the priest said acidly. "Send a page to the chapel. I shall be praying for his soul. I have written that the bleedings must cease, and the king will hear my word from the archbishop of Prague himself. It shall not be long before you are called back to Prague, Herr Doctor Mingonius."

As the priest slammed the heavy wooden door, Mingonius smiled and helped himself to another tankard of ale.

"I believe he forgot to mention that he would be praying for my eternal salvation, as well as the bastard's," said the doctor, smiling. "An oversight, I am sure."

Mingonius planned to spend as much time as possible with Don Julius without applying a leech or blade. He hoped that the prince would become convinced that he and Pichler were to be trusted, and so wean the bastard from Marketa's care. The girl would be used as a bribe to buy time with the afflicted man.

For now, Don Julius seemed addicted to Marketa as if she were opium.

~

"Good morning, Don Julius," boomed Doctor Mingonius, his voice scaring the pigeons off the thick stone windowsill. The room filled with the sound of beating wings as the birds took flight over Krumlov.

Don Julius turned languidly from the window, and seeing only the two men, turned his back on them. His movements were slow and uneven, and his hand trembled slightly.

"What are you doing?" asked Mingonius as he approached.

"I am feeding the birds," the prince said, his voice barely above a whisper. "I like to watch them eat and then fly to freedom."

Mingonius noticed the utter lack of color in the young man's face.

"Have you eaten today, Don Julius?"

"No," he said, slowly lowering himself into a cushioned chair. "I have no appetite."

Mingonius considered this. No appetite in a man who once demanded twelve or more meals a day was certainly a significant change, but not one that was necessarily beneficial. *Balance*, he thought. *We must balance the humors in his body and foster new vital blood.*

"I must prescribe that you eat a hearty breakfast and two more meals this day. You will have to consume a full bottle of red wine as well to bolster the new blood in your veins."

"I am not hungry," said the prince. "I want nothing but to be allowed my privacy."

"Nonsense," said the doctor. "What if I were to permit Marketa to enter and to feed you with her own hand?"

Julius sat up from his slouch, and his left eye began to blink.

"She is with you? Am I to be bled once more?"

"No, no. You aren't to be bled for at least another day. The new blood must course strong within your veins before we attempt to purge you again. And by that time, the new bleeding chair will be delivered by the carpenter. I have a mind to copy its design and introduce it at court. Ingenious!"

"That was Marketa's idea," said Don Julius. "You should name it after her."

Mingonius frowned.

"Send for her, Doctor. I should like to gaze upon her again." Don Julius laid a finger on the doctor's sleeve. Then he wrapped his finger around the silk fabric of the doublet, like a child pleading. "She is the only one who understands my torment. I can see it in her eyes, I can feel it in her hands. Pray, good physician, send for her."

"She is here, my lord," the doctor said, "and I could arrange for her to sit by you as you eat and drink as I prescribe. But only if you promise to be an absolute gentleman to her and permit us to remain in the room."

"She will dine with me?"

"Yes, if you agree to my conditions."

Within a half hour, Marketa sat at one end of a long table, opposite Don Julius. He stared at her intently as she pretended to eat, though in fact she merely pushed the food around her plate.

"Your manners would appall the court," mocked Don Julius, a bright tone to his strengthening voice. "Look how you grasp your fork like a peasant does a pitchfork!"

He sat back in his chair and laughed, a tinny clatter that sounded inhuman.

Marketa set her fork down and blushed. "We do not use forks at home. I have never used anything but a spoon and knife."

What little blood colored Don Julius's complexion drained, leaving his face a mask of stony white.

"Now I have embarrassed you, my sweet. You come from an ancient book, long before forks and other inventions of the court."

"What is he talking about?" whispered Pichler.

Mingonius shook his head. His attention was focused entirely on Don Julius and Marketa, trying to understand what was happening between them.

"What a fool I am!" Don Julius said. He rose to his feet, shuffling to her side.

The two guards approached the table from the wall and blocked his passage.

"Stand aside! I wish to apologize in person to the fair lady."

"Sit down," said Mingonius. "You must sit and finish your repast as we agreed. You can make your apology from your own chair. She can hear you."

"But I have wounded her," Don Julius said, trembling, his knees sagging as he tried to hold himself upright. "She will vanish into the pages once more!"

Mingonius nodded to the guards, and they took the weakened prince back to his chair.

Marketa was amazed at the thought that this Hapsburg cared about her, afraid that she had been offended by his words. The people of Krumlov never concerned themselves with hurting her, calling her "Musle" at every turn, snickering. Certainly the old brewer never worried about her sentiments, he only thought of himself, feasting his eyes on her body.

"Do not fear, Prince," said Marketa. "I am not offended in any way. You are right. I know not the ways of the court. You must teach me."

She stood and motioned to a guard to carry her chair closer to Don Julius.

"If you will behave, I shall sit beside you and you will teach me how a prince eats. Then even the king will not know that I am a simple girl from Krumlov."

Mingonius cautiously nodded. *Clever girl in her diversions,* he thought. *Where has she learned such shrewdness?*

"I give my word, O Fair Maiden. Only approach and I shall teach you and harm you not. Approach, I beseech you!"

The guards stood on either side of Don Julius as Marketa settled into the chair just beyond his reach.

For the remainder of the morning, Don Julius showed Marketa how to hold her fork, how to reach for her wine, how to drink like a lady of the court in Prague.

If I should ever reach Prague, thought Marketa, *I will amaze Physician Horcicky with my newfound etiquette. He will look upon me in amazement and ask me how I learned such courtly manners. Ha! From the king's son, himself, I will reply.*

She smiled at Don Julius, thinking of Prague. He gazed back at her, his face stunned with joy, eager to teach her more.

Marketa learned how to dab her lips and fingers with a napkin. And, finally, she learned to peel fruit and offer it to her host, briefly touching the thick lower lip that had retained a reddish tinge, despite the blood worm's bite.

Her touch sent a tremble down Don Julius's spine that he could not conceal.

"You bewitch me," he whispered. "If they were not present, I would commit such acts with you."

The smile slipped from Marketa's face. She straightened her back in the chair and pushed herself away from him.

"I will not endure such vile manners," she said. "You shall apologize or I shall leave at once."

"You dare demand an apology from a Hapsburg?" Don Julius roared, his manner shifting in an instant.

Marketa leaped to her feet and moved a few steps away. She smoothed her skirt and tucked a stray tendril of hair behind her ear.

"I think I shall go now. Good day, Doctor Mingonius. Good day, Don Julius."

"No!" cried Don Julius, struggling to rise. "Do not go, Marketa. I—I apologize. There! You have what you wished for, an apology from a king's son. Promise me now, you will sit beside me."

Marketa lifted her chin and pressed her lips together in contemplation.

"I do accept your apology for such a vulgar proposition used in my presence. But I will let you have your afternoon to consider how you will keep such foul thoughts from emerging in my presence in the future. Until another day, Don Julius."

"Marketa! Come back! Guards, you fools, stop her at once! She is my heart, my soul. My salvation!"

"She isn't coming back, Julius. You have offended her," said Doctor Mingonius.

Don Julius began to sob.

He covered his face with his hands as Doctor Mingonius and Pichler retreated into the dark hall and left the young man his privacy.

CHAPTER 24

DREAMS OF PRAGUE

The Spanish priest was right about King Rudolf's summons. Within three days, a message came by rider, mud-stained and exhausted from galloping along the half-frozen road from Prague. In his pouch was a letter with the royal seal of the Holy Roman emperor, to be hand-delivered to Doctor Mingonius at Rozmberk Castle.

In the scribed parchment, the king rejoiced at the marked change in his son, sending his congratulations and a guarantee of a generous reward for Doctor Mingonius.

But there was indication that the Jesuits had also conferred with the king. He had called Mingonius back to the court within a fortnight, to leave his son Julius solely in the hands of the Spanish priest.

One more bleeding, commanded King Rudolf. *One more bleeding and you shall be compensated upon your arrival in Prague. I await your full report on my son with eagerness.*

Doctor Mingonius had already imagined his reward—a vast tract of fertile land east of Prague, with a new manor house. The estate had rich soil, producing round, green cabbages and tender baby carrots, yellow-orange with earthy sweetness, like the ones the tenant farmers sold at the Prague market on Saturdays. The farmers also sold eggs, fresh from the landowners' speckled chickens, with downy feathers still clinging to their delicate shells, a lingering gift from the hen who had laid them, just hours before. Yes, he would have dozens of laying hens, squat and plump, pecking at worms in the yard.

But the best would be the cows' milk, so full of fat it was tinged pale yellow, frothy and fresh.

No—no, the best would be the plump red hams studded with fragrant cloves and caraway, cured in his own smokehouse. Cats would gather under the hanging meat, licking the thick drops of fat that speckled the stone floor.

Mingonius had already pictured his son and his pretty new wife settled in the estate and begun planning his visits to them on feast days.

~

Cesky Krumlov had ears at every door and eyes that stared from every window. As the citizens learned that Pichler and Mingonius had successfully treated the mad prince, more and more patients made a pilgrimage to the Pichler bathhouse for bleedings. It was now deep November, and though the transitional seasons of autumn and spring always brought more clientele for the balancing of humors, Pichler was barely able to keep up with the new crowd of eager patients.

"I'll have the same treatment as the Hapsburg prince," said the butcher, winking at Pichler. "Good enough for the son of King Rudolf, it will do for me as well."

"You mean the Mad Bastard of Cesky Krumlov," suggested a tanner, his voice low so as not to carry beyond the intended listeners.

The butcher chuckled, but wished the tanner had bathed before coming to see Pichler. He reeked of the urine and feces of the tanning vats. An hour's soak in hot water and lavender would do him and the rest of Krumlov a world of good. Whenever he did come, Lucie had to warn the regular clients, who refused to bathe at the same time as a tanner. She kept a separate barrel for him, for no one would pay to be bathed in a barrel that had once held the stinking water of Pan Ruzicka.

One by one, the townspeople came to feed the leeches with their blood, trying to pry details from Pichler about his royal patient. But Pichler would not divulge any significant information about the prince.

"How about you, Marketa? Tell us what it is like to hold a basin for the son of Rudolf II. Is he as mad as they say? Does he ask for a kiss from your sweet lips?" asked the butcher, pinching her cheek, a leech wiggling on his forearm.

"Surely he must be struck with the girl," agreed the tailor, looking her up and down. "She's far more comely than the girls up north. If only you would eat more, Marketa, and put some fat on your hips, you would be a true Bohemian beauty."

"Enough about my daughter," insisted Pichler, suddenly irritated. "Hold still and let the leeches take hold—you are making them dizzy with your gyrations. Marketa! Wash the trays and see if you can help your mother in the bathhouse. That is enough for today!"

Marketa nodded to the three patients, who blithely smiled and bid her good-bye, their limbs, torsos, and heads sporting small dark leeches. The butcher looked like a strange version of a unicorn, a water worm protruding from his marble-white forehead.

The cold waters of the Vltava numbed Marketa's fingers as she scrubbed the porcelain trays. She watched as the blood stained the coursing waters red and then dissipated in swirls, washed clean in the flow of the Vltava.

She heard a cry above her.

Looking up, she saw Don Julius staring down from the window of the castle. She stood and dried her hands on her apron. Don Julius leaned precariously out the window. She saw Doctor Mingonius at the prince's shoulder. Don Julius shoved him away and called down to her.

"Marketa! Marketa, soul of my soul. Come to me!"

The birds took flight, frightened by his voice and wild gesticulations. The guards pulled him from the window, and Doctor Mingonius reached out to pull the shutters closed. His face was riven with creases of consternation, not lost to the sharp eyes of the sixteen-year-old girl.

Marketa knew that this was the time to strike the bargain she had been planning. She set the trays in the sun to dry and hurried across the bridge toward the castle.

Mingonius seemed not at all surprised to see her as one of the servants accompanied her to the parlor where he was waiting.

"To what do I owe this unexpected pleasure, Fräulein Pichlerova?" he asked, pulling out a chair for her by the fire. "Have Don Julius's entreaties finally convinced you to take him as a lover?" he joked. "Such a passionate suitor, so demonstrative in his love."

"I want to accompany you to Prague," she said without hesitation. "I want to see Doctor Jan Jesenius perform the autopsy."

Mingonius, for once, stood silent. He stared at her as if she were mad. His hands fumbled for his chair, and he eased himself down.

"Doctor Mingonius, you must take me!"

After a moment to gather his thoughts, he answered, "Do you really think that your mother and father would approve of your traveling to Prague unchaperoned? To observe a dissection of a human body? You are a young lady, and the women of Prague do not interest themselves in the business of medicine. It is unnatural, a woman witnessing such indelicate spectacles."

"Do not concern yourself with my delicacy, Doctor Mingonius," she said. "I am sure there is nothing I will see that will not educate and intrigue me thoroughly."

Mingonius rubbed his chin. "Well then, if we are not to be concerned with you, I will have to consider myself. What makes you think that I will risk my own reputation by consenting to your mad request?"

"Because if you do not, I shall not assist you in bleeding Don Julius again. You know he will never permit you to approach him with leeches unless I am there. The cure will be halted."

Mingonius sat still, his eyes scrutinizing the girl. He had underestimated her. He wondered if Don Julius, in his madness, had sensed qualities in this girl that he could not. Why else would the son of a king be so love-struck by a commoner? Mingonius had attributed it to madness, but now he wondered if there might be something more to the girl.

He thought of the reward that King Rudolf II had promised him. If the girl started trouble, if she spoke outside the castle where the servants and guards were sworn to secrecy, the gossip would soon travel beyond Krumlov. Many of the merchants served the other Rozmberk castles of Bohemia, and the true story of the bleedings would certainly reach Petr Rozmberk himself. How gleeful he would be to share with the king the story of how a simple country girl of Krumlov could accomplish what the great Doctor Mingonius could not. Why, Don Julius had actually ordered him out of the room; he had not even been present for the bleeding!

All these thoughts rumbled swiftly through the doctor's mind and resulted in a frown that wrinkled his forehead.

"You will never be able to practice medicine, Slecna Marketa." It was the first time the doctor had spoken a word of Czech to anyone in Cesky Krumlov. "What good would an education do you? It is a waste of time and effort."

"All I want is your word that I can accompany you to Prague and see Jan Jesenius perform the autopsy. I want to see veins, the organs—"

"*Slecna*! You are indelicate in these matters—"

"Hear me, you are a doctor and I am a bathhouse attendant—what shame is there in a dead man's body?"

"Out of the question!" he said sharply. Suddenly he imagined the king's hand sweeping away his reward, his land, like an angry child knocking the chess pieces off a board. There would be no fat babies raised on warm cows' milk, no eggs adorned with the delicate tendrils of down, no succulent hams curing in the cellar. No vegetable garden with fresh-tilled loam, the earthy aroma greeting him when he arrived in his new carriage from Prague, weary of the city and the court.

Marketa saw high color flushing his face as his anger rose. He was not a man accustomed to having terms dictated to him by another man, let alone a woman—much less a mere girl.

She fingered the fringe of her shawl.

"Think as much as you like," she said, standing up. "When you finally agree, you know where to find me. But the moon is waxing, and it is time to bleed Don Julius once more. I saw how he struggled with you at the window; you have no control over him. It will not be long before he is as dangerous as he was before our treatment. His cure will be undone, and reports will reach the ears of the king before you reach Prague yourself. Imagine what His Majesty will think when he hears it was a woman who provided the cure, not his own court physician. Now, if you will excuse me, Herr Doctor, I must take my leave."

Doctor Mingonius accompanied her to the door, a stunned slowness in his polite gestures. By God, this girl had a mind worthy of the political machinations of the court itself! Had she been plotting this all along? Mingonius admired an agile mind, much as a skilled chess player appreciates a worthy opponent.

He smiled at the impertinent girl. Without realizing it, Mingonius spoke to her again in German.

"I should love to have a business partner who is so adept at bargaining—you would be an excellent horse trader in the markets of Prague. Pity you know nothing of horses, Fräulein Marketa."

"*Slecna*," said Marketa. "I prefer to hear you speak to me in Czech."

She pulled her cloak tighter and threw her shawl over her head, preparing for the cold beyond the castle.

~

Marketa knocked on the door of the little house on Dlouha Street. The good healer welcomed her in from the cold and pressed a hot cup of linden-berry tea into her frozen hands.

"Drink," she urged Marketa. "Drink and I will fetch the letter that came today."

Annabella returned with the folded parchment in her hand. Marketa pulled her lips away from the hot rim of the cup and unfolded the letter.

My Dearest Marketa:

I thank you for your last letter. I have taken your admonishment to heart. Of course I will not mention my concern for you to Mingonius, but I wince to think of you in such close proximity to

Don Julius. I cannot impress upon you the danger of the situation, were he to break loose of his bonds. You have not seen his capability to maim and destroy—I have.

Why must you be present at his bleedings?

Yes, I realize, without your cooperation I would not know of his progress and perhaps Mingonius would not succeed in his treatment.

I am torn. Torn between my need to learn of Don Julius's progress and my concern for you.

You seem to be an integral part of his treatment. Why is this necessary? I will warn you, though, you must not commiserate with this patient—it is unprofessional and dangerous. I understand from what you have written that you feel sympathy for him. You must not. To empathize too much with a patient is to become subjective. Physicians are taught to be objective and skillful in their analyses, devoid of emotion. Describe to me his physical symptoms. Do his eyes focus? Do his hands shake? Does he repeat himself or seem incoherent? What is the shade of his skin, the color in the palm of his hand? Do his gums look pink or red? His breath, does it—

These words were scratched out, with a vicious slash of ink.

Write to me of his physical conditions as well as his rantings. These observations are the most useful to a diagnosis.

As to the news in Prague. Europe is shocked by the work of our imperial mathematician, Johannes Kepler, and his revolutionary theories of astronomy. He has proclaimed his belief in Copernicus's theory that the sun is at the center of our universe and the planets all circle around it. Even our own Earth. This has been greeted with threats and howls from the Catholic Church. As a Protestant, Kepler does not concern himself with the pope and has the king's blessings in his study of the heavens, staving off the Papists in order to give his scientists free rein.

Genius! Ah, it is a privilege to be alive in this glorious age of discovery and enlightenment. Prague is indeed the sun of civilization, the glorious sanctuary of science, reason, and art.

In spite of our bright fortune and the patronage of our good king in the field of science, there is rumor of unrest. The king's younger brother, Matthias, seeks to usurp the throne. He gathers the Hungarians to his side, his allies claiming that the king's melancholy has rendered him weak and unfit to rule. Some of the Bohemian lords and Moravians are said to listen to Matthias's treasonous prattle, especially since his success in negotiating peace in Hungary.

Don Julius remains an open wound in His Majesty's heart, and I believe this contributes significantly to his melancholy. Thank heavens this mad son is locked away safely in Krumlov.

Again, in closing, stay away from Don Julius, I beg you. You must not forget whom you are dealing with or the danger he presents. Let the doctors perform their bloodletting and take your leave.

And please tell me more about this book he speaks of. I am now certain it must be the Coded Book of Wonder.

Yours in service to our king, His Majesty Rudolf II, I bid you good health and God's protection.

Jakub

More than ever, Marketa wanted to tell Jakub that it was she, and she alone, who treated Don Julius. Take her leave, indeed! She struggled with her pride, whipping it down as if were an unruly cur, nipping and begging for recognition.

She knew she must keep silent, for if the king were ever to hear that a girl—a simple bathmaid—had been treating his favorite son, he would be outraged. Her father, Mingonius, and perhaps even she herself would be thrown into the dungeons of the *hrad*.

She fancied seeing more of Prague one day than the prison walls.

Still, as she sat in Annabella's house and penned her reply to Jakub, she would reap some satisfaction. Her lips pressed tightly together in a satisfied smile as she dipped her quill into the ink pot.

My Dear Doctor Horcicky:

I have considered your words carefully—that a physician is meant to be utterly objective and not to take a patient's soul into consideration. So let me list in detail his physical condition, as well as the exact nature of his discourse.

Don Julius has lost many pounds now. It is hard to even guess how much. His appearance has changed completely. His skin is browned from his excursions hunting. His eyes are mostly focused—sometimes desperately so—on me. They are clear and as beautiful as gemstones.

His breath is—ah, but you scratched that out of your letter! Still, it may please you to know that his breath is sweet and healthful, like a baby's sigh. Yes, I have on occasion gotten this close to him. Again, he is tied, and guards stand at either side.

He proclaims his love for me. He wants me to marry him and return to Prague as his wife.

These observations I report quite objectively with no embellishment, nor empathy toward the patient. Merely the facts, reported faithfully.

I will trust you will keep your pledge of secrecy and my protection. Do not report the patient's affection toward me to the king or you will jeopardize my safety and that of Mingonius and my father.

Yours in service to our benevolent king, I bid you good health.
Marketa Pichlerova

∼

Jakub focused and refocused his eyes on the words. His hands clenched the vellum so tightly, he left thumbprints on the soft margins.

"She is in great danger!" he muttered.

He started to dismiss the courier, and then reconsidered.

"How does the *slecna* look to you? Is she in good health?"

"She is as comely as ever," replied the courier. "That one has the healing hands of an angel. No one can untie the knots of my back like Slecna Marketa."

Jakub's eyes flashed open in surprise. It had not occurred to him that the courier would be on such intimate terms with his correspondent.

"Only knots, sir," said the courier, realizing he had made some kind of mistake. "Her hands just massage my back. Her mother would beat me with a stick if I were to touch her."

The courier shifted his weight awkwardly, seeing the smoldering look in Horcicky's eye. He searched for something to say.

"Pani Pichlerova boasts her daughter's virginity will bring a pretty penny someday soon. Until then, she keeps a close eye on the patrons to see they do not sample the goods."

Jakub turned his back angrily on the courier and returned to transplanting the king's orchids.

CHAPTER 25

KATARINA AND THE GRAIN SHED

Katarina did the marketing for the Mylnar family, buying meat, roots, and vegetables for their soups and stews. Because she was so beautiful, she did better than her mother bargaining with the vendors of Siroka Street. Her father grudgingly allowed her this one opportunity to leave the mill because the money she saved was not insignificant.

But it was not because Katarina enjoyed haggling with the merchants that she was eager to shop for the family. She did it because it was a chance to catch a glimpse of Damek, the blacksmith's son, in the crowded morning market.

Her appearance at the wide mouth of Siroka Street inevitably made a ripple of excitement down the line of market vendors, who had little else to brighten their day.

"Here comes the comely miller's daughter," the grocer would say to his sweating nephew, carrying heavy crates of cabbages from the oxcart. "It soothes tired eyes to look up from the frozen muck and see such beauty coming toward us."

The smitten grocer would give the best price of the morning to Katarina and pull out his finest produce, unblemished by worms or weevils. He beamed with pleasure when her delicate fingers chanced to brush his palm as she paid a meager price for her roots and vegetables.

The butcher was the same, though his shrewd wife watched him carefully to be sure he did not throw away their earnings just for a wink of a maiden's eye. Still, Katarina would come away with the most tender cuts, and Pan Butcher always managed to sneak in some extra sausages or secretly fill her clay jar with fresh suet when his wife's back was turned.

Pan Mylnar did not like his daughter to be alone on these trips to the market. He would send his youngest son, Jiri, to accompany her. The young boy was glued to her side. Under no circumstances, said his father, was Jiri to let the blacksmith's son be anywhere near her. But there were times now when Jiri worked as a page in the castle and could not accompany her.

It was on one of these days in the busy Wide Street market that Katarina felt a hand curve tenderly around her elbow. When she turned, she saw the gentle face of Damek, whose brown eyes were shimmering in love.

"Meet me around the back of the brewery," he whispered. "I must see you!"

Katarina's lips mouthed "no," but the hunger in his eyes insisted. She looked down at her basket, suddenly bashful in his unblinking gaze, and when she looked up again, he had disappeared in the crowd.

She had a long list of purchases to make and did not know how she could possibly meet Damek and return home in time to make the midmorning meal. The bright winter sun was already warming her back, and her father and other brothers would be eager for soup and the taste of fresh bread.

Katarina hurried through her purchases, not taking the time to negotiate the best price. She did not bother to pat the butcher's hand or pull a strand of her hair from her braid, twisting it coquettishly in front of the grocer as he bartered with her. Her mother would notice that the coins she gave her were all spent, with no change to spare for the next day. She would scold her for being so careless with the family money.

The brewery was on the Latran side of the Vltava, beyond the bathhouse and the Franciscan cemetery. It was a long way from the bustling market, beside one of the Vltava's sharp, looping bends where the river twisted back on itself.

Katarina struggled with the weight of her basket. It took three heads of cabbage and many pounds of root vegetables to make soup for her hungry brothers. Beads of sweat dotted her upper lip, and she felt a trickle of perspiration work its way down her breasts. She worried whether the fresh butter would begin to melt or the thick cream would curdle from its jostling in the jug.

Why had Damek picked a spot so far away?

She knew the answer—her father would hurt him, perhaps even kill him and beat her severely if he found out the two were meeting in secret. Still, the woven reed basket cut into her tender hands. She shifted the weight onto her arms, looping them together in front of her.

A voice called from the shadows of a hovel.

"Why do you carry such a heavy load?"

Katarina looked over her shoulder to see a dark-haired gypsy sitting on a crude log bench. She wore sparkling earrings, the color of pure silver, and she was dressed in purple and red, her hair pulled back in a yellow scarf.

"I—I..."

"Ah," said the gypsy with a gap-toothed smile. "You are meeting your lover, I can see it in your eyes."

Katarina stopped breathing. Her face colored red.

"Beauty, your secret is safe with me," laughed the gypsy. "But beware of the tyrant of the brewery. He is an evil devil."

The gypsy spat into the dirt and raised her hand in a curse in the direction of the brewery.

"You can leave your basket with me," suggested the gypsy. "That way you can make better time and enjoy your lover's company all the sooner."

Katarina had been warned about gypsies and knew better than to leave her morning's purchases with her. She shook her head, thanking her politely.

"You do not trust me, do you, beauty?" said the gypsy, her smile fading. "Well, I suppose you shouldn't. Be on your way and make your lover carry your load home for you!"

Katarina hurried away, trying to make up for lost time. The sun had begun to melt the ice in the puddles, and mist was rising from the moist earth. As she approached the brewery, the stench of hops assailed her nose. She wrinkled her face at the smell, wondering how Marketa could endure the fat brewer's attentions in the bathhouse.

A voice called out from one of the deserted grain sheds.

"Over here!"

Katarina looked around, making sure no one saw her. She entered the door of the shed and looked around at the mounds of threshed barley.

"My darling," Damek cried. "I had to see you!"

He stood in the shadows of the doorway, and Katarina could only detect a silhouette until her eyes adjusted to the dark. He was, as always, blackened by the soot of the smithy's fire, and his darkened face and arms blended into the dim light.

"If my father finds us together, he will kill you!" she said.

She felt his arms pull her into the recesses of the shed. The basket fell away from her hands at the entrance, the cabbages rolling this way and that.

"I am willing to risk that," whispered Damek. He embraced her, kissing the sugar from her sweet neck.

Katarina's knees weakened, and Damek's arm slipped around her waist, supporting her as his wet kisses covered her face. He let her down carefully into the brown hills of barley. The smell of grain mixed with the musky odor of her lover, his smoky face streaking white with tears of ardor.

"My darling," she whispered through the flurry of kisses. "I thought we would never—"

"Who is there?" shouted a man's voice. "Who is robbing me of my grain?"

Damek sprang to his feet, shielding Katarina behind him.

"I do not steal!" Damek shouted. "Let me come out and I will show my face. It is I, Damek the blacksmith."

He motioned for Katarina to stay silent. She crept back into the darkest corner of the shed.

"Come out, now!"

Damek looked around, his mouth twisting with consternation. He knew he could not let the brewer know the truth, but he did not know how else to explain his presence.

He walked out into the light toward the pitchfork, his hands held high in the air.

"You! Does your father know you are a thief?"

"No—"

"And what is this?" He kicked at the reed basket, still filled with root vegetables, meat, lard, and cheese. Keeping an eye on his prisoner, the fat brewer squatted down to inspect the contents.

Fat sausages oozed their grease onto his hands. The clay cup of lard was seeping into the cloth where fresh cheese was tied.

A crock of pale yellow butter glistened, the creamy finish damp with moisture.

"A man who can afford to buy food as fine as this has no reason to steal my barley. What were you doing in there?"

Damek set his jaw and stared back at him.

"As you say, I was stealing your grain."

The brewer narrowed his eyes at the impertinent young man.

"Get off my property," he said, thrusting the pitchfork at the young man. "Go back to your sooty hovel. But leave the basket here."

Damek had no choice but to walk away, hoping that the brewer would not search his threshing shed thoroughly. He walked until he was beyond the old man's sight. He saw the brewer refilling the basket with its spilled contents, his greedy cheeks pinched up in a smile of satisfaction.

The brewer lumbered off toward his house, toting the heavy basket of food.

Damek watched as Katarina ran out of the door of the shed in the other direction, cutting across toward the Franciscan monastery toward home, without any food for her family. He wondered how she would explain what had happened.

As he plodded back toward the village square and the smithy he heard the sad love song of a gypsy, singing from within her hovel.

CHAPTER 26

TAMING A HAPSBURG

Two days after she demanded—and received—an apology from Don Julius, Marketa returned to the castle with her father. The young Hapsburg treated her with the utmost respect. He pulled out a chair for her, beckoned the servants to wait on her exclusively, and sat quietly with his hands folded in front of him.

She is remarkable, thought Mingonius. *As ordinary as peasant toast, except for that wild hair. But quick.*

A servant knocked, bringing a message for the doctor. He read it and nodded, following the servant out. Within a few minutes, he returned with three men, dressed in the satin finery of the court. They lingered in the doorway, watching Don Julius pass the time with Marketa, his face animated with good humor.

"Who is the maiden?" asked one.

"She is the bloodletter's daughter. She amuses him, nothing more," replied Mingonius.

The three court councilors whispered to each other, nodding. The girl did hold Don Julius's rapt attention.

Marketa listened carefully as Don Julius spoke of manners at the Prague court. He told her about the courtesies that were expected of both men and women. He explained how to curtsy before the king, how to remain that way until after he had passed or to retreat backward while still in a curtsy.

He laughed as he curtsied, playing the role of a woman of the Hapsburg court, an invisible fan in his hand. He fluttered his eyelashes and pretended to flirt with Mingonius, who had now returned to his chair.

Mingonius roared with laughter, and Pichler joined in warily. He could not quite believe that his daughter had brought out this frolicking nature in the young bastard prince.

"Then," Don Julius said, rushing to his bed and rooting around beneath it, "then you must bow, yes bow, in all sincerity to this."

With great ceremony, Don Julius paraded around the room with his clean chamber pot.

"Oh yes, you must bow to the king's own shit!" he proclaimed.

Pichler gasped, but Mingonius laid a hand on his arm. He then inclined his head forward to wink at the ministers, who chuckled at Don Julius's choice of court courtesies.

"So it is," said Doctor Mingonius. "I have bowed many a time to King Rudolf's discharge. After all, it has traveled through his royal person and is honorable in that account. Though our Marketa scarcely needs to know all of this."

Don Julius frowned at him.

"I am teaching Marketa what to expect when she accompanies me to Prague," he said. "She must know the ways of the court so as not to embarrass herself. A fairy from the Coded Book does not know the customs of European royalty."

"Ah yes. Well, I see. I did not know that she was to accompany you to Prague," said Mingonius, wary of what the ministers might think of this. "Of course, you cannot return until you have proved to your father that you can behave in a proper manner."

"Yes, I shall obey," he answered. "I will do anything the world asks of me now, to win the trust and love of my angel Marketa. Anything."

Mingonius stared at him, incredulous. Under the doctor's scrutiny, Don Julius covered his face with his hands and massaged his temples with his thumbs.

"I am suddenly very tired. I wish to go to my bed and rest," he said.

The guards helped him from the table.

He gestured toward Marketa.

"I wish her to accompany me to my bed."

"Certainly not!" said Pichler.

"I shall not accompany you to your bed, dear prince," said Marketa. "But I shall return to receive your tutelage. And may I say, your comportment today has made me most happy."

She approached the bed where he lay, his eyes unfocused and confused. She bent over him and kissed him tenderly on the forehead.

"Sleep now, my lord. I shall return in a few days, once you have recovered your strength."

Don Julius closed his eyes as Pichler and Marketa headed for the door. Mingonius bent over to look at Don Julius one more time.

"She is an angel," murmured the patient.

"Indeed," confessed the doctor, in a low voice. "I am only beginning to understand the extent of her charms."

With this Doctor Mingonius retreated to the door, to be greeted with profuse congratulations from the court visitors for curing the son of Rudolf II of his vicious humors.

But every courtier wanted to know more about the strange charm of the bloodletter's daughter.

CHAPTER 27

AN OMINOUS REWARD

Mingonius knocked on the door of Don Julius's apartments. In his left hand he carried a package in fine calfskin wrappings.

Don Julius, still weak from bloodletting, feebly raised his hand in greeting.

"Good morning, Don Julius," said Doctor Mingonius, bowing slightly to the king's son.

"Good morning, Doctor," whispered the pale-faced Julius. Before him was a hearty breakfast of herring, breads, cheeses, and ale. The plates were untouched. "What is this you bring?"

"It is your reward," said Mingonius, smiling at his docile patient. "The king has given me permission to let you study the book in exchange for your compliance in being bled."

Don Julius did not answer but held out his hands to receive the package, like a mother might open her arms for a long-lost child. The doctor noticed how his hands shook, as if he were ancient and infirm. The loss of blood had made him weak. Too weak, perhaps.

Don Julius set the book on a table and ordered fresh linen to be brought to clean his hands. He wiped his fingers meticulously before opening the leather coverings.

He opened the book with the utmost care and drew a breath that seemed to almost suck the air from the room. Then he sighed explosively, a man reunited with a lover.

The doctor stood beside his patient and looked at the pages. He too gasped, for Don Julius had turned immediately to the pages of naked women swimming in pools of green water. The bright colors, bizarre images, and strange text startled him.

"What is this, may I ask?"

Don Julius answered slowly. "It is the mystery of mysteries. I have not gazed upon it since I was thirteen years old. It was my first true love."

His eyes grew cold and distant. "I wonder if I have outgrown it now. It cast its spell on me a long time ago, a power that protected me as a child."

He turned to pages that depicted colorful plants, leaves, seeds, and root systems. Then to the pages of the zodiac, circles segmented by the months of the year and punctuated with still more naked women in elaborate barrels.

"What language is that?" asked Doctor Mingonius. "Is it Egyptian? What are those symbols?"

Don Julius bit his lip. "That is the mystery, good doctor. No one knows, not even I. There was one time that I was convinced that the bath maidens knew the answer but refused to share it. I asked them if it was part of the Kabbalah. Or a master alchemist's journal. Or was it the coded writing of Leonardo da Vinci, born 1452 on a Saturday night? They would not reveal the secret, no matter how I pleaded. I was so angry with the maidens when they wouldn't answer me. How peculiar that all seems now, thinking they were real."

Doctor Mingonius smiled for his patient seemed finally to be considering his own past behavior as bizarre, outrageous. What progress!

Then his smile faded.

"Bath maidens?" he said. "Why do you call them bath maidens?"

Don Julius flicked to a page where the women sat in cylinders. "Are they not all bath maidens? It is obvious. Look at the barrels, Mingonius. And this one, this one who has an impish child in the soaking tub with her, looking around her back. Does the child not look too young to be enjoying the body of such a mature woman?"

"Perhaps he is a cupid, or her own child in the tub with her?"

"No," snapped Don Julius bitterly. "He is a patron, enjoying a woman for the first time. He is smiling because he is foolish and thinks he has learned the secrets and earned favor with the king, with his prowess. But the bathmaid still holds all the secrets, and the book is forever coded. She will not whisper its secrets and laughs at his folly. But, you see, she protects him, shielding him from harm."

The prince brooded over the pages, studying the bath maidens. *He is thinking of Marketa again*, thought Mingonius. Instead of rinsing the bathmaid's memory from his patient's mind, he had only reinforced it. *Can I never rid his mind of her?*

It was at that moment Doctor Mingonius wondered if the king had made a serious error in giving Don Julius the Coded Book of Wonder, even temporarily.

CHAPTER 28

AN INVITATION TO PRAGUE

The next day, Doctor Mingonius sent word that Pichler and his daughter should not return to Rozmberk Castle before two weeks' time.

"A fortnight?" said Pichler, shaking his head. "Just when the patient has made so much progress. What could Doctor Mingonius be thinking?"

A special envelope with a red wax seal, addressed to Marketa, accompanied the brief letter to the bloodletter. Pichler was astonished to see the sealed envelope and handed it to his daughter in wonderment.

Marketa eagerly broke the seal and read the inked words on heavy parchment. Mingonius had written in Czech to make his message easier for her to read.

Make your arrangements to leave with me the day following the next bloodletting. We will travel in my coach, and I will make arrangements for a woman chaperone to be seen accompanying you as far as Prague. In exchange for this, I will expect you to keep your silence about the matters discussed.

Marketa beamed as she read the words.

"What is it, Daughter? Why does the doctor write to you?"

She clutched the letter to her breast and stood on her tiptoes to kiss her father.

"Let us walk along the river, Papa. I have some news to share with you."

~

Two hours later, Marketa and her father returned, exhausted from a heated argument. In the end, Marketa had gotten her way; they would present the news together to her mother. It would not be described as an opportunity to watch the scientific method and learn medicine, but as an invitation to visit Prague and see the court of Rudolf II.

"Mother! I am to go to Prague, chaperoned of course, and stay with Pani Mingonius in her household. And Doctor Mingonius has promised I shall accompany him to the palace, where I may even catch a glimpse of the king."

Lucie clutched her daughter to her breast and began to kiss her fingers, one by one, as if they were made of sugar.

"My daughter, presented to the king of Bohemia, emperor of the Holy Roman Empire!" she gasped. "What blessings you have brought forth for our family, Marketa."

Marketa accepted her mother's praise with grace, while her father looked on uncomfortably.

"From now on, you are not to touch the buckets," Lucie said, wringing her hands in pleasure. "No, I shall bathe you and massage your skin with tallow and herbs. Let me look at your hands. They shall know you as a simple country girl with skin and nails like this. Look at the wrinkles and creases, the redness from hot water. You must rest, you must eat more—I shall order meat every day of the week until you leave—"

"I leave in fifteen days, Mother. Not a lot of time for fattening!"

"Oh, I must pack a trunk for you immediately!" her mother said, hands flying to her face. "What clothes do I have that you could travel in? We must make arrangements with the seamstress for whatever our pennies will buy."

"Doctor Mingonius said that he will see to it that I have proper clothing once I arrive in Prague. His wife will see to it."

"And this chaperone? Who is she?"

"One of Mingonius's retinue from Prague. She is one of his wife's servants, but she came here to supervise the cooking and housekeeping at the castle during the doctor's stay."

"Oh then, a proper chaperone. Splendid!"

Marketa bit the inside of her cheek. She thought it hypocritical of her mother to worry so about a chaperone. After all, she had been left alone often enough in the bathhouse with naked men who pinched her bottom through her light shift. They spoke bawdily about their sexual prowess as she silently fetched water and dropped hot stones in their barrels to keep the water temperature warm. Drunken men—traveling merchants, horse traders, thieves—had leered at her while she served them ale, tipping the tankards up to their open mouths while their hands fiddled busily below the water. Merciful it was when the barrel lids were tapped down tight over their submerged shoulders and she could not see anything below their sweating necks and their lecherous looks.

Now her mother fussed about a chaperone to accompany her to Prague.

It was arranged that Pani Pichlerova would meet with the chaperone at the castle to be sure all arrangements were made and proper conduct was agreed upon before the journey to Prague.

Soon the marketplace buzzed with the news that one of their own would attend the court of King Rudolf. The butcher sent slabs of bacon and hams to the bathhouse, and the greengrocer sent willow baskets full of cabbages and onions. The cobbler sent a new pair of slippers to Marketa with his compliments, and the dressmaker sent an embroidered blouse of great needle skill and a matching black vest, delighted that the king himself might see her work as he glanced at the pretty Marketa. As an afterthought, she sent a petticoat, trimmed with lace and her initials embroidered into the hem.

"Show it to Doctor Mingonius's wife. Maybe she'll want something made for her here in Krumlov," she said eagerly, pressing the bundle into Marketa's hands and hugging her tight.

Neighbors loaned Marketa their finery, thinking how blessed their clothes and accessories would be once the king himself saw them.

"You must promise to wear this in sight of the king," they said.

The priest insisted that Marketa attend a special mass, to bless her departure. All the citizens of Krumlov would prepare food for a feast in her honor. The girls of the town looked at her with astonishment and admiration, and some with keen jealousy, to think that Musle would see the great city of Prague.

Only Katarina looked at her with the love of friendship, blinking away tears. The miller's daughter fumbled miserably with her hands, wishing nothing more than to hug her best friend good-bye.

Despite all the giddy preparations, all Marketa could think of was the bleeding of Don Julius she must perform, one last time before she left.

❦

The new chair, made of sturdy mahogany, was delivered to the castle in time for the next bleeding. Pan Carpenter bowed to Doctor Mingonius as his two sons carried it into the castle.

"I have done just as Slecna Marketa instructed. If I had more time, I would apply another coat of oil to its finish, but I do not want to soil the prince's fine clothes."

The doctor stepped around the piece of furniture, his finger fidgeting on his upper lip.

"Remarkably designed," he said at last. "And a fine execution, Herr Carpenter."

"Yes, I copied the design exactly as sketched. I splayed open the armrests so that you can more easily direct the leeches to the patient's sides. There is plenty of room here now to approach his body from all angles, including slats of the back to expose his spine."

"And the long leg rest," Mingonius noted. "Yes, I can apply the leeches to his inner thighs now, without fear of him kicking me when we loosen the ropes."

"It is as you commissioned, Doctor. I only followed your designs, as Slecna Musle instructed."

"My designs," repeated the doctor, realizing that Marketa had passed them off as his. "Yes, well. Your execution is commendable—you are a fine craftsman. If you would be so kind as to return my drawings to me, I may replicate this at court."

As the carpenter bowed, preparing to leave, Doctor Mingonius laid a finger to his lips, smiling.

"Herr Carpenter—you referred to Fräulein Marketa as 'Musle.'"

The carpenter swallowed, his eyes widening.

"I meant no disrespect in your presence, Herr Doctor. She is known to Krumlov by that name."

Doctor Mingonius's broad smile confused the man, and he looked down at his boots, realizing how vile the name must sound to a member of Rudolf's court, if he indeed understood its meaning.

"Yes, well it will be our secret, then. But a fine name for a bathmaid," chuckled the doctor. He winked at the furniture maker, dismissing him.

The carpenter nodded and hurried out the door of the castle, wondering when he could dare to collect payment.

Mingonius met Pichler several times during the next fortnight, as the doctor frequented Uncle Radek's tavern on a regular basis. The doctor assured Pichler that he would take good care of Marketa in Prague, but also expressed his fear that Don Julius had become too listless and that their patient needed to build up his reserve of blood before any further treatments.

But that was not the only reason. Doctor Mingonius hoped that a respite from seeing Marketa might rid the king's son of his obsession with the bathmaid. Then, if Marketa left Cesky Krumlov, Don Julius would forget about her.

A fortnight of rest and food had indeed strengthened the prince's blood and stamina. When Marketa finally returned to Rozmberk Castle, she could hear his curses lashing the air long before she reached the guarded door.

"You must restrain him," said Doctor Mingonius to the three guards. "Do not let him free under any circumstances. I will not bleed him without his consent, but we can restrain him if he is going to harm himself or anyone else."

The doctor took a deep breath. "Marketa, wait here," he said. "Do not enter until I call for you."

She noticed the creases in his face and the dark rings under his eyes from too little sleep and too much worry. *He must be struggling with the notion of my presence*, she thought. *Having a*

woman intervene goes counter to everything he considers profes-
sional, especially after receiving the compliments and congratula-
tions of the king's ministers.

Over an hour went by and Marketa could hear the scrape of boots on the wooden floor, the crash of heavy furniture, and the roar of curses. She heard the pleading of Doctor Mingonius, the curses, yelps, and wails. It sounded as if a wild beast was in the room, not a human being. Perhaps they had waited too long between bleedings, she thought, for the cure seemed to have vanished. Tonight, she thought, was the full moon—yes, they had waited too long.

Then finally—after far too much time, she thought—Marketa heard her name called.

"Marketa! My angel!"

Immediately there was a hush, an ominous silence. Then the creak and groan of the heavy door being opened.

"You may come in now, fräulein," said Doctor Mingonius, his hair tousled and his green velvet clothing torn in several places. "Be careful not to get within his reach."

"How can I apply the leeches if I am not close to him?" she said.

She strode past the doctor with feigned confidence, then stopped as she crossed the threshold: the chair!

The prince was lashed to the new bleeding chair, his body supported by crimson velvet cushions. She noticed how her patient was reclined, his body, though lashed with ropes, readily exposed for treatment, his back supported by the horizontal slats. Marketa smiled, seeing that the furniture maker had followed her designs exactly.

"Yes, your invention is quite comfortable, my darling," said Don Julius, noticing her smile. "I feel as if I am reclining on a throne befitting a king."

Doctor Mingonius stared slack-jawed at Don Julius. The doctor was still breathing hard from his struggle with the patient just minutes before. Now Don Julius had become calm and courteous, the moment Marketa walked in the door.

Marketa greeted Don Julius with a curtsy as he had instructed her to do in the lessons. Her eyes were bewitched by the sight of her patient and her creation, the bleeding chair.

"I make you happy!" said Don Julius. "Look at the charm of your smile. Let me see you, come closer, my darling."

Marketa approached him cautiously.

"Your beauty has only been enhanced since our last meeting. Is it the waters of the Vltava that perform such miracles? I watch you every day as you wash trays and towels in the river."

His hand cocked away from his rope-bound wrist, his finger indicating the direction of the bathhouse.

Marketa nodded. "I know, Don Julius. I see you above. You threw a white cloth from the window one day. Pray, what did you mean by that?"

Doctor Mingonius cleared his throat and approached with a bucket sloshing with muddy water.

"Will you let Marketa apply the leeches now?"

Don Julius wrinkled his nose at the doctor.

"I speak of love and you speak of worms. Let me be alone with the fair Marketa, and she could cut me with a blade. She could cut out my heart—"

"That will not be necessary," said Mingonius briskly. "We will follow the same plan. The guards shall attend you. If you reach out to Marketa in any way, she will leave at once and shall not return. Do you understand?"

Don Julius sneered. "Take your common stench from this room—it adulterates the aroma of the sweet Marketa."

"Don Julius, do not speak in that profane manner to your good doctor," said Marketa. "Apologize this minute."

Don Julius looked up at Marketa, wounded at her tone.

"I beg your pardon, Herr Doctor," he mumbled. "Would you be so kind as to take your leave, please?"

Mingonius ran his hand over his forehead, amazed yet again at her control over the madman. "Of course, Don Julius."

When the door shut behind them, Don Julius sighed. A sigh that reached deep, thought Marketa, from the heart.

"I am sorry, my love, for my outburst. But they represent all that I despise, those men," he said. His eyes were focused on nothing; they seemed to recede and look within himself. "They are in control, absolute control. He, the devil Mingonius, has kept you from me, though I begged to see you. They see me as a sick man, one to be managed."

"But you are sick, Don Julius," said Marketa. "That's why the bleeding must be performed."

"Do you believe that, my angel? That I am sick? Because I rage against those who imprison me? Because I despise that desiccated priest who makes me pray to a God I do not believe in?"

"Surely you must believe in God, Don Julius."

"*Surely you must believe in God, Don Julius!*" he said, mimicking her in a high voice. "No, I assure you, after what I have seen and heard from the voices, I cannot."

Marketa shivered. She had never heard a person confess he did not have faith. There were Protestants, there were Reformists, but faith was strong in Bohemia.

Everyone had faith.

But Don Julius did not.

"Say a prayer quickly to the Holy Mother to forgive you," said Marketa.

"You say one for me, Marketa. She will not hear my prayer."

Marketa did whisper a prayer. She looked at Don Julius, whose countenance was now not of a lunatic, but of a lost soul.

He was a Hapsburg, yes, but a prisoner. Perhaps he would be all his life.

Something caught in the back of her throat, and she had to cough twice to clear it.

"I know your dream, Marketa. You dream of becoming a physician, of learning and practicing medicine in Prague. I am right, am I not?"

Marketa said nothing. How did he read her thoughts?

"You dare to dream, no matter how impossible that might be. Do you know my dream?"

She shook her head.

"I dream of casting off the Hapsburg curse, this mantle of lunacy. I dream of walking through the streets of Prague without women clutching their children to their breasts and hurrying off to hide."

She touched his shoulder, not to administer a leech, not as a matter of medical protocol, but to soothe him.

"I am sorry, Don Julius," she whispered. "Truly I am."

He looked up at her.

"I do not wish you to be sorry. I wish you to love me for the man I could be. I wish with all my heart you would love me—for I know to have your love and trust would transform me now and forever."

She looked up at the guards, who watched Don Julius's every movement. Then she looked down at the bucket, where the leeches slept under the muddy water.

"I should perform your treatment now," she said quietly. She wished he did not look so forlorn. It disquieted her and distracted her from the treatment. In a way, it was easier when he was nasty and maniacal, rather than seeing this remorseful look of confusion.

He nodded as the guards adjusted the ropes so the bleeding could begin. He extended his forearms as far as he could under the restraints.

Marketa noticed the surrender, the meekness with which he offered up his body. Why was it that he was so ready to submit to her will and not to the others? When she was alone with him, especially now, he seemed to her—dare she believe?—normal.

Never had his green eyes seemed so clear and luminous. They had lost the bloodshot color that had so frightened her when he first arrived. Now they shone with a brilliance that betokened depth of character, intelligence—even, despite his blasphemy, a soul.

Don Julius had undergone a profound change in the last few months. His cheeks and face were lean after the months of a strict diet. Indeed, he cared little for food now, Mingonius had reported, and had to be urged to eat at all. His tailor had taken in the seams on his clothing several times, and the fine cloth—velvet and satin—showed off his athletic body, honed and muscled from riding the hunt.

She remembered how his erection had frightened her only weeks ago. Now there was no bulge in his trousers, only a lament in his voice and a pleading in his eyes. He looked utterly lost and childlike.

Before she applied the first leech to his forearm, she took a little knife—a fleam—out of her father's medical bag. His skin had grown thick with scar tissue over the bleeding points.

"This will only smart a moment," she said, holding the blade near his vein.

"I trust you," he said. "I trust you completely."

She looked up at his eyes.

He winced and then breathed deeply as the blade nicked the flesh.

"Now the leech will bite. The blood will arouse him," she said, dipping her hand into the cold water to fish out a creature.

"Do you trust *me*?" whispered Don Julius, his eyes wandering over her. "Do you, Marketa?"

She hesitated, looking into his eyes. His catlike stare mesmerized her. She had never seen such beautiful eyes in her life.

"Yes," she found herself saying.

"Then ask them to leave," he whispered, nodding to the guards. "I am tied. I cannot harm you. Trust me. I must be alone with you."

"My father and Mingonius would never allow it," she said. "Turn out your other arm. Bend it like this, as far as the ropes will allow," she said, instructing him with her own forearm.

He did as he was told. He drew a deep breath as she flicked the blade again into his skin.

"It seems unfair that I should be the one who agrees and surrenders constantly. There is no trust on your part. I have things I want to say to you in private—"

"Yes, I remember the topics you wanted to whisper to me one time. Vulgar suggestions."

"I will never do that again," he whispered. "But you must trust me. Look at me, Marketa. Look at me. You must trust me!"

As the next leech found the vein, Marketa raised her eyes to his. The pleading, the childlike insistence she found there unnerved her.

"Remove his doublet," she said to the guards. "I need to apply the leeches to his back."

The guards did as they were told, untying a rope at a time, cautiously pulling off the clothing, and retying Don Julius.

"I only wish they were your hands undressing me," he whispered, closing his eyes. "But you are heartless and cruel to my declarations of love."

When she said nothing, he said, "A witch and her worms—a man's heart means nothing to her."

She looked up into his eyes. He looked back at her, watching to see if his accusation had wounded her. Then the long black lashes closed, a curtain. She felt something quicken deep within her, but dismissed the sensation.

Marketa worked quietly, pulling his skin up to apply the leeches. Don Julius seemed content with the silence. His skin flushed wherever she touched him.

"Untie his feet and legs and remove his breeches," she ordered the guards. "I must apply the leeches there."

"Send—send them away," he whispered again, looking down at her between his ankles. "Or I shan't let you apply the worms to my neck and head."

"You know we must follow of the map of humors," she said. "Be reasonable, Don Julius."

"*You* be reasonable then, Marketa. I have done nothing but give—*give* my word, *give* my body, *give* my soul. Give my blood to you, and you alone. I have given up my dignity and indulged you, more than any commoner would do. Now I ask one request. But I do not think you have the courage to grant it."

Her eyes flashed, challenging him.

"What is that request, Don Julius?"

"To be alone with you. That does not seem like too much to ask. Or is it that you are a woman and I frighten you? Of course. So that is the reason women can never be physicians, for they cannot take risks and make leaps of valor!"

Marketa set her lips firmly together. She struggled with his words.

"Guards! Send in Doctor Mingonius," she said.

Don Julius's eyes flew open in alarm.

"*No!* I warn you. I will not continue treatment unless you consent. I will smash this chair to pieces if you or that doctor try to apply any more of your hellish eels to my flesh. You know my condition. Do you have real courage, or are you frightened like all the others?"

Marketa ignored him and looked at the door, her chin set.

Doctor Mingonius hobbled in, his legs having gone asleep while he waited in the straight-back chair in the hall.

"Where are the headpoints?" he said. "You must apply them to his head for the cure to work. And the thighs?"

"I am only halfway through, Herr Doctor. Now I want to complete the treatment in private."

"Nonsense! I cannot permit you to stay here alone with him."

"Those are my conditions," said Don Julius, color rising in his cheeks. "If we are to go any further, she and she alone will touch my flesh, and I will not suffer the humiliation of the guards looking on me in a naked state. Their stares sicken me!"

Marketa thought of Prague. It was her dream. If Don Julius did not accept the bleeding, the priest would report Mingonius's failure. It would be a matter of days and Don Julius would be waking the dead with his screams and rage.

The bad blood had to be drained.

"Let me," whispered Marketa to Doctor Mingonius. "I know I can do it."

"Dear girl, you do not know what you are saying! He is a madman!" Doctor Mingonius put his hand on her shoulder.

All of her life, she had been told what to do. Was she really so different from Don Julius now, bound and helpless?

"Guards, bind his wrists with more rope and leave us!" she said.

Mingonius's eyes flashed. "Marketa! Do not ask me to—"

"You will do as she says or no one, I swear, no one will enter this room to treat me again," roared Don Julius. "I will send word to my father that you are charlatans and you shan't touch me again. I swear it!" He thrashed against the ropes, making the heavy chair screech across the floor.

"Do it," said Marketa, above the din. "Do as I say and I can save us both!"

Doctor Mingonius felt the perspiration on his lip. The Jesuit would be only too happy to contradict the declarations of success carried to Prague by the king's ministers. He hoped the priest was not in earshot now.

As if hearing the doctor's thoughts, Don Julius began to shout at full lung.

"Get me the priest!" he shouted. "I shall have him dispatch a letter to the king this very night of your incompetence!"

Doctor Mingonius looked at Don Julius and then again at Marketa.

"Trust me," she repeated. "I can do this."

Doctor Mingonius scanned her face.

"Guards!" he snapped. "Remove his clothes and fasten him securely to the chair. Make sure he cannot pull away and harm Fräulein Marketa!"

"Out!" bellowed Don Julius.

With a flutter of his cape and a last doubtful look at Marketa, the doctor swept out the door.

The guards pulled off Don Julius's breeches, bowing to him as they did so. Then they retied the restraints, tighter than usual. But he did not look at them even for a second. He watched Marketa, his eyes studying her, mesmerized.

"Go now," he said to the men. "If I harm Marketa in any way, you may plunge those surgical knives through my heart."

The two guards exchanged looks but said nothing. One threw a furtive look at Marketa and opened his mouth to say something, but thought better of it and remained silent.

As the guards closed the door behind them. Marketa felt a shiver of apprehension. The room was eerily quiet. The candles flickered in the breeze that came in through the window from the river.

"Come now, Marketa. You cannot be afraid of me."

"I am not afraid of you, Don Julius."

"You are a liar," he laughed. "But a brave one. Well, here I am. Your patient. Naked and waiting for your hands to cure me."

Marketa breathed deeply. She could smell his sweat, the musky scent of his body. It was an odor she knew well from the bathhouse, a distinctly male smell, acrid and animal.

She approached his thighs and nudged them apart with her foot at his ankles.

"Why do you not just ask me to open my legs for you," he said. "I told you I would be cooperative."

With that, he spread his legs wide, his penis hanging to one side like a dog's tongue lolling.

Marketa still could not trust herself to speak, but applied the fleam to the soft skin of his upper thighs. She could tell he was a man who rode often, for there was chaffed skin that ran up the inside of his calves and thighs, where the hair had been rubbed off and the skin, once raw, had now healed over. The riding muscles were outlined distinctly, just below the blue-white skin. Her fingers touched the hard brawn, tracing a vein.

She heard his heavy breathing. His head rolled back in ecstasy. His skin twitched under her touch, and he gave a deep sigh as she applied the small leeches.

She moved, on her knees, around to his back, pulling the pail of leeches alongside. Her hand reached his spine through the heavy slats in the chair, and her finger counted the vertebrae to find the right points of contact. She opened the fleam and pierced his skin. He did not wince; he did not twitch. For the long minutes it took to apply the leeches to his back, there was nothing but silence.

Finally, she rose and stood beside him. "Kindly bring your head up, Your Highness," she said, her voice trembling.

Don Julius slowly turned his face toward her. His eyelashes fluttered open and his eyes sought out hers.

"You have to understand, Marketa. I need you. You are the only one who can quiet the voices."

"What voices?"

Don Julius shook his head and grimaced. "The ones that fill my ears, my head. All my life. To hurt, to rage…to…but you, you silence them, just as you did when I discovered you in the book as a young boy."

"I do not understand."

"You were the only one who could stand between my father and me, between the demons and me. As long as I could gaze upon you and search for the meaning of the secret language, the voices in my head were still."

Marketa pressed her lips together firmly. His voice was sane; his words were tinged with madness. She would cure him with science and dispel his bizarre notions that she was somehow part of the world of his wild fantasies.

"Look at me, Marketa. Look at me. I love you with my heart and soul. Can you not see it in my eyes?"

Marketa closed her eyes. Just for a moment, but enough time for the spell of his words to lose their power and dispel like wisps of smoke. She took a breath.

"I must apply the leeches to your temples and forehead," she said. "It will be best if you do not struggle."

"I gave you my word as a Hapsburg," he said.

He could not help but twitch when the sharp-tipped fleam pierced the skin on his forehead.

"I will not cut the skin on your temples," said Marketa. "The blood is too close to the surface and too profuse. I will just hold the leech there until he takes hold."

Her cool fingertips rested on his temples as she arched a tiny leech toward the blue veins. She thought about the tales that had been told, about how Hapsburg blood ran blue, not red. She pushed the notion out of her mind—tales for ignorant fools.

The leech's mouth strayed here and there. The worm seemed to have no interest in sucking. She could feel Don Julius's eyes study her face, her breasts, as she leaned over.

"Just a minute," she said. "I will encourage it."

She pulled out the little blade and pricked her own fingertip, and traced her bleeding finger lightly across his temple.

The leech, excited by the smell of fresh blood, bit into the vein. As the creature finally took hold, a languid drop of Don Julius's blood stained her fingers. She watched it trickle into the cuticle of her fingernail as she held the little leech steady.

The prince looked up at her, his red lips parted. His eyes shone with emotion, and she felt light-headed, her knees suddenly untrustworthy. She moved her hand from his temple to his torso and leaned over to apply a leech to his abdomen.

The leech moved languidly over the muscles, toward his navel. As Marketa moved closer and bent over Don Julius, she could see the tight muscles expand and contract with his breath. His belly glistened with beads of sweat. The droplets slid down his wet skin, one merging with the next into rivulets.

She did not know how long he had been touching her.

His forearms were bound, but this did not stop his long fingers from gently probing under her apron. She gasped. She did not look at him.

She did not move away.

He stroked between her thighs, smooth gentle movements within the range of his strong fingers. She sighed at the soft touch and blotted out the world and reason. For a second she thought where this was taking her, the risk, the folly. She did not care.

His fingers moved to a rhythm now, harder and more forceful, more direct in purpose.

She did not heed reason. She succumbed to the urge of her body, its power obliterating everything else. Marketa had never been touched in a seductive way before, never touched by fingers intent on giving her pleasure, only groped savagely.

Don Julius lifted his head and met her eyes. This time she didn't look away. The eyes of a sorcerer, she thought, as she stared back at him. The son of a king who could spin his spell while bound in ropes.

"Come to me, my angel," he whispered. His lips strained up toward her own, his fingers still prowling under her skirts, his fingertips rubbing against her moist flesh.

To her amazement, she was kissing him. His mouth was wet and his lips seemed to reach everywhere, searching for her tongue. He tasted of apples and fine wine. The king's son tasted of palaces and privilege, of possibility and love.

Of Prague.

The smell of his flesh intoxicated her. She felt her breast heaving as he kissed her neck.

"Untie me," he said.

She leaned over him, and he kissed her harder. The taste and pressure of his mouth made her feel weak, and she steadied herself with one hand on the chair.

"Marketa, untie me. I will give you pleasure you will never know with these country rubes," he said, biting her neck gently. "Just untie me, I will show you."

Her heart beat in her temples, and it was harder to breathe.

"I cannot."

She heard a low growl deep in his throat, as if it came from an animal and not a man.

"Come closer, my love, so I can feel your body close to mine."

Marketa bent her torso closer to his body. His skin was warm and smelled of a rich life, with no trace of a workman's dirt or toil. He smelled of fine milled soap and of foreign cologne, of royal privilege—of Prague.

"Straddle me, Marketa, so I can feel you close to me."

"No, I cannot," she whispered. "I cannot!"

"Untie me then," he whispered hoarsely in her ear. "Trust me."

Again that intoxicating scent that pulled her close, emanating from his breath and skin.

"I cannot. You are my patient, Don Julius."

Hurt registered in his eyes. He rolled his face away from her.

"I want to make love to you, not be pitied," he said, his voice muffled. "I want to prove to you, I—" his voice cracked.

She touched his cheekbones and tried to turn his face toward her. He resisted and her hands came away wet with tears.

"I want to show everyone—but most of all you!" His words were muffled into his shoulder. Marketa realized he was ashamed of his tears and struggled to keep them back.

She stroked his face and rubbed his shoulder. His back heaved with silent sobs.

"Hush now, hush," she said. She tried to slip her hand deeper behind his back, but the ropes left no room for soothing hands. She stroked his neck instead.

This was a boy, just a few years older than she. Yet sometimes he acted so much younger.

"Your hands remind me of my mother," he said. "I miss my mother. She writes that she cries every night for me."

Marketa worked her open palm down his back and pushed harder against the rope, feeling the tightness of the muscles between his shoulders. If she had a little more slack in the rope, she could knead them loose. He would feel comfort.

"My mother pleads with the king to release me. He will not listen to her."

The rope cut against Marketa's hand.

"But you," he said, now turning his face toward her. "You understand, I know you do. You are my guardian angel. Together we could defeat the demon voices—we would be invincible!"

This wretched knot, thought Marketa. She picked at the end of the rope to loosen it, just enough to—

Don Julius felt the easing of the rope and wiggled one shoulder loose. As fast as a snake, he worked his other shoulder free. Now he bent forward and wrenched his arms from the ropes.

He seized Marketa and covered her mouth in kisses.

"Do not scream, please do not!" he pleaded. "Let me, let me, I beg you. I will prove that you can trust me, let me!"

His legs were free now—how had that happened? She couldn't think. He cradled her in his arms and lowered her to the floor. He held her head in the crook of his elbow, and his tearstained face hovered over her.

"Shh, shh, hush now," he said, his lips brushing hers. "I only want to feel you in my arms. I will not hurt you—I could never hurt you."

As she lay quiet now in his arms, he drew back his head. His green eyes glistened above her, the black lashes still wet.

He stroked her face, and an errant tear dropped on her lips. He bent to kiss it from her mouth, and she closed her eyes, tasting the salt from his tear.

"You can trust me," he said, his lips moving over hers. "I told you I could be honorable. There is nothing else I want in this world."

He pulled her closer, and she could feel the warmth of his body. His hands moved over her breasts tentatively, gently.

"I want to make love to you," he said. "Now."

"No, I must—" she said, her mouth covered by his. "You must return to the chair. They will come in any moment!"

He groaned and pushed himself harder against her. She could feel his erection through her skirts.

"You must prove that I can trust you," said Marketa, struggling up, her breath catching in her throat. "Prove it! Prove that you are honorable! Prove it before it is too late!"

Don Julius clenched his eyes shut and pushed himself away like a wounded man. He crawled to his feet, and before Marketa could stand, he had already slipped his feet back into the loosened knots and pivoted his shoulder under the ropes.

"Tie me up," he said, his eyes open now, studying Marketa's face above him. "Tie me tight for I do not think I can withstand my passion otherwise."

Marketa tied the ropes tight against his flesh. His eyes drank in every movement she made, and his pulse quickened in his neck, making his flesh quiver.

"Tighter!" he urged. "Tighter still!"

Marketa pulled the ropes tighter, until they bit into his skin.

She straightened her blouse and kerchief. She felt a hot rush of blood flood her face, and she could not lift her eyes to meet his gaze.

She stepped away, her head still lowered.

"I do not know what came over me," she said, her hands at her temples. "I—I beg your pardon, my lord. I—"

"How can you say that? How can you deny what just happened between us?" His gasps had eased, and he studied her as his lust cooled. He snorted in derision and lay back in his chair, in exhaustion.

"What came over you is love, fair lady. Love for me. You love me!"

Marketa looked at the closed door. Her face colored a deep scarlet. How could she love a madman?

"Do not worry," he said, looking beyond her to the door. "Your secret is safe with me, my angel, if that is what you desire. And I have shown you the trust I merit. But I shall have you someday, I swear it."

A leech fell, finally gorged. Another hit the floor beside it.

"Come now, Marketa. Let us keep up the pretense. Pick up the leeches and straighten your hair, my dear. You want to look tidy and in control when they come in to see the results. You are my doctor, my darling."

She whirled around to look at him as he arched an eyebrow high. Was he mocking her? She needed to look in control, he said. Had she lost control and become as wild—as *mad*—as he was?

Once she had composed herself, Marketa called Doctor Mingonius and her father into the chamber, her hands holding a dozen gorged leeches.

Doctor Mingonius beamed at her, marveling at how much blood had been removed without a whisper of protest.

"Well now, Don Julius. How do you feel?"

"As if I have touched the heavens, kissed the stars, and fallen to earth. No, *crashed* to earth!"

Marketa turned away so that no one would see her blush. Her face throbbed, red-hot.

"Well, I want you to eat a bountiful meal and drink wine. You have to build up your strength."

"Yes. Yes, I am feeling hungry," he said, glancing at Marketa. "Some good country fare would appeal to me now. I think I have developed a taste for Bohemian delicacies."

Marketa turned to go. She had to keep herself from running out the door.

"Oh, Doctor. Would you mind if I thank Marketa in private for a second? You do not have to leave, just allow her to approach me," said Don Julius, nodding toward the girl. "Please do me this favor, good doctor."

"Of course," said Doctor Mingonius, rubbing his forehead again in wonder at these courteous words. *What a change in demeanor this bathmaid has produced in my patient*, he thought.

He speaks with such gentle humility to me, and such deference to the girl.

Marketa approached the prince, her back stiff and her cheeks still flushed hot.

"It is a marvelous thing to be out of control," Don Julius whispered, his voice hoarse. "Do not forget that. I await the moment when we can finish what we started, Marketa."

CHAPTER 29

BELVEDERE'S SPELL

The summer palace of Belvedere was adorned in snow and frost, its green-domed copper roof coated in sheets of ice. The singing fountain sang no song, but the cold winds played a shrill whistle of winter against its bronze basins. A sculpted shepherd stood atop the fount, piping silently, glistening with hoarfrost.

Jakub approached the arcades, contemplating the grace of the Italian arches.

Glorious Belvedere was the closest neighbor to his own modest house, a wooden cottage in the far reaches of the *hrad* gardens. His journey from a scullion boy sleeping on the floor in a Jesuit monastery to a resident within the royal palace gardens seemed a miracle, and Jakub said a quiet prayer every morning as he woke, grateful for the beauty of his surroundings.

It was cold and drafty inside the summer palace, but Rudolf was insistent on spending more and more time in his garden refuge, despite the season. Jakub was certain that even with all the hearths and ceramic stoves ablaze, the king with his poor circulation would be chilled and uncomfortable.

And irritable.

Jakub lifted his eyes to the copper dome where a glint of light sparkled, reflecting the sun. Tycho Brahe's observatory. Not only was Belvedere a royal residence, but the upper floors served as a platform to study the celestial heavens.

A guard stood before the filigreed portico. Jakub pulled down his woolen muffler to show his face. The guard nodded, and they walked to the west door and entered the palace. It was the first time Jakub had been invited to visit this royal retreat.

King Rudolf had moved many of his Kunstkammer treasures here. Jakub observed the collections of bezoar stones, said to have alchemic qualities—their strange mottled colors reflecting the bile of herbivorous animals in whose galls and intestines they had originally formed. Astrolabes, globes, clocks, quadrants, and mathematical instruments made of bronze and tin cluttered the corridors. A sculpture of Boreas, the north wind, abducting Orithyia, goddess of northern mountain winds, stood prominently in the great hall.

Jakub gazed about in wonder, turning slowly as he moved down the hall in a mesmerized waltz. The walls were packed, gilt frame jostling against gilt frame, portraits of naked gods entwined in passionate embrace. Dozens of seductions and ravishments illustrated with a leg slung over a lover's limb were displayed one after another: Venus and Adonis, Bacchus and Ceres, Hermaphroditus and Salmacis, and many others he could not recognize, despite his classical education at university.

He stared wide-eyed at the god Vulcan pressing a naked goddess to his pelvis, his legs tangled in the bedsheets. His fingers toyed with her nipples, and he watched as her face transformed in ecstasy.

Further on, there was Odysseus and Circe, Eros and Psyche, all who loved and lusted through the passionate brushstrokes.

Here and there, a lascivious Cupid spied on the lovers, grinning mischievously while dogs and other beasts looked on their coupling.

Despite the temptations of court life, Jakub had still remained chaste following the traditions of the Jesuit monastery, and now the sheer violence and passion of the art made his throat thicken and he swallowed hard. The erotica of Rudolf's art riveted his attention, and the guard let the king's visitor linger, gazing at the commingling of deities.

"Look at this one," whispered the guard. He inclined his head to a painting of Hercules and Omphale who were shown in reversed gender. Hercules wore a gauzy woman's shift and grudgingly twisted a spindle under the watchful eye of a dominant Omphale. The earth goddess bore a heavy club on her shoulder, flaunting her muscular buttocks and dimpled back to the viewer.

Jakub stared wide-eyed at the garish shades of pink, purple, and green and the glowing ivory flesh of the two near-naked lovers.

"'Tis to the king's taste," said the guard, raising an eyebrow. "The palace is full of these."

Jakub felt a quickening in his groin as he stared. He gritted his teeth and prayed fervently, determined to control himself.

A thought of Don Julius as a young boy shot through Jakub's mind. He had been raised surrounded by this art from the day he was born, the nude lovers looming over him even as a toddler learning to walk, speaking his first words. What influence had these violent seductions had on his childhood dreams and on his formative years?

The guard motioned Jakub to follow him from the cold hall to the audience room where a fire blazed in the hearth. The king sat in a high-backed wooden chair, swaddled in furs. Before him was a table laden with food: a fat roasted duck, a stewed pig's knuckle, pickled red cabbage, nuts, cake, ale, and wine.

"You may approach," nodded the king. "I asked the cooks to bring you food from our royal kitchens."

Even though the rich aromas of the roasted meat made his mouth water, Jakub bowed and politely refused.

"I could never eat before the king, Your Majesty. It would be wholly improper. Forgive me."

"As you wish, Physician," Rudolf said, moodily. "The servants will have it delivered to your house."

He motioned for the food to be removed, all but the bowl of assorted nuts.

"Sit, Horcicky, sit. What do you think of my art?" asked the king.

"It is quite impressive, Your Majesty," said Jakub diplomatically as he settled into a chair opposite the king. "I have never seen the like before."

"Which means with a strict Jesuit upbringing, you find it vulgar," said Rudolf, reaching for a nut on the table. He selected a walnut and handed it to his servant, who summarily cracked the shell and held it on a silver tray so that the king could pluck out its meat. "Pity. You probably judge it harshly, seeing only lascivious coupling. A tawdry display of copulation masquerading as art."

"Your Majesty," said Jakub, straightening, "I have been several years away from the monastery. I bathe in public baths and of course have seen naked women. I am no priest."

"Ah, Horcicky. The Jesuits' beliefs still haunt you. I can sense it. I see it in your rigid posture and the spark of moral judgment in your eyes—damnable Jesuit priggery has left a scar on you."

"I have left the monastery, Your Majesty. I am free to marry or conduct my life as I see fit, as long as I do so in honorable service to my king," said Jakub. He plucked at his collar, finding his neck intolerably hot and in need of airing. "I have no vows to the Church, Your Majesty."

"Complete and utter twaddle, Doctor! Have you enjoyed the intimate pleasures of a bathmaid or prostitute since you came to Prague?"

Jakub's face burned.

"I thought as much. You forget that I was raised seven years in the Spanish court and know the Jesuit order well. Their tentacles reach deep into one's soul and are not easily severed. And you who spent your entire childhood and young manhood with them..."

The king was silent a moment. He picked at his teeth with a fingernail to dislodge a bit of nutshell.

"Would it interest you to know that the art you saw in the great hall embodies a most significant premise of the esteemed Paracelsus?" said the king finally.

"Your Majesty?" said Jakub, genuinely shocked. "Paracelsus?"

"According to Paracelsus, we have the fixed and the volatile: the man and the woman, and, so too, mercury and sulfur. When they combine, it is the alchemical wedding bed and so ignites the process of purification and transformation."

Jakub thought back to the intensity of the couplings, how difficult it was to tell where Vulcan's thigh began as he pinned the goddess tight against his groin. The androgynous nature of Hermaphroditus and Salmacis had confused him. Why would the artist paint such an unsavory scene?

At least the amalgamation of the two elements mercury and sulfur provided a theoretical explanation. Still, the painting itself made Jakub pull at his collar, uncomfortable.

"Something to think about as you distill your plants and prepare your infusions," said the king. "Paracelsus lives in art and alchemy as well as medicine, Doctor Horcicky."

The king brushed the bits of nut and shell fragments from his hands, rubbing them together briskly.

"Well, enough about art. I have summoned you here to discuss your latest report from Krumlov. You say that your informant suggests a favorable change in my son?"

"Yes, Your Highness. It has been noted that he is now lean and fit from a strict diet and hunting stag in the mountains around Krumlov. He has longer periods of sanity and occasionally even shows courtesies to the bloodletters, Doctor Mingonius and Barber-Surgeon Pichler. He has even taken communion on occasion with the priest who attends him."

A smile tugged at the king's heavy lips.

"My boy, Giuglio. Ah, if he were cured, all blessings would be heaped upon the House of Hapsburg. There is nothing I would not do for him. Nothing! His mother cries and begs for his freedom."

Jakub's eyes flashed open wide.

"Your Highness, forgive me! I do not mean to insinuate that Don Julius is cured. Only that he does not lash out as he did in the beginning of his imprisonment."

The king's smile dissolved and a scowl etched his brow.

"Do not use the word 'imprisonment,' Horcicky. He is the Lord of Krumlov, and the moment he can function with dignity he shall govern accordingly. I mean to make him Lord of Transylvania someday soon."

Jakub thought of the politics of Hungary and Transylvania, of the rumors of Istvan Bocskai and his revolt against the Hapsburg rule, enlisting the Ottoman armies to fight against the Christian king. He said nothing. He had learned silence was a virtue from his days in the monastery.

Three black flies buzzed noisily overhead. They were flies of winter, crawling out sleepily from windowsill or rotting meat in the pantry. Turgid and fat, they lighted on the table, rubbing their greedy forelegs together, slowly and rhythmically.

Thud!

Jakub jumped as the king's hand smashed the insects into three dark smudges.

"Ha!" roared the king, pleased with himself. "You see my three enemies—the pope, my brother Matthias, and the Spanish king!"

"Your Majesty," said Jakub in wonderment. He was amazed at the king's disrespect in speaking of the pope. Everyone in Europe knew that Matthias sought to displace his unstable brother, but was there really a plot against Rudolf brewing in the Vatican?

As the king wiped his hands on a white serviette proffered by a servant, Jakub gazed up at the paneled ceilings painted as the celestial heavens with stars, planets, and the signs of the zodiac.

Mesmerized by alchemists, deities, and the celestial bodies, could the king be as mad as his son? Surely this melancholy man held no communion with the Christian God.

CHAPTER 30

DECEPTION AND DANGER

Marketa walked with her father to the bathhouse, her face still slightly flushed from Don Julius's kisses. She was silent, her eyes cast down upon the icy cobblestone road. Fortunately, her father suspected nothing.

"I could not be prouder of you than I am now, Daughter," said Pichler, putting an arm around her. It was a rare gesture of affection that she normally would have cherished. She could feel the warmth of his body even through the heavy wool coat.

Marketa swallowed and nodded. It was beginning to snow, and she pulled her shawl tight around her head and shoulders.

"You showed Doctor Mingonius, a court physician, that you and you alone could perform the bleeding. No wonder he wants to take you to Prague. What a special girl you are!"

The word "Prague" made her jump. Of course, the day after tomorrow she would be leaving for Prague, leaving the terrible Don Julius and his dangerous green eyes. Never would she be under his power again!

"I shall miss you, Marketa," he said, wiping his eyes. "You are my favorite, you know."

Marketa suddenly felt dirty, as filthy as the muddy water that sloshed in the leech bucket. If her father knew what she had done—what she almost had done—he would have cried out in shame. All her dreams of medicine, her noble ambition to be a physician or at least learn the skills of one, were a sham. She had almost allowed her patient to seduce her.

She had lost her head utterly and thoroughly to a lunatic.

"I shall miss you, too, Papa," she said. "But it is better if I go away."

"What a curious girl you are!" said Pichler, stopping and staring at her. Then he noticed her finger was bleeding into his hand.

"Oh, yes," she said, wiping her finger quickly. "I had to prick my finger and encourage the leech. I must have struck more deeply than I should have—it should have stopped bleeding by now."

The barber-surgeon's face beamed, so proud was he of his daughter's wit and skill at bloodletting.

That night, Marketa walked out of the bathhouse and onto the Lazebnicky Bridge, the Barber's Bridge. Her footsteps made the boards creak softly, nothing like the thunderous boom of the horses.

She looked up at the castle, to Don Julius's apartments. The chandelier was lit, and she could make out the constellation of candles that burned within. The dark water of the Vltava flowed below her, and the early stars above etched brilliance in the darkening December sky.

In two days, she would leave Cesky Krumlov to see the great capital of Prague. It really was to happen. She wished it would happen immediately and she could forget what had occurred earlier in the day.

She turned and faced north, thinking of Prague and Doctor Horcicky—no, not "Doctor Horcicky," she thought of "Jakub" who had written to her, who had trusted her, who had kissed her. What would he think when he heard that she was in the city as Doctor Mingonius's guest? Would she ever be able to confide to him her secret of having been the one who truly treated the king's son, or would sharing such a confidence be too perilous?

She heard a whistle above her and looked up.

Don Julius was standing at his window, looking down at her. He pointed up to the emerging stars.

Then he opened his arms wide, beckoning to her to come.

A shiver ran down her spine. She remembered another time that she had seen someone—a white apparition that had beckoned her.

"Marketa!" rang out a voice. It was the voice of her mother. "Marketa! Do not stand in the cold like a fool! I've been looking for you." Then she too looked up, squinting, and saw him.

"Is he calling to you?" she whispered eagerly. "Your young eyes can see better than mine. Is that the Hapsburg prince?"

A wild laugh echoed across the river, and Don Julius retreated within the castle.

"He was! He was calling to my Marketa."

"Mother, *please!*"

"No. Listen!" Lucie said, pulling Marketa's arm so the girl swung around and faced her. "Do not be selfish! Do you know what a liaison with the king's son could do for our family? Think of the twins growing old hauling water for the baths. Think of your reluctance to marry any of the town's boys. Do you really think, Marketa Pichlerova, that you could do better than a Hapsburg?"

Marketa dropped her eyes to the cobblestones.

"Has he made any amorous gesture to you?"

Marketa blushed and turned away.

"He has, hasn't he! Well, missy, you cannot always think of yourself. If the prince has given you any indication of interest, you must reciprocate."

"He is mad, Mother," she whispered. "He is a madman!"

"He is a Hapsburg!" she said, shaking Marketa hard. "A Hapsburg who could change the very course of our lives forever. Who are you to deny us that!"

Her mother's strong fingers dug into her arms.

"Do not disappoint us, Marketa. We have been good to you! I have indulged your time away from the bathhouse to work with your father. My back cannot take many more years of lifting buckets."

Marketa's face crumpled in anguish. She knew that her mother's hard work and sweat in the bathhouse offset her father's excesses in buying books and making trips to Vienna. It was she who made sure the family was fed and clothed.

"Can you not find a woman's heart to give a man the love he craves?" whispered her mother. "Maybe your love and trust would provide the cure he needs. Surely God would punish you for not giving him that chance."

Marketa looked back toward the castle. She remembered his lips and the rich pleasure of his smell and taste. A quick shiver shook her body. From somewhere, the thought of Jakub Horcicky arose again. She saw his face—was he warning her or welcoming her? She forced his image out of her mind. Don Julius wanted her. That she knew for certain.

And Jakub's letters were mostly filled with news of Prague and science. Not one single personal word. Not even a hint. Was the imperial chemist only using her as an informant to the king? She thought of his gentle kiss, his touch on her throat as he tied the scarf. It had been so long ago.

Her mother watched her carefully, and a slow smile rose to her lips.

"The prince is a far better catch than the brewer, is he not?"

Marketa sought out her mother's eyes in the darkness. There would always be the brewer and his groping hands, waiting for her.

"Come, Daughter, make us proud. I have a plan," said her mother. "You shall capture a Hapsburg's heart."

An hour later, Marketa emerged from her hot bath, smelling of lavender and rosemary. Her mother had dressed her in the new white blouse the seamstress had made for her trip to Prague. She wore a new blue skirt and a pretty red vest, and her mother tucked lemon verbena in her camisole.

"There. Now go up and deliver these cakes to him," she said, handing her a basket lined in a checked cloth.

"But—Mother! I am not allowed alone with him unless Doctor Mingonius is just outside the door."

Pani Pichlerova hurried Marketa out the door. "Your Doctor Mingonius is at Uncle Radek's tavern, drinking his fill. I just saw him there when I delivered Radek's dinner."

"The guards will not let me past them unaccompanied. It is impossible!"

"You are a shrewd girl. Find a way. Do not disappoint me," Lucie said, her eyes taking a hard edge. "And if you do not come back tonight, I will understand. Think of our family. I shall dream of you and the king's son."

With that she gave her eldest daughter a kiss on the forehead and a hasty shove out the door.

Was it fierce loyalty to her family that urged Marketa to do her mother's bidding? Or was it the full moon over Krumlov, the memory of Don Julius's soft lips and playful bites, the smell of fine Italian perfume mixed with sweat, the taste of good wine and sweet cakes on his breath? There was not anyone in Cesky Krumlov who could ever smell like that, taste like that…touch or kiss like that. Ever.

Without knowing how it had happened, she realized that she longed to be out of control with him, to feel the surging tide of pleasure carry her away, like a twig pulled out to sea.

She knew it was wrong. She knew it was impossible. And yet she knew she wanted it to happen.

And she knew that her mother did too.

When she knocked at the castle gates, the sentry Chaloupka was surprised to see her.

"You are working late," he said. "Doctor Mingonius is not in."

"No matter. I am just bringing some cakes to Don Julius that my mother baked."

The sentry's face revealed his hatred of the son of the king. He sniffed crookedly as if there were a foul smell in the air.

"He is the devil, *slecna*. I know you assist your good father in bloodletting, but if you know what is good for you, Marketa, you will stay away from that monster."

He opened the gates and called to a page.

"Escort Slecna Marketa within and see that she is greeted by the housekeeper, Slecna Viera."

The boy bowed to her. He was the greengrocer's youngest son. His shoes were too big for him and his tunic was too small. His skinny white forearms dangled far below the sleeve cuffs.

"Hello, Wilhelm," she said. She reached in her basket and pulled out a cake.

"Thank you, Marketa," he said, his eager hands reaching for the treat. He stuffed a piece of cake in his mouth, chewing as they walked. His tongue rolled around his mouth in pleasure, for Lucie Pichlerova's baking was as fine as anyone's in Krumlov.

They walked together to the courtyard, and Marketa looked up.

She froze stock-still, and Wilhelm had taken three paces before he realized she was left behind.

"Are you all right, Slecna Marketa?" he said, wiping the crumbs from his mouth with his sleeve. "What is it?"

Marketa's eyes opened wide, and the moonlight played upon them.

"Do you see her?" she asked the boy.

"See what?"

"Look—"

Marketa turned the boy around with her hands and pointed to the second story of the castle. There in front of them Marketa saw a woman dressed in white, her hands and arms obscured by long black gloves. She was lit by a faint light that seemed to emanate from her flowing gown and followed her like a shadow.

"I—I do not see anything, Slecna Marketa. Nothing!"

The woman disappeared down the hall, and the light faded away.

A shiver overtook Marketa. What was happening to her? She was desperate to see a madman and feel his kisses. She had just seen a spirit.

What of her dreams of Prague and the great reason of science?

"Wilhelm, would you do me a great favor? And I will give you another cake."

"Anything, Slecna Marketa."

"Do not announce my presence to anyone. I want to deliver these cakes to Don Julius's door myself. I do not want anyone to spoil the surprise."

"But Pan Chaloupka said—"

"I know. But he does not know it is Don Julius's birthday. I do not want anyone to know but you. And no one to spoil the surprise, all right?"

"Well, all right," he said, his toe digging at a loose cobblestone.

"I will not tell anyone, so do not worry that you will get into any trouble, Wilhelm. It's a surprise, you see."

Wilhelm's face brightened a bit. Marketa was sharing a secret with him and no one else. He had always had a crush on the pretty girl of the bathhouse.

"Here, we will go in the servants' entrance," he told her. "You can go up the stairs, or if you really want to surprise him, you could use the pulley platform."

"The what?"

"There is a platform to haul up food from the kitchen. The guards upstairs take the trays directly to Don Julius's table so the food remains hot."

"How ingenious."

"They say it was built for Wilhelm von Rozmberk so he could eat in his apartments. He hated cold food and would punish the cook and servants if his meal wasn't hot from the oven."

He looked over his shoulder to check again if anyone was listening.

"The other boys and I have played there when Don Julius is out in the courtyard for air or on a hunt. We pull each other up and down, riding on the platform."

Suddenly his face tightened in distress. He had said too much.

"You will not tell anyone, will you, Slecna Marketa? They will whip me and the other boys if they find out! I will lose my position!"

Marketa smiled at the thought of the young boys of Cesky Krumlov playing games in Rozmberk Castle.

"Of course not, Wilhelm. We will keep each other's secrets."

Marketa insisted that she wanted to deliver the sugar cakes properly, to Don Julius's door, flanked by the guards. It was part of the trust she was building with him.

Wilhelm showed her through the servants' door and pointed to the wooden staircase that led up to second floor. His face was smeared white in sugar, and he licked his fingers in happiness, accepting a kiss on his cheek from Marketa.

The guards, alert to even her quiet steps on the stairs, met her at the top of the staircase.

"Slecna Marketa! Are you looking for your father? He is not here."

"No, no. I am to finish a treatment on Don Julius. It is part of the trust Mingonius speaks about. You are to bind him and I will feed him cakes, to show friendship and goodwill."

The guard looked at her, astonished.

"Doctor Mingonius said nothing to me about this. I—"

"It must have slipped his mind. He said to make sure I told you to tie the patient tightly, so there is no chance of him leaping for me or hurting me in any way. Just in the manner you did earlier today."

The guard rubbed his hand over his face and then gestured with his torch for her to follow. He spoke to the second guard. Then they both bowed to Marketa and entered the room. She waited in the hall.

She could hear a laugh beyond the great oak door, and then a murmur of pleasant words. She smiled, thinking of the change that had slowly come about in Don Julius in the past few weeks, the—

Down the hall she saw a sweep of white. It was her!

The ghost looked down the corridor at Marketa, beckoning to her with black gloves. What did she want?

The guards emerged from the door suddenly, before Marketa could respond to the specter's demanding gesture.

"He was amenable," they said, looking puzzled at Marketa's wild-eyed stare. "Perhaps today's bleeding has calmed him. He held his arms out to be bound, as meekly as a child."

"Thank you," Marketa said, and she held her hand up to warn them not to follow.

"I will cry out if I need any help," she said, shutting the door behind her.

She breathed deeply to steady herself. The room smelled of beeswax and polish. The aroma of roast mutton and the tannic smell of red wine laced the air. The room danced in the flickering light of the tapers. Don Julius sat tied in the bleeding chair as he had just hours before. His face was illuminated in the candlelight.

"Welcome, Marketa. To what do I owe the honor of this evening visit?"

Suddenly Marketa was speechless. She wondered if she really knew why she was here. Because her mother wanted her to take a Hapsburg as a lover? Because she wanted to tell him that she was leaving for Prague in two days? Because she wanted to apologize for what had happened this morning? Because—she remembered the taste of his kisses?

"I—I have brought you some cakes my mother made this morning."

Don Julius laughed again.

"Cakes? Ah country cakes, fresh and moist, like a certain young woman of Cesky Krumlov. Did I tell you I thought I tasted sugar on your lips this morning?"

"Shhh!" said Marketa, looking at the door.

"Oh, your secret is safe. They cannot hear unless you shout. But come closer. Then we can whisper."

Marketa settled in a chair close, but not too close.

"Come now, Marketa. How can you feed me those cakes if you sit so far away? Look, I am bound. I cannot harm you."

Marketa pulled her chair closer, causing it to screech across the floor. The sound unnerved her. She could smell the wine on his breath. He must have been drinking heavily.

"Now be a good girl and feed me a cake," he said, his eyes glittering in the candlelight. They were the color of the Vltava on a cloudy day, dark green and forbidding, but mysteriously beautiful.

She reached into the basket and pulled out a cake. She leaned over and suspended it in the air.

"I do not want you to choke," she said. She broke off a small piece of the cake and reached it out toward his mouth. He snapped at it, and she pulled back in horror.

He laughed at her. "You still do not trust me, do you, my angel? Come, feed me again and I will be good. I swear to you."

This time he took the morsel of sweet cake and rolled it over in his mouth, his tongue flicking out to sweep the bits of sugar and flour from his lips. His eyelids flickered and he seemed to be in a trance, all but the gentle smacking and savoring of the cake.

"She is a good cook, my mother," stammered Marketa. "My uncle Radek says she is the best cook in Cesky Krumlov."

"I do not care about your mother's cooking," he said, opening his eyes at last. The deep pools of green glittered up at her, urging her. He was the most handsome man she had ever seen.

"I do not care about any other woman on this earth but you."

Marketa found herself staring into his eyes. She blinked and looked away.

"Why do you say I am the woman from your book?" she asked. "You must know I am flesh and bone, a common Bohemian bathmaid."

"A bathmaid, yes. And you are certainly that in the book. But common—no, never! You are the angel sent to save me."

"No, my lord, there is no magic in me," she said, looking down at the crimson rug. "I am a poor girl from Krumlov. You want too much of me, to be some fantastic creature who can cure you, protect you. I can do none of this."

"You think you cannot, but what do you know of my mind, Marketa? You have always been with me since I was a child, whether you know it or not. There are some things we cannot know. You asked me if I believed in God and I said no. But I do believe in a spiritual world that is far beyond our comprehension; I believe that what you call 'coincidences' are reminders from the other world."

Marketa grasped the edge of the table, slightly dizzy. She was not used to this kind of talk. He spoke almost like a priest of an invisible world, one she could not see or touch.

"Do you not think that these are fantasies of a diseased mind?" she said.

Don Julius did not answer her right away. He stared beyond her. Finally he said, "Fantasies? Call them dreams, if you like. But the coincidence, Marketa, this is what we must seize upon! You are a bathmaid. The bathmaid in the book comforted me as a child. Now you are here and you are the only one who can comfort me. There is a message here from the spiritual world. Events that arrive cloaked in mystery—we as mortals can only wonder, 'What is this?' What a strange coincidence, a bathmaid in a magic book, a bathmaid in Krumlov. A simple twist of fate, nothing more than happenstance, we laugh. We are fools—no!— we are *cowards* not to recognize the presence of the Other World. We ignore the divine message in our mundane lives, paying no heed to the heaven-sent tidings, worrying instead whether we shall have a boiled turnip with our midday meal."

His eyes gleamed with fervor. She noticed beads of sweat on his upper lip.

"I choose to recognize the message," he said. "You are my savior—the only being on earth who can help me."

She approached him cautiously, hardly daring to breathe. She could barely follow his words, but he spoke to her of God and the meaning of life. She thought of her fate with the brewer in the months to come, how he would brutally take her virginity, his sour breath in her face, his old stubby fingers prowling her body.

And here was a Hapsburg who talked of the sublime.

"Do you truly believe I am a messenger from the heavens?" she whispered. "That I am something other than a bathmaid from Krumlov?"

"Come here to me, my angel."

Marketa lost herself in his eyes. She leaned down and met his lips with hers. All the sensations she had felt that morning came flooding back to her, and she cradled his aristocratic face in her hands. It was so finely chiseled, as if she were holding a classical sculpture.

His body surged toward her, straining at the ropes.

"Release me, Marketa," he whispered, his lips still wet against hers. "Did you bring your bloodletting knife to cut the ropes?"

She nodded, pulling her lips away from his mouth.

"I knew you would. I knew you loved me," he said, his eyes shining. "I have never doubted you."

Marketa reached in the pocket of her apron and flicked open her fleam. She severed the ropes that restrained his hands—and those hands suddenly, fiercely pulled her down on top of him, pressing her face, her throat, her breast against him with such force, it took her breath away.

"Cut me loose, all of me!" he whispered to her, his words urgent and hot in her ear.

She quickly cut through the ropes, and while she was still trying to finish the last strand on his ankle, he tore free and placed his hand over her mouth. The fleam dropped to the floor with a clatter.

In a second, he had sprung to his feet, and his arms enveloped her, pressing her body tight to his.

"You! Yes, you are my angel. Should any man touch you or offend you, I will kill him. I swear I shall!"

He held her close to his breast, to his thumping heart, and stroked her brindled hair. "I knew I could trust you," he whispered in her ear. "You have proved to be who I always knew you were. My angel!"

He knelt now at her feet, clasping her knees.

"You defeat the demons who assail me. They cannot approach when they hear the sound of your voice."

Marketa stood motionless with the young prince at her feet. Then she dropped to her knees.

"You ask too much of me, Don Julius. I will stand with you against your demons, but I fear I have not the power you see in me."

Don Julius lifted his hand to her cheek and pushed back a strand of her hair. "You cannot know what power you wield, for you are in mortal form. You must remain humble, modest as you are. Your innocence of the dark world is your force."

His words made little sense to her, but she heard this Hapsburg prince say that he worshipped her, he believed in her strength. She thought of the stinking bodies in the bathhouse. She thought of the brewer. A shiver of repugnance shook her spine.

He took her hand and drew a picture with his fingertip into her palm. Marketa found it curious that he should cease his adoration and lovemaking so abruptly and play such a childish game. His touch on the flat of her hand began as a tickling light pressure, a series of squiggles. Then she winced as the point of his finger drove harder into skin.

"What is that, my lord?"

"It is an illustration from the Coded Book," he laughed, his eyes wide in excitement. "Tell me which one."

"How could I know when I have never seen this strange book?"

"Do not mock me," said Don Julius, his voice terse. "Tell me!"

"I have not the knowledge, my lord. Is it a squirrel?"

"A squirrel! You do mock me, you imp. Tell me! You know!"

Marketa felt him squeeze her hand harder now, bending it closed like a clamshell. A pulsing vein grew prominent, throbbing in the center of his forehead.

"You know what it is!"

"I do not!"

"It is the Turkish bathhouse, the tiled arched roof of a harem. You are there, among the others."

He stopped abruptly, his eyes widening as if he had seen some horror. Then his eyes narrowed to angry slits in his face.

"You—you whore! You are standing among them in the green water—waiting your turn for the sultan to take you!"

"Of what do you speak! What sultan? What green water?" Marketa cried. He was hurting her. "Let go of my hand—I pray of you!"

He seized her by her shoulders and shook her until her head rocked.

"You betray me!"

He dragged her to his bed, his voice a hoarse whisper. "You whore! You shall not be his or anyone else's but mine!"

He threw her down on the bed and buried his face in her throat and bosom. He was everywhere on her body at once. His kisses licked her and then he began to bite, and bite hard at her breasts.

"Ouch! You are hurting me! Don Julius!" she said, stifling a scream.

He flattened his hand over her mouth.

"Silence!" he said, cold anger in his voice. "You will spoil everything."

He pulled her skirt and petticoat up over her head and tore at her undergarment.

"Don Julius! No! No!"

This was not the lovemaking she had envisioned.

She felt a hard thrust between her thighs.

"No!" she cried. There was no response but a panting, the panting of an animal.

There was a rough, searing pain between her legs. She felt her tender flesh being torn.

She twisted and rolled her hips to the side, pulled at his shoulders and arms to loosen his grip. He only bore down more violently, making a growling sound deep in his throat.

"Give me the secret to the Coded Book!" he gasped in her ear. "You bitch of the Netherworld, give me the answers!"

"I do not know!" she cried. "I swear it."

"You *shall* give me the code!" he said, driving himself into her harder and deeper. "How do you quiet the voices? Tell me!"

Marketa whimpered in pain, and she stared up into his eyes glinting in madness and fury. He bit her neck hard, pulled her back close to him. All she could hear were his gasps, rough and surging in her ears.

She shut her eyes tight, refusing to look at the beast who raped her.

Within minutes he shuddered above her. Was this was what her mother had wanted for her? Now she had had a Hapsburg between her legs. She felt nothing but pain and emptiness. And terror.

Don Julius rolled off her, breathing hard. She smelled something rancid on his breath.

She felt hot tears streaming down her face. She watched his eyes lose their mad gaze, the muscles in his forehead relax, the throbbing vein in his temple retreat until it was only a faint green-blue line.

He lifted himself up and looked into her face, studying it with bewildered eyes.

"Why—why are you crying?"

"I—I did not want this to happen. Not like this."

"You untied me!"

"I thought—the lovemaking you promised."

Don Julius rubbed her tears away with his fingertips.

"I am deeply and forever in love with you. Is that not enough?"

Marketa thought, *No! No, it is not enough.*

This was the lovemaking he had in mind. Warm blood stained the sheets, a souvenir of his violence.

She stared at him.

"I came to tell you something," she said. Blind fury surged up from a place deep inside her; she wanted to hurt him. Hurt him and pierce his heart, just as he had ravaged hers. She felt foolish. Beyond foolish. She had believed in love, that she was his angel. He had raped her.

"Tell me what?"

She spat the words in his face.

"I am leaving for Prague. I never want to see you again in my life! And I shall tell them what you have done to me!"

There was a great gulf of silence, a terrifying silence, as if a violent summer storm approached.

"What—*what* did you say?"

"I am going to Prague with Doctor Mingonius—"

He slapped her in the face hard with an open palm. The demon was returning; she could smell the sulfur growing stronger.

There was a blackness tinged in yellow and blue; she could see only fragments of the room around her, floating in the dark swirl of color. She could hear his voice rage.

"You would desert me now? You—the only one who can make the voices cease! I need you! I love you!"

She screamed for help.

"Silence!" He cupped his hand over her mouth. "You would betray me to my enemies?" He looked at the door. "Leave me at the mercy of the voices? You are not going anywhere with anyone! You have just made love with a Hapsburg, and now you are mine! You will never leave this room again without me. Do you hear me? Never!"

He pushed her away, and she stumbled across the room.

"I will not have a bathhouse whore make a fool out of me!" he said, coming after her again, his mouth flecked with spittle.

Marketa's hands covered her face to protect her from more blows. She felt a violent movement and heard a heavy thud as one of the guards threw Don Julius to the floor.

"What happened!" the guard said, not comprehending. "Slecna Marketa, are you all right?"

"Look, Marketa! See what you have done!" cried Don Julius. "It was our secret."

"Seize him," said one guard.

Through the curtain of darkness, she could make out movement below her. Don Julius was searching frantically for something on the floor.

"The fleam!" she shouted as a form rose up behind the guard.

It was too late. Don Julius had sliced the guard's ear with the fleam and seized Marketa again.

He looked into her eyes, searching desperately.

"Marketa! Do not leave me!"

She tried to struggle free. His eyes were wild, frantic, and he screamed again.

"Can you feel their wings brush your face, their claws at your breast? Do not let them enter your heart!"

Still holding her tightly, he slashed at the invisible demons. The blade caught just in front of her ear and sliced up across the top of her cheek and into her scalp.

"Away! Leave her in peace!" Don Julius ranted. "It is me you want, you devils!"

The tip of the flailing knife cut into her breast and she stumbled back, falling to the floor.

The second guard clubbed Don Julius with a cudgel, stunning him temporarily. He stumbled a few steps and knelt to the floor, the fleam still in his hand.

The guard helped the bleeding Marketa to her feet. "Are you all right, *slecna*?"

Don Julius jerked her away, sending her reeling toward the wall and the open window.

Don Julius roared, coming at her with the bloodletting knife.

"I will protect you! No demons shall touch my angel!"

"No, Julius! No!"

She backed up against the window, raising her hands, trying to protect her face.

"Cease, Don Julius!" shouted a voice. It was Doctor Mingonius. There was a quick scuffle and the smell of Don Julius's wine-sour breath in her face. She jumped back and suddenly the night air flooded her senses, cold and dark, the wind rushing in her ears.

As Marketa fell, she screamed. It was not a loud scream. Only she could hear it. She had nothing left to say to the world.

PART II

After the Fall

CHAPTER 31

A MIDNIGHT DEPARTURE

"Marketa! Marketa!"

What voice was this? She knew she was dead. But then, how could she still feel pain? Every part of her body screamed in pain. She could not breathe. Her chest felt as if it had collapsed.

"Dear girl, Marketa. Speak to me!"

She opened her eyes and saw the face of Doctor Mingonius floating before her eyes.

Then a stench filled her nostrils, and what little air she had in her lungs was forced out in a burst of coughing. She felt something heavy and furry run over her leg.

"You have fallen on the rubbish heap," said Mingonius. "Just lie still, try to breathe."

Long minutes passed. Doctor Mingonius willed her to breathe, whispering encouragement in her ear as he knelt beside her in the stinking heap. He placed her hand over her chest so she could feel the rise and fall of each aching gasp.

Dazed, she looked at him, hovering just above her. Blood was still running down her face from the slash to her cheek and scalp.

When he at last helped her to her feet, she saw her new white blouse was soaked red from the cut on her breast.

"I tried to trust him," she said and fell again to her hands and knees and began to sob. She could smell the spoiled food of the kitchen and the human waste of the castle, slimy and putrid under her hands. The stench assailed her as she tried desperately to breathe.

God had condemned her to hell before her spirit had even left the earth.

The doctor knelt beside her and drew her into his arms. She convulsed in sobs.

"You can never trust a madman," he said. "Never. But I blame myself for this. I never should have let you treat him. I was worried about my reputation, my failure as a physician. And now look. All this sorrow is of my creation."

"No, I wanted to cure him. I thought I had. I thought—"

"That your patient could love you. That is my fault, too. I have failed your family, and I have failed the king. But most of all, I have failed you, Marketa. Let's get you up and take you back to the bathhouse where your mother can care for you—"

"No! I never want to see my mother again! This was her idea—she thought I could be his mistress and she would never have to work again."

Mingonius didn't say anything for a few minutes.

"Do you still want to leave with me, Marketa?" he said in the darkness.

She turned and lifted her face toward him as far as the pain would allow.

"I want nothing more in this world than to go to Prague."

Doctor Mingonius looked up at the moon, blinking back tears as the first snowflakes of the winter hit his eyes.

"Marketa, I cannot take you to Prague. Especially now. We must find safe haven for you. You need care—you are badly hurt."

"I—I must go to Prague! I need to escape him."

"Shh! Shh!" said Mingonius, stroking her hair.

He looked up to the window, the torches still burning bright. He could hear the howls of Don Julius within the castle.

"Do not talk, *slecna*. Rest. We will talk later of Prague."

They rested there in silence a while longer until, at last, Doctor Mingonius thought he could move her safely, and he pulled her gently to her knees and then to her feet. He was relieved to see that she could walk or, at least, limp with his help. Once they were back in the castle, in his apartments, he ordered Viera, the housekeeper, to bathe Marketa and clothe her in some of Viera's own garments.

He spoke to the guards, swearing them to secrecy, lest the priest learn what had transpired during the night. For their part, they were terrified of being assigned the blame for what had happened to Marketa and eagerly swore an oath of secrecy.

"We must make him think she is dead," said Doctor Mingonius. "And it is only by the grace of God she is not."

～

It was two hours past midnight when the coach was brought round. The clatter of iron horseshoes on the cobblestone shattered the dark silence, striking sparks in the courtyard. The wild-eyed horses, snorting great puffs of white vapor into the cold air, gave urgency to the departure. The trunks were hastily lashed to the back of the coach, and two guards carried Marketa out. Doctor Mingonius and the servant Viera helped settle the girl into the velvet seat.

The road was snowy and rutted. The carriage rocked and jumped, jostling the passengers like dice shaken in a gambler's hand.

Marketa's face throbbed from being battered by Don Julius. There were sharp, searing pains from the blade wounds. But for the most part, the shock numbed her gashes and bruises. Soon she felt nothing but the deep aching pain in her head.

Doctor Mingonius had given her a potion to calm her, and despite the rough, jarring ride in the carriage, she found herself falling asleep.

When she opened her eyes again, sunlight was streaming in through the open curtains of the carriage. She saw the hard frozen ponds of the Rozmberks, where fat carp slumbered in the deep, cold water. Soon they would be harvested for Christmas dinners and sold throughout Bohemia, for what good Christian mortal would not feast on the white flesh of that fish in honor of the holy day?

Her eyes were heavy with sleep, and her face throbbed rhythmically like the beat of a drum. Doctor Mingonius, seeing that she was awake, steadied himself beside her in the rocking carriage. His fingers inspected the knife wounds that he had stitched up before they left Rozmberk Castle. They had already begun to pucker a bit and ooze, but the work had been done with a steady hand and he thought it would hold together, God willing, and heal.

He smiled gently at her.

"We will stop in Cesky Budejovice," he said. "There is a good little inn, clean and simple. I've sent a rider ahead to notify the innkeeper of our coming. His wife is a good cook."

He looked at her, worry etching his face. "You do like brook trout, Marketa? Fresh from the river?"

Marketa tried to smile, but when her skin stretched across her wound, she winced.

"It will take time to heal, Marketa. Viera will take good care of you."

Viera smiled and reached over to clasp her hand gently.

"You have gone through too much in that wretched little village."

Marketa wondered through her haze just how much Viera knew. She looked at her warily, but saw the woman's kindness shining in her soft blue eyes.

"You will love Prague. There is no city like it in the world. You will see!" Viera squeezed her hand. "A world of reason, medicine, and science," she said, stealing a quick look at Doctor Mingonius. "The finest artists, astronomers, and poets. You shall see. You will never want to return to Cesky Krumlov again!"

Doctor Mingonius put a finger to his lips.

"Enough, *slecna*. Marketa is too ill to go to Prague now. Budejovice will have to do."

Slecna Viera looked crestfallen and stroked Marketa's damp, blood-crusted hair.

Marketa closed her eyes against the pain. When she woke again the carriage had rolled to a stop in Cesky Budejovice and it was late afternoon, less than a day after she had walked through the heavy wooden door, into the madman's chamber.

CHAPTER 32

CESKY BUDEJOVICE

Marketa's eyes were swollen nearly shut, yet the chance to see Budejovice made them widen enough to glimpse through a squint that made her wince in pain. She could not help herself. This was the first town she had ever seen other than Krumlov. It seemed another world, full of movement and life.

The coach had pulled up in the main square, colorful as Krumlov but immense. The houses rose in peaked roofs, crowded tight around the square. It was alive with people—boys carrying buckets of water from the nearby river, Bohemians selling hemp bags and casks of salt to rich foreigners in fine clothes, men driving long wagons stacked with beer kegs. In market stalls, men and women were selling squawking hens, root vegetables, secondhand woolens. Packed down by the march of feet, the snow had become a gray sheet of ice.

Steam rose from the backs of the coach horses, and they snorted onto the cobblestones. The trio had traveled many hours at a fast pace to reach Budejovice before dusk.

Viera and the doctor helped Marketa descend from the coach into the strong arms of the innkeeper and driver. "She is in bad condition," said the beefy innkeeper. He spoke German with a fluency that indicated it was his native language, not Czech. "My wife can tend her, if you like."

"Thank you for your kindness," said Doctor Mingonius. "Fräulein Viera will care for her and sleep in the bed by her side."

Marketa was unsteady and thankful for the support of the two men, who helped her limp into the warm inn. There was a crackling fire in the main room and diners eating at long tables. The yeasty smell of good beer and roasting meats on the fire made her stomach tighten and complain with hunger. She had not eaten in almost two days.

The innkeeper's wife saw Marketa's face and gasped, her hand flying to her mouth. She stopped serving beer to her customers, set down the pitcher, and wiped her hands on her apron.

"What in God's holy name happened to her?" she asked. "Was she in an accident? Are those knife wounds?"

Marketa groaned and touched her swollen, battered face—was it so hideous to everyone?

"You ask too many questions, Wife," grumbled the innkeeper. He picked up the girl from Krumlov in his arms in one sweeping motion, like a bridegroom carrying his bride across the threshold.

"She shall have the best room in the inn, toward the back, where it is quiet and she will not be disturbed. The linen has just been washed and the mattress stuffed with fresh straw, as you requested, Herr Mingonius."

Minutes later Marketa was in a room with homespun red curtains across a shuttered window, a large straw bed, and a goose down pillow. The coverlet was quilted of colored squares, some of material that was familiar and others dyed in colors Marketa had never seen in Krumlov. In the corner was a little table and stool where a ceramic basin stood beside a pitcher of water.

Viera helped Marketa remove her shoes and stockings and pull off the woolen dress. She lay down in her shift on the fresh straw mattress, her back, neck, and limbs as stiff as frozen branches on the trees of winter. When Marketa had been under the spell of the medicine the doctor had given her, she had slept in a contorted position and felt nothing. Now she was acutely aware of the constant pain in her battered body.

She cried into the linen ticking while Viera tried to soothe her. Marketa's tears wet the bedclothes, making the material translucent, exposing the yellow blades of straw. The fresh-made bed smelled of autumn fields and made her drowsy.

When Marketa was tucked under the comforter, Doctor Mingonius came in to inspect her wounds. She could tell by his worried face that he did not like the look of the throbbing gashes. She ran her fingers over the stitches in her cheek and winced. She wondered if they looked the same as the one on her breast, angry red puckers between the black thread stitches.

"Do not touch them, Marketa," said the doctor. "Sit up, *milacek*."

She smiled weakly as he called her *dear* in Czech.

"Good. You need to drink beer—a lot of beer and water from the jug. And I will send for some soup. I want you to try to finish it all. The beer will induce sleep and help you heal. The hops give rich nourishment, and with rest, your body will take care of itself."

The innkeeper's wife brought in herbs that she swore reduced swelling and brewed an infusion for Marketa. She called it Mountain Daisy and told the girl she kept stalks drying in the kitchen, along with other wildflowers and herbs that hung from the rafters. Viera prepared a poultice of the leaves and dabbed the paste on her wounds.

Doctor Mingonius inspected the plant and crumbled the leaves and flowers between his fingers, sniffing it, and then taking a lick.

Then he nodded his approval. "Arnica," he pronounced. "Yes, this and beer will help you heal. We will stay here in Budejovice until you are well enough."

With that the weary doctor bid Marketa good night and left her in the care of the women.

~

They told her she slept for three days. Even after she awoke, everything was still muddled and vague as a dream. Steins of beer were brought to her lips. She ate broths of beef bones and barley soup flavored with dried marjoram. The innkeeper's wife spooned beef marrow into her mouth between sips of arnica tea. Marketa drank in the smell of her hair—perfumed with the smoke of the wood fire and the essence of roasted poultry. The woman's hands were red and cracked from washing dishes all day in her stone sink, but they were moist and soft on Marketa's forehead. She stroked her skin as she would a favorite cat, and the girl fell asleep again under the spell of her touch.

Besides these soothing moments and Marketa's struggle using the chamber pot—for her torn flesh still stung when she urinated—she remembered nothing. It was warm under the quilts, and she sensed the warmth of Viera's body at night.

At last, one morning, Marketa opened her eyes and realized the swelling had diminished. She looked around the room and saw a stub of a tallow candle, rosary beads, and a pitcher of beer sitting on a rough-hewn table. There were thick fingers of frost around the cracks in the shuttered window. The water in the bucket beside her bed was frozen, an uneven crust of chipped ice revealing the depression where Viera had been dipping the cup.

"You are awake!" said Viera, entering the room with an empty chamber pot in her hands. "We have been so worried about you, so worried, *milacek*!"

Marketa pulled herself up to a sitting position and shivered. The cold made her teeth ache.

"Here, you must put a shawl on," Viera said, rummaging through her bag. She put a clay-colored shawl around Marketa's shoulders.

"Here, drink some beer. I'll have Ivana make some tea to warm you. There is a blizzard raging outside."

Marketa could not talk, but nodded her head. All day and all night long the storm blew, and when they woke in the morning, snow powdered the stone floor in drifts blown in through the gaps in the shutters.

CHAPTER 33

DON JULIUS GRIEVES

For days, Don Julius moved as if he were in a stupor. Don Carlos Felipe, the Spanish priest, was hopeful for the first week, thinking that perhaps the crafty Doctor Mingonius had done them all a favor and bled the bastard dry. The blood would not be on the priest's hands if the boy died a day or two after bleeding. Then he could leave this godforsaken backwater and perhaps even return to the good red wines and sherry of Spain.

Yes, perhaps he will die, thought the priest, *and God will have his revenge so much the sooner. As men of the holy cloth, we can only provide spiritual salvation to the willing. This whore's son of Rudolf II spits in the eye of God and laughs. He will pay at the gates of hell.*

The ghostly pallor of Don Julius's skin made the priest think the youth had been leeched to death. On the heels of this observation came the thought of morcilla, his beloved sausage of pig's blood, rice, onions, and spices. With a good glass of bone-dry rioja, not the sweet, flowery swill of the Austrian lands. That was a meal for real men, not the perfumed white wines and sweet beer and damnable caraway seed that scented every dish in Bohemia.

Die, bastard. Die.

Still, now that Mingonius was gone, the health of the king's son was in his hands. The Jesuit could not let the boy die, damn it. But if Don Julius did return to robust health and his accompanying madness, the Spaniard would have no peace with his thundering roars and wails piercing the night.

He would see that the lunatic hunted by day—escorted by legions of guards—and he would find ways to keep him out of Rozmberk Castle as much as could be managed. Maybe he could obtain some opium to make the boy sleep at night. It was sold by apothecaries in the alleys of Prague, but he was not certain where to search for it in Krumlov. He loathed having any contact with the town below.

The priest was still puzzled why Doctor Mingonius had left before dawn, without so much as a farewell. Still, there was no love lost between them, and Mingonius had performed the last bleeding as promised. Perhaps he had been summoned by King Rudolf to report personally on the health of his patient.

The priest questioned the guards, but they said they knew nothing—only that they were ordered to fetch the coach and ready it for the journey. The men were predictably tight-lipped with him, and he was certain they talked about him to his face in that damnable gibberish of a language. These Bohemians rogues, he thought, were not to be trusted. He was sure they were lying to help Mingonius.

He enlisted some of the Jesuit monks to help in taking care of his charge. The bastard had not protested when he was brought to the chapel to pray for eternal salvation. He refused to say confession, but the fact that he had stayed two hours that first morning in the cold chapel on his knees was accounted a victory—a holy victory.

But at the end of the second week, Don Julius complained of pain in his breast and his scalp. He winced when the priest inspected his body, as if there were an invisible wound. He yelped in pain, not letting the priest touch him. He waved away the Jesuit brothers and cursed at their incense orbs, coughing and sneezing and cursing, in German, Italian, and Latin.

He begged incessantly for the Coded Book, but it had disappeared with Doctor Mingonius.

And then there was the infernal commotion about Marketa. Lucie Pichlerova insisted on seeing Don Julius to find out why her daughter had left for Prague without embracing her or even fetching the beautiful trousseau the village of Krumlov had assembled for her stay in Prague.

"Quite impossible," said the priest. "No one can see Don Julius but the doctors, guards, and priest assigned to him."

"What do you mean?" said Pani Pichlerova, crossing her stout arms in front of her. "We see him weekly riding to his hounds. My daughter has seen him many times, including the night she left for Prague."

Were they really bleeding again that same night? thought the priest. *No wonder he has no wits or color to his face. Pity they hadn't finished the job and sent him to the devil.*

"It is out of the question," said the priest. "And if you had any sense in your head, you would realize how dangerous the man is and never permit your daughter near him."

"He is a Hapsburg," sniffed Lucie. "Is he not?"

The priest closed the door on the indignant woman and ordered the guards to escort her out through the courtyards and beyond the gate. She lingered on the far side of the moat, throwing the fattened bears covetous looks and bitterly begrudging them their supper.

The end of the second week brought wails and high screeches again. Don Julius had found a small lock of hair near the window, where he had plunged the fleam into Marketa's scalp. When the priest arrived in response to the racket, he found Don Julius clutching the strands of hair.

"What have you got there, Don Julius?" asked the priest.

"None of your God-cursed business, you withered maggot!" the bastard prince snapped, hiding the strands in his clenched fist. The priest could see a few long hairs emerging from his fingers.

"Did you touch her?" the priest muttered, realizing what he had in his hand. "Is that why she left so precipitously?"

"No!" roared Julius, leaping to his feet and lunging at the priest. The guards seized him just in time as his outstretched hand reached for the priest's neck. The priest jumped back, placing his own hands over his throat.

"No, no, no!" cried Don Julius, struggling against the guards. "I did not mean to kill her! It was the demon that possessed me. I love the Angel of God more than my own life! I shall be damned to hell and never see my Marketa again."

The priest's mouth puckered as if he had bitten into a Malaga lemon, and he flashed a bitter look at the guards.

"If she is dead, she has at least escaped this godforsaken town," said the priest, gathering his composure. He narrowed his lizard eyes at the madman. "And that is a blessing."

The guards' faces turned stony, and they considered letting their hands relax their grasp on the royal lunatic. *"Do prdele,"* they cursed the priest, and spat on the ground. *Go fuck yourself!* The Spanish priest thought he heard the word "crucifix" uttered in their profane litany of Czech curses, and that offended him more than all the other unknown vocabulary that sputtered out of their outraged Bohemian mouths.

~

Barber Zigmund Pichler read and reread the letter Doctor Mingonius had sent him. The looping letters were written in haste, not at all the usual fine penmanship of the great doctor.

December 5, 1606
Herr Pichler:

I am sorry that I cannot say my farewell in person, but we must leave Krumlov in the utmost haste. There has been a terrible situation—accident?—concerning your daughter. She secretly arranged to enter Don Julius's chamber alone, apparently with the blessings of your wife. Could this be true?

What followed was a disaster! The results were miraculously not as tragic as they might have been, but still she was stabbed and fell out the window of the castle. God be praised, she landed on the castle rubbish heap and was saved, but she has suffered greatly and will take a good many months to heal.

I have taken her to a good inn in Cesky Budejovice and will remain with her until I think she can travel back to Krumlov to continue her recuperation. Is there a safe haven for her, someplace other than your home? I fear that Don Julius will learn she has not died and will demand she return to the castle. The first place he would look is the bathhouse.

In the meantime, I shall treat her as a member of my own family. I have much to atone for and shall be honored to care for her health and help her heal.

I will send her back to Krumlov at my own expense in a carriage, when she is well enough to travel. Please tell me the address I should give the driver. Obviously it would not do to take her to your residence, as she might be seen from the castle above the bathhouse.

By My Heart and Truest Confession with the Greatest Apologies,
Doctor Mingonius

Pichler fingered the creased parchment. He did not trust himself in his great sorrow and rage to broach the subject with his wife. He knew how much she coveted the wealth and status of the noble class, but had not had an inkling of how far she would push Marketa. Instead he wept alone, quietly, in the dark recesses of his barbershop, staring into the muddy buckets where the leeches slept peacefully in the cold, dark water.

CHAPTER 34

RETURN TO KRUMLOV

When Marketa's father wrote to her, she was relieved. After two weeks at the Gray Goose, her contusions had faded to a sickening yellow-green, the color of daffodil shoots that stupidly push their tips through the snow and ice in early spring. Her body no longer ached to the hollow beat that had seized her bones and muscles. It was true that her stitches had festered and puckered for a week, but the innkeeper's wife had a magic touch with her herbs, and the throbbing pain subsided and the inflammation diminished. Marketa's body began to heal.

The innkeeper's wife reminded Marketa of Annabella, with her knowledge of herbs and flowers, though her work maintaining a lodge and tavern had left her little time to study and collect medicines. There were sausages to broil on the hearth, soups to simmer, ducks and geese to turn on the spit and baste. Her hands were crimson and rough. Vinegar from the sauerkraut had etched its way into the red cracks in her skin.

Still, Marketa sensed her ability to heal with her potions and rough hands. It was those same chapped hands that had initiated

Marketa's own healing, along with Doctor Mingonius and Viera's caring touch.

Dearest Daughter,

I was greatly grieved to hear of the news of your injuries and what transpired in the castle. Grace be to God that you are still alive, for it is nothing short of a miracle!

Doctor Mingonius wrote to me asking where we could find you a safe haven here in Krumlov, since returning to the bathhouse is out of the question. I thought of course of the Poor Clares. I asked your aunt for permission to hide you there. But she worries that a nun would confide to a priest that you were there and the Jesuits would come hunting for you.

Is there anywhere else you can take refuge?

Your Loving Father

Marketa left smears on the parchment as her fingertips dragged over each letter, making out the sounds. It was a struggle to decipher the words in her still wounded state.

She asked the innkeeper for a quill, ink, and parchment, asking him to charge Doctor Mingonius for the costs, as Marketa had not a coin in her pocket.

Dear Father,

Please forgive my foolishness. I have lost your trust, I am sure, and almost lost my life.

There is one person who might agree to let me take shelter with her, where no one would look for me. Could you please approach Annabella, the witch, and see if she would take me in?

Your Loving Daughter,

Marketa

Within the week, Marketa was whisked away in a carriage back to Krumlov to live with the witch.

~

Annabella opened her door to Marketa, taking her by the arm and sweeping her in as fast as possible. Marketa heard the clatter of the horse-drawn coach turn the tight corner toward the marketplace and the drawbridge beyond.

"Marketa!" Annabella pressed her close in an embrace. Marketa could smell the smoke from the open fire in her hair and bitter, strange herbs on her skin. She must have been performing a spell just moments before. Marketa wondered with a shudder if it had to do with her.

"You know it is a miracle that you still breathe on earth, and you must give thanks and praise for the rest of your life!"

Marketa had started to be accustomed to this miracle, for she had fought hard to survive, but she nodded her head.

"Yes, a miracle," she mumbled, her eyes beginning to tear. "Don Julius tried to kill me."

"Oh, and he will finish the job if he has the chance! He is a wicked one—the demons possess his very soul."

Marketa said nothing, but gazed at the fire ring in the center of the room. If demons indeed possessed his soul, perhaps she had seen—and been led astray by—the last remaining shreds of his true, untainted spirit. Perhaps she had been battling the demons for the prince's soul. The thought made her feel a tiny bit less ashamed. She had done battle—and paid a terrible price.

Annabella lifted Marketa's chin, and they gazed into each other's eyes—Marketa's blue-gray eyes, the witch's hazel eyes, the sprinkling of brown proportioned differently in the background of green, from left eye to right, like the random speckles on a trout.

"Yes," Marketa murmured. "Annabella, I know I was unspeakably foolish, and my folly nearly cost me my life. But... there was something there. I felt something, some trace of love, some hint of tenderness in him. I only—"

Annabella's eyes blazed and she seized Marketa's arm, dragging her to the looking glass, warped and dusty. She polished it with her sleeve, watching Marketa fiercely in the glass as she burnished the reflection. She pulled the girl's hair back and made her look at the swollen scars where the fleam had sliced her flesh.

"Does this look like love and tenderness to you?"

Marketa's fingers traced the red, puffy flesh. She felt the ridges left by the doctor's stitches and the healing flesh that was developing a hard, raised scar. In the glass she watched her eyes grow red and wet as the tears spilled down her cheeks.

Annabella nodded in the reflection, her hands relaxing their grip on Marketa's temples. The two young women exchanged looks in the mirror, and their eyes spoke silent words.

Marketa placed her hands upon Annabella's and slowly pulled them off her face, all the while watching her in the mirror. She turned and kissed the witch's fingers.

"You are a true friend," Marketa said. "I could not think of who would risk taking me in."

Annabella's face melted, and she pulled the girl to her in an embrace.

"I am pleased to give you shelter. My fate is to help those who ask for succor, as it has been for all the women in my family before me. That is the requirement of a good witch, to protect the innocent from evil. Come, let me make you some chamomile tea."

And so began Marketa's life with Annabella.

Under the house was a strange stone cellar, ancient catacombs filled with dried plants, bottles of potions, and shriveled animal parts—vital organs, desiccated paws, and gnarled talons. The floor was made of bones, pounded into the dirt, so tightly packed they resembled a whitish-gray cobblestone. Marketa shivered as she looked down the dark tunnel, having been told that the remains of ancient Celts—her Bohemian ancestors—lay in the rocky earth beyond.

Annabella had made her a bed stuffed with fresh sweet-smelling straw and given her a coverlet filled with soft goose feathers to keep her warm in the dampness of the cavernous cellar.

The only entrance to the cellar was a trapdoor, hidden under an oak chest in the kitchen. Sometimes Marketa wondered whether anyone would ever find her if anything happened to Annabella or if she would just be lost—until her bones had worked their way into the floor among all the others.

That first night, as she drifted off to sleep after a good supper of carp fried in suet, Marketa thought she saw a flash of light in the far end of the cave.

Just a few months earlier, the curious girl would have set out to investigate, plumbing the depths of the catacombs with her smoking tallow candle. She would have scrutinized the light with scientific eyes, determined to find its origin. She would certainly never be afraid.

But that night, Marketa blew out the candle with a puff and pulled the coverlet over her head, refusing to open her eyes again until she heard Annabella drag the heavy chest away at dawn.

CHAPTER 35

KEPLER AND THE HEAVENS

Jakub Horcicky should have had no trouble finding 5 Karlova Street.

Only a hundred paces from the Charles Bridge on the Old Town riverbank of Prague, the home of Johannes Kepler would have been easy to find on a clear day. But the evening fog rolled off the Vltava, stretching its back like a cat above the winding streets and settling down cold and raw on the cobblestones. Jakub walked past Kepler's home twice, doubling back and casting a furtive look over his shoulder to see whether any petty thieves had followed him, a stranger lost in the serpentine streets of the city.

In this mystic world cloaked in gray fog, Jakub heard the tolling bells of the astronomical clock in the town square. He listened to the mournful clang and thought of the animated specter of death, a skeleton with a bell in one hand and an hourglass in the other, standing guard at the right of the clock tower. Twelve pious disciples appeared and disappeared in the two windows above, marking the hour.

Below the holy path of the disciples, Death kept company with a turbaned Turk, a hook-nosed Jew with his sacks of gold, and Vanity who studied his own fair countenance in a looking glass. But it was Death who tolled the hour.

Jakub finally stopped and asked for help at the Jesuit residence and university, the Clementinum. He yanked the bell cord hanging outside the great wooden doors.

"*Pax vobiscum*," Jakub said as the great door creaked open on its ancient hinges.

"*Pax tecum*," responded the monk, bowing his head, his hands forming a temple of blessing.

"Brother, could you tell me where I can find 5 Karlova, the home of Johannes Kepler?"

"Ah, Herr Stargazer," mused the monk, his hood pulled up against the damp night. "He lives just across the street. But you will not find the answers in the stars, my son. Only in God."

A dank odor rose from the monk's wet woolen robe, and his eyes sought Jakub's.

"Of course. It is the king's business that brings me here," said Jakub. "Thank you for your assistance, and good night to you and the brothers."

"Good night, my son. And may God bless you and the king's errand."

What did the Jesuits think of a staunch Protestant living a stone's throw from their center of learning? Jakub wondered if Johannes Kepler looked over his shoulder every night as he unlocked his front door.

But perhaps he had no fear, given his high standing in King Rudolf's court. This was the privilege of being the king's chief astronomer—religious protection. No one trifled with a member of the court.

But in the heavy fog of night without witness, a heretical Protestant ran a risk, as religious factions became more and more polarized.

A thief had pried off the knocker from the door of 5 Karlova Street. Jakub rapped his knuckles against the small brown door, noticing the chipped paint and splintered wood.

Frau Kepler answered the door, a scowl on her face. Her hair was pinned under a white linen kerchief. The smell of food clung to her and beads of sweat lined her upper lip.

"Yes," she said, her voice full of impatience. "What is it?"

"Is Herr Kepler at home, please?"

"He is not well," she said, pushing the door closed. "If you want your astrological chart done, come back in a week or so."

"No, you misunderstand, Frau Kepler," said Jakub, putting his hand on the door to keep it from shutting in his face. "I am sent by our king to prepare an elixir of plants and herbs to ease your husband's condition. He is missed in court."

Frau Kepler pulled the door wide open.

"Forgive me," she said, covering her mouth. "Please come in, Herr—"

"Horcicky. Jakub Horcicky de Tenepec."

"Ah, the imperial chemist," she said, clapping her hands against her temples in recognition and straightening her kerchief. "We are honored to have you visit our house."

"May I see your husband?"

"Of course," she said, stepping back to allow him to enter.

Jakub ducked low to keep from knocking his head against the lintel. The stone floor was still wet from Frau Kepler's scrubbing and a reed brush lay against a bucket of dirty water. Jakub wondered why a courtier's wife would be washing her own floors.

"Would you be so kind as to wait here, Herr Doctor, while I announce your visit?" asked Kepler's wife.

"Certainly, thank you."

Frau Kepler walked up a staircase barely wide enough for her big hips. Kepler must have been in the attic, where he could best observe the stars. Jakub could hear a hushed discussion and then footsteps across the groaning floorboards two stories above, as Frau Kepler tidied the room for the visitor.

"Please. Come upstairs. You must excuse the condition of the house. We were not expecting visitors. Our servant is off today," she said, her face reddening as if she were caught committing a heinous sin.

Jakub followed Frau Kepler's ample hips up to the attic. She knocked softly on the little door and ushered her visitor in.

Johannes Kepler lay on a cot, his room littered with drawings of circles and ellipses, diagrams of orbits of the planets, and a wooden replica of the solar system.

The astronomer was not elderly—in fact, Jakub estimated the scientist to be his contemporary—but Kepler's prodigious forehead was furrowed with stern lines and his sharp beard jutted out in a stubborn, righteous manner that spoke of a Protestant cleric.

"Welcome, Herr Chemist," said Kepler despondently from his bed. His tunic was rumpled as if he had slept in his clothes for several days. "To what do I owe the honor of this visit?"

Jakub bowed and produced a letter from the king.

"Tell me its contents, Horcicky," said Kepler, propping himself up on the pillows. "I will open it later when I can locate my letter opener."

"The king sends me to gather information to cure your illness," said Jakub. "He expressed great consternation at your absence at court."

"Ah, yes. Does His Majesty wish me to send his astrological chart for next month?"

Jakub noticed Kepler's mouth puckering in distaste. He had heard that Kepler despised using his precise mathematical observations of the stars to produce the gibberish of a horoscope. The astronomer considered it a bastardization of true science.

"The king only mentioned his concern for your health…and his hope that continued work on the Rudolphine Tables might not be suspended for too long a time."

"That is most kind, Doctor Horcicky. Of course, my assistants chart the position of the planets each night, even when I am absent. Their eyes are sharper than my own. I make the calculations based on their clear-eyed observations."

Jakub shifted his weight, making the old floorboards creak. The king would not tolerate an absence from court from his imperial mathematician and astrologer for much longer.

"Your symptoms, please?"

Johannes Kepler looked beyond Jakub's shoulder to the window. He waved away the question.

"Please be so kind as to draw open the shutters and open the window."

Jakub pulled open the wooden shutters, latching them back. Kepler had designed the window so that it could be opened to observe the night skies.

The fog rose to the windowsill, its gray back climbing no higher. Jakub looked out to the clear sky, the stars glittering sharp against the black night. The damp fog formed a horizon for the starry heavens.

"My symptoms, you say?" said Kepler, rustling under the bedclothes. "Ah, Doctor Horcicky, I was born a sickly child and my hands are crippled. My eyesight has always been poor, and without the help of lenses, I see little of the world others take for granted. The night sky, which is clear to your naked eye, is a haze to me without my lenses."

Jakub drew a breath. This patient would be difficult.

The doctor's gaze fell to the optical instruments on the table by the window. He bent down to admire the spyglass. "Ah, but Herr Kepler, what eyes you now possess! You must see the very heart of the universe through this glass! May I?"

Kepler gave a curt nod, and Jakub pressed the scope to his eye.

The stars leapt into sharp focus.

"What wonder!" said Jakub. Then, as he removed the spyglass from his eye, he froze. His eyes scanned the conical shapes, the painted adornment. He turned the spyglass around and around in his hand.

"What is it?" asked Kepler.

Horcicky lowered the eyeglass and turned it over in his hand. "Is this an antique?"

Kepler laughed. "I should say not. The Dutchman Jansen has only invented it. I am lucky to be in possession of it. It was a gift to the king."

"I have seen it before," said Horcicky quietly.

"What?" said Kepler. "Nonsense!"

"No. I swear I have seen it. And something similar, but even more complex," he said, looking into Kepler's skeptical face. "May I use your ink pot and parchment?"

"Of course."

Jakub sat at Kepler's desk and drew a series of tubes that were recessed one into another. He shaped the top of the tube in a curve to denote a convex lens. He brought the rough sketch to Kepler's bedside without stopping to blot the ink.

Kepler rubbed his red-rimmed eyes, staring at the crude drawing.

"Where have you seen this?" he demanded, his face pallid and strained. "Where?"

"In the Coded Book of Wonder, a manuscript in His Majesty's Kunstkammer. There are many sketches similar to this in its pages."

"It possesses the same design as Galileo's telescope," said Kepler.

"It is baffling," said Horcicky. "How could the author of this ancient book know of the instrument that one day a great astronomer would make?"

Kepler looked at the drawing with hunger in his eyes.

"I need an advanced telescope, Herr Doctor. I cannot make proper observations without the Italian instrument of Galileo. I must see this book!"

"It is currently in possession of Don Julius, the king's son, incarcerated in Cesky Krumlov. But surely Galileo would furnish King Rudolf's astronomer such an instrument."

Kepler shifted uncomfortably, situating the pillow to better support himself.

"No. Galileo does not want competition. Especially from a Lutheran. Despite my letters to confirm the accuracy of his observations and to prevent his imprisonment, he refuses to share his great stargazing glass with me, even as he begs me to confirm his theories."

"I am astonished that another scientist would willfully retard scientific progress."

"Greed, Jakub. Greed, politics, religion, and vanity. They all forsake science to protect power." Kepler's rheumatic fingers balled in a fist. "Even the most brilliant scientist is not immune to the allure of power."

Jakub found himself thinking of the astronomical clock. He thought of Vanity staring at himself in a looking glass.

Then he remembered the reason for his visit.

"Your symptoms, if you will, Herr Kepler."

"Extreme melancholy. I cannot bear to leave my bed or venture beyond the threshold of my house. I do not care whether I live or die."

"Herr Kepler?" said Horcicky, genuinely astonished. "You, who are esteemed throughout Europe, who have so quickly filled the shoes of the great Tycho Brahe."

"Brahe? I stole his observations. From the moment of his death, I hid myself in our observatory and copied his star journals. I am no better than a petty thief, according to his heirs."

"Brahe was your master and you his collaborator. I am surprised he did not share all his findings with you."

"No. He wanted my mathematics, my calculations—but he denounced my theories. Tycho Brahe was not immune to the disease that shrinks the human heart and impedes science. A fellow Lutheran and my collaborator, but he did not believe in the Copernican universe. He clung to the notion that the planets revolved around the earth. Still a brilliant mind, however warped by convention."

Kepler sighed and his crippled finger reached clawlike for the earthen flask of water by his cot. He swallowed, quenching his thirst.

"And now, I live penniless. The emperor has not paid me in a year. I have debts I cannot pay and no savings. My wife bickers with me over money while I peddle personal horoscopes to courtiers and rich merchants to pay the bills. It barely suffices while I try to discover the key to the universe."

"The key?"

"The sun and planets have a soul. A force, if you will. Not only is the sun the center of our universe, but the sun compels the planets to follow in their individual orbits—spinning elliptically around the great force, as a pagan would dance around a bonfire, mesmerized."

Jakub felt a sudden emptiness in his chest. Planets with a soul? What force is there in the universe but God himself, who by his hand alone set the orbits of planets and fixed the stars in the sky?

"But that is heresy," he protested. "Completely contrary to scripture."

"Ah, but I believe it is the truth," said Kepler. "And I shall prove it one day. There is a force in our sun, a force in our planets. Each follows its own course, but each is inextricably bound to every other."

Kepler studied Jakub standing before the open window.

"Come closer, Horcicky," he said. "I want to see your face."

Horcicky approached the bed and reluctantly bent close to the imperial mathematician.

"Ah, as I suspected. I see the reproach of the Jesuit in your eyes. You are torn. Jesuits, of all orders, seek learning and enlightenment, yet the traditions of the Catholic Church hold them back. Such a pity in an otherwise bright mind."

Jakub drew back and straightened. He swallowed his anger at the insult.

"Jesuits respect the scriptures, Herr Kepler," he said. But even as he spoke his protest, his mind was seizing on Kepler's theories as a hungry man wolfs down a loaf of bread.

"Respect scriptures? Pah!" said Kepler, his sharp beard flicking out to punctuate his remark. "Would it surprise you to know that I have had several Jesuit friendships in my life? They cannot help themselves. Their search for knowledge, for truth, often triumphs over their damnable souls. They are attracted to the light of science, like moths in the night."

Kepler smiled. "The king's confessor, Johannes Pistorius, is among my closest companions. His sharp mind and eloquence exercise my spirit, while Galileo turns his back on me."

Jakub blinked and stared back at Kepler. Pistorius, the king's confessor, befriending a heretical Lutheran? The doctor knew the esteemed confessor, who in addition to theology held a degree in medicine.

"Pistorius finds my theories of harmonious spheres heretical but tantalizing," said Kepler, his face animated. "The planets travel not in perfect circles of the divine but in elegant elliptical curves, adulterated by the physical force of the sun, God's own cosmic soul."

"Your words are dangerous," Jakub protested. "The confessor does not report your heresy?"

"Of course not. We argue hours on end, as civilized men should do. Besides denigrating my theories, he works on his dissertations of the Kabbalah."

Jakub gazed out at the stars and the quarter moon rising through the bank of mist into the clear night sky.

Kepler rubbed his arthritic hands together. He watched Jakub's face as it absorbed his words.

"Harmonious spheres?" said Jakub, his voice soft. He watched the rising slice of moon mingle with the stars.

"Yes," said Kepler. "If you listen with your heart and pure soul, you will hear the music of the cosmos, in perfect harmony. It is only the sins and arrogance of man that obscure the sound."

Jakub thought about Krumlov and the king's son locked in the castle. Pride, greed, power. The distant drumbeat of war and religion already echoed in Eastern Europe, the Reformation clashing with the Counter-Reformation, and one Hapsburg brother against another in a struggle for power.

He thought of the bathmaid living on the banks of the Vltava and thought of her innocence, her thirst for knowledge to cure the sick. He had laughed at her, pinching her cheek, dismissing her ambitions as naïveté.

Yet he had been thoroughly charmed.

Jakub raised his eyes to the stars. He wondered if she could hear the music of the planets, while powerful men heard silence.

Johannes Kepler stirred under his coverlet and threw off the bedclothes.

"You are a good physician. Your visit has purged my bad blood and returned my humors to balance, better than any bloodletter. It is high time I returned to court to see Johannes Pistorius. I am eager to argue again against his theological pretensions. Some lively sparring would do the stubborn old priest good."

Johannes Kepler stood up and approached Jakub. Putting an arm on his shoulder, he turned his face to the sky and they both looked out at the star-filled heavens.

SPRING 1607

CHAPTER 36

CRIES IN THE NIGHT

Gradually the word got out to the village that Marketa was living once more in Krumlov. She was not afraid that they would tell Don Julius, because, whether man, woman, or child, they all despised the brutal Hapsburg. It was their Bohemian duty to protect her—one of their own—and Marketa soon became comfortable moving among them in an almost normal life. The seamstress made her a long, hooded cape of black boiled wool that she wore to hide her face and distinctive hair, should Don Julius spy her from the castle.

Barber Pichler came to visit several times a week and begged to study Annabella's Book of Paracelsus. He had for so many years traveled to Vienna to study, at great financial hardship to the Pichler family. Here was a great treasure of medicine only a few minutes' walk from the bathhouse.

Marketa refused to go back to the bathhouse, determined never to speak to her mother again. The rumor that her mother had urged her to approach Don Julius on that fateful night enraged the townspeople and they ostracized her, from the butcher to the soap-maker to the women hissing curses whenever she crossed their paths.

The business in the bathhouse had dwindled until there were barely enough clients to make ends meet. Lucie Pichlerova was sold only the puniest fish, the toughest ends of meat, and moldy bacon when she went to the Wide Street market. The greengrocer refused to sell to her altogether, and she had to procure vegetables and other necessities from the gypsies and Jews beyond the gates of the town.

Marketa refused to see her mother but welcomed the twins to visit her at night, when they would not be seen. She also begged her father to protect them from their mother's rough hands and not let her barter their "favors" to the bathers. He hung his head in shame and promised he would defend their honor with his life. Marketa was sure if he could have afforded to do so, he would have shut down the bathhouse altogether.

Then, as the patches of snow melted and the ice cracked along the shores of the Vltava, the shrill wails of Don Julius returned to haunt the night.

As the bloodletting had ceased, his strength—and his madness—had returned. Across the little valley they heard his cry from atop Rozmberk Castle.

"Mar-ket-a!"

It was a beseeching cry, one that would make a mother's heart wither. He shrieked only at night when the wind was calm and the screams cut through the early spring air. His cries startled flocks of birds from their roosts, sending them to fly blindly into the night.

The men cursed his name and their eyes were bloodshot from lack of sleep. The women suffered nervous conditions and begged Annabella for calming tonics.

Marketa gulped down mugs of Annabella's teas and stuffed woolen yarn in her ears, but somehow she heard her name still reverberating in the air. The high-pitched scream slipped through the cracks of the door and even down into the cellar, like a snake that writhed and slithered into her ears. Her dreams were filled with huge red lips and a cavernous mouth that screamed her name, consuming her as she drew closer and closer and, finally, too close.

When she could stand it no longer, Marketa would leave the house with a lantern and sit in Saint Vitus Cathedral and stare at the altar. Since she had been a young girl, the church had been a peaceful refuge, built of granite at the very edge of the Vltava. The raging roar of the river drowned out every sound, and the priest was forced to shout above its thunderous din.

Those long years ago, Katarina would cry in fear, crawling into her mother's lap because she thought they would all be swept away by the water and drowned. But Marketa fell asleep under her father's arm, finding the water's roar a lullaby.

She smiled sadly, thinking of her old friend Katarina. It seemed decades ago the two had sat peacefully by the river, Katarina braiding Marketa's hair.

Now, at night, the river's voice echoing through the vast space of the cathedral gave her solace. Here and only here, Marketa could not hear her name carried through the air from a man she once foolishly considered a lover. She would focus on the painting of the Madonna of Cesky Krumlov and beg her intercession. Could this Hapsburg not return to Prague and cease this torment? Surely, if the Bohemian lords were to pass a single night listening to Don Julius's mad lament, they would petition the king to remove his son from their lands. The Madonna remained motionless on the canvas. She had nothing to say in return to Marketa's prayers; she only looked demurely at her holy child.

Katarina cried copiously and often. Too often, worried her mother. But ever since the day her daughter had come home from the market that winter without her basket and without an explanation or excuse and her father had punished her, she could not be persuaded to smile.

Pan Mylnar had forbidden her to ever leave the house without the escort of one of her older brothers, her mother, or himself. And since she had insulted Marketa, Katarina doubted her friend would ever want to speak to her again. So she was alone. And lonely.

The miller noticed that his beautiful daughter, his pride and joy, was losing weight. His wife baked extra breads and sweets for her, but she could not be persuaded to eat more than a nibble. Her cheekbones stabbed through her once plump flesh, and while she was still the most beautiful girl of Cesky Krumlov, she no longer flourished.

Pan Mylnar had always suspected that the disappearance of the basket had something to do with the dirty scamp, the blacksmith's son. Although there was nothing to prove his suspicion, the miller heard the rumor that the boy was a thief and was caught red-handed in Pan Brewer's grain shed.

"I told you he was no good," he declared to his daughter, jutting out his lower lip in justified satisfaction. "The scoundrel is a thief and is not to be trusted."

Katarina opened her mouth to answer, but quickly shut it again.

"Think what you like, but he is an honorable man," she said, scowling at her father. She ran to her pallet, throwing herself on the straw mattress to cry.

The days were long and repetitious for Katarina. She sewed and knitted when the family could afford to buy woolen yarns. She cooked and baked alongside her mother, whose spirits mirrored her daughter's, for the good woman could not be happy unless she saw her beloved daughter smile.

"Daughter, is there nothing I can do to make your spirits rise? You torture me with your melancholic nature. It is so unlike you."

Katarina looked toward the thick crystal window, toward the castle. She sighed, her lip quivering.

"There is one thing," Katarina said at last.

"Do not mention the blacksmith," said her mother quickly. "You know it is beyond my power to change your father's mind."

"No, something else," she said, staring at the tower of the castle. "Could you send word to Annabella's house that I want to visit Marketa?"

"Oh, my darling! You know that your father would never let you see her, now that there is so much danger. You must stay as far away from her as you can!"

"But I miss her," said Katarina in a small voice. "I want to see her again."

Her mother bit the tip of her tongue, thinking.

"You could write to her," she suggested, her plump face creasing up in enthusiasm. "Yes, we could pay a scribe to send a letter to her."

For the first time since she had run away from the grain shed, Katarina smiled. "Yes, I could write her! And she can read my words. She would think that fine and learned. I will ask for her forgiveness in a letter."

"Oh, Daughter," said her mother, drawing Katarina's head to her breast, caressing her. She squeezed her hard in an embrace. "Daughter! When a girl suffers as much as Marketa, she learns to forgive."

The next day Katarina accompanied her mother to the market where the scribe stood behind a little bench that served as a desk, with furls of cheap parchment too dark and flimsy for official documents, but appropriate for more perfunctory book-keeping and correspondence.

"My daughter wants to send a letter," said Pani Mylnar. "How much would you charge?"

"It depends how many words."

"Words?" worried her mother. "How many words make a proper letter?"

The scribe saw his advantage. "One hundred make a noble epistle. Anything less than that would offend the recipient. I charge a half thaler for a good letter."

"A half thaler?" gasped Pani Mylnar in astonishment. She turned to Katarina and whispered, "We cannot afford that—your father would notice that the food we bring home is too scarce and of poor quality if we spend a half thaler on a letter."

"Of course, Mother," said Katarina, disappointed. She narrowed her eyes at the scribe, who pared his quill nonchalantly as the women suffered the shock of the price of his services.

"Surely there is something we can barter for your services, sir," said Katarina. "We cannot afford to spend a half thaler on some ink and animal skin."

"Ah, that is the price of literacy," replied the scribe, admiring the fire in the pretty girl's eyes. "In literate eyes, these squiggles are transformed into meaning and convey essential information—or, I might guess, the depths of the heart."

Pani Mylnar realized what the scribe was saying.

"No, you rude young man! My daughter is not writing a love letter. She wants to write a simple communication to her friend. Her best friend—another girl."

"Oh," said the scribe, chewing at the rough nib of his quill. He seemed pleased. "Well, in that case, perhaps we can strike a bargain. You bring me fresh bread for a month, and I will pen the letter."

"A month!"

"Or...what if you bring me a loaf of bread for two weeks and I receive a kiss from your lovely daughter."

"You gypsy of a swindler!" cried Pani Mylnar, turning on her heel to leave. "I shall send my sons back to pummel you for your impertinence!"

Katarina caught her mother by the arm and whispered in her ear. "Only a kiss, Mother. I want to write to Marketa so badly."

"You will not kiss that despicable man."

"We could afford to bring him a loaf of bread for a fortnight. You know we could."

Her mother looked at the sad face of her daughter, her imploring eyes fixed on her own.

Pani Mylnar squinted hard at the scribe, setting her teeth together as she bit off her words.

"A kiss? What kind of kiss?"

"A kiss. A lovely kiss on the lips."

"Impossible!" said Pani Mylnar, the fat of her cheeks jiggling with indignation.

The scribe shrugged his shoulders in indifference. Then he took another look at Katarina and her long blonde hair.

"All right. For her, a kiss on the cheek. Slowly so I can smell her breath on me. And a loaf of bread for a fortnight."

"Done!" exclaimed Katarina, who was used to bartering and knew when to seal a deal.

And so the unlikely threesome disappeared just behind Uncle Radek's tavern, and once it was assured that no one could witness the transaction, Katarina kissed the young man slowly on his cheek, making sure her breath wafted toward his nose.

She was secretly satisfied when the young scribe blushed redder than the greengrocer's beets, promising her he would write a letter that would melt her friend's heart. But, he said, it could not exceed a hundred words or he would demand another kiss, this time on the lips for certain.

~

Two days later a letter was delivered to Annabella's house. It read:

Dear Marketa,

I am sure you have not forgiven me for my foolish words. I have suffered in your absence for there is no friend truer to me or more beloved than you.

My father forbids me to see you. It is too dangerous, he says. The two Austrian companions of Don Julius watch me in the streets and insult me, even when my older brothers are present. I could easily lead them to your door and your death. Please know I love you still.

I have no more words left, the scribe says.
My love and friendship forever,
Katarina

Tears welled in Marketa's eyes to see her friend's words inked on parchment, and she wondered how the baker's daughter had been able to pay the scribe. She missed Katarina's friendship and often thought of her raucous laugh, late at night in the depths of the catacombs.

She would send word to her friend, the first chance possible.

~

Annabella was behaving strangely. The young healer seemed restless as a cat and paced the earthen floor of the house on Dlouha Street. She would begin a spell and forget her words, wandering off into the cellar calling to the spirits, her voice echoing through the depths.

"What is the matter, Annabella?" Marketa asked one night when she found her friend conversing intensely with her cats.

The witch sighed.

"It is time for a new Annabella to come into this world."

Marketa stifled a laugh, knowing that Annabella had never shown the remotest interest in men. Except her father, Pichler, who came to visit and read the great Book of Paracelsus, no man had ever crossed the threshold.

The house smelled of women—generations of women. Women's presence infused the sheets, and the packed earth floor preserved their sweat and tears. The sweet breath of girls and the rattling coughs of old crones lingered in the close air of the ancient house.

"You do know how children are begotten, do you not?" teased Marketa.

Annabella looked exasperated. "Yes, yes. I know a man must be involved." She twisted a strand of her flame-red hair around her finger, her eyes distant.

Marketa sat next to her on the wooden bench and stroked her friend's long hair. Annabella's fingers fidgeted now in her lap.

"I cannot picture you with a man, Annabella. Any more than I can picture Aunt Ludmilla with a suitor."

Annabella's voice was distant.

"It must be just the right man. The future Annabella must be conceived in a perfect union. He must be a man of great virtue, a man of learning and of compassion. Alas, I see no mortal who could father such a brilliant child."

Marketa almost laughed but thought better of it. Annabella had begun to lose weight and color; she bore a frightening look of distraction. It was obvious that this dilemma weighed heavy in her heart.

"You will find the father one day, Annabella. You will know when you have found the right match. Why the rush?"

"She must be conceived this spring, as the earth awakens from its sleep," said Annabella, a shiver rocking her body. "The spirits demand it."

Marketa fetched a warm blanket and threw it over her friend's shoulders. She stoked the fire and put the iron kettle on to boil.

It was clear that the good healer of Cesky Krumlov was delirious.

~

Jakub Horcicky looked down from the royal gardens at a pair of newborn fawns in the deer moat. They were no bigger than large foxes, matching four steps to their mother's one. The spotted fawns accompanied the graceful doe through the young spring grass, the pale green blades parting as the mother deer foraged.

Jakub loved spring. His carefully tended bulbs shook off the winter mulch, poking their tender tips up through the wet soil. He smiled at a tulip that wore a ridiculous cap of dead leaves and bark, so intent on blooming that it pushed its way through winter debris weighing more than the bulb and stem combined.

Fighting to be born. He pressed his thumb to his lips, smiling. He could smell the earthy scent of loam on his fingers.

Spring came weeks earlier in Krumlov than in Prague, he mused, and he thought of the long, solitary walks he had taken when he was a boy. Often the Jesuit brothers would send him to gather mushrooms and ramps in the hills, and he would look down from the forest's edge at the town, the Vltava meandering on the valley floor. He could make out the market on Wide Street, the carts and salt wagons, the pigs and fowl herded into makeshift pens. The street was usually crowded with eager vendors and haggling customers, and the multitude spilled out into the side streets, the taverns, and the main square where there was a steady line of villagers, filling their buckets with water from the town well.

Jakub's mind wandered. Why had he not heard from Marketa in the past few months?

A deep, doglike growl followed by a sucking sound filled the air and broke his reverie. The king's camels complaining. It was feeding time in the royal zoo, which stood within the botanical gardens. The roar of the lions and leopards soon drowned out the camels. Out of the corner of his eye, Jakub watched as the doe lifted her head, alert to the danger, and stealthily led her fawns back into the grass and sheltering trees.

"Beautiful, are they not?" said a voice.

Jakub turned, and standing next to him under a pomegranate tree was the king himself.

Jakub bowed low.

"Yes, Your Majesty."

The king nodded toward them.

"See how she does not run, but simply fades into the forest. True grace. I wish I could do as much."

"Your Majesty?"

The king turned and caressed a low branch of the pomegranate tree. It had only been recently exposed from its winter wraps, and small lime-green buds had emerged on its limbs.

"I have recently gotten word of a tragedy that happened four months ago in Krumlov. You are from that town, are you not, Physician Horcicky?"

"Yes," said Jakub, his eyes riveted on the king. "Pray, Your Highness, would you tell me what transpired?"

The king hesitated.

"It seems a girl fell to her death from the window of Rozmberk Castle. My son's window, in his apartments. The news only reached me now, months after the wretched event transpired. My ministers did not wish to raise my ire when they heard the rumor—and my son now howls day and night for the dead girl, they say.

"If this were not enough, my brother Matthias has spread the news throughout Europe, hoping to gain sympathy to challenge my throne."

"Your Majesty!" Jakub ceased breathing. "If you please, who was the girl?"

The king worked his lips together in consternation. "A girl who assisted her father in bloodletting. Mingonius contracted him in Krumlov. What the devil a girl was doing in a chamber with my lunatic son, I do not know. I have summoned Doctor Mingonius to court when he returns from Poland, accompanying Jan Jesenius. It seems it happened a day or so after the last bleeding. Doctor Mingonius had already departed for Prague. The girl was alone with my son, and he raped her. She plunged to her death from the castle window."

Jakub could feel the blood drain from his face, and he shifted his weight on his feet to keep from losing consciousness. He willed himself to breathe.

As soon as he could politely disengage himself from the king, Jakub ran to his cottage. He wrote to Annabella, asking if it was indeed Marketa who had fallen to her death and how she had ever been left unguarded with Don Julius. He hurried to the castle and paid an exorbitant fee for a rider to carry the missive directly to Krumlov.

A few days later, a response arrived, scribbled in beet juice on the same parchment of his letter. One word. In Latin:

VIVIT.

She lives.

Mingonius appeared in court, dressed in a fur cape and carrying an ivory staff. He had not even had time to wash after the long, cold ride from Poland when the royal guards appeared with a summons to appear before King Rudolf at once.

As he approached the king he looked up at the vaulted ceilings of the cavernous Vladislav Hall. This was the moment he had dreaded for months.

Mingonius feigned surprise when King Rudolf told him of Don Julius's apparent murder of the Bohemian bathmaid.

"Your Majesty! I am shocked beyond all reason. When I left him, he was as docile as a lamb, as witnessed and recorded by your ministers who visited. It was only then that I took my leave to return to Prague."

The king's mouth tightened. Mingonius could see the workings of the muscles, tight around his jaw.

"My son slashed the girl, the guards said, and threw her from the window. They swear she said it was by your order that she visit him."

Mingonius gasped. He worked hard to show utter surprise.

"She lied! Would I send an innocent maid into such danger?"

The king's eyes scoured his face for betrayal. Mingonius revealed only dismay at the terrible news.

No, it was ludicrous for the king to think that this prestigious doctor would allow an unchaperoned midnight visit by a female. And, after all, by the guards' own reports, the doctor had already departed for Prague.

There was no one to blame but the maiden herself. But now there was suddenly strong cause for the king's brother Matthias to instigate more trouble.

"No, I cannot hold you responsible, Doctor. You were already on your way back here. The guards have been lashed for their incompetence. But how did my son know this maiden? And why did the guards believe her, unless she was quite familiar with Don Julius?"

Doctor Mingonius had prayed he would not be asked this question. But he had prepared himself as best he could.

"She was the virgin whose blood attracted the leeches. And—forgive me, sire, but she was useful. Don Julius believed she was a maiden from the Coded Book of Wonder. Only when she was present would he allow bloodletting."

King Rudolf stared at his physician.

"He believed she was an illustration from the book?"

"An angel, my lord. And Don Julius believed himself deeply in love with her."

The king looked out the window toward the gardens. "Why was I not informed of this strange maiden? Who was she?"

"Marketa Pichlerova, the bloodletter's daughter."

The king stood and turned his back on his physician. He paced the floor.

"To imagine a common bathmaid may be my undoing! Matthias is biting at my heels, howling for my crown. And now he may have his way. All for the death of a simple commoner, a foolish maiden who does not recognize a madman when she sees one!"

Doctor Mingonius lifted his chin, standing rigid before the king. He had practiced this over and over. Let the king do the talking. Let him decide for himself what had transpired.

But suddenly the doctor found himself saying, "She was a good girl, sire, kind and benevolent. I think that is why your son was so at ease with her."

"Kind? Benevolent? What words are these to use in the presence of your king, when his empire is at risk! The girl was a simpleton, damn her soul!"

The king slammed his fist hard on the stone windowsill, impervious to the pain.

"You are dismissed, Physician!"

"Yes, Your Majesty."

As Mingonius walked backward, bowing to King Rudolf, the guards opened the door to the hallway.

A pair of hands grasped him as the doors closed in front of him. Mingonius turned and saw Jakub holding him fast.

"We must talk, Doctor Mingonius," he said, hurrying him down the hall and out into the gardens.

~

"Why didn't you tell me?" raged Jakub. His anger overwhelmed his deep respect for the older man. "How dare you keep this secret from me?"

"If you had heard of her fate before the king, you would have been in grave danger. I kept it from you because I knew you might do something rash."

"Something rash? I would have galloped to Budejovice to be at her side."

"Exactly. And do you think the merchants who travel the route from Budejovice to Prague would not have wagged their tongues to the king? Two of the king's doctors lodging at the Gray Goose with a mysterious injured girl."

"She needed my help! I should have been there all along!"

"You do not understand, even now. What would you have done but bring her back here to Prague, where she would surely be noticed? Her face is battered, and the sutured slashes still scar her. You think the court would not put two and two together? Doctor Horcicky nursing an injured girl with a Krumlov accent! How odd."

Jakub drew a breath. He knew Mingonius was right. But his anger still raged. He took another deep breath. He had not realized how deeply he had come to care for that simple Bohemian bathmaid until he had feared she was dead.

He felt the doctor's hand grasp his shoulder and realized Mingonius was shaking him to get his attention. "Here," said the doctor, holding a folded piece of parchment up for Horcicky to see. "Read this."

He recognized Marketa's awkward writing immediately.

My Dearest Jakub:

Forgive me. You offered me wisdom. I chose to ignore it and have paid dearly.

You warned me to beware of Don Julius, that he was a dangerous—deadly—man. I thought I saw more to him than just a madman. I thought I had glimpsed his soul. What a fool I was, and how I have suffered for it.

Doctor Mingonius and I have decided you will read these words only if the news reaches the ears of the king, and thus you. Fool that I still am, I hope that comes to pass. I know it will mean more danger lies ahead, but I would rather face the wrath of the king than have you think I have disappeared from your life as if I did not care about you.

It is for your own protection that we have left you in ignorance. I owed you that much for your warnings and concern for my life. But now that you are reading this, you know the truth. You know of my foolishness. You know of my suffering. And you know that I do care.

I write this in deep gratitude to you for your wisdom, which I ignored. And for your concern, which I am only now beginning to appreciate.

Marketa

Jakub read the letter twice, then folded it away.

Mingonius spoke gently, grasping Jakub's shoulder. "Marketa was an informant to the king, was she not? She has confessed as much to me now, in order to protect you. We both agreed I could not deliver this letter unless the news of Don Julius's assault on her had reached Prague.

"Had His Majesty learned that the spy you had contracted was the same girl that Don Julius attacked, he would have imprisoned you in his wrath. As it is, he has almost directed his ire at me, even though the guards and staff have sworn I had already left for Prague before the attack happened."

Jakub felt tears start up in his eyes.

"You are a true friend to both of us. Tell me what she suffers and how I can help."

"I am not sure how any of us can help now. She makes her home with the cunning woman of Krumlov, and the people of Krumlov protect her. The guards and staff have sworn secrecy to protect her. But she will never be truly safe until Don Julius's death."

At that moment Jakub knew he had to travel at once to Krumlov. He would make arrangements as quickly as possible. He unfolded the letter from Marketa and read it yet again.

CHAPTER 37

THE LIBERATION OF DON JULIUS

The day Don Julius was released from his confinement in the castle brought threatening clouds on the horizon and ominous winds that whipped across the Vltava and bent the budding trees of spring. The king's impulsive decree came without warning to either castle or town. The villagers in Latran and beyond in the Old Town learned only when they heard whoops of triumph as Don Julius galloped his black stallion down the steep hill, across the Barber's Bridge, and into the town square.

Disguised under her woolen cape and hood, Marketa was bargaining for a head of cabbage from the greengrocer when Don Julius's horse clattered into the square. Riding beside the prince were two churlish youths, one blond, one dark-haired, dressed in satin doublets and fine riding breeches.

"Stay down, *slecna!*" warned the greengrocer, pushing Marketa to her knees and piling the pyramid of cabbages higher. "Do not rise until I say so!"

The crowd backed away from the galloping horses, mothers pulling their children close.

"Lock up your women, Krumlov! The rutting goat of the House of Hapsburg is loosed once more!" shouted the blond rider in slurred German. He swung about in his saddle, letting one foot dangle, and took a swig from a silver flask. "Hear me, oh white beards! There will be no honor in this shit pot of a Czech town when Don Julius cuts his swath!"

Exhausted by his speech, he slumped back in his saddle and belched.

"Well said, Heinrich!" cheered his companion. "Our wenching days are upon us again. Is that not so, Don Julius!"

Don Julius wore a forlorn look for a man in his moment of triumph. He turned his head away from his two rowdy companions and gazed down at his outstretched hands. He flexed them open and closed, his fingers undulating to his breath, pulsing like water grass in the river.

"Where is the girl with hair the color of the many leaves in the fall?" he wailed. "How I would love to sleep beneath her sweet-tressed forest!"

"Pick another," said the black-haired companion, peevishly. He, like the blond youth, spoke German with a Viennese accent. "Find another wench and drink away your woes. Forget the dead whore."

"Franz, you villain! Brilliant!" hiccupped the yellow-haired youth. "We shall sup on the wenches of Krumlov and drink to oblivion! That is the cure for you, Don Julius!"

But Don Julius seemed not to have heard. He looked up into the stormy sky and spread his arms wide.

"Where is my Marketa?" he cried as scattering raindrops fell into his eyes. He blinked up at the sky, wet-faced. "Can angels not fly? Can they not forgive as they look down from heaven?"

Marketa sucked in her breath. Now he called her an angel. This same madman who had raped her, slashed her, and caused the fall that should have been her death. How had she been such a fool as to believe even for an instant that he was anything but a murderous beast?

"Here," said Heinrich, the blond Austrian, dismounting from his horse and grabbing Katarina from the crowd. "Here is a fair maid to make you forget any who came before."

He heaved her over his shoulder. She kicked and screamed, beating his back with her fists.

The Austrian youth dumped her on the ground her like a bag of grain in front of Don Julius.

"Take this wench and bury your woes between her legs!" he said, panting with the effort. He slumped down beside a barrel of ale.

Katarina scrambled to her feet and tried to retreat.

Don Julius seized her elbow and swung her toward him. He kissed her neck and explored her bosom with his groping hands, kneading her breasts. His hands moved roughly under her skirt.

She shrieked, "Let me go! It is not me you want!"

Suddenly he dropped her from his arms, as if he had no idea she was there. He gazed about the town square with a haunted look.

Katarina scurried away to hide in the crowd.

Don Julius staggered over to the brewer's barrels, kicking the kegs.

"Beer!" he shouted. "To rinse the memory from my head." He rubbed his temples. "My angel has cast a barb in my heart. It aches for her still."

Marketa swallowed hard and remembered his kisses, hot on her mouth and neck. What a fool she had been!

Don Julius's companions looked at each other, wagging their heads. Franz staggered toward the brewer and his kegs.

"You heard the king's son. He asked for beer, you old simpleton!"

Pan Brewer hastily drew a deep tankard of beer and proffered it to Don Julius, bowing. The prince's friends kicked the fawning man in the butt and collapsed in howls of laughter.

"And us? Are we not his companions? Where is our ale, man?" Don Julius sat down heavily on a barrel.

"Where are the Bohemian beauties?" he cried. He seemed to have forgotten that he had been mourning Marketa just moments before.

A ripple of whispers worked through the crowd. Two whores of Virgin Lane—one with bright red hair—were pushed out from the ranks of townspeople. They were only a few years older than Marketa. For all their professional experience on their backs, they now quaked like wet lambs before the lecherous son of the king.

The girls' hair hung matted for it had been a season since they had properly bathed, other than the splash of a whore's wash, straddled over a splintered bucket. The matrons of Krumlov urged them on, whispering it was their duty to satisfy the lust of Don Julius and spare the innocent girls.

"Go on, show him your shoulders," said the fisher's wife, pulling down the red-haired girl's blouse until her white skin was bare, just above her nipples.

The girls took two or three steps toward Don Julius, but their forced smiles died on their beet-stained lips.

The two Viennese companions hooted and howled at the exposed flesh of the women's shoulders. Don Julius joined in, gesturing wildly at the bawdy women who approached him.

"You, red-haired whore!" called the shoemaker's wife. "Show him your bosom! You have shown it enough times to my husband and sons to pave Virgin's Lane in silver!"

Don Julius's lecherous laugh stopped suddenly as he regarded the two whores who stood before him. The drunkards beside him stopped their catcalls.

No one spoke, and the only sounds were the screeching of crows circling above Krumlov and the plop of light raindrops on the cobblestones.

"You dare to offer me your leavings?" Don Julius growled ominously. "You foist these common whores on me?"

With a roar, he seized the brunette. He caught her neck in the crook of his elbow and pulled her head close. He sniffed her and curled his lip in disgust.

"You smell of Czech spunk!" he said, pushing her to the ground. He drew his rapier and made a feint at the girl, making her scream in terror.

Then he dropped the sword. It clattered on the cobblestones and he walked over it, blindly as a sleepwalker.

"Fetch me beer!" he demanded.

The brewer complied quickly, and Don Julius raised the tankard to his lips, draining it in one go.

"Bring me the yellow-haired wench," he shouted.

The Austrian youths parted the crowd with rough shoves, making their way toward the bakery, where Katarina had run.

The blacksmith's son jumped in front of them, blocking the way. In his hand was a dagger.

"Leave her alone!"

Despite his great size and blackened face, they laughed. "You would force us to do your bidding with that little prick of a knife?" sneered Franz, reaching for his rapier. "Let us show you what nobles carry as their members!"

Krumlov acted in a heartbeat. The fear that had lodged in the townsmen's breasts melted and they reached for weapons. The air filled with the hiss of daggers unsheathed, the clatter of clubs seized from under crates, of hammers, scythes, and pitchforks raised.

The wind whined through the marketplace, and big raindrops pelted down on the angry mob. Their jaws set, they blinked away the rain from their white-ringed eyes.

The two Austrians suddenly sobered as they heard the crack of the stablemaster's whip and saw the sharp gleaming hooks of the hay-balers. All around them they saw eyes burning with hatred and faces quivering with bloodlust.

Only Don Julius failed to register the danger of the situation. He yawned.

"Let us go to the hills. Tell the huntsmen to ready the hounds. I lust for blood!"

A boy who had latched onto Don Julius's horse hurried it to him and held it steady as he mounted. Don Julius settled into the saddle and reined his horse through the crowd, and his companions eagerly followed.

"Out of my way, half-wits!" he growled. He spurred his horse and charged at a gallop, racing to the walls of the city and out toward the hills.

As Marketa stood up from behind the pyramid of cabbages, every eye of Krumlov was pinned on her.

∼

"She is a witch, I tell you," said the castle housekeeper in German, tucking a greasy strand of hair under her white kerchief. "That hellfire red hair, the gleaming green eyes of a cat."

The old Viennese cook crossed herself and kissed her fingers. She stared at the red-haired stranger at the entrance of the first courtyard.

"What does she want with Doctor Horcicky? Did he not attend the Jesuit seminary? Surely he cannot admit a woman like that to cross his threshold, into the king's sanctuary?"

One of the king's own personal guard approached them, walking swiftly with scorn on his face, his heels clicking on the cobblestone. The women scattered like clucking hens.

"You do best not to gossip in the presence of the king's guard," he called after them. "Perform your duties to our king and bite your vicious tongues. Do you think your voices do not carry in the open air?"

The guard spat on the gray cobblestones and returned to the comely stranger wrapped in wool scarves and a black cloak against the cold spring weather. He found the woman who awaited Doctor Horcicky quite attractive, and unlike any woman he had ever seen in Prague.

But even the guard was amazed when Jakub entered the courtyard and received his visitor. He rushed to her and pulled the woman into his arms.

"Annabella! You have come, just as I am about to depart for Cesky Krumlov."

"Hush," she whispered, motioning to the guard. "Let us go where we can talk in private."

Jakub regained his composure and signaled to the guard.

"Thank you, guard, for welcoming my sister to the *hrad*. She is most grateful for her warm reception."

With this, Jakub offered his arm to Annabella and they walked toward his cottage in the far corner of the gardens.

~

It took Annabella long into the night to calm Jakub's fears and answer his flood of questions about Marketa.

"Is she not in great danger in Krumlov?"

Annabella shook her head as she cut a wedge of cheese with a small knife. The flames of the hearth licked their reflection on the shiny blade.

"To the contrary, the safest place for her is Krumlov. All Bohemia knows now how he slashed her and how she plummeted from the castle window, thanks to the howling laments of Don Julius. We want to preserve the lie that she died in the fall. No one in Krumlov will ever whisper the news; they will keep her secret to their death. Oh, how they hate the Hapsburgs!"

"But what if the secret is discovered? The gossips at Budejovice? What if the king learns—or worse yet—Don Julius learns that Marketa lives?"

Annabella took a bite of her cheese and a long draught of ale.

"We will deal with that when we have to," she said, wiping the froth from her lips with her sleeve. "For now, as she recovers, she is safest among her own people."

Jakub shook his head. "I cannot rest until I see her again. It was my fault for asking her to report on Don Julius's treatment. I must return with you at once."

Annabella studied him as she pared the molded rind from another chunk of cheese. She shook the knife at him, a red glow flickering with its movement. "Oh you shall see her. There will be plenty of time for that. But it will not be until deep winter, Jakub. To see her now will bring spies from Prague. For now you must let her be if you truly value her safety."

Jakub walked to the window and stared out at the stars and the moonlight on the budding apple trees through the thick, warped glass. Spring was so late this year, bestowing little comfort for the earth's tender shoots and bulbs.

"I should have protected her from that monster," he said, shaking his head sadly. "She wrote of her compassion for him. I should have responded more strongly. I should have forbidden her. I will never forgive myself!"

"She lives, Jakub, she lives."

"Yes, but how she has suffered. And now…"

Annabella put down her knife and wiped her hands on her apron. "And now *what*, Jakub?"

Jakub could not face her. He stared again out the window.

"I meant to make her my wife. But now it is impossible."

Annabella rose and walked toward the window. She seized Jakub by the shoulders and turned him around.

"And why would that be? Why could you not marry her?"

Jakub hesitated. "Because she has been raped by the king's son."

Annabella's face buckled with scorn. "What difference does that make?"

"You don't understand, Annabella. I cannot help it. It is my upbringing. And what if the king discovers my wife's past with his son. That she was raped—"

Annabella turned on him in fury, her hands clenched in fists.

"Does her virginity matter? You confuse the bitter teachings of priests with God and goodness. Do you really believe bloody sheets are the banner of purity and innocence?"

"Annabella! You cannot understand. Those 'bitter priests' were my life, my childhood. I can't just forget everything I ever believed. I would have to begin my life, my beliefs again from nothing." He blushed and tried to steer away from the black abyss of life without belief. "And the king—"

Annabella slammed her hand on the table, the noise like a sudden explosion. "Don't talk to me about the king! We are talking about love. Love risks all, fears nothing! Do not be a fool, Jakub."

She thudded her fist on the table and narrowed her eyes. "Would I have the power in my spells, as potent and blinding as religion!" Annabella narrowed her eyes. "And do not pretend that your own virginity does not play a part in your fears. You are too proud, Jakub."

Jakub turned on her, furious. "You have no right to say that, Annabella."

"Aha! I have touched upon the truth. It is indeed your own 'virtue' that stands in the way of your heart. I know you, Jakub.

You are a good man, a forgiving man. Release yourself from the tyranny of cloistered men. What a dark shadow these vicious men in robes of sackcloth have cast upon your soul."

"But it is my faith, Annabella!"

"Faith? Ah, see how the Church has blinded you, crippling your own true spirit? You must throw off these fetters, find your own courage."

Jakub turned away and looked out at the darkness. He was so absorbed in his despair that he did not notice the Krumlov witch reach quickly into her cloth bundle and draw out a tiny, blue glass vial. She removed the stopper with her teeth and sprinkled the contents of the liquid into the jug of dark ale.

She gave the jug a quick swirl, watching Jakub's back as he stared out into the night.

Jakub drew his finger across the condensation on the windowpane. Spring was still as fragile as a newborn, here in the north of Bohemia, fragile to the point of sacrifice to the lingering winter cold.

Annabella sighed. "Come away from the window, Jakub. You worry too much about Marketa and the past. Come drink to her health, for she is in the safety of my own home. Besides, I have a plan, a way to save not only Marketa, but all of the innocents of Krumlov, should the spirits help me."

Annabella poured Jakub ale from the pitcher. When he asked if she would join him in a drink, she refused.

"I have sated my thirst. But there is a favor I will ask tonight, though not quite yet. Drink, Jakub, drink. Let the good ale rinse away your worries."

Outside the cottage, an owl hooted in the moonlight. Annabella smiled as Jakub downed his mug of brown ale and poured himself another draught.

WINTER 1607-1608

CHAPTER 38

A Dark Winter

By early winter of 1607, the Jesuit priests of Krumlov had learned the story of Marketa's rape and the near miracle of her survival. Abbot Bedrich Prochazka prayed fervently for God's advice, begging for wisdom. He spent days on his knees, his old bones soaking up the chill of the ancient stone floor of the monastery.

The abbot ultimately decided it was God's will to protect the innocent, and he said nothing to the Spanish priest. Though the Jesuit order was a staunch supporter of the crown and the Catholic Hapsburgs, the Krumlov priests could not bring themselves to betray one of their own and give comfort to Don Julius.

The Jesuits knew how to guard secrets.

Abbot Prochazka felt he owed his allegiance above all to God, then to Bohemia, not Rudolf II. The king's obsession with the occult had left a sour taste in the abbot's mouth. Better to protect an innocent girl than please a Hapsburg and bring about her certain death. Abbot Prochazka believed there was a higher reckoning in heaven than the judgment of the Hapsburg dynasty here on earth. If God had spared the girl's life, He must have another plan for her.

Abbot Prochazka sighed, remembering his boyhood. Marketa's aunt, Ludmilla of the Poor Clares, had been his childhood sweetheart, before she renounced him one night and took her vows. There was a special aura about Ludmilla that had passed to her niece. Marketa had been spared by divine intervention, of this the abbot was certain.

Abbot Prochazka was not convinced that Carlos Felipe would feel the same way. He thought the priest worked a bit too hard to cultivate favor with royalty, and the fact that he had once been confessor to the Spanish court of Felipe II made the abbot doubt his commitment to God's work among the poor and innocent. Abbot Prochazka doubted that the Spanish priest would protect a simple Krumlovian girl, a bathmaid. Her fate would seem inconsequential to him in the great chess game of European politics and religion.

On the next occasion when the two priests met to discuss Don Julius's soul, Abbot Prochazka mentioned nothing about Marketa's plummet from Rozmberk Castle.

∾

Under the leaking roof of the Poor Clares convent, Mother Superior Ludmilla Pichlerova was confined to bed. The old nuns whispered this disease had been long in coming, for her rattling coughs had echoed ominously through the convent for months.

As the summer days shortened toward autumn, the nuns knew she had little time left on this earth. They were certain she would not make it through these last hard winter months before God called her to Him.

Ludmilla coughed continuously, spitting up bright blood. She was so weak she could barely sit up for the nuns to spoon-feed her broth brewed of pork bones and marjoram. She invited her brother to visit her often, even though the rules of the convent prohibited men. As she was the mother superior and the other nuns, the Jesuit abbot, and the church priests made no trouble about her requests, her brother, Zigmund Pichler, spent many an hour by her sickbed.

"And how goes the healing process with Marketa?" she asked, as her own health diminished day by day.

"Splendidly, dear Ludmilla."

"Ah, that is good."

Ludmilla's brother twisted his beard between his fingers.

"You know I only wanted the best for her. To protect her from the raging lunatic—that is why I brought her here."

Ludmilla nodded weakly, a slow rocking of her head in rhythm to her ragged breath.

"Of course, Brother. You did what a good father should. You tried to protect and defend your daughter."

Ludmilla struggled to focus her fever-glazed eyes on her brother, for she thought she heard a sob cracking his voice. When she reached her hand for his face, she touched his cheek, hot and wet with tears.

"Oh, Sister! I was a bad father, a selfish fiend! I let my wife sell her to a patron to procure gold and feed the twins better cuts of meat! I used the money earned by her body to purchase books!"

"I know," said Ludmilla, turning her eyes toward her statue of the Holy Virgin on a shelf on the wall. She considered the saint's forgiving smile, a woman who mourned her son but nevertheless faithfully protected wretched humanity and heard their prayers. Christ's mother lived her entire life among the sinners, but she spends eternity forgiving them, her kind love intervening in their despair.

Sinners—humanity. Ludmilla heaved a sigh from the depths of her lungs, striking a sharp pain in her chest. She winced, clutching her breast. After a few shallow breaths, she composed herself to speak again.

"The nuns told me that the brewer was her patron," she said. "They said she would lose her virtue to him if we did not intervene. I, too, wanted to protect her and bring her into our flock." She looked toward the faint light that strayed through the leaded window, playing on the gray stones. This time of year, the sun offered only the weakest rays of sunlight to the Bohemian lands.

"You know my time is near, Zigmund," she said, her voice barely above a whisper. "I am called to meet Jesus and his Father, our God."

Her brother sniffed back his tears, realizing what she was saying and wanting to be stronger for his sister, as strong as she was at this moment.

"Let Annabella brew a cure for you, Sister. She has cured even the sickest among us!"

"No," said Ludmilla, coughing. She dabbed a white linen cloth to her white lips. "Annabella would look at me and ask me if I wanted to be cured, if I had a dream to pursue. I have heard of her ways. My dream is to meet Jesus our Lord and Savior. I am on that path."

Pichler grasped his sister's frail hand across the coarse woolen blanket. He was amazed how fine and white her skin remained, even after so many years. There were no wrinkles on the creamy skin that had rarely seen the sun or wind and snow, sheltered for a lifetime within the walls of the convent.

"We will not dwell on my future in the other world," she said, "but in this world we live in, you and I. There is something I wish. It will shock you, I am sure. But hear me, I am adamant about this."

"What, dear Sister? I promise you, I swear to you. Anything you wish," said Pichler.

Ludmilla lifted her free hand to her eyebrow and scratched it, her arm trembling.

"Truly. You would swear?"

"I swear it."

She let her hand fall, exhausted from lifting it to her face. She cleared her throat as she reached for the handkerchief on the coverlet. Pichler winced as crimson drops stained the linen.

"I want to give my body to your science, to Marketa and to you to further your investigation of anatomy."

"Never!" said Pichler, his spine stiffening in revulsion at the thought. "I could never consent to that!" He squeezed her hand so hard, he could feel the fragile bones crush together.

His sister mewed in pain and drew back her hand, pressing it protectively against her concave chest. Then she gathered her strength and drew herself up, shaking with effort. She looked at her brother, her blue eyes deep in their sockets, wild animals in a cave.

"Marketa is right. What have I ever accomplished by not setting foot outside this convent? My last act should be to help humanity in the search for cures for the body's disease. I have always attended scrupulously to my soul and that of others in my prayers. If I were to donate my body once the soul has departed, then I serve one last time, in a way I never could in life."

It was all too much for Pichler. He convulsed with sobs, his big shoulders shaking as he wept for his sister.

～

Ultimately, it was neither a Jesuit nor a Krumlov citizen who told Don Julius that Marketa still walked the earth. He learned that news in a small tavern—a hunting lodge and salt traders' rest stop—nestled in the dark pine mountains of Sumava, a long, cold day's ride from Cesky Krumlov.

It was there on a cold February day that Don Julius overheard a drunken conversation between two salt traders.

Don Julius had become darkly morose, more melancholy than choleric. The Spanish priest, at wit's end with his wailing, finally acquiesced to his companions' pleas to take their swollen-eyed friend on a week's hunt in the wilds of southern Bohemia, where bears roamed the pine-studded mountains and wild cats prowled the steep embankments.

"He must be persuaded to forget this common girl! Her memory haunts him like a phantom!" they pleaded. "What good is it to watch the man cry like a woman for the loss of a simple bathmaid? Let us take him away on the hunt. His soul will be recharged with the excitement of chasing prey where good winds blow with the scent of pine. The chase and blood-lust will restore his health so that he sleeps once more at night. As shall we!"

Finally Carlos Felipe agreed. He was to accompany them in a coach and lodge in the tavern in a room close to Don Julius.

The inn at Smrcina was large enough to host a dozen men, many of whom were salt traders from Austria who wended their way with mule trains to Prague or Cesky Budejovice. The food was simple, game roasted over an open fire, eaten with a knife, something all travelers carried with them, often around their necks. The Spanish priest found the fare simple and agreeable, reminiscent of the spit-roasted meats of Spain: fire-licked and unseasoned, except for salt.

Still the days of hunting in the cold mountain air had no effect on Don Julius, thought the priest. Carlos Felipe watched his morose charge brood, hunched over his ale, examining the tankard as the froth lost its vigor, receding slowly below the rim. He refused to converse with his companions or the priest and snapped that he was to be left alone.

But Don Julius and his party were not the only customers in the tavern, and those who shared the room were drunk and loose-tongued.

The two brawny salt merchants had swallowed jar after jar of ale and were slurring their words in loud voices as they exchanged gossip.

"He pitched her from the castle, screaming for mercy!" said one, his powerful hands clenched in a fist. "The bloody Hapsburgs think nothing of tossing a Bohemian out a window! To them, we are expendable as apple peelings and kitchen scraps!"

"He cut her, that's what I hear," answered his friend, a dirty scrap of leather worn as a patch over his eye. "My friend says he saw her enter the Gray Goose, her face stitched up with black thread. Eyes swollen—puffed up like she had been pummeled. Couldn't walk on her own, the innkeeper had to carry her back to her room like a sack of salt. It was a miracle she was alive."

He paused, taking a long gulp of beer and rubbing at his greasy eye patch with his knuckle.

The priest squinted hard at Don Julius to see how these words registered. At first, the melancholy eyes seemed to blink, as if struggling with a bad memory. Then Don Julius jumped up, snarling like mad dog, knocking over his ale.

The crash of broken crockery alerted the two traders. Suddenly a disheveled man with wild eyes stood before them with his rapier drawn.

"Where is she?" Don Julius demanded. "If you value your life's blood, you will tell me this moment!"

The men jumped up from their table and unsheathed their own weapons, crouching, ready to spring at their attacker.

"Stop!" shouted the priest standing beside Don Julius, along with his two companions.

"This is the son of His Majesty King Rudolf II. To harm him will bring you to the dungeons of the *hrad*!"

The traders kept their swords unsheathed and at the ready, but lowered them several degrees.

"Tell him to drop his weapon and we will do the same," shouted the man with the eye patch. "We have not done him harm. By God, why does he menace us?"

"Where is she?" roared Don Julius, slicing the air with his rapier.

The priest drew close to his charge and whispered in his ear, "If you drop your sword, we can discover the secret. Dead men cannot talk, Don Julius. Secrets die with them."

At this Don Julius moved his head, more of a sequence of trembles than a nod. He lowered his rapier, his movements as wooden as a marionette. The priest slowly and cautiously removed his hand from the hilt.

"Now," said the priest, panting, "would you allow us to sit with you, and we can discuss the matter of the bathmaid."

The two men quickly pulled out stools so that the prince and his priest could join them at the table. The stupor that the ale had cast just minutes before had evaporated. Everyone in Bohemia knew about the dungeons of the Prague Castle, the rack and the other machines of torture. The two salt traders had no intention of visiting those underground cells. They told Don Julius and the priest everything they knew of the mysterious bathmaid of Krumlov.

CHAPTER 39

A Man in Annabella's House

Marketa could smell him as she cracked open the trapdoor from the catacombs. A man's sweat, a strong male musk permeating a house that had been so thoroughly scented with women for centuries.

Annabella no longer took the precaution of sliding the chest over the trapdoor—all of Krumlov was committed to Marketa's protection. That, and her screaming nightmares of being sealed alive forever in the catacombs below made Annabella agree to leave the trapdoor covered with only with a coarse woolen rug.

Annabella had gone to the mountains two nights before to visit the graves of her dead mother and the previous Annabellas from throughout the centuries. It was a secret place in the depths of the forest, known only to the coven of witches who had lived in the house on Dlouha Street. Annabella had explained, flames leaping in her eyes, that she needed the spirits' counsel to be prepared for the days to come.

That morning, Marketa arose at dawn. For months she had slept late, having no light underground to wake her. Those long hours of sleep had helped her heal, but now her body had adjusted to the rhythms of the sun and moon. She climbed up the lashed wooden ladder and pushed the trapdoor open as far as she could manage on her own. Even without the heavy chest to block the door, escape from the catacombs wasn't easy if there was no one to help. She had to slide along the kitchen floor, wriggling under the massive weight of the door.

Her plan that morning was to make some tea and eat a heel of black bread for breakfast and then start her studies of the Book of Paracelsus by the first rays of the morning light. But as soon as she emerged, she was stopped by the scent of a man—and then, just as immediately, by the sight of a man.

He lay on the floor asleep, still in his muddy clothes and riding boots. The hard ride from Prague had left him exhausted.

As she stared, Jakub shuddered awake and blinked open his eyes.

"Marketa!" he cried, helping her from the gaping hole in the floor. He embraced her, pulling her tight to his chest. His lips kissed her hair as he rocked her in his arms.

"You are here! But Annabella warned you not to come."

"I could not stay away any longer. I had to see you, I had to explain. There is something that weighs on my conscience. But first, where is Annabella?"

"She has gone to the mountains to visit her ancestors' graves. She said she must confer with them about her plan."

Jakub looked at her with wild eyes.

"Plan? What plan? If it involves Don Julius, you must not take part in it. Come away with me to Prague at once!"

"No," said Marketa. "I have not yet heard the plan, but I trust Annabella. She has cared for me in my hour of need."

Jakub dropped his gaze to the floor, and his face burned with shame. He thought how he and Annabella had both betrayed Marketa on that spring night in Prague. When he awoke that next morning to find the naked red-haired beauty beside him in bed, he grabbed his aching head in disbelief. He smelled the unfamiliar scent of lovemaking in the sheets.

"You have bewitched me!" he said, struggling to his feet.

Annabella only laughed. She pulled a long strand of her red hair over her breast. Her fingers worked at untangling the knots Jakub had made as his fingers raked through her hair in passion.

"Bewitched you! That is my profession, dear friend. But be not so accusing—I have taken your damnable virginity, and you will give us both a child. And an extraordinary one at that! An Annabella the likes of none before her!"

Jakub held his head in his hands, his fingers clutching at his hair in despair.

"Do not look at me with the eyes of a complete innocent," she chided him. "Dare not feign that you cannot remember our night together. Such passion and prowess, such hungry desire cannot be attributed solely to my potion. I shall have the child I long for, and you—you no longer have your priestly virtue to confuse your heart and deny love. I have set you free."

As Jakub now remembered that night for the thousandth time, he looked at Marketa in his arms. He thought of the child that grew in Annabella's womb and opened his mouth to begin a confession.

The door flew open, and Annabella stood before them.

"Enough!" she said, drawing them apart. "We have not the time for affairs of the heart. Stay hidden, Marketa. Jakub, come with me. I fear the time approaches more quickly than we expected."

Don Julius galloped his horse so hard he almost killed the stallion. Over the rutted roads and snowy trails through the forests of Sumava, he urged his mount forward at a cruel pace, lashing at its flanks until the whip came away bloody.

Carlos Felipe made no attempt to chase the three riders down. He could not hope to compete with the equestrian skills and athleticism of a young man born in the saddle and trained by the finest horsemasters. He sent the two companions to pursue the king's son and followed in the small surrey, which clattered over the rough roads of the Salt Trail.

The sharp rocks of the hills slashed at the fetlocks of the stallion, but the horse had a bold heart and clearly sensed the way to the Rozmberk stables. The mad rider who sat atop him demanded ever more speed, and the galloping madness became one between rider and steed. The iron clang of horseshoes and the shouts and mad ravings ricocheted over the dales.

As they approached Krumlov, Don Julius did not ride to the stables, but galloped over Barber's Bridge, straight to the bathhouse. He leapt off the horse, his legs buckling after so many hours in the saddle.

"Where is she?" he bellowed, struggling to his feet.

Lucie Pichlerova and a few half-dressed bathers rushed to see what the commotion was about.

"Where do you hide her, you miserable old whore!" shouted Don Julius, staggering toward her with his hand on his dagger.

Lucie shrieked and ran inside, bolting the door behind her. The naked bathers scattered in all directions, clothing abandoned, hands pressed to their breasts and genitals.

Don Julius pounded on the massive door.

"Whore of a whore, where is she? I will kill you and every member of your family if she is not returned to me!"

By now, citizens were gathering by the bridge to watch the wretched Hapsburg pounding against the door. When Lucie refused to open it, he unsheathed his dagger and stabbed the wood savagely, over and over again, gouging and splintering the heavy oak planks as if it were living flesh and a mortal enemy.

With a clamor of thundering hooves, the two Austrian companions finally caught up with their lunatic friend. They surveyed the scene, still gasping for breath from the rough ride, and exchanged a few words in German. The blond rider took off at a gallop for reinforcements from the castle while the dark-haired one dismounted, throwing his reins to the nearest bystander.

"Don Julius, come! We will find your bathmaid, I swear it! Come away from the door and let us return to the castle to make our plan."

Don Julius threw him a murderous look and continued his violent attack on the door, his hands bleeding now from sharp splinters that scored his skin.

As he slashed feverishly at the door, Jakub and Annabella came running, for the news of Don Julius's attack on the bathhouse had flown from mouth to shouting mouth the length of crowded Wide Street. All Krumlov pressed near to see, making the old Barber's Bridge creak under their weight. Jakub and Annabella pushed through the crowd.

"Don Julius! Cease!" shouted Jakub in German. "Let me through, I am a court physician to Rudolf II!"

The people of Krumlov pressed back against one another, clearing a narrow passage for him, staring at the well-dressed stranger.

At the sound of Jakub's voice, Don Julius stopped mid-gouge, his dagger plunged deep into the wood. He did not turn around, but pressed his forehead to the door.

"Jakub!" he shouted, the name resounding. "You too seek the maiden of the Coded Book. Well, you shan't have her. She is mine until death and beyond!"

"Come away from the door, Don Julius. She is not within those walls."

Don Julius grasped the hilt of his dagger with all his might and pulled the blade from the splintered wood. He grunted mightily with the effort and swung around, facing the physician with his weapon in his hand. He crouched, ready to attack.

"Go away, Physician. You shall not have her and her secrets!"

Jakub skirted the edges of the crowd, approaching the lunatic from an angle.

"Drop the weapon, Don Julius. Listen to reason, sir."

"Reason? I know why you are here!"

"The Coded Book is back at court in the hands of your father. Doctor Mingonius has delivered it there safely."

"God curse the swinish king! His greedy hand caressing something he cannot comprehend!" shouted Don Julius, his hands trembling. "The book is mine! It is I who will read its secrets, not a thickheaded sot!"

A collective gasp issued from the gaping mouths of Krumlov. Never had they heard such treasonous blasphemy shouted in their streets. Treason shouted at full lung by the king's own son.

"Come, Don Julius. Doctor Mingonius will return. Once we calm the bad humors that possess your body and mind, he shall return with the book. I will write to him tonight, you will see. Come now. We have gone through too much to let it end like this, Giuglio."

At the mention of his childhood name, Don Julius began to tremble, the dagger shaking like a child's rattle in his hand.

"All I want is the maiden, my angel!" he cried. "She lives, they say, and she must join me to be my mistress, my wife! My soul bleeds for her—the voices will not be stilled!"

His legs buckled and he collapsed, the exhausting ride and emotion finally taking their toll. He began to sob, phlegm running from his nose and mouth.

"With her, I can fight the demons. She silences the voices in my head with her touch. Nothing else can save me. No one!"

He scrabbled at the filthy ground with his bloody fingers.

The clatter of horseshoes ricocheted off the cobblestones, heralding the approach of the guards and coach. Jakub kicked away Don Julius's dagger and knelt by his side.

"Come, Giuglio. I will attend you at the castle and prepare hot baths to soothe you. The demons that haunt you murder your soul."

The guards dismounted and helped the sobbing Don Julius into the coach. The grief-stricken Hapsburg offered no resistance.

Jakub crouched in the slick muck of the cobblestones. He picked up the dagger and returned to Annabella as the crowd watched his every move, trying to identify this new stranger to Krumlov.

"Bring some red oil to the castle and your most potent sleeping teas," he whispered to her. "Make sure Marketa stays hidden. This is a very dangerous time."

He jumped into the coach and shouted to the driver. He comforted his blubbering patient as they rode back up the hill to Rozmberk Castle.

CHAPTER 40

JAKUB HORCICKY DE TENEPEC AT ROZMBERK CASTLE

The carriage clattered up the cobblestones. The short ride up the hill to the castle was punctuated with wailing sobs from Don Julius. Jakub Horcicky, who had known the king's son almost all his life, was shocked to witness such despair from a young man who had always prided himself on his strength and the cruel power he could wield over any who crossed his path or thwarted his desires.

What humor had seized him with such force as to render him a weeping mockery of a man? Had Marketa opened the veins of the emperor's son and stolen his soul along with his blood?

In the castle courtyard, Jakub flung open the carriage door and told Don Julius, "Do not worry, my lord. All will be well." Then he stepped down onto the cobblestones and told the guards, in Czech, "Take Don Julius to his chambers and draw a bath." They looked at each other in surprise when they heard his distinct Krumlov accent. He had spoken perfect German when addressing Don Julius. Now to hear the royal physician speak to them in their own tongue and dialect left them dumbfounded.

"Yes, I was born on a farm near Krumlov," he said with a nod. "I am one of you."

The guards had no time to converse further. They seized the quivering Don Julius and half carried him through the castle doors and up the stairs to the Rozmberk apartments where he now insisted on living in luxury rivaling the king's. One guard barked an order to a servant for water to be drawn for the bath.

Jakub left orders for Wilhelm the page to await Annabella's teas and potions, with strict instructions to bring them immediately. He followed the guards up the stairs and watched them deposit their charge on his bed and prop him up against the pillows so he wouldn't choke on his own saliva.

Don Julius's eyes rolled in his head. He gulped at the air as if it were something foreign, a maritime creature dredged out of the water, gasping.

Jakub had no pity.

"You attacked her and she fell to her death," said Jakub in a low voice, his teeth grinding in anger. "You murdered that innocent girl."

"NO!" shouted Don Julius, his eyes focusing past Jakub. "She lives! They deceive me, these wretched pigs of Krumlov. They hide her. They have hidden her from me all along!"

Jakub looked at the guards and then back at Don Julius. The thought that Don Julius knew she was alive made his blood chill.

"No, Don Julius, she died in the fall," said Jakub. "No one could survive from such a height!"

"She could if she landed on the rubbish pile," said a Castilian-accented voice. The Spanish priest stood at the threshold of the door. "A miracle, perhaps, but a miracle that was concealed from us by these deceitful Krumlovians!"

Jakub watched the desiccated priest approach the bed. His cassock was rumpled and mud-splattered. He looked weary, but angry.

"And who are you?" Carlos Felipe asked rudely. "What business do you have conversing with my charge, the king's son?"

"I am Jakub Horcicky de Tenepec, a physician to the king," replied Jakub. "I might ask the same of you—you seem to have wandered away from your monastery. The Jesuits are down the road in Old Town."

"How did you know I was a Jesuit?" snapped Carlos Felipe.

"I spent my childhood scrubbing plates and fetching water for the brotherhood," replied Jakub. "There is a certain aura about Jesuits one does not soon forget."

The two men eyed each other warily.

Don Julius struggled to his feet. "I shall imprison her father the barber until she surrenders herself to me!"

Jakub's eyes narrowed. "Imprison the barber? On what cause?"

Don Julius's face wrinkled in furrows as he cast about for reasons.

Then the priest committed the greatest of sins. "That he conceals the truth from the Hapsburgs!" he said in a cold harsh voice. "That is clearly treason. This entire wretched town is an accomplice to treason!"

Jakub stared at the priest. How could this old man of the cloth condemn Marketa to certain death?

The priest stared back in defiance, his nostrils pinched and his mouth hard and small. Jakub thought, *This man is no friend of Krumlov or Bohemia.*

Don Julius shouted, "Treason! Yes, I am the Lord of Krumlov, by order of the king. I shall do whatever I choose with the miserable village and its people. They are my subjects." He set his lower jaw forward, grinding his teeth in a maniacal grimace.

"She loves her father. She will come back to me!" he said, twisting his dirty hands together. "I—I shall have a nightgown made for her. Trimmed in bearskin so I can tear it from her body and ravage her power. I shall ravish her until—"

"I think that is quite enough, Don Julius," said the priest, a sudden pallor overtaking him. "Have you forgotten your grief, your repentance? God has performed a miracle in—"

"Shut up, you miserable old man!"

To the priest's horror, the young man who had crawled on the floor of the chapel, proclaiming his sin and profound regret, declaring his love for the girl, now had the hard sheen of mad cruelty in his eyes.

The proud, vicious madman had returned, after months of remorse.

Carlos Felipe had only thought of revenge for the collective deceit of the Krumlovians, who had lied not only to Don Julius, but to him. In his burning spite, he had been blind to the girl's peril. Gone was the remorse, the tears, the confession and pleading for absolution for killing the girl, the pitiful bleating of a man in grief. Instead the hard glint of bestiality had returned.

The priest's old eyes grew large. He left the room genuflecting, his dry lips whispering a fervent prayer as Don Julius declared, atrocity by atrocity, exactly what acts he would commit on Marketa. Jakub's mind rocked with the diatribe, and he rushed for the door when the scullery boy arrived with the bag of teas and potions that Annabella had brought to the castle.

Jakub was able to keep Don Julius sedated for eight days, but he knew that he could not prolong the treatment any longer without running the risk of killing his patient. He did not wish King Rudolf's hooded executioner to dull the royal ax on his neck bones.

Jakub pleaded with Annabella to send Marketa away, and he warned of the certain arrest of her father, Zigmund Pichler. When Marketa refused to leave, he hurried to Annabella's house.

"He told me exactly what he would do to you, Marketa," said Jakub. His body was tense with emotion and his stomach churned with concern for the bloodletter's daughter. "He has ordered a night robe to be made for you out of the finest silk, trimmed in bear fur from the hunt. Then he will approach the bed and..."

"And what?"

"He shall cut you for your deceit to punish you. He shall rape you as you scream for mercy, bleeding from your wounds. I think he intends to kill you for not coming back to him at once," said Jakub, staring down at the worn planks of the table. He looked up again at Marketa. "He has always been brutal, and when the humors seize him, his bestiality knows no boundaries."

Jakub pulled Marketa toward him, his hands grasping her shoulders. "I beg of you, do not return to him. Let me hide you—I will take you to Prague under my protection."

Annabella watched the two from her stool. She said nothing.

Marketa looked back at Jakub, holding his gaze. There was tenderness mixed with terror in his eyes.

"I thank you for your offer of protection, Jakub. It is charitable, given your station at court, to risk intervention," said Marketa.

"Marketa! It is not charity. I could not bear to see harm come to you."

Marketa held his gaze as long as she could bear. But then she broke away from him.

"He will imprison my father? Does he mean to execute him?"

Jakub's silence was all the answer she got. Or needed. Marketa frowned, savagely twisting her hair around her finger.

"How can I let my father rot in the dungeon? How can I abandon him to face death for my foolish deed?" she said finally.

"I have already sent word for him to flee. Your mother must accompany him. There is no telling what Don Julius might do to her."

Marketa said nothing. Annabella reached for her hand and gently pressed it. She had been silent all evening.

"Annabella, help me. What should I do?"

The witch looked at the fire in the hearth.

"It is nearing Masopust, when we prepare to fast and the bad spirits run riot. They will be purged as spring finally comes, but now is a dangerous time as they rebel and walk among us. No good comes of this time. It is the bad month of February."

Marketa looked at her friend, her eyes welling with fear and disappointment. She had come to trust Annabella's prognostications, and now there was nothing but a bleak omen.

"But what of the plan? What did your coven of spirits tell you?"

"They told me to await your decision. First you must determine the course of destiny, and I must not intervene until you have chosen the path."

"But—I—what can I do? I am powerless!"

Annabella lifted her hand to Marketa's fear-stricken face. "You will lead us, Marketa. Somehow—the spirits have disclosed as much."

Marketa closed her eyes in despair. She had no idea what her friend was saying.

"In the meantime, bring me a lock of his hair," said Annabella to Jakub, her eyes turning back to stare at the fire. "I shall do what I can."

Jakub knew better than to argue with Annabella, for he had witnessed her cures and strange spells. Yet he still felt exasperation with her turn to witchcraft at such a dangerous crossing point, when reason and logic were clearly in demand.

"I doubt I can collect his hair, Annabella. The man will not let anyone touch him, save Marketa."

"Find a way. I must have his hair," she said, staring hard into his eyes. "The hair that grows from his crown and obscures his vision."

Jakub was certain he saw the leaping flames of the hearth still reflected in her gaze, even though she had turned away from the fire.

~

The warning came too late to save Barber Pichler. It was not a Krumlov guard who arrested Marketa's father, but the two Austrian companions of Don Julius, Heinrich and Franz, eager to put an end to the spell the Bohemian bathmaid had cast on their lord. They longed for their old friend, the king's son, to accompany them as he once did, sparking fights, drinking to excess, and whoring in the streets.

The Austrians seized Barber Pichler roughly and dragged him to the carriage. The coach driver cried out his remorse in Czech in the darkness as he watched his old friend pulled from his home. The Austrians shouted at him to stop his incomprehensible prattle or they would whip him and throw his old bones in the dungeon to keep his friend company among the rats.

Lucie Pichlerova's screams brought the neighbors running from both banks to the bridge. Heinrich shoved the barber's wife to the ground and spat on her.

"Mother of a whorish witch!" he shouted, running a hand through his greasy blond hair. "Surrender your daughter to Don Julius or you will never see your husband again!"

The carriage pulled away, leaving Lucie sobbing on the ground.

No one in Krumlov came to comfort her. They turned silently back to their affairs.

CHAPTER 41

LUDMILLA

When word reached the convent of the Poor Clares that Barber Pichler had been arrested, the news was quickly brought to the dying mother superior. The aged Sister Agnes knelt by her bedside and whispered the news.

"My brother," Ludmilla cried softly, her eyelids pressing closed. "I may be too late to help either of them."

The old nun who had brought the news nodded her head, resigned to the will of God.

"It is in the hands of our Lord," she said, fingering her rosary. Her face was set in hard lines, and she thrust her lower jaw forward. She was accustomed to the cruelty of the mortal world and comforted by others' misfortunes. The fact that Ludmilla had sullied the convent's sanctity with a male presence other than a priest made her despise the mother superior.

Ludmilla opened her eyes slowly and focused on the nun's tight mouth, etched in lines of bitterness. There was no trace of kindness in that face. It was as harsh and barren as winter's frozen ground.

The mother superior brought her hand to her own face and traced the contours with trembling fingers. Did she wear the same hard countenance as this pious but embittered sister?

"Send me the novice, the one who sings in the halls when she scrubs the floor."

"I have punished her for this, Mother Ludmilla," said the nun. "She will not do this again, I assure you."

"Pity. Send her in at once." She paused to regain her strength. "And thank you for bringing me news of my brother, Sister Agnes. Now I need you to promise me that you will follow my wishes for my death arrangement. Follow them exactly."

At the mention of death, Sister Agnes's face hardened even more and her chin tucked in obedience to the mother superior.

"I swear I shall do as you instruct, by God's name."

"And by the Holy Virgin's?"

"By the Holy Virgin and the Holy Trinity. By God's own blessed hand and our Lord Jesus Christ."

Ludmilla swallowed. She winced, for swallowing now hurt her; she almost preferred to drown in the mounting waters of her mouth.

"I shall send my instructions then through the voice of the novice who sings in her loneliness. You shall carry out the plans I lay forth as you have sworn to do, by holy witness."

The ancient sister's face wrinkled in offense that a novice should hear the last requests of the mother superior. Her lips pursed in wrinkled protest.

"Send the girl in immediately," whispered Ludmilla before Sister Agnes could say anything more. She turned her gaze away from the nun and up to the statue of the Holy Virgin.

Zigmund Pichler's hands were bound tightly behind his back. He was shoved forward into Don Julius's chamber and went sprawling on the floor.

"So! The barber-surgeon pays me a visit!" said Don Julius, kicking Pichler hard in the ribs. "Where are your leeches, my friend?"

"Why have you arrested me?" pleaded the barber, wincing. He struggled to roll on his side. "What crime have I committed?"

"You have deceived me and hidden your daughter. She did not die in the fall, for she is a witch! Any mortal would have perished falling from such a height! But she is indeed a witch, a witch who has possessed my soul!"

Pichler grunted with pain. "She is no witch. She is an innocent girl! I swear it!"

"Ha! Innocent? You lie, Barber! Do you think I have not heard her nickname? They call her Musle in the streets of Krumlov. She is the fat brewer's whore and yet refuses to share my bed! I am a Hapsburg!" he thundered. "She will open her legs to a stinking beer monger but spurn me, the son of the king?!"

Pichler said nothing, but closed his eyes in misery.

"Send him to the dungeon!" roared Don Julius. "I shall have my Marketa back or you shall die, wretched barber!"

The novice Fiala smoothed her wimple before she entered the mother superior's chamber. The old nun who had brought Fiala to the door was as angry as the young novice had ever seen her, even worse than when the old woman had caught Fiala singing as she scrubbed the floors. The young girl trembled as she pushed open the heavy door and approached Mother Ludmilla's bed.

She curtsied and then bowed and curtsied and bowed again.

"Your grace," she said, her eyebrows furrowing in consterna-tion. "I am sorry! Pardon me for I have sinned."

Ludmilla rolled her face slowly toward the girl. "Whatever for?"

Fiala's brows relaxed and she began to stammer. "Sister Agnes—she was so cross—I thought—I thought I was—"

"No, no," said Ludmilla, stretching out her weak hand to grasp the girl's. "I called for you because I have heard you singing."

"Forgive me, Mother, for I have sinned—"

"What sin is singing while you work? No, the song is why I have summoned you. You still have the scent of humanity and joy about you. You have not lived so many years in the confines of this convent as to erase that pure zest of life, God's own embrace. I have a favor to ask of you, and through you I ask that my last request on this earth be followed faithfully. Will you swear it?"

"Of course, Mother," said the bewildered novice.

"I want you to go to the livery and have a carriage take me to the home of Annabella, the healer. I must reach her house before I die or all is lost."

CHAPTER 42

KATARINA'S NIGHTMARE

Katarina walked along the roaring Vltava and, remembering last summer's thicket of wild leeks, took a turn into the woods, off the monastery path. She touched her face and neck where the skin was still flushed from her lover's kisses. Those kisses had been so intense, she wondered if her complexion would bruise and her father would suspect that she had not spent the afternoon gathering ramps, bulbs, and roots.

She did not care. Katarina tossed her blonde hair defiantly in the rare winter sunshine. How could he punish her? She was already virtually a prisoner in her home.

Her mother had begun to worry. Just that morning she had begged, "Please, eat something, Daughter. You are growing too thin—look at how your dress sags on your bosom!"

"I do not want to eat, Mother. I have no appetite. No appetite for food…no appetite for life."

Her daughter's sadness consumed Eliska. She could think of little else.

That morning she had decided that things must change. The girl needed to walk beyond the confines of the millhouse. But her older brothers were working beside their father at the mill. There was only little Jiri to accompany her.

Eliska had relented, sending Katarina and Jiri out to cut roots for stews and soups along the path to the old monastery. Eliska had thought that the fresh air and the beauty of the frosty meadows and the sparkling ponds might cheer her sad daughter.

Katarina had set off in the early morning in a stiff winter cloak, carrying a straw basket. She had strict instructions to be home in time to help with the dinner chores. Jiri stepped beside her, thoroughly annoyed at having to accompany his older sister in such a boring chore.

Katarina had trudged through the streets though she felt her step lighten as she crossed the town square near the blacksmith's shop.

"Oh, Jiri," she said, looking down. "I have forgotten to bring the little spade to dig the roots. Run home fast to fetch it. I promise to stay here at the well until you return."

Jiri cast a suspicious look at his sister.

"Run!" she commanded. "What harm is going to happen to me in the center of the town square?"

Jiri ran back to the mill down Panska and Soukenicka Streets, the soles of his worn shoes slapping against the cobblestone.

For the first time in months, Katarina drew a deep breath of freedom as she waited by the well.

From the smithy, Damek watched her every move as she bent to drink from the ladle in the bucket at the well. He pounded bits of iron from a red-hot horseshoe as she pressed the ladle to her lips to drink.

"Oh, that I were that ladle!" he moaned to himself.

He rubbed his eyes hard to see his beloved walk away from him, without uttering a word. His father chided him roughly when he saw the sadness in his son's eyes.

"Be a man and forget the maiden," he growled, passing the boy red-hot metal from the forge. "Pan Mylnar will find a rich man for her to marry."

"It is only soot in my eye," Damek answered defiantly and turned to pound the hot iron, until he could stand his torment no more.

He hurried across the square to her, not caring if anyone saw him or not.

"Where are you going?" he said in an urgent whisper. "I must see you!"

"You must leave me alone, Damek! Jiri will be back in a minute and will tell my father you approached me."

"I do not give a damn about your father—where are you going?"

Katarina looked over his shoulder, down the road toward the mill. She still did not see Jiri returning.

"To the hills on the road to the monastery. To gather ramps and roots."

"Find a way to wander away from Jiri," he said. He darted a look toward the tavern, wondering who else was witnessing this meeting. "I will come and find you."

With that he turned around, not waiting for her reply, and walked back to the smithy to finish his work.

A few minutes later a breathless Jiri ran down the street, a small spade in his hand.

～

It was not hard to slip away from Jiri once they began hunting roots. They agreed to stay in calling distance of each other and reunite at the travelers' shrine of the Madonna when they grew hungry for their packed meal of buttered bread and cheese.

Damek caught her on the path through the meadows and Katarina shrieked with pleasure and then with fear that someone might see them.

He pulled her into the frosty grass, behind a stand of trees. He took her into his arms, declaring his love and covering her face with kisses, marking her fair face with black smudges.

Damek acted honorably, and though their lovemaking was passionate to the very edge of fulfillment, he never fully compromised the woman he had sworn to make his wife.

They lay in each other's arms, the frozen grass thawing with their heat. They planned their future together, in hot gasps and whispered promises. If need be, they would run off together to Budejovice and start life anew. Katarina could not imagine her life without her beloved parents, but she could not bear to marry another man.

Before long, Katarina heard Jiri calling her name.

"I must go at once!" she said, giving her lover a quick kiss.

She hurried to the travelers' shrine, where Jiri had already begun to eat the buttered bread and cheese their mother had packed.

"You go ahead, Jiri. I am not hungry."

"Not hungry?" he said, his mouth stuffed with food. "Can I eat yours then?"

"Yes, eat mine. I have not had much luck finding roots. I will wander a bit more and try another section of the woods."

"Do not wander too far," he warned.

She cast him an irritated look as she headed off.

She knew she must fill her basket quickly to make up for lost time. She knew a place deeper in the woods where leeks grew in the shade of the towering pines. It was near a little brook, and though it might be beyond calling distance from Jiri, she was sure she could fill her basket quickly.

Katarina walked in the brilliant winter sunshine, feeling her lover's kisses still brushing her skin. She smiled as she knelt beside the tree trunks and dug with her fingers under the frosty canopy of fallen leaves. Every spring this area yielded scores of succulent wild leeks, and those that were not harvested during the spring and summer lay like hidden treasures for the lean winter months.

Her fingers ached in the cold, and she reached for the little spade to dig at the half-frozen ground. Lying under the earth like a white thumb was the elongated shape of a wild leek ramp. Beside it were several more, smaller and hidden under the mulch of twigs and leaves.

Katarina was digging up the bulbs when she felt vibration beneath her knees and heard the sound of horses galloping toward her along the wooded path. She looked up to see three riders on fine horses, dressed in rich-colored silks and velvet. One reined in his horse and stopped beside her. He was a blond and spoke in German. She gasped when she realized who it was.

"Are you on your knees praying for my arrival, fair maiden?" he chuckled. Katarina jumped to her feet and curtsied, tying her kerchief tight under her chin.

"I am gathering ramps for my family," she stammered.

The two other riders had now caught up with Heinrich, and she recognized one as the Hapsburg prince. Her heart pounded.

"Harvesting ramps? And who harvests the harvester?" said Heinrich. He dismounted from his horse, throwing the reins to his companion. He approached her, his eyes narrowing with lust.

"Jiri!" she screamed, although she knew it would do no good. "Jiri!"

"Who do you call for, maiden? It seems no one answers."

"Good sir, please, leave me in peace! I am the daughter of the miller, and my father will thank you to see that I am protected."

"Thank me! What does a Viennese count need with the gratitude of a Bohemian peasant? But you are a beauty, despite your ill-breeding."

"Stop!" shouted Don Julius, his horse prancing under him. "Do not lay a hand on her, Heinrich."

Heinrich wrinkled his brow in irritation, but he halted all the same.

Don Julius dismounted as the third rider, Franz, took the reins of his horse. The bastard prince snapped at the air, muttering, as if he were arguing with an invisible being. He pulled his tangled hair, his hands trembling with rage.

He stared at Heinrich, standing next to the pleading girl.

"Take her!" urged Franz. "She will cure you of the demons, Don Julius."

Don Julius stared at the girl, his eyes unfocused in the light that filtered through the pine trees. His haunted look terrified Katarina, who shivered uncontrollably.

Heinrich gritted his teeth and echoed his companion's words. "Take her! Take her!"

The voices surged inside his head. Don Julius clapped his hands over his ears and screamed, his roar echoing through the frost woods.

Take her! Take her!

"She is mine," growled Don Julius at last, unlacing his breeches as he approached Katarina. His eyes had lost the faraway look and had focused in a glinting stare, savage and cold.

"Fair one, we meet again!"

Katarina's virtue was taken brutally on the cold, leaf-scattered ground of the leek field, her head and neck pressed against the rough bark of a tree. The rape was witnessed by two cheering brutes, who felt sure that the taking of a maiden in such a lusty manner would cure the prince of any demons that haunted him.

A part of Katarina died that day. As she heard the hoofbeats retreat into the depths of the forest, she pulled her battered body from the mulch. Leaves and twigs clung to her damp skin where she had been crushed against the ground.

Her face had been pummeled, blood's salty taste on her lips.

Gone was the sweetness of sugar that clung to her skin, her mouth. In its place was the foul smell of men's sweat and seed.

She gathered the shreds of her torn blouse together, stumbling toward where she and Jiri had parted.

As Katarina licked her bloody lips, she feared she would never taste the sweetness of life ever again.

CHAPTER 43

MATTHIAS AND TAMAS OF ESZTERGOM

The soot-faced boy poked the embers with a stick, trying to coax a flame. He fed the fire dry grass and chips of wood, slowly. Patiently.

When a small flame finally leapt up, he blew gently, trying to keep it alive.

But the fire was not the only thing he was trying to keep alive. His brother groaned a few feet from him in a tent of tattered, dirty cloth.

"Water," the wounded man croaked.

The boy lifted up his brother's head and pushed the spout of the jug against his parched lips.

"Drink, Adam," he said. "Drink."

Adam sucked at the water, though most of it splashed down his chin and neck.

"Thank you, Tamas," he gasped, sputtering.

"Now rest," the boy said. He knew that was what their mother would say.

≈

Astride his fine Andaluz steed, Matthias watched the scene from a hill with his spyglass. He handed the glass back to his escort.

"Get me a blanket," he ordered. "I am going down to that camp."

The commander's face wrinkled and he shook his jowly chin.

"I will send a scout down. It is too dangerous for Your Highness to go unescorted and on foot."

Matthias raised a hand to silence him.

"Get me a blanket from one of the troops immediately," the Hapsburg snapped. He dismounted and threw the reins to an attendant. The commander watched in disbelief as Archduke Matthias rubbed his boots with handfuls of mud and streaked his hands and face with filth.

≈

Matthias pinned the blanket around his shoulders and walked into the makeshift camp.

"Who goes there?" shouted the boy in Hungarian, grabbing a pike.

They did not even leave him a firearm, thought Matthias.

"I am from the Bathory division of Transylvania," he said. "Do you speak German?"

"A little," said the boy, still pointing the pike at Matthias's heart. The boy was so puny he could barely lift the spear at all. The handle dragged on the muddy ground.

"I have come to inspect the camp to make sure you do not harbor any deserters."

"How do I know you are not a deserter?" challenged the boy, pushing his dirty blond hair from his eyes. "How do I know that you have not come to steal what little we have and kill me and the wounded?"

Matthias smiled grimly at the boy's spunk, especially given how pale and weakly built he was.

"Help me!" cried the man lying behind the young boy. A deep wound in his neck bloomed like a red rose against his dirt-caked skin.

"Prove your worth," said the boy, dropping the heavy pike with a thud and grabbing a pitcher of water. "Help me with the wounded."

Matthias nodded and followed the child to the groaning solider.

The boy wadded a dirty rag against the man's neck. "Hold this against his neck, tight. And help me lift him so he can drink."

Matthias helped the boy tilt the man's face toward the jug. As Matthias shifted the weight of the man's head to his opposite hand, the filthy bandage slipped and the water gushed out of the wound in the man's neck.

Matthias stared at the spilling water and remembered a white dove he had wounded as a boy. He had wanted to keep it as a pet, but every time the dove drank, water dribbled out the wound his arrow had made. At last the bird died. He had to hide his tears from his father and his older brothers as he stroked its white feathers.

"You must hold it tight or the water will not reach his belly," the boy said, his voice fierce. "Otherwise he will not survive."

Matthias held pressure on the wound and waited. The rag came away wet but not soaked.

They settled the man back onto his blanket and let him sleep.

"I am sorry I have nothing to offer you to eat, but I can offer you the warmth of our fire. I can add more wood to the flames. My brothers and uncle would be angry if I did not show hospitality to a scout for Royal Hungary's troops."

"No, I do not need more warmth. Save your fire for your patients and for cooking. How is it that you are here?"

The boy hunched near the flame again, feeding it twigs with his dirty fingers.

"I was too young and weak to fight against the Ottomans. When they laid siege to Esztergom, my uncle spirited me from my home, to teach me to be a man. I think my mother must cry every night, but we fight to protect Esztergom from the infidels and keep our women safe."

Matthias's shoulders drooped as he heard the boy's words. Esztergom had fallen to the Ottomans that very morning. The women and children had been raped, killed, or abducted.

There was nothing left but rubble and charred ruins.

"And your father?"

"He fights with the armies of Archduke Matthias," the boy said, sitting up straight and pushing his grimy hair from his face. "The king says that we are the shield of all Christendom."

Matthias winced. The boy would learn soon enough that his family in Esztergom was now dead or became concubines to the Ottomans. There was no shield. Only the wounded and the dead were testimony to the battle.

"You say you are too weak to fight, and yet here you are alone keeping the fires burning, caring for the wounded, preparing food. Hard work you perform here. What gives you the strength?"

The boy shrugged, then took the stranger's hand and placed it against his chest.

"Keep your fingers there—to the right," said the boy, directing his hand with his own. "Can you feel it?"

Matthias nearly snatched his hand away. As royalty, he was not used to being touched, but he played his part. And he was curious. The boy's chest was concave, the flesh seemed hollowed as one would scoop out the meat in a melon.

Under his fingertips Matthias felt the beat of a heart. A faint pulse on the right side of the boy's chest.

"My mother used to tell me that it was a secret gift, to have my heart on the right side of my body. She said it gave me unnatural courage and strength. That is why I can help the wounded, I think. My uncle thought it would be better than staying home with the women."

Matthias's hand slipped from the boy's chest. He looked around at the campsite, littered with broken, wounded bodies. Another man cried out for water.

"I'm coming," called the boy.

"I must report back to my commander," said Matthias. "I will remember meeting you—"

"Tamas."

"Tamas. Tamas of the Right Heart. I hope your other brothers and father come back to camp safely."

Tamas looked at his brother Adam, his mouth wide, sucking for breath.

"I pray they do," Tamas said. "I want to return to Esztergom and see my mother and sisters. I fear I was not made for battle, yet they tell me there has been war since the year of my birth."

Matthias studied his face. "How old are you, Tamas?"

"Thirteen. Just."

Matthias nodded slowly. "Yes, they tell you the truth. Every year since your birth."

Tamas squatted on his haunches and poked at an ember until it blazed. Then he fetched the jug of water.

"Too long. We all pray for peace. They say Matthias may defy the king and sign a treaty with the Ottomans."

Matthias stared at the boy.

"Do you think that would be a mistake, Tamas? Would it not show a lack of courage?"

Tamas shook his head. "My father says it is the peacemakers who take the biggest risks. He says any fool can start a war. It takes courage to stop one."

"Your father sounds like a wise man."

"Water, boy! I am dying of thirst," cried the wounded man from his pile of rags.

Tamas nodded toward him.

"Oh, he is, the wisest man in the world. And I hope the war ends soon," said the boy. "I miss my mother's cooking!"

Matthias nodded his thanks and climbed the long, steep hill toward his horse and escorts. He turned once more to watch the boy lift the clay jug to a dying man's lips.

CHAPTER 44

THE REUNION

Gripped by fear, Marketa shook with terror, but one thought burned bright through all the cold bewilderment she felt in her soul.

She would not let her father die in the castle dungeon.

Marketa had heard he was kept in cavernous blackness, chained to the rocks, given only hard crusts of bread to eat and whipped daily.

Some of the servants risked their life to bring him scraps from the kitchen and news from the outside world. Barber Pichler begged them to send his love to his daughter and tell her she must not surrender herself to Don Julius.

"He will murder her. Tell her!" he implored. "She must flee Krumlov. Otherwise the madman will find her."

The servants noticed that the barber never inquired about his wife.

~

It was Masopust, the final days of feast before the Lenten fast, a Christian celebration stretched thin over ancient pagan roots. The streets of Krumlov were filled with townsmen in animal-spirit costumes, carrying offerings for fertility, both in soil and womb. They knew evil spirits ran wild, indulging their last chance for mischief before the faithful partook in the holy fast of Lent.

It was a time for frenzied excess, gorging on the last of the winter's meats and ale, and parading wildly and reeling drunk in the streets. The tavern was packed, and the savor of roasting meat wafted through the winding lanes.

It was traditionally a festive time, the full breath of merry-making in the bleakest month of the year. But not a soul in Krumlov greeted the holiday without a shiver of apprehension in the winter of 1608.

It was still bitterly cold, and the banks of the Vltava were crusted in a brittle wedge of ice. The howls of the royal madman above pierced the winter wind. The mad Hapsburg ruled from the ancient castle, and one of their own innocent citizens was locked in the depths of his dungeon. Now they heard that the miller's daughter, Katarina, had been raped savagely in the forest and left bleeding and half-dead by the bastard prince. The townspeople of Krumlov spit down on the cobblestones, looked up to the gray skies, and wondered what kind of spring could be birthed from such terrible omens.

Don Julius hunted everywhere for Marketa with a murderous glitter in his eyes. Slit-mouthed gossips whispered that she should surrender herself to the Lord of Rozmberk Castle and save their town.

Destruction, vice, and terror reigned in Krumlov. What cheer could the coming Holy Easter tidings provide when the world reeled from such sin and iniquity?

∾

Marketa was alone in Annabella's house when the coachman knocked on the door and a young novice entered, her head humbly bowed.

For a novice about to take the holy orders, entering the house of a professed witch was unthinkable. Fiala knew she risked damnation, but she did as she was bidden by Mother Ludmilla.

"Why are you here? Who waits in the coach?" Marketa asked her, bewildered.

"It is your aunt, the mother superior. Her last request is to be at your side when she dies," said the novice in a meek voice. "I have sworn to carry out her orders. She begs you let her enter to pass her last days—perhaps only hours—with you."

Marketa stared—the novice stood before her, her young eyes set on the bathmaid's face, waiting anxiously for an answer.

"Of course," Marketa managed to say at last. "Bring her in immediately—it is cold and bitter outside!"

Marketa pulled together some coverings and placed them on Annabella's mattress. She drew a deep breath. Would a mother superior really lie in a witch's bed? Would she draw her last breaths on the sheets of a sorceress?

The coachman carried the light bones of Ludmilla into the house. She winced as he moved her to the bed, for she was in pain and the withered folds of her skin were pinched in the coachman's grip.

"Aunt Ludmilla, welcome," Marketa said, kissing her dry cheek. "But I beg you listen, this is Annabella's bed I offer you. Mine is in the catacombs below."

"She is good to share it with me," whispered her aunt, and she put a hand out to touch the linen ticking as they laid her on the mattress.

After the novice and coachman had left, Marketa covered her aunt with quilts and fanned the embers to flames. Then she placed the clay kettle on the firehook to make some tea.

"Annabella is digging for roots, Aunt Ludmilla," she explained. "She will assess your health when she returns. She has marvelous knowledge of plants to cure sickness. I have witnessed it time and time again."

"Come closer, child," said her aunt. Marketa knelt by the side of the bed, and she grasped Ludmilla's hand, the nun's fingers a bird's claw.

"I did not come here seeking a cure. I came to see you and make things right between us before I die."

Marketa's eyes welled with tears. Her father was in a dungeon because of her, and now her aunt risked her soul to cross the threshold of a witch to see her. What good had she, Marketa Pichlerova, ever brought to this world?

"I want to ask your blessing, dear niece, before I die. I fear I have not intervened in the world of sin and mankind. I have indeed been a poor servant to our Lord."

It took Marketa a second to understand what she was saying. When she did, she gasped.

"Oh, no! Aunt Ludmilla, you are a good, pious woman. I beg you to forget my spiteful words!" Marketa crossed herself in genuflection, a habit deeply instilled in her by the Catholic Church.

Before Ludmilla could answer, the door creaked open and Marketa caught a glimpse of red hair trailing below an indigo scarf.

"Annabella! Come here—my aunt is very ill!"

Annabella hung her cloak on a peg. She did not look surprised to see the mother superior of the Poor Clares convent lying on her bed. She bent down and kissed Ludmilla's hand.

"I have been waiting for you, Ludmilla," she said. "I was afraid you would wait until it was too late. As I wrote you, time is of the essence."

Marketa narrowed her eyes at Annabella, wondering what madness she spoke of now. But her aunt nodded her head and smiled weakly.

"It is almost too late," she said. "Tell me how I can help."

~

Don Julius had gone days without bathing. His hair was matted and his face streaked with greasy food and filth. He refused to use the chamber pots and left puddles of urine and mounds of excrement on the parquet floor. He screamed and threw vases, clocks, and fine ceramic figurines at the servants who dared to enter his chambers.

His behavior had deteriorated to a point that was close to the condition in which he had arrived in Krumlov a year ago. There was no trace of the studious young boy, of the handsome prince, of those last shreds of his true soul that Marketa had fought to rescue.

Jakub had ridden north to Prague to plead with the king to revoke Don Julius's powers over Krumlov and to free the poor barber Pichler. The king had refused. He trembled with fury to learn that Marketa's reported death had been a lie.

"Let Krumlov deal with my son—these are the consequences of their deceit!"

But the king did worry about his son's mental collapse and bade Jakub to discuss the matter with the other court physicians.

Jakub had ridden straight back to Krumlov, with only one night of rest for his horse and himself. Before he even opened the door of Don Julius's chamber, he could smell the stench.

"Don Julius, pray let me enter," Jakub called, covering his nose with a handkerchief. He did not wait for an answer, but pushed open the door to the filthy room.

"You traitorous physician!" Don Julius shouted. "You know the whereabouts of my love and you betray me by keeping silent! You conspire against me like all the others!"

"Don Julius," Jakub said, "I bring tidings from your father. I bring tidings and—I bring the Coded Book of Wonder."

At this the snarling expression of Don Julius faded like a wave receding from washed sands.

"You possess the book?"

"Yes, I have it in safekeeping," he lied, for the book was still back in Prague in the king's possession. "And I shall give it to you if you release the barber from your dungeons and cease your search for the girl Marketa."

"Never!"

"Your father is very distressed at the news of your behavior. He is sending Doctor Mingonius back to Krumlov to help me treat you. There are two other doctors who are to attend you, for your father is afraid for your health."

"That devil does not worry himself about me!"

"His Majesty is very concerned about the rumors that have spread throughout the land, throughout the empire. Your actions have shocked the civilized world. Matthias, your uncle, is using the outrage to fuel a rebellion to overthrow your father, our king."

"Ha! It will serve the swine right."

Jakub stared fiercely at him.

"And you do not think your own protection and privileges will end should your father be dethroned? I think Matthias would relish the thought of beheading you to prove his power."

Don Julius furrowed his brow. His uncle Matthias had always hated him and would stop at nothing to possess the throne of the Holy Roman emperor.

"The Coded Book. Where is it?"

"As I say, it is kept in a safe place where no one can find it. Your father promises you may have it if you cease this behavior. He loves you as his favorite son, but your behavior has caused a scandal that endangers his throne. You have gone too far."

Don Julius said nothing. He rubbed his hand over his itching crotch.

Jakub looked at him in disgust. He had tried hard to contain his temper and to convey King Rudolf's word as clearly as he had been commanded to do. But he could no longer contain his fury.

"Good God, man, clean yourself! What woman would ever want to be in your company? Your apartments smell of shit, and your body is filthy. Your hair is matted as an ape's."

Don Julius reached up and touched his knotted hair, feeling the thick snarls for the first time. He sniffed at his doublet, raising his arms.

"I must bathe then," he mumbled to himself. "She must fall in love with me as she did for one day, one enchanted day!"

Jakub's eyes flashed wide. Could Marketa have ever loved such a man? He thought of her blue-gray eyes and how her gaze might soften in love. Was it possible this man had really seduced her?

True, Don Julius had proclaimed his eternal love for her. The night air of Krumlov carried his desolate torment, crying mournfully for his lost love. What woman would not be affected when the favorite son of the emperor shouted her praises and celebrated her beauty, when he declared himself so lovesick at her absence that he could barely breathe? Don Julius shouted to the world that he needed Marketa with a desperate passion.

Had his passion once been desperate enough to sway her judgment? Was it now desperate enough to end in murder?

"I must bathe. I must shave and cut my hair," Don Julius decided. "I must look my best for her. She must fall in love with me again!"

Jakub remembered Annabella's request. A lock of hair.

"Yes, I will send for the barber after you have bathed, Don Julius."

～

Marketa watched as Annabella stared at the blood spots on Ludmilla's lips and touched her finger to the red droplets. Annabella brought the blood to the candlelight to study it, turning her finger this way and that. Then she disappeared into the catacombs to rummage through the dried herbs, bones, roots, and talismans. Marketa stood over the passage, the trapdoor flung open against the stone floor. She could see the witch's candlelight dancing against the walls.

Marketa turned away to stoke the fire under the cauldron. The water was boiling by the time Annabella emerged from the dark hole with a bundle wrapped in her apron. She spilled the ingredients out on the floor by the hearth.

Among the litter Marketa recognized a dried rat's tail and a desiccated toad. There was a bulbous root much like the one Marketa had seen when she encountered Annabella that first time in the cemetery, digging by a child's grave. The root had an uncanny resemblance to a tiny man, its tendrils reaching out in four limbs and its wrinkled face sneering at her with squinted eyes. There were two glass vials of black potions Annabella poured in the cauldron. They boiled up in a sulfurous cloud that made Marketa gag and turn away, coughing.

Annabella did not twitch, immune to the smell. She added the bones and skull of a small animal and some fresh organs, perhaps an animal heart. Then she asked for Ludmilla's blood-soaked handkerchief and tossed it into the brew.

Finally she coated the inside of a mug with a thick black tar. "Essence of poppy oils," she told Marketa. "The sweet oblivion of the magic flower."

Marketa could not understand the murmurings and incantations. They were in a tongue she didn't know—not Germanic or Latin or Slavic, for there was not a word she could decipher.

At last Annabella poured a dose from the cauldron into the mug and brought it to Ludmilla's bedside.

"You will die soon," she said, holding Ludmilla's hand. "You know this, of course."

Ludmilla nodded, and her white lips stretched into a peaceful smile.

"Annabella!" Marketa cried. "What of your potions, your cures?"

"There are some things a healer can do. But the others, the vast majority of life and death, we cannot pretend to tamper with, for there is a much higher spirit who determines our fate. Your aunt knows this, Marketa, the difference between our mortal world and the world beyond. That is why she has come to us."

"But what of this brew?"

"It will bring her peace and strength for the brave deed she is about to perform."

Marketa looked at her aunt Ludmilla, white as death's own pallor. Then she turned to Annabella. "What deed can she possibly perform?" she whispered. "She is barely alive!"

"A deed of great nobility and sacrifice. I only give her this potion to carry her through these few remaining hours, without the torturing pain she endures now."

~

Pichler dug his filthy knuckles into his eye sockets against the blinding light of day. He stumbled on the stairs to Don Julius's apartments and was helped up by the two Krumlov guards who had known him since they were in Latin school together as children.

"The lunatic wants you to cut his hair," Chaloupka whispered to him. "The stinking animal has finally bathed and wants to look presentable."

"For whom?" asked Pichler quickly. "For my daughter?"

The other guard said nothing at first but then set his lips on the rim of the barber's ear.

"Let the blade slip, Pichler. Save yourself, your daughter, and all of Bohemia from this devil!"

Jakub came out of Don Julius's chambers, closing the door quietly.

"You are Barber Pichler?"

Pichler nodded, bowing to the well-dressed man.

"We must speak quickly. I am a friend of your daughter—"

"My Marketa! Oh, sir!" Pichler gasped. "How is she?"

"I saw her last night and she is in good health. She has just received a visitor at Annabella's house, your sister Ludmilla, who is dying."

"Ludmilla in the house of a witch?" The barber's face stretched wide in astonishment, his eyes blinking. "I cannot believe it!"

"Annabella has hosted you, I understand," said Jakub.

"Yes, but I am not mother superior of a convent! Why would she venture outside the confines of the nunnery?"

"They seem to have an understanding, your sister and Annabella. But Annabella needs something that only you can provide."

"What could that possibly be?"

Jakub leaned closer, whispering in his ear.

"Hair clippings of Don Julius—from the crown of his head. You must procure them and give them to me to deliver to her hand, or all is lost."

Pichler had no time to respond, for he was ushered into the apartments where a basin and barber set were laid on a table next to the freshly bathed Don Julius.

Don Julius studied himself in the polished looking glass, tilting his chin this way and that. He moved to the window where the winter light illuminated his newly shaved skin.

"You look particularly good from the right profile," said Jakub, nodding surreptitiously at Pichler.

As Don Julius angled the mirror away from his barber, Pichler stooped and swept up strands of new-cut hair and stuffed them in the pocket of his coat.

"You are quite right," pronounced Don Julius. "I shall remember to present that profile to Marketa when she arrives." At this his lip curled down. "And she shall arrive by sunset, before my beard grows back, or you shall die, Barber."

Pichler swallowed but otherwise said nothing. He had already resigned himself to this fate and only hoped that it would be a Krumlov guard who dispatched him mercifully and quickly rather than having to suffer death at the hand of the Hapsburg.

Before Don Julius could offer more threats, he was interrupted by Guard Chaloupka, who begged entrance.

"My lord, I bring urgent news," he said, his eyes skipping nervously from the Hapsburg to Pichler. "The maiden Marketa sends word that she shall surrender herself this very day."

Don Julius jumped up, his eyes bright and feverish.

Pichler buried his face in his hands.

"Miserable barber," muttered Don Julius, dismissing him with a wave of his hand. "Guard, take this man out of my sight!"

As Chaloupka led Pichler away, Don Julius gave another order.

"Send for the seamstress at once. And bring me the skin of the bear I slayed on the hunt."

~

A small box containing the royal hair clippings was delivered within an hour to the house on Dlouha Street. Wilhelm had been dispatched with the errand, and he ran barefooted through the frozen streets as fast as he could to Annabella's door.

"Doctor Jakub Horcicky de Tenepec awaits instructions," he said, panting. He rubbed his sore, cold feet. "What should I tell him is your reply?"

Annabella nodded curtly. "My work should not take long. Tell him to look for me at the castle by late afternoon."

Marketa heard this exchange and the closing of the heavy door. She held her aunt's hand and whispered her good-byes.

"I cannot let him kill my father," Marketa said. "It was my folly to trust a madman. My father should not sacrifice his life for my horrid mistake."

Aunt Ludmilla squeezed her niece's hand with more strength than Marketa thought possible. Annabella's potion was working.

"He will harm you if you return," whispered Marketa's aunt. "Do not go!"

"I have no choice. I am the only one he wants. He will kill my father. Good-bye, my beloved aunt."

Marketa left her weeping against the bedsheets and walked across the room to stand beside Annabella.

"He intends to murder you."

"Yes. Unless he falls in love with me again. I can at least try to make him remember. He thinks of me of as an angel."

Annabella looked at Marketa, her eyes sad and hollow.

"Lunacy is fickle. He may believe you are an angel to love and then, in a blink of an eye, a demon to destroy."

"What else can I do? Tell me!"

"You could refuse to return to him, Marketa," said Annabella.

"What life would I have?" Marketa's voice was suddenly strong with conviction. "He would always search for me, kill my loved ones to force me back. You can say I am foolish to return to him. But everyone I love is in danger from that madman! He is a Hapsburg who can kill, rape, and maim without fear of reprisal. The demonic voices have returned to seize his soul."

Annabella drew a deep breath and let it escape slowly.

"You cannot silence the voices, Marketa. All your tenderness will not quell their screams."

Marketa shook her head.

"What else can I do, Annabella?" she repeated. "What choice do I have? And if he kills me, his father will lock him up forever or even execute him, to save the throne from further disgrace. It will be the end of him and this nightmare."

Annabella looked back in silence, Marketa's words still ringing in the air. She took Marketa's hand and kissed it, pressing it to her heart.

"That is why you saw the White Lady, Marketa. Ludmilla and your father as well. The three of you will make a sacrifice for the good of Krumlov. I do not argue with you. I question you only to be certain. I find great courage in your decision. I have anticipated it, my friend, and already made preparations. But now, as the critical moment draws near, you must know that there is a good man who loves you. The best man I could find," the cunning woman said. "He loves you well and truly. But you must also know that I have chosen well in finding the father of the future Annabella."

Marketa's eyes flew to Annabella's rounded belly. How could she have not noticed the bulge under her woolen skirts and apron?

Annabella smiled back at her bewildered stare.

"It was only one night. One night to ensure the birth of my child. You are the one he loves."

Marketa stared again, stunned. She remembered the green scarf that Jakub had tied around her neck, his long fingers grazing her skin.

No! Her dear friend had made love to the doctor in Prague and now carried his baby. Marketa reeled as she imagined the two together, limbs entwined.

Marketa felt a quick flash of jealousy, sizzling like a drop of water in a pan of hot grease. Her breast tightened and bitterness filled her mouth.

Annabella saw the glint in Marketa's eyes.

"Think now before you speak, Marketa. Heed me well," she said, gently placing her hands on Marketa's shoulders and shaking her once to break the spell of anger. "You are the one he loves. I swear it is true!"

Marketa looked into Annabella's face and saw the love that shone there.

This was no rival. The woman who stood before her was her true friend.

Marketa's chest released and drew in a deep breath. She closed her eyes and nodded slowly.

Now there was no time to think of Jakub. Marketa's dreams of the handsome, gentle physician and the great city of Prague receded, like sunlight disappearing behind a bank of clouds. She had to think only of what she must do to atone for the sin of believing a madman capable of love.

Annabella turned and scattered the hair clippings into a boiling cauldron of calf's blood she had procured from the Jewish butcher outside the walls of Krumlov. She watched as Don

Julius's hair mingled with the liquid and the rolling boil sucked the strands down, into the depths.

Marketa shivered but gave her friend a long embrace.

"You have given my aunt and me protection. I do not know why your heart is so generous and why you have risked so much. But it is my time now to give."

Annabella nodded. "Since you have decided this is your destiny, I will now help you, if I can. You must be ready tonight. Jakub will help me execute my plan, but you must find a way to be alone in Don Julius's room tonight. We will meet once more, and I will take a prized possession from you."

"Anything! Take it now!"

"No, the time is not right. We will take care of the rest when the moment is ripe."

Annabella walked to the door and pulled the green scarf from the peg.

"Wear this. It will remind you of the true course," she said, placing the scarf around Marketa's neck. Her hands lingered on her friend's shoulders and she closed her eyes, whispering an incantation.

Then Annabella abruptly turned away to stir the potion. She wore the faraway look she possessed when engrossed in her spells.

As Marketa left, she realized she had not asked for whom this sorcery was made.

~

As Marketa walked past the bathhouse, her mother ran out into the street. Lucie Pichlerova's hair was untidy and her dress tattered. Under her eyes, dark pools cupped her tired skin.

"You will surrender to him and save your father?" she pleaded, her eyes white-ringed in frenzy. "Tell me you will save my husband and bring him home to me before we all starve to death!"

Marketa said nothing, but her mother followed like a stray dog up the winding cobblestone to the castle.

"I knew you could not let him die, the good man, the good father he is!" she said, dancing like a wild woman beside her daughter. She knew better than to embrace Marketa or take her hand, but she rushed from one side of her to the other, just beyond striking distance.

"You can charm the Hapsburg prince, you can subdue his choler!" she chanted. By now there were other curious citizens following the two up the cobblestone street. By the time Marketa looked around for one last sight of the Vltava, there were easily a score of people following her solemnly up the hill, like a crowd of mourners.

"Do not enter the castle!" shouted a voice, choked with sobs.

Marketa turned to see the bruised face, the eyes only slits in purpled flesh. It took Marketa a second to recognize her friend Katarina.

"I beg you, Marketa! He will kill you. Look what he did to me," she said, clasping her friend's hand.

Marketa stared in horror. Her other hand reached out to trace her friend's swollen face.

"Leave her alone, Katarina," said Lucie, pushing the girl away. "She must save her father!"

Katarina was held back by the crowd as Lucie pulled her daughter by her arm.

They trudged up the steep hill to the first courtyard, the crowd pressing close behind.

~

As Marketa approached the door to the Rozmberk apartments, she drew a deep breath. The guards who accompanied her murmured in Czech.

"You sacrifice yourself to save your father—may God's salvation be yours, faithful daughter!" said one.

The other whispered, "You do this to save all Krumlov." He crossed himself and kissed Marketa's hand. "Your sacrifice will put an end to this fiend."

"God bless you, Slecna Marketa," the guards both whispered as they approached the threshold of the apartments.

Neither of them addressed her as Musle.

The seamstress curtsied and curtsied again. She had been frightened to the cold bone of her skull by the summons, knowing the stories of Don Julius's brutal outrages. She hoped that her faded looks and buckteeth would prevent rape, but she worried that her thin neck would be too easily broken by the force of his cruel hands.

Jakub whispered to her. "Do not be afraid, just do as he asks." She nodded nervously, swallowing hard the fear that had lodged in the back of her throat.

"Seamstress—what silk can you procure today?" said Don Julius.

The old woman looked at Jakub and then answered. "Any fine fabric you desire, sir."

"Blue. I want blue silk, the blue of a pool of fresh water. No, the blue of a lake, placid and generous. I want it to be so cool and light that it washes over a maiden's skin, refreshing her as if she were swimming naked in the moonlight."

"Yes, my lord."

"And," he said, pointing at the blood-encrusted bearskin in the corner of the room, "I want you to trim the robe with that. Clean it until it shines, like the living bear it once was. Fierce and proud."

"Yes, sir," she said, staring in horror at the bloody, matted hair.

"And it must be ready tonight."

"Tonight, sir?"

"Are you deaf, old woman? Yes, before the moon rises or your scrawny neck shall be on the chopping block along with the chickens come morning."

"Yes, sir. It shall be finished tonight. I will have my daughter and daughters-in-law all help me, but it shall be finished tonight, I swear it."

"It must be beautiful. Befitting a princess—no, a goddess!"

"Yes, sir."

Don Julius waved her away.

"Right profile, is that what you said, Jakub?"

Jakub sucked in his breath, knowing that Marketa was waiting just beyond the door.

"Yes, Don Julius. The right profile is your best."

"Send her in. I am ready to greet my angel."

~

Marketa had imagined the moment many times, the moment she was to again see her patient, her lover. The man who had raped her. The man who had nearly killed her. She had wondered how she would greet him, whether she would cry, whether she would attack him, whether she would beg for mercy.

Now she simply worked to steel herself, to summon the courage to face him. She knew that sooner or later he would decide to kill her. She bent her head in a silent prayer, her hands clasped in front of her. The fringe of the green silk scarf entwined in her fingers as she pressed them, pleading.

"Dear God! Give me the courage to do what I must," she whispered. She thought about running down the corridor, out of the castle to hide in the depths of the catacombs forever.

"Give me courage," she repeated. "Oh God, please!"

An errant ray of sun pierced the clouds and illuminated her clasped hands in prayer through the leaded windows. Gentle steps sounded in the corridor. Marketa turned her head. The guards did not react at all.

A woman dressed in a long white gown made her way down the hall.

She walked toward Marketa, her chin held high. She smiled down at the girl, for this noblewoman was quite tall. She took Marketa's hand.

"Be not afraid," was all that the woman in white said.

Together they approached the door. Then she kissed Marketa on the top of her head. "Heed my promise. I shall never leave you."

Without another word, she walked away, down the long hall of the castle.

The door swung open.

"Bid her enter!" shouted Don Julius.

Marketa thought of the touch of the stranger's hand, the feel of the satin gloves. For an instant she struggled to remember, what color were those gloves? But in her shock she hadn't noticed and now it was too late.

She approached Don Julius silently and noticed a spot of blood on his neck where he had been nicked in shaving. She watched the drop work its way slowly down his throat, his skin still brown from the days on the hunt.

He looked at Marketa with his right eye, his head cocked at a curious angle as if he could not shift his gaze to see her. He looked like a rooster eyeing a worm, ready to peck. She could avoid his eyes as he posed in this curious position, and she focused her attention on the blood as it stained his skin. She remembered the leeches. She remembered too much.

Then, as Marketa removed her kerchief, he saw her hair, and his strange posture vanished. He reached for her, stifling a sob. He pulled her tight against his chest, one hand knotted in her hair, the other embracing her.

Marketa stiffened. She fought to control herself as his lips covered her mouth, her face, her throat. He tore the green scarf away from her neck, letting it fall to the floor, his lips working over her skin. He groaned and grew unsteady on his feet. He fell to his knees, worshipping her with kisses.

"My angel! You have returned to me," he cried. "I thought you dead!"

She said nothing, but bent to retrieve her scarf from the floor. It was her talisman now, a source of strength, a reminder of love and sanity. She stood again, looking down in disbelief at the man whose arms encircled her knees. His breath was warm on her skin.

Finally, he rose, taking her face in his hands with tenderness and care. Marketa looked into his eyes. The madness had retreated into the depths of green, and what she saw was love, pure and clear.

Out of the corner of her eye, Marketa saw Jakub staring intently at her.

"Prepare a feast!" ordered Don Julius, his voice full of joy. "My woman looks wan and pale. We must fatten her up before she returns with me to Prague my princess!" He kissed Marketa's hands, and then kissed them again, his eyes drinking in her presence as if he were a holy man at the altar of Christ.

He led her to a chair and bid her to sit down and sip wine. He removed her slippers and massaged her feet, looking up into her face like an adoring child. His lips, ardent and wet, kissed her toes and ankles, purring endearments.

"A feast, I said, Horcicky!" ordered Marketa's lover. "Why do you stand there?"

Jakub signaled to the page at the door to convey Don Julius's orders to the kitchen. Marketa did not notice when the page returned with another message just for Jakub. A special crate, carried in the alchemist's carriage, had been delivered to the castle, accompanied by the witch Annabella.

While Annabella waited in the courtyards, she comforted Abbot Bedrich of the Jesuit monastery, who appeared unaccountably distressed.

CHAPTER 45

AN AFTERNOON OF LOVE AND BLISS

The rest of the day was an all-encompassing embrace: an embrace of the body—chaste and adoring; an embrace of the spirit—the secrets of his soul that Don Julius bared only to Marketa. He did not attempt to take her, to force himself between her legs as she had feared. Instead it was his soul and mind, talk of love and devotion that he bestowed upon her. He held Marketa's face between his hands and stared into her eyes.

"Tonight I shall take you as my lover, the way I should have before, when you released me from the ropes, when you gave me my chance and I betrayed you. You, the only one who trusted me, how could I have forsaken you? I shall make up for it tonight. You shall have lovemaking no woman has known. I shall make you swoon, I swear it!"

Then suddenly he began to weep. "How could I have treated you so cruelly, my angel? How can I make you understand, it is the voices that drive my very hands. The voices—"

His head was bent over her breast, and she felt the hot tears soak her blouse. Soon he was sobbing as a small child would, into the soft flesh just below Marketa's shoulder.

Marketa wrapped her arms stiffly around him and let him cry. He cried for his betrayal, he said, for having injured her. He cried for the great loss he felt when he thought Marketa was dead.

His words were clear and made sense. Though they tumbled from his mouth with great force, a burst dam, it was not the incoherent babble of a lunatic. German, a brutal language to Krumlov ears, conveyed his passionate longing for Marketa's return, the utter bleakness of his soul when he thought her dead. German conveyed the anguish of his solitude and inconsolable grief in a way Czech could not.

His words, his pleas, were not without effect. These were not the words of a madman, Marketa told herself as she held him to her heart and kissed his salty, burning tears, the tears of a feverish child. For a moment—for a long moment—she allowed herself to think perhaps she could still save his soul from the demons that tortured him. And perhaps she did deserve his love. Did she not have the heart of a woman, a woman who had never truly been loved? Her body had been traded for meat, salt, and beer into the hands of a fat, stinking brewer. Never had she known love or respect. Here before her was the son of a king, an emperor, proclaiming his love for her above all his possessions or kin. Love, wealth, life in Prague.

She longed to let herself believe his declarations of love, and she bathed in the adoration. She so desperately wanted Don Julius to be normal, a sane man. Just as desperately as he did.

And then she bit her lip and cleared her mind. She knew better. The moment would come when he would turn back into the monster. He was not a sane man and never would be. Behind the jewellike eyes lurked a demon, a demon who would strike when she least expected. He had raped her, slashed her with a knife. He had attacked her best friend, a sweet, defenseless girl, in the woods beyond Krumlov.

She closed her eyes, hard. When she opened them again, she was strong, immune to his pleading—and too smart to let him see her strength. She was prepared to meet her fate and prepared to play her part until that final moment came.

The afternoon feast was laid in the crimson dining hall under the blazing chandeliers. Don Julius insisted Marketa sit at his side so that their elbows touched. He could not abide being apart from her.

He poured her wine, fed her with his own hands, licking his fingers after they touched her lips. He served her sweet oysters from the faraway seas, wrapped in sea grasses on ice shavings.

He squeezed lemons from Spain on the translucent flesh of the mollusks and asked her to let the flavors mingle on her tongue before she swallowed the essence of the sea, the clean salt taste of the ocean Marketa had never seen. They ate a fruit called an orange, which he peeled with a sharp knife in one long continuous coil. He fed her this with a devilish dark sweet that tantalized the girl's mouth.

"Chocolate," he said. "Brought from the Americas. A delicacy of my father's court."

Marketa licked her fingers, marveling at the rich taste. The wine had entered her veins and she smiled. If this was to be the end of her life, she thought she would enjoy every moment as best she could.

Don Julius indulged her until she could eat no more. He kissed the palms of her hands and gazed into her eyes. Then he excused himself for a moment. When he returned, he carried a book in his hands.

Through a haze of wine, Marketa thought, *At last I shall see the Coded Book and know the woman I resemble!*

But it was not the Coded Book at all, but another. He opened it and the title page read, *Malleus Maleficarum, the Undoing of Witches' Spells and Incantations.*

"What is this?" Marketa asked.

"Someone is practicing witchcraft," he said, his voice low and secretive. "A witch has cast a spell on me, I am certain of it. I can feel the evil eye cast my way. And when I find her, I shall destroy her. She will be burned at the stake, and my demons shall go up in smoke, along with her flesh. Then we will leave for Prague and be wedded at the *hrad*, and live a happy life at last."

Marketa's mind reeled. She thought of Annabella and her dying aunt. She remembered how Annabella had demanded the prince's hair clippings and recalled the potent reek of a boiling potion over the open fire as she left the house on Dlouha Street.

The castle's vast dining table stretched into the distance. At the far end, she saw Jakub, watching intently from the dim hall. And she could see a portrait hanging just beyond him under the light of a flickering wall sconce. A woman dressed in white with a gray sash, with the palest skin she had ever seen.

Marketa set down her crystal wineglass and stared at the portrait. She recognized the woman immediately and studied her sad eyes, cast down at Jakub, standing in the shadows of the hall.

CHAPTER 46

THE LAST NIGHT OF MASOPUST

The sounds of the Masopust procession obliterated any other in the town of Krumlov. Perhaps that is why no one noticed the sudden absence of the Hapsburg wailing, now that he had been rejoined with the love of his life.

In the processions, the ratchets' rattling whine competed with the enormous cowbells, drums, horns, and whistles. The ear-splitting cacophony shook the birds from the trees and drew cheers from the festive crowd. Almost everyone wore a disguise of some kind. Beaked birds and colorful clowns, men masked and horned as deer or bulls, others furred in bearskins and bear heads to frighten children. Some men hid under piebald cow skins, the heads laced with rawhide to wooden racks hung around their shoulders like yokes. The farmers wore traditional garb from centuries before, wooden clogs and white shirts, open-necked despite the cold, dragging their plows and scattering the streets with seeds for fecundity and good harvest. Their three-pronged wooden pitchforks lifted women's skirts and made them scream and giggle.

The parade lurched through the tight, winding streets of Krumlov to end as always at the first courtyard of Rozmberk Palace. Festivities had begun on Sunday night and by now, riotous Tuesday, there were Krumlovians everywhere with spittle and greasy food staining their disguises. The town was strewn with drunken bears, goats, sheep, dogs, and chickens who rolled in the snow, inebriated and thick-tongued, struggling to keep up with the clamorous procession.

Bruna, one of the most frightening beasts—an amalgam of a giraffe, goat, and camel—tipped over into a snowbank at the castle gate, weighed down by its own sodden costume and too much strong drink. Its many attendants dressed in ribboned hats, beaks, and pointed shoes wrestled the beast to its feet, heavy bells clanging at its waist. A jovial stablemaster whipped its flanks until the huge monster roared and leaped on its assailant—coming to blows, which did not last long with such cumbersome garb and drunken unsteadiness. Again the beribboned attendants pulled the beast to its feet, and the two combatants shared a flask and roared their eternal friendship, beast and master.

A horned devil pointed at the towers of the castle and spat copiously on the ale-splashed cobblestones, while a mare's-head phantom tried to calm him. The devil shook off the cajoling arm and roared blasphemous insults through the cold winter air. Beaked and horned heads turned toward him, crying "Ne, ne," for his words could cost him his head and bring the wrath of a Hapsburg down upon all of them.

A subdued blonde maiden, dressed in ribbons and jovial face paint that belied her mood, began to cry, her bright rouge smudged and streaked with tears. The devil came to comfort her, putting a black furred hoof around her heaving shoulders.

～

The seamstress measured Marketa, her speckled hands shaking, and then turned to her three helpers. She saw the puddle of fine blue silk that lay in their sewing basket, and she reached out to touch its coolness.

"For you, *slecna*. For tonight," said one of the younger women. She met Marketa's eyes and then turned away.

Following her glance, Marketa saw a thick black fur wrapped in damp sheets of linen.

She shuddered. "What is that?"

"The fine silk is to be trimmed in the bear the master killed on the hunt. It was the master's order."

The fur, in contrast to the luxurious silk, glistened ominously, raw and savage on the white sheet.

All four women looked away from Marketa now. They gathered up their fabric and hurried out the door to begin desperate work on the robe.

~

Jakub met Annabella at the servants' doorway. His mouth brimmed with questions, but she shook him off with a hard cluck of her tongue.

"We have no time. We must bring in the crate. I have spoken to the kitchen women. They are to store it in the pantries, out of sight. They did not question me as to what it contains. They are terrified of Don Julius."

Jakub nodded and directed the attendants to carry the wooden box to the cavernous kitchens, alive with preparations for the night's feast.

"Now, find Marketa at once. She must come immediately."

Jakub hesitated and his face twisted with jealousy, eyes narrowed to slits. "It may be difficult to pull her away from Don

Julius. He is like a drunkard in love with her, impossible to pry away from the liquor. I have never seen a more disgusting display of besotted love."

Annabella studied his face, her mouth almost curving in a smile. Then she turned deadly serious, her eyes allowing no excuses.

"Find a way. Bring her to me. At once."

Jakub mounted the carpeted stairs toward the drawing room where he had left Don Julius when Marketa had been whisked off to be measured for her robe. Now she was returning, escorted by a guard down the long hall toward the royal apartments again.

"I will escort Slecna Marketa to Don Julius. You are dismissed."

The guard nodded and turned down the hall toward the servants' steps. Jakub waited until he heard his footsteps diminish down the stairwell.

"Come quickly," Jakub said, squeezing her arm. "Annabella waits for you."

Then he stopped. His hand reached for the scarf around her neck. His fingertips toyed with the fabric and then stroked the soft flesh under her chin. She felt her neck and scalp tighten at his touch.

He pulled her tight to him, his lips covering hers.

She kissed him with a fervor that rivaled his own.

"Come away with me," he begged, pulling his lips away only enough to look at her eyes. "I love you with all my heart. Come with me to Prague."

"I cannot," she said, through the kisses, her lips trembling over his. "He will murder the entire town in revenge if I should leave him now!"

"Marketa!" called Annabella from the lower steps. "Jakub, release her at once. We have no time to lose."

Marketa and Jakub ran down the stairs to the kitchens. The cooks and attendants bowed and curtsied, their eyes soft in sympathy and respect.

Annabella waited with a gleaming pair of scissors.

"Sit," she said. "I must cut your hair at once."

"But, but—it's my hair he loves the most!"

"He shall see it again, I promise," Annabella answered, and cut the first swath of hair, before Marketa could protest or struggle.

Marketa's face crumpled in despair. "If he sees I have cut my hair he will kill me in rage!"

"He will try to kill you anyway, no matter what you do," the witch snapped. "Trust me, this is your only salvation."

"I have no salvation, Annabella. Your potions will not cure his madness. I am doomed."

Annabella cut deftly and quickly, shearing the brindled locks that fell into her open hand and were laid carefully on a linen sheet on the table. When she finished, the table was covered with glossy, thick strands of hair.

Marketa felt the cool, dank air of the castle on her bare neck. She shivered, her fingers touching the exposed skin that puckered with the cold.

She looked up at Annabella and Jakub, her eyes burning, fighting back tears.

Jakub put out his hand to touch her shoulder, but she shook it away.

"What have you done? You've destroyed me! You are both mad, as mad as he is!" Marketa shouted.

"You have to trust us," insisted Jakub. "Annabella's plan is your only hope."

"I have no hope." Marketa was suddenly calm again. She knew how all this was going to end, and she refused to be fooled again. Not by Don Julius. Not by Jakub or Annabella. Not even by her own spirit. She had to be strong and confront her fate.

"I will pay for my sins with my life," she whispered. "I will not live beyond tonight."

"No!" roared Jakub, his hands seizing her shoulders and shaking her hard, as Annabella had once done. "Do not be a fool. Come with me!"

Annabella had remained silent, but now she spoke sharply.

"Enough, both of you!" she said. "Marketa, take this."

Her hand dipped into her basket and retrieved a glittering jewel: a pearl-beaded snood of celestial blue silk and pure gold ribbon. The exquisite hair covering was befitting a queen. Marketa thought she had never seen anything so beautiful in her life.

"Put this on and tell him your hair is to be concealed until tonight, to heighten his pleasure," she said.

"But once he sees I have been shorn…!"

"You must trust me. Put it on."

Marketa's hands shook as she adjusted the snood. Her fingers ran over the pearl strands and crisscrossed ribbons of pure hammered gold. How had Annabella ever procured such a treasure?

Annabella folded the linen carefully around the thick strands of hair and tucked it in her basket.

"Be ready tonight," she whispered. "We will take care of the rest."

Marketa drew in a breath and closed her eyes.

"Courage," Annabella said. And with that she turned and disappeared into the dark recesses of the servants' quarters.

CHAPTER 47

AN ENCHANTED EVENING

Marketa refused to speak to Jakub as he escorted her back to Don Julius's apartments.

Before he opened the door, he cleared his throat and hesitated. Marketa pressed her hands at her temples, adjusting the snood, her fingertips touching the smooth ropes of pearls.

"Marketa—" he began.

"No!" she snapped. "There is nothing to say. I will not be fooled. It is too late for hope."

"Is it even too late for love?" he whispered, fighting to control his voice. His eyes were blurred with tears.

Marketa felt her lip quiver. "Don't say that! What choice do I have?" she whispered furiously. "My father beheaded, my friend raped again and again until she is murdered? Leave me in peace!"

Jakub put his hand on her cheek.

"Let me protect you," he said, his voice urgent. "Come this minute and I will hide you where he will never find you. I will teach you to become a real physician. I will—"

Marketa never heard what Jakub proposed, for the great door swung open and Don Julius stood before them. He had heard their voices in the hall, passionate voices. His eyes narrowed and his cheek began to twitch as it did in the days when Marketa first met him.

"What are you doing alone with my Marketa?" Don Julius growled. "You traitor!"

"I was only escorting her from her fitting—"

"You damnable swine! You think I cannot smell your coupling, your seed on her leg?"

She opened her mouth to protest, but he seized her arm and pulled her into the room so violently, she could say nothing.

"She is mine, Jakub. Mine. And tonight she shall tell me the secrets of the Coded Book. She shall teach me to decipher the text that no mortal has read before! She is mine!"

The Coded Book! thought Marketa. The touchstone of his lunacy. He had lapsed into choler.

He slammed the door on Jakub and pushed Marketa roughly onto the divan.

"What is this that covers your hair?" he said. "You know how your locks bewitch me." He reached to pull the snood away.

"No!" she said, turning away and mustering the courage to be coquettish. "I want to save my hair for you tonight, when I am dressed in my new night robe. Do not spoil the pleasure I have planned for you, my sweet surprise." And even as she said this, she realized she was still hoping that somehow she could be saved, that somehow Annabella's mysterious plan would work.

He contemplated her and slowly smiled.

"Is it not the most beautiful headdress you have ever seen?" Marketa said, turning her head this way and that, but keeping one hand clamped tight over her head. "Look how it glitters in pure gold and the perfect luster of the pearls."

"It is fetching," he said, fingering the gold. "But when it covers your hair, it offends me—take it off."

"How could I do such a thing to spoil tonight's tender moment?"

Suddenly his eyes glinted, like a hungry wolf.

"We do not have to wait until tonight. I will take you now!" he said, his voice hoarse and low.

Cold sweat pulsed down Marketa's spine, and she fought to compose herself.

"But, my beloved, no, we must wait. We have waited all these months. I want it to be right. Wait until my robe is finished. It should be the way you planned it."

Please, oh God, she prayed, *do not let him remove my hair covering! If he does, I am done for.*

Don Julius stared at Marketa now, his eyes cold, the warmth of love extinguished.

"Where did you get such a costly adornment?" he said. "I have never seen anything like it, even in my father's court. How does a poor bathmaid possess such a treasure? And where did you acquire this silk scarf?"

"It was a gift," she answered quickly.

"A gift from whom?" he snarled through his clenched teeth. "From Jakub Horcicky?"

"A gift from a dear friend, Don Julius—"

He raised his hand to strike her.

"You lying whore! You open your legs for an old brewer, and you open your legs for my father's physician. Do you think I do not know your nickname? *Musle!* Musle, they call you, the bathmaid whore."

"No, Don Julius. Do not call me that name!"

"Musle!" he roared. "Yes, and they laughed that my heart broke for you when I thought you dead. All the while, you lived among them, the fornicating swine!"

"I was frightened, my lord. I was frightened of you and your temper! Have mercy!"

"Why can you not understand how I love you! You betray me at every turn, you harlot!" cried Don Julius. He held his hands over his ears, driven mad by voices that Marketa could not hear.

"Look at me, Don Julius. Look at me—do not listen to the voices, my darling. I beg of you!"

He turned his eyes, red with tears, toward Marketa. His face was a map of anguish. The shadows of the tormented boy washed over his countenance, like a moonbeam through a web of midnight clouds.

She pulled his hands away from his ears and whispered, "Stay with me, Don Julius. Do not listen to them!"

But Marketa could see that the voices had won. The demons had seized his soul.

"Get away from me, whore!" said a strange, cold voice.

Marketa covered her face and waited for a blow to hit her.

Instead, she heard a key rattle and the grinding of a lock. She looked up. She was alone. He had locked her in his chambers.

Marketa ran to the window where she could see the banners of the Masopust procession waving over the bright costumed revelers. Throughout the late afternoon, the town had carried out the traditional celebration of Bacchus, which would end with his burial. The fat brewer was this year's Bacchus, and his wife and a child stood at his side. In one hand, he held a mug of beer; the other clutched a huge greasy drumstick from a goose. Bacchus ate and drank in excess, singing bawdy songs while the crowd cheered. A sexton and a grave digger, a priest and mourners followed him, for tomorrow, Ash Wednesday, he would be buried, according to the tradition, and the hard days of fasting would begin.

Suddenly, as she watched, a horseman charged into the scene. The women screamed and clutched their children to their sides.

The rider, Don Julius, headed directly for Bacchus, trampling him. The brewer shielded his head with his arms as the horse trod his legs and torso, but within seconds the livid rider reined the horse toward the town square, the clang of iron horseshoes competing with the screams of the injured brewer.

Marketa knew it would be hours before Don Julius returned, drunk and murderous. And those hours were all that she had left to live.

~

Doctor Mingonius's coach arrived at the castle when the sun was a bloody streak on the horizon and the first stars had begun to emerge. The doctor shared the coach with two other physicians, one being the great Jan Jesenius.

Jakub walked swiftly out to greet them. He sympathized with the older men for the grueling journey at such a relentless pace. But there was no time to waste.

Doctor Mingonius embraced the younger man.

"Where is he?" he said without any other word of greeting.

"He locked Marketa in his bedchamber and took off at a gallop down the hill into Krumlov. Trampling a townsman—"

"Marketa?" Doctor Mingonius broke in. "Marketa is held prisoner?"

Before Jakub could answer, Jan Jesenius, a stately man at forty, cleared his throat, interrupting them.

"May I present myself, Doctor Jan Jesenius, and my assistant, Doctor Jelinek. I believe, Doctor Horcicky, we have had the pleasure of meeting at Court, but you may not remember me."

Jakub nearly smiled despite the dire circumstances to hear the self-deprecating charm of the illustrious physician, known throughout Europe and beyond. Of course any learned man of medicine knew Jesenius.

"Of course, Doctor Jesenius. It is an honor to have you here. And I believe we have met, Doctor Jelinek."

Doctor Mingonius nodded anxiously at the pleasantries, but his face was a wrinkled map of worry.

"We must get her out of the room at once, before he returns! Has he harmed her in any way?"

"After a cloying display of affection, he struck her across the face and called her a whore. He has returned to his maniacal rage about the Coded Book—"

Doctor Mingonius was already charging up the stairs.

~

Don Julius left his horse in the square. The townspeople had returned to their festivities, drunk and stumbling, after the injured brewer had been carried away in a litter.

Bacchus had been lost to them a day early. He would not be buried tomorrow after all. Bad luck, they grumbled, and staggered back to the tavern to ease their disappointment with strong drink.

Last year's Bacchus, a merry tanner, had died of the cold when the townsfolk buried him in the wet snowbanks of the Vltava. And what a year they had endured, a Hapsburg raping their women, their grievances ignored by the king. Could the coming year be worse? Was a wounded Bacchus more of a dire omen than a dead one?

Enough! The most important part of Masopust was to gorge oneself with meat and drink. Appetites must be sated, and the rest of the world could take care of itself. The oblivion of strong spirits washed over them, carrying away their fears and woes, making them stupid and happy for the remaining hours of the feast.

Under the mind-numbing effects of mead, medovina, and ale, they barely noticed the lord of Rozmberk Castle sitting among them. It wasn't until he pounded his fist on a wooden barrel, demanding mead, that the surly tavern-keeper even threw a look at him.

Don Julius drowned his thirst with mugfuls of the honey wine, one after another, as if he were parched. The strong spirits rose from the wine and burned his eyes. He blinked back the tears and tipped up the clay vessel, downing it in one draught.

The women, not as drunk as the men, hurried from the streets to hide in their homes, for they had seen Don Julius's horse in the square. But the men of Krumlov were not going to leave their tavern on the most festive night of the year—Hapsburg be damned—and they drank all the more.

Don Julius felt his face grow numb and spirit rise in his veins. The fermented honey smelled of flowers and he thought of Marketa, of burying his face in her thick hair. He gave a lopsided smile to the beaked rooster who served him, and pounded his fist for more.

"Bring a goodly pitcher!" he shouted.

A spool of spittle fell from his mouth, and he wiped it with the back of his hand.

Around him the other drinkers spoke Czech, a language he could understand but could not speak fluently. Don Julius considered it a barbaric tongue, fit only for peasants, a language to be extinguished and replaced with German, the language of God and intellectuals. His nose and lips wrinkled up in a sneer as the Czech words grew louder and louder. The repetitive buzzing of syllables annoyed him, and his mood grew dark again.

A huge bear slammed his massive human hand on a barrel, hissing violently to a horned devil. Both men uttered curses, their tempers flaring as their tankards emptied.

Would a bear defeat a devil? Don Julius wondered, the wine buzzing in his head. *What of that bearskin—it would be the trimming for—ah, the night garment of Marketa. Marketa, my angel—*

No! The whore!

He would teach her tonight who is master! How could he touch her when she had sat naked before the piggish brewer, the stinking fat brute. She would give her maiden favors to a commoner, a man not worthy of a Prague whore. And then she had seduced a Hapsburg.

She deserved to die.

How could his true love have betrayed him?

And had he not seen lust in the eyes of Jakub Horcicky? His hand on her cheek when the door swung open. Coupling. There in the dark hall, right outside his own door.

He would teach her not to make a fool of him again!

And the Coded Book. Had she whispered its secrets to her new lover? With his magic potions, his dedication to herbs and flowers, a sorcerer.

Would the two of them poison him now? Was that the secret of the Coded Book, a recipe for his death? His father and Jakub and Marketa—all of them plotting his death.

The words of the book, unreadable—they held the key to his destruction! All the strange plants, the flowing waters where the maidens bathed. His blood. The green water in which the women played? Greenish-blue as the veins that ran under his skin.

He stared in horror at his hand, cold with sweat, examining the veins that pulsed just beneath the flesh. Look! The same color as the waters that flowed through the book. Maidens laughing, in the waters, maidens round-bellied with another man's seed, swimming in his blood.

"I will kill her!" he shouted.

The devil leapt unsteadily from his seat though the bear struggled to pull him away.

"You Hapsburg shit!" spat the devil, his breath stinking of sour beer and boiled eggs. "Foul villain who preys on innocent girls! Coward!" The blacksmith's son tore off his mask as he shouted.

Don Julius blinked to see a devil become a red-eyed, soot-faced man, screaming insults. He had never had anyone challenge him in his life.

"You dare insult a Hapsburg?" he shouted, reaching clumsily for his rapier.

The blacksmith already had his dagger in his fist. With a quick jab, he slashed Don Julius's face.

The riotous talk ceased and silence filled the cellar as royal blood was spilled. Only the crackle of the wall torches could be heard, licking the stone walls with their flames.

Don Julius raised a hand to his cheek, his fingers coming away bloody. He stared at the sticky redness as the bear and the rooster pulled the devil-man away, now shouting and kicking him out the door as he screamed insults.

The wound to Don Julius's face was not mortal, a horizontal glance of the blade. Still, it bled copiously. He sat fingering his blood, dumbfounded and remembering the leeches.

All around him swirled stumbling ghosts and stags, gawking chickens and fish monsters. They shoved each other to get a closer look at a bloody Hapsburg, haunting him with whispers and curses in a guttural Czech he could no longer understand. The closed air of the tavern was sour with fermented hops and men's sweat.

"The devil curse all of you!" he screamed, waving his rapier at the crowd of ghouls. The drunken mob parted as he struggled to the door.

He stumbled out into the square where he found his horse, attended by a barefoot boy.

"Out of my way!" he screamed at the hapless boy, kicking him in the ribs.

He threw himself into the saddle, still swinging his rapier. The horse shied and he lurched forward, nearly toppling from the saddle. With a dig of his spurs he galloped away to the castle, muttering the name of Marketa between his clenched teeth.

≈

"Marketa, can you hear us?" shouted Doctor Mingonius.

There came no answer.

"She must be in the furthest recesses of the rooms," he said to Doctor Jesenius. "Where is Jakub?"

They both looked around. Jakub Horcicky had disappeared.

≈

"I must get back to the doctors," argued Jakub. "I think Mingonius means to break the door down."

"What?" said Annabella. "Release her and have Don Julius extract vengeance on the entire village? *Ne,* listen to me, Jakub. This is a true solution, which will settle the matter once and for all."

"How can you be sure it will work, Annabella? What if he—"

"It is her last wish. Trust me," she said. "Dismiss all the kitchen servants and forbid them entry."

Before she heard his reply she was already working a metal wedge into the wooden crate, prying it partly open with great care. She looped a rope around the box, securing it with a knot.

Jakub helped her lift the box onto the platform in the shaft, the device that had once been used to ensure Wilhelm Rozmberk's meals were delivered piping hot from the kitchen.

"Are you sure you can pull the cable without me?"

"It will not be just me but Marketa. We are strong and the load is light, compared with the strength of our necessity. Go! Stop him before he reaches the door or all will be lost!"

Jakub hurried out of the kitchen, his winter cape drawn over his shoulders.

Neither of them noticed the sweep of a dark robe and the glitter of a crucifix in the shadows of the servant hall.

CHAPTER 48

A Confession

Carlos Felipe Sanchez de Miramar had heard the snap and creak of his knees as he lowered himself to pray on the cold granite of the monastery chapel a few hours earlier. He had heard the screams and protests of Marketa as she had been locked in the room, and the howls of the brewer trampled in the streets, the wretched man clutching at the broken bone of his leg.

I have helped the bastard prince play Satan against the people of Krumlov, he thought. *He will murder the girl now.*

The priest lowered himself to his knees, folding his hands in prayer, his stiff knuckles protesting. The harsh Bohemian cold was unmitigated by tapestries, rugs, or heat, and the old priest shivered under his coarse wool tunic. The dim light that strained through a leaded glass window only partly illuminated the altar and the worm-eaten wooden statue of Christ on the cross.

The priest bent his stiff neck in prayer. He remembered how fervently he had prayed as a young man, how the mystery of Christ and the aura of the Blessed Virgin had enthralled his soul and left him ardent to serve God. He was from a wealthy family in Ronda and did not have to join the order, but he had heard the call as clearly as a man stricken with love, a stirring in his heart that had urged him to dedicate himself to the Jesuit brotherhood. The erudition of the Jesuits suited him, for he was a man of books and learning. He counted himself many times blessed to have been given the honor of tutoring the young Hapsburgs, Rudolf and his younger brother Ernst, when they had come to the Spanish court.

It all seemed so long ago now. The future had shone with untold brilliance then, the strengthening of the Holy Roman Empire, where God's word would educate and guide the hand of an emperor, and Jesuits would administer holy discipline to the continents of Europe and the Americas.

But Hapsburgs bred weaker and weaker monarchs with each generation. They bred amongst themselves like caged rabbits. Despite the Jesuit's tutelage and his Uncle Felipe II's stern hand in his education, Rudolf II's fancy turned to collecting art and clocks, frivolities, and fanciful inventions. He spent the empire's treasure on alchemists and practitioners of the occult, astronomers and astrologers who predicted his future from the position of the stars, instead of leaving fate to the hand of God. It was rumored that Rudolf had left the faith entirely, too occupied with his fanciful pastimes to find time to pray to his Maker.

Then the king had bred haphazardly and prolifically with the Italian wench to produce this devil, Don Julius. The bastard, who, under Carlos Felipe's own charge and supervision, had planned to rape and possibly murder an innocent girl.

The priest winced as he thought of his part in this tragedy. His temper had betrayed him; his pride had made him suggest that the barber should be seized and punished for having lied to a Hapsburg.

And to him.

Suddenly, Carlos Felipe's chest contracted in a spasm of pain, and he pressed his tight fist against his heart. What had become of the man who served God so willingly and who had shyly asked favor of the Blessed Virgin Mother, like a schoolboy with a crush? When had his heart shrunken like a withered apple in winter? His faith and soul had been pure so many years ago, praying and studying in the monastery. Now he was an accomplice to murder, an embittered old man who had helped a madman procure his blameless victim.

His heart tightened again, and he gasped. He looked up for someone to help him and saw a pale white light hovering over the niche that held the statue of the Virgin. He thought he heard a rustle of skirts, the stiff cloth an aristocratic lady would wear, but all he saw was the light illuminating the niche. He was dying, and this must be the Holy Spirit gliding away from him.

He cried toward the light, "Forgive me!"

Suddenly the light was extinguished and he heard shuffling footsteps behind him.

"Brother," a voice called from the shadowed recesses of the chapel.

Carlos Felipe gave a little cry, clutching his chest.

Abbot Prochazka hurried to his side and pleaded for the old man to lie down, kneeling beside him and propping up his head. The chill of the stone floor soaked into the old priest's back, but his heart ceased its clenching pain as he felt the kind hands holding him in the darkness. He began to breathe a little easier, though terrified the pain would return.

"I am dying," Carlos Felipe gasped. "God punishes me for my actions, for my betrayal."

"How have you sinned, my brother?" the abbot whispered. "I shall give you absolution."

"Yes," the priest admitted in a small voice. "Let me confess my sins, for they weigh heavy in my heart."

As the weak winter sunlight had faded in the western windows of the chapel and vespers began, Carlos Felipe's heart and soul had been unburdened. Abbot Prochazka, who had suspected the Spanish priest's complicity in Don Julius's search for Marketa, listened, reminding himself to hear the confession with compassion and forgiveness, as he had been taught to do in the name of Jesus Christ.

But he had already thought of a plan to heal the damage that had been done.

"It is not your time to die, Brother," the abbot said. "The blood is returning to your cheeks."

The priest sat up, amazed.

"The pain has stopped! Blessed be our Lord. But there is a weight in my heart, a sin, that must be expunged."

Abbot Prochazka stared at the priest through the darkness of the late afternoon and said, "I have a way. If you will listen...

"Once there was a young girl named Ludmilla," he began. "She had the bluest eyes and the creamiest skin of any girl in the land. But this young beauty resisted the advances of all the men of Krumlov, even the one who desperately loved her the most. She had only one suitor—Jesus Christ. She renounced her worldly goods and joined the Poor Clares. After many years of tireless service, she became the mother superior.

"Now she is dying," the abbot said, his voice breaking. He tried hard to swallow back the tears and the hard lump in his throat. "But she is not finished with her work to serve God and mankind, and she is determined to perform one last unselfish act. There may be yet a way to rinse your soul of your sin against Marketa and save her life."

"How can I serve?" the priest whispered, straightening up now and looking into the abbot's face. "I cannot abide this stain upon my spirit—it will burn my path to hell."

The abbot drew a deep breath. When he first mentioned the flame-haired witch, he thought Carlos Felipe surely would denounce him as a blasphemer. But the priest only listened quietly, staring into the darkness toward the statue of the Blessed Virgin. It seemed as if she looked upon him with kindness at last.

CHAPTER 49

An Act of Contrition

"Marketa!" Annabella called. The icy-cold air of the shaft stung her face. Her voice echoed up through the dark to the apartments above.

The witch heard the scamper of light feet as Marketa approached the vertical shaft. Then a voice: "Annabella! I saw him leave the town, galloping this way!"

"We have no time to waste," the witch said from below. "Pull the rope on the pulley and help me lift the platform."

"What are you doing?"

"Trust me. Pull!"

"Perhaps you need a man's help," said a voice beside Annabella. She turned to see the Spanish priest.

"I need no help from you," snapped Annabella. "Why do you not attend your master?"

"My master is God."

"Then your God is a murderer," she snapped. The priest said nothing, but watched her frenzied efforts.

"Pull! Marketa, pull!"

But the box on the platform was wedged against the wall of the shaft, jammed against an outcrop of stone.

"He's coming! I can see his horse running back to the stable!"

Annabella clenched her teeth.

"Pull!" she screamed. "Pull!"

The crate only wedged more tightly against the rock.

"Let me help," said the priest. "I will pull. You get on the platform to guide it through the shaft."

Annabella looked at the priest, uncertain. Her eyes studied him, not knowing whether she should trust him, or whether he would let go of the rope at the last minute and send her plunging to her death.

He met her eyes, and she read his intentions. With a nod, Annabella handed him the end of the rope and climbed onto the platform.

"Pull, Priest! Pull as if your soul depended on it!"

And this time, with the strength of an old priest who had one last chance to seek God's salvation and a witch guiding the way through the dark stone shaft, the box made its way to the light, carrying its burden, light as a sparrow, within.

CHAPTER 50

MALEVOLENCE

The flaming sconces illuminated the madman's face as he galloped his horse through the courtyards of the castle. He saw the black seal of the double-faced eagles on the lacquered coach standing empty in the first courtyard.

He rode his horse into the second courtyard, screaming obscenities at the guards. Horseshoes echoed through the arched gates and the horse shied at the guards' warming fire in the corridor leading to the main entrance of the castle.

"Have you been enjoying Masopust, Don Julius?" said Jakub, standing in the doorway, blocking his way. "What is the wound you have on your face? A souvenir of Krumlov's respect for you?"

"Out of my way!"

The tall physician stood solidly in front of the bleeding man. "You have earned that wound and more!"

Don Julius raised his dagger and lunged.

Drunk and frenzied, he was handled easily. Jakub blocked him and grabbed his right arm. He twisted it savagely. Don

Julius howled in pain and the dagger dropped to the stones with a clatter.

"You are a disgrace!" Jakub shouted. "You will not harm her—do you hear me?"

"Release him, Physician!" shouted a Viennese voice behind him. Jakub whirled, trying to keep Don Julius between him and his enemy, but the two men jumped behind him again.

"Let him go or we kill you and the girl right now!"

Jakub felt the iron of their blades against his back.

"I swear we will. Where is the key to the chambers, Don Julius?"

"In my—my pocket."

"Give it to me and I will kill the girl now!" said Franz.

"No!" cried Jakub, pushing Don Julius away, whirling around and drawing his sword. Don Julius ran through the door and up the stairs.

Jakub lunged for Franz, his sword seeking flesh. The clang of metal rang out over the courtyard.

Jakub was late to fencing, for it was not a skill the Jesuits taught. Still, he had trained with the same instructor who had tutored Don Julius, and his ability had been honed quickly.

Franz lunged and feinted, then lunged again. Jakub heard a noise behind him and turned his head slightly, his eyes searching for Heinrich.

Franz saw his opening and thrust his rapier into Jakub's shoulder.

As Jakub recoiled, Heinrich thrust his blade into the doctor's back.

Jakub crumpled to the ground on his stomach, the hilt of the rapier waving out of his back, a futile banner of surrender.

"You have killed him!" cried Franz. "Quick, get our horses! We must escape Bohemia. The king will hang us for murdering his physician."

"Don Julius will protect us," protested Heinrich.

Franz spat. "That mad fool can't even save himself." They ran for their horses.

$$\sim$$

The key lay heavy in Don Julius's pocket. He ran bleeding, gasping for breath. As he bounded up the stairs, he heard the sounds of men at his doorway.

Then he heard the sound of splintering wood.

"What is the meaning of this!" he roared.

The big guard Chaloupka grunted as he pulled the ax from the heavy oak door. It had bit deep into the wood.

"Drop that ax at once!" cried Don Julius. "By order of the king's son!"

The ax clanged to the floor, striking sparks on the hard stone.

Don Julius stooped to pick it up.

"Back!" he ordered, fishing in his pocket for the key with one hand, the other hand holding the ax. His sudden appearance had startled the men, and for a second they stood speechless.

It was enough time for Don Julius to find the key. He fitted it into the lock and heaved the door open.

"Julius!" cried Doctor Mingonius, leaping toward the door. "Leave her alone! She has done no harm!"

Don Julius slashed at him with the ax, and the doctor jumped away from the swinging blade.

"She is a murderous whore who couples with devils in my absence! She plots my death in her green blood!" he screamed as he slammed the door shut, the froth from his mouth mixing with the blood from his wound.

The clang of the heavy bolt from within echoed through the dim hall.

~

"Marketa!" Don Julius shouted, his body shaking with rage. "Where are you?"

His voice echoed in the stone depths of the apartments.

The hall was lit with blazing sconces, and the fine chandelier with its thirty-six candles flickered overhead. The floor was scattered with rosemary and other sweet-smelling herbs.

Fireplaces in the entry and the inner chamber had been lit. The flames crackled in the silence. As he looked around the room, the light from the fires splintered, dancing in front of him.

He rubbed his eyes hard. Then he smelled something foul and sharp, like the smell of singed hair. His eyes blurred with tears so that he could barely see.

He whirled around, looking for the source of the smell. It was so close it smelled as if his own hair was aflame.

Don Julius saw a small caldron bubbling away on the hearth.

"Marketa!" he shouted again.

Don Julius heard his own ragged breath, the only reply. As he entered the bedchamber, he saw the robe—blue silk trimmed with the black fur of the bear he had killed—lying across the bed.

Then he saw her, lying beneath the covers.

He saw the smoothness of her hair spread across the coverlet, its brindled colors shining in the firelight. She was turned away from him, the white nape of her delicate neck the color of fine ivory.

His eyes welled.

He heard her shallow breathing in rhythm to the slight rise and fall of the bedcovering. She sipped less air than a sparrow, he thought. Should he wake her before he took her into his arms, before he—

The voices whispered in his head, urgent and brutal. He fought them, clapping his hands over his ears. They would not scorch his love for his Marketa, not this time.

His face crumpled in agony, like dry parchment in a tight fist. He reached for her, his fingers spread wide like a blind man, hot tears blurring his vision. He reached for her as a drowning man reaches for the shore.

His outstretched arms breeched a decade, reaching to a past where his beautiful mother had loved him and his father had doted on him—a child lingering in the royal Kunstkammer, the prodigy who reassembled clocks and intricate mechanical toys, astonishing his tutors with his prodigious intelligence.

Don Julius smiled, his blinking eyes staring across the years—again for an instant, a lonely adolescent whose fingers traced the colorful pages of a mysterious manuscript. A tormented boy, cursed with the blood of a mad grandmother.

Don Julius's hand hovered over the shining hair, spread over the coverlet. His fingers touched the strands with the lightest caress, as a mother would stroke a baby in sleep. He longed for her to turn toward him and show her face, tear-streaked and contrite for her sins against him. All would be forgiven, for he had loved her with shy, boyish passion since the day he had first seen her on the page, so many years ago.

She would smile, knowing—certain—of his love for her.

And her smile would silence the voices, echoing in the dark, twisting corridors of his mind. He waited for her to turn to him.

He waited.

The smile slowly faded from his lips as he felt his heartbeat in the veins of his temples, drumming out the seconds in the stillness of the room.

Still she did not turn toward him. The coverlet rose with the shallow draw of her breath. *Why doesn't she turn? Why? I need her!*

He heard a murmur.

He held his breath and listened. A chorus of voices, an impossible army of demons, their chant growing louder and louder, unchallenged.

Why won't she turn to me?

He shivered uncontrollably. He was defenseless without her. There was no one to keep the voices at bay.

"Marketa!" he screamed. "Marketa, help me! Awaken!"

The hellish screams roared full-throated now in his ears. He could not fight them alone. Don Julius clutched at his temples, his nails scratching at the blue-green veins throbbing under the thinnest veil of skin.

The whore! Ignoring a Hapsburg. The insolence of her refusal to wake and greet her lord.

Rape her! Before she can open her eyes, mash her face to the pillow and take her from behind like the beast she is.

He began to pant. His lips were slick with saliva.

He tasted the bile in the back of his throat as he had that night long ago when he wrestled his father's hound in the bloody straw, knife in his hand.

He staggered and fought for his balance, reaching down blindly.

The ax. Its blackened blade called to him, ominous in the wavering light of the wall sconces. His face contorted, his teeth tight in a grimace. The angry voices roared in his ears above the quiet sobbing of a boy whose father had struck him.

He raised the ax high in the air and brought it down across her exposed neck, white and creamy in the dim light.

"You whore!" he screamed. "Witch!"

She uttered a moan, and he thought he heard her call out a name—her own name and then the name of the Holy Virgin. He saw a glow of moonlight on the moonless night, a sweep of white silk, a lingering scent, a waft of perfume.

"Receive me!" cried the muffled voice from the bed.

Then there was no sound at all. The sheets stained red, blood creeping silently across the bed, a rising tide.

Don Julius stared at the blood, his pulse throbbing against his temples. He felt leeches sucking at his flesh. He pulled madly at them, plucking them from his skin, from his scalp. He squinted at the mad devil of the tavern, the one who had cursed him and cut him, his sour breath in Don Julius's face. He saw the bear, the bear that spoke Czech, and he slashed at the beast's shoulders, hacking at him with all his might. The stag who danced with the torch in his hoof. Bacchus who returned from the grave to haunt him. They screamed together, in wailing chorus to revenge Krumlov.

He murdered them all. He chopped them into pieces, each time smaller, the ax biting into skull and flesh and bone. He cut at the leeches and gouged out their hideous eyes, eyes that had lusted for his blood. He cut his mother's breast, the Italian whore who had coupled with his lecherous father, leaving him the legacy of bastard to haunt his life.

He murdered his father, the fiend who possessed the Coded Book. Oh yes. He butchered his father most of all, again and again.

When the guards and doctors managed to break down the door, there were no pieces left of the body larger than the butcher's scraps that were tossed to the dogs of Krumlov.

It was Doctor Mingonius who led the muttering Don Julius away from the gore. He had gazed around the blood-splattered room in horror, to Don Julius crouched in a corner, fondling a scrap of matted hair.

The physician closed his eyes and uttered a prayer for the strength to face the scene in front of him.

"Come," he said. "Take my hand, Giuglio. I will fix a tea for you and a warm bath."

Don Julius would not answer but continued to stroke the hank of hair as if it were a beloved pet.

"She is gone," he said in a hollow voice. "And with her goes the code. No one will ever decipher the book. No one will ever quiet the voices. Ever."

The other doctors crowded forward, murmuring at the spectacle of the bloody room.

"Giuglio," said Doctor Jesenius. "Come. Come away from here."

"Draw a hot bath immediately!" cried Doctor Mingonius to the guards. He covered his eyes and felt his knees buckling.

"Oh, Marketa!" he wept. "I have failed you!"

Mingonius felt a hand on his shoulder and a gentle tugging. He opened his eyes to see the old priest, who nodded solemnly.

"We must talk," he whispered.

"How could you let her enter his chamber?" Mingonius cried, wiping back tears in anger. "In the name of God, how could you?"

"Was he not Lord of Krumlov by the king's command? Would you have me beheaded? How could I betray the king himself? I, too, have been frightened by this monster."

Mingonius could not answer. Tears had not wet his eyes since he was boy, and now they would not stop. It was not befitting a doctor, he knew, a personal physician to the king, but he could not control the flow of tears any more than he could stop breathing.

The priest watched him, and his shoulders sagged.

"Come, Doctor. There are some things that must be explained to you."

Doctor Mingonius looked into the priest's face and saw a serenity he had never seen before.

"You must trust faith," whispered the priest.

"Let me take him," said Jan Jesenius, laying a comforting hand on Doctor Mingonius's shoulder. "You are not well, my friend."

Mingonius nodded, wiping the tears from his face.

Jan Jesenius took over, guiding Don Julius by the hand. The madman's eyes were vacant and his gestures wooden. He walked stiff-legged beside the physician, docile as a child's pony.

"I am going to bathe Giuglio myself," pronounced Doctor Jesenius. "I will take care of this, gentlemen," he added slowly and clearly, his voice taking an ominous tone.

"Of course," they murmured together. "So it should be, by the king's own command."

"By God's own grace," mumbled Doctor Mingonius.

Then Jan Jesenius and Don Julius descended the stairs, following the guard Chaloupka, who led them to the bathing room, the deep marble tub already filled to the brim with water, warm and fragrant with rosemary, the herb of remembrance.

Don Julius dreamed he was floating. Above him entwined all the strange plants and flowers he had seen in his childhood, their roots tangled in a squirming mass.

He squinted and looked closer. Below him swam maidens, their bellies swollen with child, their breasts heavy. They laughed and frolicked in the waters, spilling down chutes and slides, splashing into the never-ending, overflowing pools.

He floated on his back, along with them, drifting to some magical tide. He felt love, the love of the water angels next to him, drifting with the slow current. Above him he saw the face of Jan Jesenius looming, his hand reaching out.

Rest in peace.

He felt a pain, sharp but brief. Then the doctor faded. A pale-skinned woman took his place, dressed in a white gown from a century before. She beckoned to him and slowly smiled.

The last thing Don Julius saw was the water suddenly flowing red. Finally it ceased flowing at all.

CHAPTER 51

THE FUNERAL FOR THE SAVIOR OF KRUMLOV

The people buried the pieces of the body in the Franciscan cemetery, next to the Vltava River. Marketa's father was inconsolable, and his big shoulders heaved as he wept over the grave. Lucie Pichlerova's hair had seemed to turn white overnight, and it was whispered she was not right in her head. When the barber died a few years later, the people of Krumlov tried to drive his widow from the village. Finally they relented, for she had become a pathetic old crone, devoid of reason. Lucie was left to live out her remaining years in the bathhouse adjacent to Barber's Bridge, and her twin daughters cared for their deranged mother.

The Poor Clares mourned the death of Mother Superior Ludmilla Pichlerova, on the same day of Marketa's interment. The nuns clasped their hands white-knuckled in prayer for her eternally damned soul. It was said she had died in the bed of a witch and was buried below the witch's house in the ancient catacombs like a pagan. They could never accept how their abbess had so betrayed the Lord with her heresy.

It was announced sixteen months later that Don Julius had died of an abscess in his throat, which explained why he ceased his wailing, never to be heard again, after the night of the murder. It was rumored that he had been locked in barred rooms of the castle, seen by no one but his attending doctors, because he was deemed too dangerous. A privy was built out from the wall of the castle, so that no one would have to enter the bedroom to remove the chamber pots, and only the old guard Chaloupka and his wife, an assistant cook, were able to enter the apartments, to clear the trays of food and clean Don Julius's chambers.

Don Julius's body still lies in an unmarked grave in Krumlov's cemetery.

SUMMER 1608

CHAPTER 52

THE CORONATION OF MATTHIAS

The Hapsburgs called it Pressburger Schloss, but in Royal Hungary it was known as Bratislavsky Hrad, Bratislava Castle. Either way it was the capital of what remained of Hapsburg-ruled Hungary, after the Ottomans had torn away three-quarters of the kingdom in war.

"Hah!" gasped Archduke Ferdinand, Matthias's younger brother, as he pulled up his sweating horse on the grassy road flanking the Danube. His horse danced under his tight rein, swinging its rump against his son's mare.

"Heh, stand now," said the archduke, calming his mount. "Look, son, it rivals the *hrad* in Prague. Here in the wilds of Hungary!"

The massive castle commanded a view of the Hungarian lands and beyond to the green hills of Austria, regions that would now both be governed by the new king, Matthias of Hapsburg.

Arriving guests—those who were brave enough to show their support publicly for Matthias in hope of future favors—stared up at the imposing castle. First built by the Celts and then sacked and restored by the Romans and subsequent Hungarian, Polish, and Austrian kings, the ancient stone fortress had stood for more than a millennium on its hill overlooking the Danube. It had served as the seat of the Holy Roman Empire under King Sigismund in 1433. And the Hungarians boasted the *hrad* would rule an empire again, Prague and Vienna be damned.

And on this day, a coronation—that of Matthias II, king of Hungary—would be celebrated here at the Cathedral of Saint Martin. Many swore it was the beginning of a new era when Matthias would justly wear the crown of Rudolf II and the Holy Roman Empire, once and for all.

Down below the castle, on the banks of the Danube, carts loaded high with mounds of soil from all regions of Royal Hungary were arriving. Together the piles of earth would form the "Coronation Hill," where the new king would swear to protect all Hungarian lands.

"Good riddance to the recluse king who hides in Prague while we fight the Turks," muttered a laborer from Esztergom, shoveling his load of dirt onto the growing hill.

"The senseless fool cowers in his bed if an astrologist foretells an ominous shadow," rejoined another man, raking his dirt smooth on the mound.

"A coward who does nothing as his own son butchers an innocent girl," said a matron, selling cups of mead to the thirsty men.

Word of the tragedy at Cesky Krumlov had traveled along the salt routes, traders carrying the gruesome story of an innocent girl's murder at the hands of a Hapsburg to any land that salted its meat. The story had so shocked Europe that there was little support left for the eccentric Rudolf II, among the nobles or the commoners. Matthias had marched on Prague four months after the murder at Cesky Krumlov, Rudolf yielding the Hungarian throne only when Matthias's troops were five miles from Prague's gates. Matthias had accepted that and turned back. But that was only the beginning of his ambitions.

The pile of soil grew to the size of a hillock, cresting over the Danube's shore. Hungarians from throughout the kingdom stood back to admire it, pointing out their region's soil by the color and location.

Meanwhile, above the town, the entourage of guests had arrived at the gates of the stone castle, pleased to find a fortress befitting a king at the European crossroads of the mighty Carpathian Mountains and the snowy Alps.

Hapsburg brothers, cousins, and powerful Protestant lords who had chosen to cast their lot with Matthias craned their heads to look at the towers above them, the yellow-and-black silk banners of the Hapsburg Empire flapping over the Hungarian kingdom.

"Look at the courtyard," marveled Archduke Maximillian, another Hapsburg, brother to both Rudolf and Matthias, who had thrown his support behind Matthias. He gestured at the view with a wide sweep of his arm.

Archduke Ferdinand's young son threw a stone in the courtyard well.

"Is it bottomless?" asked the boy as he let the stone slip from his hand.

There was a faint splash.

"Almost," smiled the Slovak-Hungarian escort. "It is over eighty forearms deep to reach the sweet waters."

The archduke pulled his young son aside. "Do not go near the well again, do you hear me?"

He wanted his eldest son to remember the day of this coronation and for Matthias to remember his son's presence, but a cold shock touched his spine when he thought of the depth of such an abyss.

First he threw her from a window. But she returned. The tale of the bloodletter's daughter had already taken on the ring of legend.

As the nobles gathered in the cobbled courtyard, the conversation flew. Times as important as these were moments for alliances to be forged and affirmed, and for gossip to flourish.

"Is it true he slashed her face and threw her from the window?"

"I have heard worse. He took the girl by force and then stabbed her. Cut her into scraps and then cried over the pieces, like a child with a broken toy."

"A curse upon his wretched soul! And Rudolf has taken no action?"

"Against his bastard son? Not sufficient. He keeps him in Rozmberk Palace. No one sees him but the caretakers and physicians."

"Perhaps the king means to make him monarch one day—Rudolf is mad."

"The sordid deed must weigh heavy in a father's heart. The king must be mad with grief."

"His huntsmen swear the king tried to kill himself with a shard of glass, slashing his own wrists."

Much of the vicious gossip was true. Rudolf had shut himself up in the *hrad*, turning out Minister Rumpf and putting his valet, Philip Lang, in charge of external affairs. His closest confidant was a stable boy, who, some gossiped, had taken Anna Maria Strada's place in his bed. And an old toothless lion prowled the darkened halls of the *hrad*.

In contrast, Matthias had led the campaigns against the Turks for fifteen long years. Today he would wear the crown he had earned.

Matthias and his entourage descended in a procession from the castle to Saint Martin's Cathedral. The Hungarians cheered and bowed their heads to the man who had negotiated peace with the Turks and who would now be their king.

Matthias climbed the long stairs, his robes trailing behind him. He approached the dais and stood before the Bishop of Esztergom, dressed in an ermine-collared cloak. The Hungarian palatine, the Lutheran Stephen Illésházy, stood by uneasily, his velvet tunic reeking of sweat.

He probably thinks I will execute him as my first order, thought Matthias as he considered the miserable Illésházy. *He stains his fine clothes with the reek of sweat and garlic, red wine oozing from his skin. A nervous constitution for such a rich and powerful man.*

The Catholic bishop placed the heavy gold crown on the head of the new king of Hungary. Matthias stood tall as the throngs cried, "Long live the king!" He mounted the waiting chestnut stallion, tacked in royal livery, and rode through the gates of Saint Michael to the front of the city wall and approached the soil of Coronation Hill.

Astride his prancing horse, Matthias swore the coronation oath and laid the tip of his sword north, south, east, and west to indicate his resolve to protect all of Hungary and its people.

The soft earth clung to the tip of the glinting sword, and Matthias smiled. Rudolf had dug his own grave. The Hungarian crown was only the first of many Matthias would wear. Others would come soon enough, as he marched with his new allies into Prague to seize the throne of the Holy Roman emperor.

EPILOGUE

The sun warmed the scalp of the young doctor, her short-cropped hair glistening in the brilliant light of a late summer morning. A thick book lay across her lap, open to a wildly colorful page of medicinal herbs and potions. She looked up every now and then at His Majesty's botanical gardens as her fingertips moved gracefully just above the words on the pages, a ghostly caress of the strange text.

Her fingers were stained all the colors of the rainbow from herbal potions and distillations to cure the sick. Though she never personally attended the king, one of her potions this year had cured him of a disease of the liver, and in gratitude he never inquired from whence she had come. It was simply understood that she was the loving wife of Jakub Horcicky de Tenepec, and worked at his side creating potent medicines that cured the ill, both rich and poor.

The young woman contemplated her tinted hands, hands that could at last heal the sick. She felt the warmth of the sun on her skin and looked with gratitude at her surroundings.

In the August sunshine, the drone of bees in the wisteria competed with the call of the nightingale and the chirping songbirds in the garden. The butterflies flitted from one exotic flower to another in an explosion of color no painter could capture. In the coolness of the deep pond, multicolored carp swam slowly under the lavender and white blossoms of the lily pads, making gentle ripples on the surface of the water.

The doctor stretched her arms, breathing in the fragrant air. When she lowered her arms again, she brushed the scar on her cheek that disappeared into the thicket of her short hair. The fingers of her hand lingered there, tracing the raised flesh of the old wound. She closed her eyes, her mouth twitching with a memory.

A throaty call from the gates made the woman's eyes fly open, and her mouth broadened in a smile. She set the book down on the bench and ran toward a woman with flame-red hair, accompanying a child perhaps two years of age, an exquisite pale-skinned girl with dark auburn hair and glowing green eyes.

The women greeted each other with kisses and an embrace that lasted far longer than any casual greeting. They stared into each other's eyes and wept. Then together they looked down at the book on the bench and the tears dried, their mouths drawing up once more into smiles.

The red-haired child begged to see the book, and the doctor spread its pages wide so the toddler could examine it.

The little girl stared open-mouthed at the women sliding down chutes of green water, splashing into the deep pools below. Then she suddenly laughed, the sun gleaming off the white of her baby teeth.

A tall man came out of the garden house with a flowering plant in his hands. Seeing the visitors, he set the plant down carefully and strode slowly but urgently across the tall grass, one hip swinging broadly in a limp. He embraced the red-haired woman and kissed her wrist. Then he bent down and swept the toddler up in his arms.

The little girl whispered "Papa" to him shyly, and he kissed her twice on her pale cheeks.

The short-haired woman carefully closed the book and took a deep sigh as she tipped her chin toward the blue sky, her lips moving in a silent prayer. The red-haired mother nodded and clasped her friend's hand.

Together the four walked into the house.

AUTHOR'S NOTE

History records that the scandalous butchery of the bathmaid Marketa Pichlerova rocked the European royal courts in 1608. Rudolf II fell into a deep melancholy and dismissed his advisers and ministers, leaving his valet, Philip Lang, in charge of state affairs. In June 1608, Matthias and his allies marched toward Prague and forced Rudolf II to yield the kingdoms of Moravia, Hungary, and Austria. In 1611, Matthias seized Bohemia and left Rudolf with only the titular crown of Holy Roman emperor.

Rudolf II lived out the remainder of his life in seclusion surrounded by his personal servants. He became a recluse who puttered about his botanical gardens and his beloved Belvedere. His heart broke at the death of his beloved lion, Mohammed, and the king himself died two days later, on January 20, 1612.

The subsequent Thirty Years' War, involving most of Europe in the struggle between Catholics and Protestants, devastated Bohemia. In the course of the battles of religion, Doctor Jakub Horcicky de Tenepec, a Catholic prisoner, was exchanged for a Protestant prisoner, Doctor Jan Jesenius. Jan Jesenius was later shot along with twenty-six other Protestants in Prague's Old Town Square in 1621 after the Battle of White Mountain.

Doctor Horcicky, taking the Catholic side of the war, wrote a pamphlet entitled "Catholic Confession, or Description of the Right Common Christian Confession, about Hope, Credence and Love." He was quite successful professionally, creating a medicine from the distillation of plants called "aqua sinapii" that proved quite profitable. He held the title of imperial chemist both under Rudolf II and Emperor Matthias.

A curious discovery was made in Rozmberk Castle, in the year following Don Julius's death. Among his possessions was a copy of the *Malleus Maleficarum*, a two-tome book explaining sorcery and witchcraft. This is explained in H.C. Erik Midelfort's *Mad Princes of Renaissance Germany*:

"Surely this was the well-known *Malleus Maleficarum* which we can surmise was purchased not to amuse Don Julius, but on the suspicion that he, like his father, was bewitched and perhaps some further steps toward locating the witch needed to be taken."

The Coded Book, which plays an important role in this novel, is known as the Voynich manuscript and is housed in the Beinecke Rare Book and Manuscript Library at Yale University. The mysterious tome, written in an indecipherable text, somehow passed into the hands of King Rudolf's personal physician and director of his exquisite botanical gardens after the Hapsburg's death.

The name Jakub Horcicky de Tenepec, botanist and personal physician to Rudolf II, was inscribed on the first page of the manuscript.

A CONVERSATION WITH LINDA LAFFERTY

1. What inspired you to write *The Bloodletter's Daughter*?

My husband and I hiked through the Czech Republic on a self-guided tour with Greenways Travel Club in 2005. We spent a couple days at Cesky Krumlov, a picture-perfect village in Bohemia. Rozmberk Castle, rising from the Vltava River, looked like an illustration from *Grimms' Fairy Tales*. We took a tour and learned the legend of the Lady in White, a Rozmberk ghost who walks the halls at night.

Another tale, which was absolutely true and quite disturbing, was the story of Don Julius, bastard son of Rudolf II. He was imprisoned for his unsavory conduct and for stabbing his servant. This mad prince became obsessed with Marketa, a Bohemian bathmaid and the daughter of the local barber-bloodletter.

I couldn't wait to get home to write!

I subsequently learned that King Rudolf II, Holy Roman emperor, had among his treasures an illuminated manuscript in a secret code. It is called today the Voynich manuscript.

Now I *really* had a novel.

2. How long did it take you to write?

About three years total. This was including many rewrites. The initial draft took about a year.

3. What's your writing process like (Do you dive in? Do you carefully plot? Do you need music or silence? Do you write at night or in the morning?

I always look for an intriguing story, a fascinating character. Once I have that character (or characters) I start out with a conflict, and see how the person reveals his or her character through thoughts or actions. For example, with Marketa—I knew she was a bathmaid. How would my Marketa react to bathing stinking bodies and performing sexual favors?

I tend to write in the morning, but when I really get going, that stretches into the afternoon and even editing in the evening. When I work on a book, I try for one thousand words a day, but sometimes it is more. A good day is four to five hours of solid writing, and then a few hours of research and editing.

I write all year long, but I especially love to write in the winter. My schedule is to write for four hours in the morning and then take my dog on an hour to hour-and-a-half cross-country ski. I usually cross-country ski four or five days a week and downhill ski on weekends.

I have found the repetitive motion and solitary experience of cross-country skiing is one of the best ways to find inspiration. There are places over the hill where I have come up with flashes of clarity, seen a new plot point, or figured out the motives of a character.

4. What's your favorite part of being a writer? What's the most difficult part?

My favorite part of being a writer is the actual writing. I love the "deep zone" when the story takes off, when I hear the characters' voices, and especially when the language is flowing.

The most difficult part of writing? Ah, that is easy...nearly three decades without being published!

5. What was your favorite scene or character to write? Did you have any difficulty with a particular scene or character? If so, what made it difficult, and how did you overcome it?

The most difficult scene in the book to write was the chapter where Marketa cuts Don Julius's ropes. I had to show how she was truly falling in love with this madman, and convince the reader (and myself) that she really thought she knew what she was doing. Marketa cut his ropes because Don Julius had found a way into her heart. Yes, it was foolish, but haven't we all done crazy things in our lives?

I particularly like writing scenes with magic and folklore. And, curiously, I loved writing the historical scenes with Matthias. Great fun!

6. What sort of research did you do for *The Bloodletter's Daughter*?

I spent a great deal of time researching the Hapsburg reign of Rudolf II, the history of Don Julius, and Marketa Pichlerova. I traveled back to Cesky Krumlov and walked the streets for days in the middle of February. I was accompanied by my Krumlov guide, Jiri Vaclavicek, who had done a great deal of research himself and could point out landmarks—the market, Annabella's house, Marketa's house, Barber's Bridge, the cemetery, the old Jesuit monastery. He also told me the sordid name—Musle—that was Marketa's curse in the novel.

Jiri dared me to use the epithet in my book, saying, "You Americans are too prudish. Don't make this the Disneyland version!"

I also worked with Zuzana Petraskova, a guide and at the time a graduate student in Prague. She had access to the University of

Prague's library and brought me lots of historical records to help me with my research. (Both guides also translated for me.) I contacted Prague's television station for a copy of a special on Don Julius. A Czech friend in Aspen helped me translate the contents. (By the way, the one portrait of Don Julius shown on the show made him look very handsome.)

7. What sort of advice would you give to aspiring authors?

Enjoy the process of writing. Thrive on it, rejoice! No one can take this joy away from you. That passion is what we live on as writers, what feeds us. (Otherwise I would never have lasted twenty-seven years as an unpublished writer.)

8. What are you working on now?

I am working on a story of Virginia Tacci, the fourteen-year-old girl who rode the Palio horse race in Siena in 1581—bareback! She is Siena's heroine to this day.

QUESTIONS FOR DISCUSSION

1. In *The Bloodletter's Daughter*, which character did you find most compelling? Most loathsome? Most sympathetic?

2. Marketa has two very strong, very different friendships: one with Katarina and one with Annabella. Which character would you gravitate toward as a best friend, and why?

3. Was Annabella right to take Jakub to her bed, knowing her friend loved him? How is Marketa able to trust her, especially when Annabella and Jakub hold Marketa's life in their hands in the attempt to liberate her from Don Julius?

4. Don Julius was brought up in the castles of his father, Rudolf II, while Marketa was born into a Bohemian bathhouse. Who would you say had a more difficult childhood, and why?

5. Would you have freed Don Julius from his ropes?

6. In the historical record, Lucie Pichlerova actually did accompany her daughter Marketa to the gates of Rozmberk Castle, in order to exchange her daughter for her husband. How do you think a mother could reconcile such an act? As a reader, do you feel any sympathy for her?

7. Rudolf and his brother Matthias engage in an epic battle for the throne. Who would you have wanted as king and emperor, given their individual strengths and faults?

8. Is there anything that has ever fascinated you or enraptured you like the Coded Book of Wonder did Don Julius?

9. Czech folklore plays a role in the story. What did you think about Krumlov legends, such as the White Lady, being included?

10. What did you think about the ending, both in the final showdown with Don Julius and the epilogue? Were you surprised?

ABOUT THE AUTHOR

The daughter of a naval commander, Linda Lafferty attended fourteen different schools growing up, ultimately graduating from the University of Colorado with a master's degree and a PhD in education. Her peripatetic childhood nourished a lifelong love of travel, and she studied abroad in England, France, Mexico, and Spain. Her uncle introduced her to the sport of polo when she was just ten years old, and she enjoys playing to this day. She also competed on the Lancaster University Riding Team in England in stadium jumping, cross country, and dressage. A veteran school educator, she juggled teaching and horse training while writing this book. She lives in Colorado.